Barrera, Joseph E.,author.
Confessions of a golden dragon

2016
33305249303524
sa 01/20/21

Confessions Of A Golden Dragon

by Joseph E. Barrera

Suite 300 - 990 Fort St
Victoria, BC, V8V 3K2
Canada

www.friesenpress.com

Copyright © 2016 by Joseph E. Barrera
First Edition — 2016

Some names of persons have been fictionalized. Certain factual references may be somewhat inaccurate due to failure of memory. Depictions of incidents, places and sequence of events were derived from letters sent to Donna by the author from Vietnam.

All rights reserved. No part of this publication may be reproduced in any form, or by any means, electronic or mechanical, including photocopying, recording, or any information browsing, storage, or retrieval system, without permission in writing from FriesenPress.

ISBN
978-1-4602-9222-8 (Hardcover)
978-1-4602-9223-5 (Paperback)
978-1-4602-9224-2 (eBook)

1. FICTION, HISTORICAL

Distributed to the trade by The Ingram Book Company

To any American soldier
who has been in combat,
my deepest sympathy
and highest respect.

Table of Contents

Confessions Of A Golden Dragon

Chapter 1

Turn of Fortune

"Jive-ass motherfuckers," Garcia, Hernandez, or whatever the fuck his name was, repeated for about the fifth time. A fleeting thought went through Defurio's mind. "Jive-ass motherfuckers." Jive-ass was an unusual term to use. Fitting, but unusual. It wasn't Vietnam jargon, or even current USA jargon.

Defurio and the three strangers he was with had been ordered to advance to the top of the hill and throw smoke grenades on the dinks who had been mortaring them for twenty minutes... or was it fifteen minutes?...or two minutes? Time and life are ephemeral when you're trapped at the bottom of a hill in a bamboo forest.

Chunks of shrapnel tore through the trees. Defurio flattened himself tighter against the ground, his face paralleling the jungle floor. At the limit of his reason, he became fascinated by balls of breath moistened earth rolling back and forth in front of his nose, some entering and tickling hairs inside, some keeping cadence with his heavy breathing. Strange. Of all places on the planet, the hundreds of millions of acres, this grave-sized plot had become his total world.

Another crashing shell and zinging metal. He squirmed. Patches of reddish dirt stuck to eruptions of sweat on his face, hands, and arms.

More explosions. Defurio winced reflexively and clung harder to the earth. He inhaled deeply and choked on swirling residue of atomized jungle kicked up by the shells. Could it get any worse? He was breathing in Vietnam; it mixed with his sweat and clogged his pores, and unknown to him...seeping into his essence... never to leave.

He half turned on his side, holding the M-16 between his legs as if it were his hardened, swollen member wanting to hold something intimate, familiar, and reassuring. Jagged hunks of shells were hitting six feet high in the bamboo. Finer pieces drifted down around him like spent buckshot.

"Fuck, fuck, fuck!" Defurio screamed, his voice an empty echo made silent by the bamboo, bursting shells, and the shriek of his own senses. He shut his eyes, a child hiding under a blanket in a lightning storm. No use. Shells were hitting closer. He came to a bitter acceptance of his fate, ready to submit to a force over which he had no control. He felt a release. Life suspended to a dreamy slow motion interrupted by a split second paroxysm of introspection raising an irony and a question. How the fuck did he get here?

Four months prior, he had been at the Alameda holding station near Oakland, California. The facility, a converted naval warehouse, housed a thousand graduates of advanced infantry training waiting in rotation to be bussed fifty miles to Travis Air Force Base and from there flown to Vietnam. The prevalent feelings among those assembled were of disbelief, fear, confusion, and a new-found piety.

The latrines were painted in pinks and blues. A feminized décor helped soothe the jittery assemblage. In contrast to the usual scatological material common to men's rooms, here pastel walls displayed scribbled religious epitaphs.

There wasn't any of the FTA graffiti found throughout Ft. Lewis, Washington, where Defurio had done his basic training. FTA were initials for "Fuck the Army."

When peeing at Alameda, a man could read inscriptions such as, "My savior will look over me," "God is my salvation," or "I love Jesus and He will protect me." Given the uncertainty of the future, the messages were especially poignant when holding on to your most prized possession.

At the end of basic training, inductees received a military job designation, the most dreaded of which was 11B40, light weapons infantryman, commonly referred to as a grunt. Later it became evident the designations were made at random. A person with a master's degree in biology might end up as a radioman. An illegal immigrant could receive training as a welder. These were anomalies. The imperative was for infantrymen. The Army needed hundreds of thousands of warm bodies to pull triggers.

Jack Defurio, age twenty-six, two years of law school, high test scores, working as a probation officer when drafted, married nine months, had expected to be assigned as a legal clerk, the military occupation for which he had been recommended at the close of the testing and evaluation process.

Notification of MOS (Military Occupational Specialty) was done verbally at hurried open air meetings at the end of basic training. Individual training companies were called, names were shouted, and notifications made. Three quarters of the way through the list, a beefy sergeant bellowed, "Defurio. 11B40." He became lost in a whirlpool of panic, helplessness, and anger. He hadn't anticipated this. Could there have been a mistake? Factors of age, education, marital status, work experience, and high test scores should have precluded him from an MOS of light weapons infantryman.

Defurio had steeled himself to the prospect of wasting two years in the Army. Maybe he would be given an interesting job at an embassy or the Pentagon. What a delusion. In an act of misfortune, he was being condemned to battle for his life ten thousand miles from home in an Asian wasteland.

He should have known the Army would give him the same thoughtless consideration as the draft board in his hometown of Fresno, California. He remembered the head of the board, a wealthy furniture dealer with the dimensions of a walrus. This unctuous man sat on the committee hearing his appeal for an exemption. The walrus spoke for the board. Defurio listened as he pontificated on how important it was for Americans to answer the call to duty. Easy for him to say; none of his chubby-assed children would be serving, nor those of his white bread cohorts. Vietnam had become an unpopular war with massive casualties. This kind of dirty work was for the lower classes. This war would be fought by poor whites, Mexicans, Puerto Ricans, and Blacks. It didn't make any difference what their age, education, experience, or marital status.

The cold refusal to his plea for an exemption wasn't unexpected. Defurio knew the game and that he would lose. He went through the charade hoping against the odds he might find some sympathy. He hated the hypocrites controlling his life. Ruefully, he pictured himself as the oft-depicted Mexican peasant in old movies, the one fingering the brim of his straw hat while those in power dumped all over him. Listening to the walrus, Defurio did what he'd always done when confronting highly placed bigots or misusers of authority. While they sermonized, he smiled benignly and mentally repeated, "fuck you." This allowed him to maintain self-control, a technique he had used since grammar school.

The appeal to the draft board did have one positive effect: it postponed his induction for two months. His draft notice had mistakenly been sent to his former address in San Francisco.

He utilized the two month reprieve to contact legislators in an attempt to obtain an exemption. In the interim, he and Donna moved to an apartment in Bakersfield, California, where her parents were living temporarily.

He gathered college transcripts, personal endorsements, employment history, and supportive information and sent them to state and federal congressmen. These efforts were in vain. A typical response came from the harebrained eccentric, the Tam O'Shantered academic, California State Senator Hayakawa. He'd recently been elected in a blaze of publicity. In 1968, politicians still considered it patriotic and advantageous to support the war despite growing student demonstrations. Therefore, Hayakawa, basking in electoral stardom, didn't mind fucking Defurio by sending him a form letter refusing any action by his office. Defurio had received less attention than a pesky fly. It wouldn't be the last time he would deal with a Jap bastard.

His orders were to report for basic training at Ft. Lewis, Washington. He would depart from the Fresno Air Terminal. He had never flown before. This would be one of many firsts.

He began making conclusions on how and why the Army did what it did. For one thing, he had determined three quarters of the way through basic training that any useful instruction could probably have been taught over a couple of weekends in a rural backyard. Squeezing triggers on hand-held weapons is not that complicated. Overlooked were subtleties involved in fighting a war in the tropics against a clever enemy. Instead, trainees were immersed in World War II tactics employed within sight of snow-topped mountains. Where the fuck was the wisdom in training in the snowy regions of Fort Lewis for a war being waged in rice paddies and tropical forests?

Hours of bayonet practice emphasized an archaic form of combat not performed effectively since the age of Napoleon and the single shot rifle. In any event, the object of the Army wasn't to produce skilled rapiers. The purpose was to inculcate a man to follow orders whether they made sense or not, which it did with extreme efficiency. The Army endlessly drilled recruits to condition them to obey orders without hesitation. This approach didn't include developing a sophisticated, well-prepared fighting man.

Throughout basic training, personnel officers pestered Defurio to attend officer candidate school. There were significant drawbacks. First, it required a four year stay in the Army. Second, available positions were restricted to combat roles. Third, he didn't have a desire to lead men in combat. He wanted responsibility solely for himself. Another consideration was that he had grown to dislike senior officers. As a lieutenant, the beginning rank for an officer, he would be at the bottom of the officer corps, subservient to the hacks up the chain of command.

At the end of basic training, Defurio received a weekend pass. He and Donna rented a hotel room in Tacoma. She was shaken to see her already thin husband skinnier by twenty pounds. He had become emaciated from having contracted pneumonia a month earlier.

There had been a nighttime training exercise, and he had been ordered to stay in a four foot deep hole. A freezing rain filled the pit with chest-high water—good training for a war being fought in jungles and rice paddies. He had been released from the hospital one week earlier after suffering fourteen days from high fever and delirium.

They arrived late in the evening to the hotel room. Defurio fumbled with the keys, anxiously unlocking the door. Entering without a word, they fell on the bed grasping, touching, kissing, sucking, and attaching together with the abandon of wild animals. Try as he might, he couldn't sustain his ardor past two initial outpourings of pent up desire. The Army's attempt to build up his body had had the opposite effect. He had been reduced to a shadow of his former self.

The lovers were half asleep, entangled in an amorphous union of torsos, arms, and legs. She reposed on her side. Morning light slanting through a blind crossed her forehead. He looked at her as though studying a work of art. She batted her blonde lashes. They were coated with day-old lumpy mascara, which somehow made her more alluring. Her lashes closed pleasingly on her pinkish skin drawn tightly over high cheek bones. Her right hand, feathery as a baby's touch, rested on his left thigh. This aroused him. He ran his fingers down her shoulder following the line of her body to her waist across her hip to below her navel. She responded. He savored her acrid taste, the taste of early morning sex.

The hours went by until the weekend raced to a close. Defurio returned to Ft. Lewis for three months of advanced individual training. None of the months of vigorous training, except for the firing and maintenance of weapons, would be applicable in Vietnam.

A big pink curler sprang loose from her hair onto the bed. Although not a regular churchgoer, he knew Donna knelt by her bed every night and prayed for him. She didn't necessarily take the flying curler as a sign from God, but she wondered. Jack could imagine her big eyes flash open when it happened. Reading her letter, his lips spread into an affectionate smile.

Taking over command midway through Defurio's training cycle, Lt. Col. Hackworth was the most decorated man in the military. He had fallen out of favor for his open criticism of the military's conduct of the war. In response, the Army had given him the degrading assignment of overseeing the training of recruits. At an introductory talk to trainees, the lieutenant colonel announced a decidedly unmilitary policy. Any soldier having a problem could bypass the chain of command and talk to him directly.

As he approached, Defurio being an insignificant recruit, expected to be verbally abused and rudely abolished from the legendary man's office. Instead, they talked man to man. Intelligent, selfless, straightforward, and honorable, Lt. Col. Hackworth was everything an officer should be. A man of action, he then and there wrote a recommendation to reclassify Defurio's job designation to that of legal clerk. Regrettably, the recommendation was rejected at the next highest level of command.

Three months of AIT lapsed with the speed of a melting glacier. Ft. Lewis had become a depressing grind. Finally, the training concluded. Completion of AIT resulted in a mixed blessing. He would receive one month vacation before leaving for Vietnam. He spent the bittersweet month with Donna in the apartment in Bakersfield. A cloud of uncertainty hung over them. Their lives would be shaped by what ensued in the coming year—or less, if something bad happened.

There were questions. Would he return a broken or fractured man? Would Donna be subjected to viewing a flag-draped box containing his body? These contemplations were left unsaid.

Denied a foreseeable future, they chose to live in the moment. The shabby Bakersfield apartment became a romantic playground. They loved in full measure; eye to eye, voice to ear, and skin to skin, day and night for the entire month, pausing for meals and short family visits.

There hadn't been any need to discuss the harm that could come to him. Daily newscasts made the reality plain enough. The war came to everyone's living rooms, brought in graphic detail by celebrity reporters.

Vietnam had become more controversial since the 1968 Tet offensive. Casualty rates had skyrocketed. Public support waned.

For Jack and Donna Defurio, the last grains in the hour glass were running out. The war and its juxtaposition with Private Defurio was speeding to its inevitable conclusion. The myths and madness of Vietnam awaited him.

Not just yet. He would be held a week or so waiting for deployment at the holding facility in Alameda.

Defurio ignored orders not to leave the premises. To his astonishment, the Army did not lock or guard the Alameda facility. He took advantage of this oversight and every morning snuck out after roll call, met Donna at her car, and drove across the Bay Bridge to San Francisco. He had family there, and it was where he and Donna had met and were married. Presently, family connections and personal history were not of paramount importance. San Francisco was home to the Presidio, the U.S. Army post responsible for conducting the war in Southeast Asia. This is where he traveled in a quest to avoid combat duty.

On his fourth day at Alameda, he dejectedly climbed stairs to yet another headquarters at the Presidio. The high stairs were part of a veranda running the width of a boxy two story wood edifice. Army buildings tend to have an appearance of temporariness. The ones at the Presidio resembled dilapidated country estates ready for demolition. On Friday at 4:30 pm, Defurio opened the flimsy creaking screen door. Adjusting to the light, the place seemed as empty and hollow as a college library on a weekend. He walked through the hushness and came across two non-commission officers chatting casually. They were at the back of an array of deserted desks. Defurio apologized for interrupting and began his tired presentation. One of the NCOs, a master sergeant probably in his late forties, arose from a squeaky chair and reviewed Defurio's paperwork. Polite and professional, he didn't behave like the average career non-com. Impressed with Defurio's qualifications, he showed dismay that there weren't any available openings. However, he observed Defurio would be arriving in Vietnam at Bien Hoa airbase. The master sergeant called over the other personnel sergeant. Defurio would come to discover that PSNCOs were personnel specialists who represented the cream of the crop of lifer-sergeants. They were responsible, competent men.

The two PSNCOs confirmed they had a good friend, a warrant officer in personnel, stationed at Bien Hoa. The men delved through file cabinets and determined where he could be contacted. They gave the information to Defurio. In the meantime, the friend would be notified by telephone with the recommendation Defurio be placed in a legal clerk position. Jack gratefully thanked them.

On the fifth day at Alameda, they called his name. He would be leaving for Travis Air Force Base in the morning. There would be a midnight roll call for those scheduled for departure.

The last evening became a torment of doubt and desperation. He and Donna had eight hours. By a contorted confluence of factors, he was being dragged through a quagmire without any assurance of coming out alive, or figuratively speaking, partially alive. Would or could he and she ever be the same? Would Vietnam destroy them?

On their way to the motel room, Jack and Donna dropped off John Walters in Oakland. Defurio knew Walters from Ft. Lewis. They retrieved him and returned to the Alameda facility at 11:30 pm. Donna said goodbye to Walters and gave him a kiss on the cheek and a warm hug. Walters made for the barracks, soon disappearing into a settling fog.

In a parking lot down an alleyway a block from the holding facility, they were alone inside Donna's Chevy Nova and surrounded by a heavy fog. There weren't any signs of life other than the groan of a foghorn. Defurio wrapped himself around her and her with him.

"I love you, Donna."

"Oh, Jack. I love you too. Please come back to me."

"I will, I promise. Write me."

"I will, every day. Be careful."

"I'll be careful. I'd like for you to be pregnant."

"Oh, I hope so."

"If you don't hear from me, write anyway. There'll be times I won't be able to write."

"I'll write to you every day."

He reassured her he would take every precaution. He also had the possibility of being reassigned when he reached Bien Hoa.

With words straining and choking, she continued to promise to write every day and send him food or anything else he requested. She pleaded with him to let her help him in any way she could.

Words were inadequate to describe a rampaging sense of desperation, of utter helplessness and impending irreversible loss.

Five minutes to midnight. He had to go. Why? Why was he doing this? By what rational deliberation could he have chosen the obscenity of Vietnam over her? They could have fled to Canada or Sweden, changed names and gone underground. He could have declared himself a conscientious objector, or faked an injury or illness.

By nature, a cynical, anti-authority iconoclast, Defurio had found his once-in-a-lifetime love. What stake or belief did he have in this war? None. He was in danger of losing everything and gaining nothing.

He had struggled with the absurdities of his predicament. This country had provided his family sustenance, education, and opportunity. His father and uncles had served in World War II. He was brought up an American.

He had the dilemma of a deformed man trying to shake the hump from his back. He can't. Defurio couldn't escape a sense that he had an obligation to the country. Right or wrong, for better or worse, that's the way it was.

With an unwilling motion, he gently put his hands around her wrists and removed her arms from him. She wept the subdued tears of a farewell she prayed would not be permanent. For his sake and hers, she restrained herself.

She stared at the narrowing outline of his angular frame. He moved stiffly, a puppet manipulated by invisible strings. He hesitated, wrought by disconsolation. Would he see her again? Would he be a whole person? What if something happened to her, an illness or injury?

He stopped beneath the diaphanous glow of a streetlight and looked back. Her brown Nova had become a blurry outline obscured by a silvery curtain of condensing moisture. He knew she was crying. He dropped his head and moved on wooden legs.

She watched as he was absorbed by the night and the fog. When the last hint of his presence was gone, she collapsed in a convulsion of shaking sobs.

Chapter 2

Between Heaven and Hell

Buses jerked from the navy shipyard and sped eastward on highway 80. In an hour, they came to a stop alongside a runway at Travis Air Force Base. A jet waited, its engines idling impatiently. Emblazoned on its side, the name of a newly created commercial airline indicated a corporation had scored a huge military contract.

That morning, Pvt. Defurio and the other Vietnam bound soldiers were required to dress in semi-formal summer tan uniforms. The creased trousers and shirts were topped off by a soft narrow cunt cap, so-called because in the active imagination of a GI when held with the open side up looked like a desirous part of the female anatomy. Although a sunny day, in short sleeves he developed goose bumps walking to the bus in the early morning chill.

Defurio had assumed he would be conveyed overseas by military aircraft. A welcoming squad of well-formed stylishly coiffured stewardesses furthered this misconception. At the plane, there wasn't anyone present to admire his impressive uniform. Families, friends, and well-wishers were uninvited and nowhere in sight. Representatives of the media were absent. Plane loads of luckless troops being hauled to Southeast Asia was no longer considered newsworthy. America had tired of the war.

Defurio and Walters, his friend from Ft. Lewis, sipped from a bottle of Bourbon Deluxe they had purchased in Oakland. They sat back and tried to relax. Defurio noticed a minimum of conversation. The words "Vietnam" or "Nam" never passed anyone's lips. The words themselves conjured up fear like a hatchet poised to come down on their outstretched necks.

Sporadic talk between Defurio and Walters dwindled in between swallows of the cheap whiskey. It soon stopped altogether. Within four hours, Walters passed out.

In route to the stopover in Hawaii, he recalled how Donna reacted to reports of hundreds of GIs and Marines killed and wounded every month. She became teary-eyed when casualty reports were announced. The buildup of U.S. forces had increased to above five hundred thousand. Casualties at the close of 1968 had risen dramatically.

They spent an hour in Hawaii refueling. The next refueling stop would be Guam. Somewhere in between, the soon-to-be-jungle fighters were closer to Vietnam than the States. A soul-searching quietness predominated. Some prayed, although not openly. Most went inside themselves...questioning their fragile mortality... questions usually held in abeyance by the optimism of youth. Heads with ears exaggerated by military haircuts seemed to belong to innocent choirboys rather than real soldiers going to war.

Meals were distributed. Defurio, trying to doze, became aware of two opposing sounds: the drone of jet engines and the irritating scratch of plastic eating utensils.

He and Walters continued drinking. Jack had improved the quality of whiskey, having bought Jack Daniels at the Honolulu Airport. They had asked for proof of age. It struck him than an underage conscript could be forced to fight for his country and not be allowed to buy a libation to alleviate worry of the possible consequences.

One hour from Guam, he woke to a thunderous headache. He and Walters had finished the bottle. A pendulum swung inside his skull and his mouth had the taste and texture of dirty sweat socks. The familiar whine of the jet's engines had become the buzz of a giant mosquito.

Defurio's head tilted toward Walters, who slept peacefully. Walters represented an exception to the rule, a middle class white guy swept up in the draft who didn't do anything to get out of it. College educated, he had a good sense of humor and an easy going manner. Besides succumbing to shots of whiskey, he rested in the afterglow of his frolic with a prostitute. On their last night in the States, Jack and Donna had dropped him off and later picked him up in downtown Oakland. He spilled out his gratitude. Apparently, one of the denizens of downtown Oakland had satisfied his every prurient wish. Presently, he appeared dead but for a slight snore and drool escaping from a corner of his overbite. He reminded Defurio of a large bunny. "He's a good guy, I hope he doesn't get killed," he thought.

At 4:00 pm, waves of heat shimmered from runways at the Guam airport. A heavy oily smell came from the adjoining Air Force base. He saw rows of B-52s. Drooping wings seemed to touch the ground at the tips. The huge resting birds huddled over bomb loads, waiting for the call to release them somewhere over South Vietnam.

A newlywed Guamanian couple were taking Polaroid pictures on the lawn outside the terminal. Jack asked if they would take a picture of him and Walters. The shy couple nodded in agreement. They refused payment.

A decent picture showed the rumpled figures in dress uniforms looking upstanding and respectable, belying the fact both had mind-bending hangovers.

They embarked on the last leg of the trip. Leaving Guam, Defurio stared out the window. A cloudless sky. Reluctant embers of sunlight simmered behind the Western horizon.

Attitudes began to change. Hours of self-doubt reverted to curiosity, an emboldened sense of adventure, and a mounting eagerness to prove one's manhood in the tradition of Americans having never lost a war. The threat of death or injury at the hands of a bunch of small boned gooks began to burn from impatient brains. Assertions of "kicking Viet Cong ass" spread through the cabin. This momentum had been gathering since Hawaii; timid butterflies transforming to soaring eagles in the course of a single day.

Post pubescent males generally consider themselves invulnerable; willing believers in glorified tales of warfare handed out by militarists, politicians, and sunshine patriots; tales reinforced by personal accounts from fathers, uncles, and ancestors having fought valiantly and victoriously in America's wars.

In the lexicon of U.S. history and in John Wayne movies, the American fighting man had been extolled and revered as a conqueror of good over evil. History and God were on the side of the Americans.

Not for Defurio. He didn't give a damn about the legacy from previous wars, nor did he relate to God. He had faith in neither God nor the Army. However, he didn't blame God for his problems, he blamed the Army. In his short tenure, he had been the victim of poor training, indifference, and negligence. He could have died of pneumonia before leaving the country. They had made him an 11B40. As a private, the lowest rank in the Army, he was vulnerable to being buried under an avalanche of incompetence. As a system and institution, clearly he could not trust the Army. He would have to fend for himself.

Defurio sat at the rear of the plane. He surveyed the crop of shaved heads with protruding ears and calculated his chances for survival compared to these clueless neophytes. Six to eight years older, his maturity and life experience should come in handy when making decisions concerning his welfare. Moreover, he was familiar with adversity and conflict. War is conflict in the extreme.

At home, he had been subject to stringent rules applied by a stern, fiery mother and a hardworking, rigid, and aloof father. His parents bickered constantly. He had never gotten along at home and at the age of fourteen, a bruise to his left cheekbone put there by the fist of his father, he ran to the streets.

Defurio had an inborn capacity to go to the absolute limits of convention and authority without crossing the line. Both of them knew he could have kicked his father's ass. His dad never again physically challenged him.

A marginal student in high school, he had periodically been disciplined for fighting and classroom misbehavior. Although frequently in trouble, he avoided suspension.

This background hadn't helped him much in polite society. However, his personal travails had developed in him a toughness and sharpened awareness of reality; of adjusting to untoward circumstances, and a talent for independent thinking. In the challenges that lay ahead, he would not be distracted by foolish notions of duty, glory, sacrifice, or bravery. Like a well-conditioned athlete, Defurio would be set to achieve his ultimate goal: to come home alive and unhurt.

What if he were killed? He was unafraid of death. There would be no pain, no feeling, no anything. Instead, he feared being crippled or disfigured. His vanity and ego wouldn't abide ugliness or pitifulness of permanent pain. He recalled seeing a veteran in a wheelchair, legless, half a man. He shuddered and wished he hadn't finished the whiskey. He leaned his neck on the crinkly white cloth covering the headrest. How nice, to protect his head from getting dirty—or was it to keep his head from getting the headrest dirty? Why these disjointed ruminations? A fitful slumber overcame him. The image of the legless veteran lingered, then vanished.

Pieces of the past came and went, then settled as always on her. He drifted through an inner sanctum of memory, reliving when they'd met at the hole-in-the-wall Safeway supermarket.

In his second year of law school in San Francisco, he had moved in with a widowed aunt. He had gone to buy basics at the Safeway on Nineteenth Avenue. The supermarket, tucked between high-rise apartments and musty shops in an ethnic neighborhood, had the intimacy and informality of a corner grocery.

Only blindness could have prevented attention being drawn to the tall, lithesome blonde working the middle check stand. He hastily threw a few non-personal items in a basket and queued up in her line. He needed toilet paper. That purchase would have to wait.

Working the cash register, her head moved from side to side, keeping up animated conversations with customers. Her face had classic features of a renaissance sculpture. Her carefully arranged thick hair swept up to reveal a white neck gracefully curved like that of a swan. The champagne color of her hair caught the light. Filipinos, Germans, Russians, and other heavily accented people crowded her line.

Defurio waited uncertainly, not knowing what to say to her. His turn. He, the hopeful law student and she, the pretty checker, came face to face. Both became flustered as with the beginnings of a mating dance, which indeed it was. He introduced himself, somewhat hampered by the presence of amused customers. Radiant and talkative, her name tag identified her as Donna. Taking a direct approach, he asked her out for coffee. She replied affirmatively, and surreptitiously wrote her phone number on the back of the sales slip.

Within a year, they were married.

With sweet recollections and a feeling of contentment, he awoke and reached to touch his wallet, the sales slip and number still inside.

Walters nudged him. "How long before we get to Bien Hoa? I'll be glad when we get there, I'm tired of this goddamn ride." Walters expressed a widespread shift in outlook. Notwithstanding the looming horror of Vietnam, a restlessness had overcome trepidation as the prevalent state of mind. The length of the journey had fomented a transition, a crystallization of acceptance and inevitability. A curiosity pervaded. Fearsome impressions of jungles, poisonous snakes, leeches, punji pits, and meeting Charlie faded to the background. Defurio wasn't immune from the syndrome. What would be would be.

Over the intercom came the announcement, "stewardesses prepare for landing." The slender women in white blouses and blue blazers and matching skirts moved unhurriedly before seating themselves fore and aft.

In a protocol made unnecessary by obliteration of enemy vantage points, the jetliner corkscrewed down in an elaborate and gut wrenching effort to avoid non-existent anti-aircraft fire. Other than upset stomachs, the landing proved uneventful.

Defurio was in Vietnam.

Chapter 3

In-Country

There weren't any loud mouthed non-coms on the plane, so except for metallic clinking of seat belts being unfastened, it was fairly quiet. The front side door opened and a flood of sunlight poured through.

A setting sun blinded him. What happened? Hadn't it already set coming from Guam? Restless, sleepless hours aloft had made a confusion of night and day.

He sagged momentarily when taking in a breath of thick, heated Vietnam air. He became soaked in perspiration. Temporarily light headed, Defurio recovered his equilibrium. Curiosity overrode any physical discomfort.

The Western fringe of sky beyond Bien Hoa crackled with activity. Defurio detected the subdued beating of faraway helicopter blades. Three helicopters were working an area of cleared field stretching from the border of the base, an area called no-man's land. Every so often one of the choppers would lean sideways and spew intermittent streams of orange-red fire, followed by a guttural clap reaching the ears seconds afterwards.

Bien Hoa rivaled the immensity of San Francisco's Golden Gate Park. From its depths, surly sergeants assigned to the newcomers were pried from the local beer hall. They were indistinguishable from a honking flock of waddling, overstuffed geese.

"Get the fuck over here, privates." "Shut the fuck up." "Get your asses over here and sit down." Same old bullshit. Defurio and his companions were led to a piece of graveled ground. Jack noticed the gravel. Where did it come from? Old fashioned Mexicans made kids kneel in it for punishment.

Since the newcomers were on their way to infantry companies and a year of hardship, with many sure to die, Defurio had expected a surcease of the stateside military caste system. He had anticipated from lifers a certain amount of man to man, soldier to soldier respect and empathy. To his chagrin, in-country lifer sergeants appeared to be what they were in the states: an in-bred family of empty headed misfits.

Defurio and his mates were members of the current class of newbies, the lowest form of life in the military. Privates, cherries, fresh bodies in-country, without practical knowledge or credibility, so far down on the food chain they were looked down upon by the pathetic dregs of the Army...safe duty lifers.

What a fucked up way to start his tour of duty; seated on gravel in the middle of nowhere, dressed in a semi-formal uniform, street shoes, without gear or a weapon, taking orders from retarded assholes.

Oh well, fuck it. With nothing else to occupy them, the newbies made themselves comfortable as best they could and enjoyed the show. On this clear, sultry night, they looked at, listened, and sniffed the sights, sounds, and smells of Vietnam.

While watching aerobatics of the helicopters, the newbies listened to outgoing 81 mm mortars resonating from somewhere within the bowels of the base. A mile away, illumination rounds from the mortars popped high in the air and danced earthward on silk parachutes. They heard the banging of outgoing artillery rounds. The smell of cordite hung in the heavy air.

This was Alice in Wonderland. Defurio had dropped through the rabbit hole to an unreal realm inhabited by fire breathing creatures, some hidden on land, others commanding the skies.

Named Cobras but imitating supersized flying insects, two slender-bodied choppers lit up no man's land. Thousands of bullets a minute shot out from mini-guns tucked beneath their noses. Broken red lines weaved back and forth, like water squirting from the end of a thumb-held garden hose. Torrents of bullets cracked down in a crimson Morse code of vacant spaces alternating with elongated orange-red dashes, every fifth round being a tracer. If it weren't for the spitting of bright and deadly poison, it wasn't difficult to imagine the darting machines as translucent winged dragonflies flitting over lily pads during the last steps of day.

"What are they shooting at? There can't be any VC activity around here," Jack asked, as if he were knowledgeable on the subject.

"Maybe it's suppressive fire along a convoy route," Walters responded in uncharacteristic military parlance.

The newbies were arranged in a cluster fuck, referred by lifers to describe two or more privates sitting or standing together. Occasionally someone would break from the cluster and go to the side. There weren't any available latrines. The subsequent splatter of piss off the gravel added an interesting pitter-patter to the ongoing fire dance of bullets, artillery, and mortars. Enhancing the peculiar aspect of the setting, the arching splashing fountains of urine, as though by an artist's hand, were tinged amber by luminance from bobbing flares and incandescent tracers.

Hours crawled by until the newbies were haphazardly lined up and marched to a mess hall. Walters accurately described the food: "tastes like shit." Jack would discover the greasy meatloaf, dried out mashed potatoes, and canned vegetables were gourmet dining compared to field rations.

At 2:00 am, buses, steel mesh covering the windows, came for them. The caravan careened through the outskirts of Bien Hoa. Vietnamese could be seen in neighborhoods of frail looking shacks. What were they doing here? It seemed to Defurio the buses were traveling through the narrow streets of a Chinatown.

Walters broke the groggy trance that had befallen him, the kind that overtakes exhausted vacationers on a cheap tour. "I wish I knew where the fuck we're going." As usual, there wasn't any information or purpose given.

Eventually, the procession parked in front of an administration headquarters somewhere within the depths of Long Binh Army Base, which ran contiguous to Bien Hoa. The weary travelers were ushered inside an unpainted plywood building. Standing upright at a row of podiums, the new in-countries were instructed to complete paperwork.

One question captured his interest. It asked the date he had come in-country. Didn't the Army already know this? Jack saw an opportunity and wrote down November 7, 1968. A tour of duty in Vietnam was a year. Perhaps he could shave off one month.

Fuzzy headed from the force of events, Defurio had missed the fact he had come in-country on a historic and ominous date, December 7th, the anniversary of the attack on Pearl Harbor. Aside from the historical implications, the relevance of the date to him was that it established his deros date. This was the day he would be officially eligible to return home, December 7, 1969. Deros: date eligible to return from overseas. If good fortune smiled on him, Defurio's deceit would fudge the date to November 7, 1969.

They finished the initial processing at 3:00 am. The lifer overseers decided to save themselves the trouble of relocating to barracks. Newbies were told to bed down on the gravel. Lifer's stayed inside the processing center, likely using six packs for pillows.

Breakfast at a post mess hall wasn't bad. The oily coffee was tolerable and a standard feature of Army mess halls. That afternoon the newbies would be informed of their division assignments.

After breakfast, Jack withdrew an empty folder from under his shirt and made a beeline for the nearest administrative headquarters. Ostentatiously flaunting what appeared to be a packet of important documents, he wasn't stopped or questioned. Jack maintained an uneasy confidence searching for the warrant officer whose name he had been given at the Presidio. He was warmly received by the officer. Finally, Defurio caught a break.

The warrant officer separated a file from hundreds contained inside a tall avocado green metal cabinet. Tugging at the folder, the officer made a call to Division. His sanguine expression turned sour. Defurio's mouth and brow tightened. The file disappeared under the pat, pat, pat of the officer's extended fingers. The fingers may as well have been a fist punching Defurio in the face.

"I'm sorry, Defurio. We usually need legal clerks. Unfortunately, we're full up. The last position was filled yesterday. Try again at the division you're going to."

"Thank you, sir," Defurio replied feebly.

In the afternoon, the in-countries were amassed before a bloated master sergeant. The unceremonious role call reminded him of the end of basic training when he was branded with the MOS of 11B40. Life-changing events were apparently done in an off handed, trivialized way as part of a process of dehumanization.

Waiting to hear which division they were going to, the newbies grouped like a pack of hungry puppies waiting to be thrown contents from a garbage can. At least it would be something to chew on, something definite. In fact, newbies didn't know one division from another.

Names were called, followed by division. Men peeled off and formed up in front of sergeants. Names were verified and the in-countries put on buses.

"Walters… Ninth Division." Jack remembered reading in the newspaper about the Ninth Division. He believed they operated in the Mekong Delta. Jack waited anxiously for his name to be called. He wanted the Ninth Division so he could stay with Walters.

"Defurio… Fourth Division."

"Fuck! Goddamn it!" Fourth Division! He'd never heard of it. Defurio was about to be separated from the one friend he had in the Army.

Without delay, they were gathered up. Walters had been waiting with Jack until he got word. A sergeant yelled for Walters. He had to leave.

Jack accompanied him. Walters seemed pleased to be in the Ninth Division, but Jack didn't know why. They shook hands and wished each other good luck. Walters got on the bus and soon fused within a glob of tan uniforms, elbows, and asses moving and taking seats inside the bus.

An unmerciful wind had blown out the candle of friendship. Jack would never see or hear from Walters again.

Defurio traveled from Long Binh in a C-130, a World War II cargo plane. The interior had the appearance of an exposed rib cage, the open walls revealing its framework. The racket and vibration from propellers made it as relaxing as a sawmill. From a modern commercial jet to this?

He sat next to Fox, a rare familiar face from Ft. Lewis. "Do you know where we're going?" Defurio asked the 6'2" darkly handsome kid, given to brooding. Defurio had to shout over the dentist's drill decibels coming from the propellers.

"Central Highlands," Fox answered in a low, throaty voice.

From this meager tidbit, Defurio deduced he was on his way to a mountainous section in the middle of South Vietnam. His assumption proved correct.

In dead of night, the C-130 touched down at the Pleiku Air Force Base located ten miles from Camp Ennari, site of Fourth Division Command Headquarters.

The tired recruits were transported in two and a half ton trucks and deposited at a transit billet. The bare-walled billet reminded Defurio of YMCA housing where he had stayed on a weekend outing in grade school.

The 7:00 am fall out formation found him ridiculously clad in the same slept-in semi-dress uniform, stinky and matted after two days of extended wear and travel.

The transit billet occupied one of several barracks astride a wide pathway. Across from the barracks, a thinly graveled area was where daily formations were held. The gravel here was of lesser quality and abundance than Bien Hoa or Long Binh.

A nasty-tempered master sergeant with responsibility for the formation made cursory announcements and arbitrarily chose a handful of unfortunates for guard duty and work details. He kept a roster attached to a clipboard on which he agitatedly penned notes. Clerks, people leaving or returning from leaves, medical appointments, and the like were dismissed. New in-countries remained standing at ease and were told to report to supply after breakfast. There they would receive necessary clothing and equipment as a final step prior to leaving for the field.

Before dismissing the formation, the master sergeant came to his favorite part of the briefing, the order to police the area. This continued as a well-worn form of servitude from the days at Ft. Lewis. Defurio wondered why they did this before and not after meals. Eating with fingers made filthy from picking up spit covered cigarette butts seemed a prescription for a gastronomic catastrophe. The problem was minimized by the fact that almost everyone went through the motions without actually picking up anything.

After breakfast on his way to supply, Defurio passed a wide sign. On it were painted the interesting sobriquet and curious insignia of the battalion. Diverted by unfamiliar sights and sounds, he ignored the sign and its irrelevant inscriptions.

At supply, personal belongings like razors, deodorant, mother's mittens, and similar reminders of home were confiscated, supposedly to be returned upon the completion of their tours. Jungle fatigues, boots, underwear, and an assortment of gear were distributed. The next day, M-16s would be issued, sighted, and test fired. That evening they would hear a welcoming speech by a senior officer relegated to this irksome task by higher ranking officers.

The dowdy, uncamouflaged fatigues were disappointing. The roomy garments lacked any semblance of dash or style. Quite the opposite. Donning them, one looked like a balloon character painted pea soup green. Within a couple of days, the fresh fatigues would become deflated by sweat and humidity.

A dispassionate, bored major gave a half-hearted welcoming recitation. Subsequent to the rah rah bullshit, another officer verbally presented official mailing addresses for individual companies. Defurio's was:

Company A, First Battalion,
Fourteenth Infantry, APO San Francisco
Written as:
Co. A, 1st /14th
3rd Brigade, 4th Inf. Div.
APO. S.F.

On the succeeding day during a break in orientation, Defurio sought out the battalion legal clerk. Woods was laughable concerning anything military. Gaunt and about 6'2", he had an unauthorized Fu Manchu moustache hanging down edges of his mouth to his jaw line. At 11:00 am, Woods, already woozy from repeated hits of marijuana, tottered when he stood up to shake Defurio's hand.

Sergeant Woods had a fuck the Army mentality, which made him instantly likeable. He was impressed with Defurio's qualifications and attitude, especially his efforts to get out of the infantry. He was genuinely sympathetic to Defurio being married. "Fucking Army," he kept saying.

Woods was rotating back to the States in April. He promised he would arrange for Defurio to replace him. The two nonconformists spent a pleasant half hour deriding the Army before Defurio had to return to orientation.

Woods reiterated his promise. There wasn't any doubt about his sincerity. However, Wood's drug-fried brain made it difficult to believe he possessed the memory, cognition, or wherewithal to help him. What the hell though, it was nice to have found a kindred spirit.

Leaving Woods, Defurio's feet cramped inside his stiff leather canvas topped jungle boots. He felt conspicuous in his flapping sailcloth of jungle fatigues.

December twelfth. Barely noticeable or appreciated were half-assed Yule decorations scattered about on barrack walls. At half past midnight, he stepped outside and scanned the countryside. In a deceiving trick of distance, far away moonlit ridges to the west appeared as gentle slopes. Countless ranges of mountains interspersed the thirty to seventy miles from the highland plateau to the Cambodian border. Cambodia provided the hiding place for the Ho Chi Minh Trail, the lifeline sustaining the communist war effort. The trail ran in serpentine lines near the South Vietnam border. Well-traveled trails branched from the main route and traversed throughout mountains of the central highlands. Defurio would be in those mountains in a couple of days.

His first convoy. The uncovered trucks got underway early in the day passing under the shadow of Dragon Mountain, a rock promontory dominating the southwest corner of Ennari. The trucks accelerated through an opened reinforced barbed wire gate straddled by guard towers. The towers were links in a chain circling Ennari.

The greenery along the convoy route had been eradicated. The flat, open pastoral countryside could have been anywhere on the west side of California's San Joaquin Valley.

Defurio sat on one side of opposing benches occupied by twenty newbies and in-country veterans. They sat holding loaded

M-16s loosely between knees, rifle butts on the floor, muzzles pointed up. Dust flew everywhere. Particles penetrated every uncovered opening of the body. Defurio discovered a fact of life. That is, dirt and its permutations are the intimate, miserable, and inseparable companions of a foot soldier.

The road was rutted and rife with pot holes. Drivers frantically wheeled and downshifted trying to avoid larger holes. The normally reddish soil alongside the road had become yellowish from the application of defoliants. Drivers used sides of the road as much as the road itself. Soon the alfresco passengers became beings from outer space; helmeted heads, hooded eyes, and flak jacketed bodies swaddled in sulfurous powder.

To Defurio, the relatively slow moving convoy offered a perfect target for snipers. A Huey helicopter giving protective cover did not alleviate his concern. A sniper's bullet could slam through someone's body without knowing where the shot came from. No one seemed to worry about the possibility. Neither did he. There wasn't anything he could do about it anyway, so fuck it.

The trucks came to a thatch-roofed village and wound through it without breaking speed. A drunken GI returning from R & R stood up at the rear of the truck and began urinating in the direction of curious Vietnamese children lining the street. He laughed derisively. He seemed to enjoy pissing on the popular image of friendly GIs throwing candy to war torn children. There wasn't any move to stop him, including from a lieutenant sitting nearby.

There were thirty or forty pre-teen boys wearing grungy long sleeve GI shirts that hung to their knees. The boys were flipping off the GIs with impressive enthusiasm. Middle fingers of both hands jutted up shoulder high, thrown up from the waist so forcefully as to raise the boys to their tip toes. They were yelling and gesturing with every ounce of energy their scrawny bodies could muster. "Fuck you, GIs." "GIs numba ten."

"Numba ten?" Defurio asked.

"It's a numbering system, one being the best, ten the worst," explained a veteran in-country soldier.

"Great," thought Defurio. "This asshole is provoking people who already hate us."

The convoy continued down the highway. In addition to snipers, Defurio perceived a danger from ambushes and land mines. Shallow craters from past encounters attested to the possibility of land mines.

He was a prisoner inside the truck, helpless to protect himself from these potential hazards. So why worry about it? He threw his concerns in a mental trash bin already overflowing with a multitude of unresolved doubts and misgivings.

The boyish lieutenant sitting across from him had allowed his M-16 to slip. The rifle rested at a dangerous angle, straight at Defurio.

"Sir, would you mind pointing your weapon elsewhere?"

The shave-tailed lieutenant responded, "Oh, yeah, sorry. No offense." No offense had been given or taken. The inexperienced officer and Defurio were similar in age, both just trying to get through the day.

It took less than two hours to get to Firebase George, or St. George as it was sometimes called. Reinforced gates like the ones at Ennari had been opened to allow the convoy to cruise in without stopping. Outside the gates, they passed a Montagnard woman taking a break from sifting through garbage. She sat on her haunches. The old woman used her back teeth to crack open a boiled chicken head and proceeded to suck out its contents.

George, the forward support firebase for Fourth Division, rested on a rise of land wrapped in cleared fields fifty to one hundred yards wide. Four feet high looping strands of razor edged concertina wire covered the cleared spaces. A circular line of bunkers manned by infantrymen formed a defensive perimeter.

The firebase served as command post for the lieutenant colonel responsible for the division's field operations. An artillery battery and mortar platoon were stationed here. A mess tent and generators for electricity gave further evidence of a well-developed, well-protected military outpost.

Getting off the truck, Defurio's ears were assailed by the deafening sound from Huey helicopters. For a moment, he became sightless from dust whipped to cyclonic speeds by chopper blades. Wind whipped particles flew into his eyes, nose, ears, and mouth.

Wiping the grime to clear his vision, he was flabbergasted by what he saw. A non-stop line of Hueys were coming in and out bringing in supplies, troops, and mail and taking out personnel to the rear area. Firebase George had the noisy stop and go busyness of a subway station.

Always alert, Defurio pilfered a quantity of unattended provisions. He packed his ruck with freeze-dried rations—superior meals made especially for scouts doing long range reconnaissance.

A sergeant appeared. One of the functions of FB George was as a jumping off place for GIs linking up with their respective companies. He began bunching men according to company. He directed Defurio to form up with an eight man contingent flying to B company. B company? What the fuck? At Ennari he'd been assigned to A company. This mix up would have far-reaching consequences.

This should be interesting. Defurio had assumed he would be humping to his company. Isn't this what had been shown in countless war movies, infantrymen marching to the front? It seemed inconceivable at this point that he had been unaware he'd be airlifted to his company. He readied for his inaugural flight by helicopter.

Hueys were flying in and hovering for a couple of minutes. GIs struggled to get on, many of them burdened by loads of beer, soda, and a variety of goods purchased at the PX in Ennari. Sometimes a red canvas bag of mail would be exchanged between a door gunner and a member of the landing pad crew.

Hand gestures and shouting got messages across. Defurio would be getting on a Huey currently banking and decelerating to a layer of sandbags that composed the landing pad. Upon landing, the Huey performed a jig, gently rocking and rolling on its skids, the torque of the turbine engine preventing the skids from completely coming to rest.

Clamoring in and out of the copters, bodies were bent at the waist. There seemed to be an unreasonable fear of decapitation. For that to happen, someone would have to be eight or nine feet tall.

Four troopers entered from each side of the open compartment, sliding past door gunners seated behind mounted M-60 machine guns positioned at the doorways behind the pilot and co-pilot.

On spongy legs unconditioned to sustaining a burdensome ruck sack, Defurio climbed aboard. There wasn't any room in the interior so he swung around and dangled his legs over the side.

Better than a carnival ride, the suspense and drama of dropping at tree top level then zooming sideways and upward was exhilarating. The Huey thwacked skyward and leveled high above undulating vegetation. From above, the jungle canopy had the rounded, bumpy appearance of a grocer's rack of stacked broccoli.

Defurio enjoyed the view. Chopper blades produced a cooling downdraft. Fox, also on his way to B Company, slid next to him. Fox cupped his hand to the side of Defurio's head and managed to relay a rumor. B Company sought two or three newbie infantrymen to train for mortars. Important information. Mortarmen were usually exempt from humping—a big advantage in terms of safety and avoiding physical hardships.

Although Fox and Defurio came from entirely different backgrounds and circumstances, they shared a tenuous bond from being from the same AIT training class. They agreed to present themselves as a tandem to the leader of the mortar platoon.

Two naked hills became visible. The high flying band of copters assumed a linear formation, decelerated, and dipped towards them. The hills were connected by a narrow saddleback.

Descending in a curving, graceful approach, the scattered dirty-green rooftops of bunkers became visible. At midday, layers of heat made it difficult to see clearly. At first, the site seemed uninhabited. Coming in closer, they saw an agitation of filamented specks. The specks moved like insects around a morsel of food. One flat square in particular attracted attention. This rectangle is to where the Hueys aimed themselves.

At the apex of the banking maneuver, the Huey paused, then dived rapidly if it were a bird of prey catching its breath before swooping in for the kill.

Hilltops came rushing up to meet them. Indefinite shapes magnified until they became identifiable forms of people and structures.

The Huey came in hard, braked, and touched down lightly, never shutting its engine.

Last on, first off. Defurio shifted his cumbersome rucksack and scooted off the side, dropping less than a yard onto the landing pad. He ducked his head and went a short distance teetering under the weight of his pack.

He stumbled through a dust storm caused by rotating helicopter blades. He attempted to see through the fouled air but couldn't make much out. What he could see looked like a squatter's camp. He attributed the discouraging scene to poor visibility. When he recovered his vision, the picture was worse than he could have imagined.

A majority of the population seemed afraid of daylight. Those few who presented themselves were in various stages of slovenliness, many of them shirtless. Soldiers casually loafed or strolled about impassively. Strains of rock and soul music coming from a dilapidated patchwork of bunkers added an auditory disconnect to the depressing sight.

Ramshackle, unevenly placed sandbag dugouts served as underground dwellings for the inhabitants.

Defurio summed up his first impression. He had arrived at a sandbag shantytown populated by a tribe of shiftless, unkempt subterraneans.

The seedy outpost had the discordant lyrical name Charmaine, the present home of B Company of the 1st Battalion, 14th Infantry.

Chapter 4

Charmaine

Defurio and Fox huddled with other replacements in front of the captain's command post. Rather than waiting and listening to an insincere pep talk, they went in search of the mortar platoon. Asking directions from a man urinating in an upright tube, they located the mortar platoon CP.

They stepped around and down a four foot high sandbag wall. All bunkers had these step down protected entrances. A three foot high wall attached to a side of the entrance ran perpendicular to a four foot long wall standing in front of it. A man had to step down, then turn at a right angle to enter. Defurio, trailed by Fox, hesitantly pushed through the poncho liner covering the opening. They crouched their way inside.

Defurio struggled to gain vision inside the darkened hole. Wavy flames came from a solitary candle resting on a wood ammo crate. A PRC 25 radio, batteries, two flashlights, and maps were sitting on another ammo box. He saw two lieutenants reclining on bunks. "Lt. Duke?" Defurio asked. "Yeah." Lt. Duke, head of mortars, seemed mildly amused by the unannounced visit.

He was a short, almost girlish southerner, a shock of brown hair falling to a side of his bulbous forehead on a porpoise shaped face. He had been talking to his sidekick, Lt. Flack, the fire control officer. Duke got up. "What do y'all want?" he asked without rancor. "We want to join the mortar platoon, sir," Defurio answered. "I have two years of graduate school and he," Defurio pointed to Fox, "has two years college." Lt Duke showed a friendly smile. "Okay." Without further comment, he told them in a lilting mint julep voice to rejoin their group. Lt. Flack ignored them altogether.

Squeezing from the CP, Defurio readjusted to sunlight. He glanced at Fox, then at himself. They looked like shit. It amazed him how grimy they'd become in five hours. Fox, furrowing his brow against a hellish sun, stared ahead. "I think we're fucked," he said in his usual paucity of words. Unrattled, Defurio replied, "Fuck it." Already developing a fatalistic GI attitude, he capped his reply with, "It was worth a try."

Returning to the captain's CP, they went past a disarray of mortar pits, artillery emplacements, and other military hardware spread amongst four to five feet high flat roofed underground living quarters. In due course, the captain emerged and driveled about how happy he was to see them. While he spoke, a commotion broke from somewhere in the interior of the camp. "Short round! Short round! Short round!" Defurio spotted a mortar shell coming at them in a lazy arc as if shot putted. The babbling captain had his back to the oncoming round. He also happened to be blocking the CP's entryway. Defurio knocked the captain aside and dove inside. The misfired round landed harmlessly outside the perimeter.

Replacements had taken cover. Some were shaken up, some weren't. Defurio had remained remarkably unruffled. The bewildered captain wordlessly stole back within the CP. He grimly passed Defurio coming out. Sour fumes of liquor expended by the gasping captain wilted Defurio for an instant.

The replacements were re-grouping when Lt. Duke showed up. He asked if any of them were interested in joining mortars. A unanimous show of hands sprang forth. Lt. Duke discreetly selected Defurio and Fox. Lt. Duke had just become Defurio's favorite officer.

The mortar platoon consisted of three squads. Defurio carried his ruck to 1st squad, which was led by Sgt. Colmes. Fox went to a different squad.

Defurio could hardly see through the gloom of the bunker. Sgt. Colmes stayed reclined, observing the newcomer trying to find his bearings. "Is Sgt. Colmes here?" Defurio saw six indistinct supine bodies on the floor. None made a move to greet him. Quietly Colmes uttered, "over here." Defurio strained in the candlelight to see the inert figure of Sgt. Colmes. Colmes, a lanky, laconic guy, had an Uncle Remus black drawl. Without arising, he introduced Defurio to the squad. Initially names didn't stick, his mind too busy familiarizing himself with faces and living arrangements.

At the far end, propped against a wall, sat a freckled-face Tom Sawyerish kid who stood out because everyone else in the room was black.

No one bothered to shake his hand. They said hi and hey and kept doing what they were doing; rolling marijuana cigarettes, reading skin magazines, bullshitting, smoking, and listening to Motown.

Colmes pointed to a frame made from scrap wood, a jerry-rigged platform hanging from a corner of the ceiling by trip flare wire. "That's your rack." Defurio hoisted his pack onto it. "Put it outside, dude". He went out, setting his pack next to the hooch with the others. He came back in and sat down on the dirt floor and lit a cigarette. He had stopped smoking when he finished college. Irritations of the Army had caused him to resume the habit. He released a prolonged tension relieving puff, alleviated that for the time being, he was rescued from infantry duty, out of the line as it was called.

His current residence consisted of a 7' x 12' by 5' high earthen pit. His cigarette fumes added to existing smog from tobacco and marijuana smoke. The combination of smelly bodies, damp earth, and smoke wasn't unpleasant, somewhat like the smell of garden mulch.

Dying rays of sunlight slipped through a flap covering the entrance. Someone opened it from time to time to let out old air in exchange for fresh. The inside offered a cool respite from the 110 degrees outside.

Defurio threw his sleeping bag on his rack. Putting his left foot on the bunk below, he swung his other leg and rolled onto the swaying rack. Good. He had a box seat view of the bunker. He rolled a towel around spare underwear and socks to fashion a pillow and lit another cigarette.

Listening to banter among squad members, Defurio concentrated on associating names with faces. Tom Sawyer's name was Couch. He and Turner, a bantamweight black guy having two missing upper front teeth and purple tinted granny glasses worn at the tip of his nose, industriously manipulated cigarettes, replacing tobacco with opium-laced marijuana.

Defurio took an immediate liking to the squad and the closed-to-the-outside-world setting. Life and conduct within these walls was simple, direct, confidential, and without pretense.

The squad's passiveness to his presence did not offend Defurio. He realized intuitively that the lack of responsiveness derived from the pull and strain of combat duty. One didn't waste emotional collateral gushing over the unheralded arrival of a newbie.

Defurio went on smoking, listening, looking, and learning.

Ward, a teenager who seemed wise beyond his years, drew Defurio's attention. Ward sat in a corner and wore a knowing smile as if he were a keeper of important secrets. He stayed quiet and non-braggish, in contrast to usual displays of braggadocio by blacks.

On the other hand, Simpson and Jones fit the typical stereotype; thick tongued, jive-talking ghetto types, offensively loud, having affected high pitched laughs to emphasize foolish points of conversation.

Defurio generally liked blacks. As a busboy at the Hacienda Inn in Fresno, he had worked, partied, and fought with them. The Hacienda, a relatively famous high end restaurant and entertainment center on Highway 99, is where Defurio worked on weekends while attending Fresno City College.

He worked the dining room. Except for him and an occasional white guy, the busboy crew of fifteen was entirely black. The title of busboy was misleading. These were full grown men, many of whom were heads of households.

At the Hacienda, Defurio became part of the black social milieu, sharing many a pint of Bourbon Deluxe on and off the job with his fun loving, uneducated, street wise black friends. He respected them and was saddened by their lack of opportunity and unrealized potential. He empathized with their attempt to offset emasculation at the hands of white society by overcompensating with displays of aggressive manliness.

Inside the bunker when night time came, a pipe bowl of marijuana was brought out, lit up, and passed from man to man, calling to mind Indians passing around a peace pipe. The bowl was offered to him. He deferred. There wasn't any objection or recrimination whatsoever. Defurio would never be questioned or cajoled for not participating in the nightly ritual.

In the course of the evening under the influence of hi octane weed, conversation swung around to Defurio. Someone asked where he was from and how long he'd been in-country.

"California. Six days," he responded.

Jones and Simpson cracked up.

"Beaucoup days left in-country, dude," Simpson ribbed good naturedly.

Couch's interest perked up. "California, cool. I always wanted to fuck a surfer girl." He related how he frequently masturbated to Mouskateer Annette Funicello, imagining her with nothing on but mouska ears.

That got the black guys talking and settling on Tina Turner as their wet dream date. Defurio had never heard of Tina Turner.

Interaction with Defurio lapsed as dream dates became the dominant topic. He had been accepted and included as a member of this non-exclusive club. Membership did not require initiation. They needed him. Until proven otherwise, nothing else mattered. They were outcasts and they knew it. Theirs was a togetherness born of necessity and mutual dependence.

For one night at least, Defurio felt safe. Ignoring the idle chatter, rhythm and blues, and giddy laughter, he went to sleep thinking of Donna.

At 3:00 am, he awakened to rustling movement and saw two men rise like apparitions and were gone. He realized he was by himself. He needed to take a piss. Peeing near the gun pit, he saw squad members silently moving inside a flat area encircled by a two layered sandbagged fence. In the middle sat a 81 mm mortar on a heavy base plate. Several feet apart on either side were two nearly unbendable thin, red and white striped, seven foot metal aiming stakes. A scope attached to the mortar's shaft sighted on aiming stake markers setting the angle of the mortar tube.

In an economy of motion and dialogue, the squad fired off seven high explosive rounds. They were adjusted by Lt. Flack, who gave verbal directions to Sgt. Colmes according to information by whoever called in the rounds. The firing rattled Defurio's head. He couldn't see the squad putting fingers in their ears when firing rounds. Finished, the squad returned to quarters, passing by Defurio without wasting time or energy acknowledging him.

What the hell happened? Had the squad saved an endangered patrol? Had intruders been killed closing in on a listening post? Defurio didn't have a clue. These questions would go unasked and unanswered. Seems this was business as usual. Who gives a fuck what the purpose, or how many killed or wounded? They had completed a fire mission. Nothing more or less. Let the night count the dead.

That was fine with Defurio. He didn't give a damn either. He didn't go inside for a while. He became captivated by the panorama he beheld. An ink dome sky displayed innumerable pinpricks of starlight, providing a background for far off flashes falling from the sky before being absorbed into the earth. Far away firing from mini-guns and other ordnance carried in the air.

At Bien Hoa and Ennari, fire shows occurred to the west, toward the mountains, where Defurio now found himself. Here, no quarter of the sky held dominance. Action occurred anywhere on an 180° cinemascopic screen of black sky.

Morning brought an unexpected hot breakfast. Charmaine housed a 105 Howitzer battery. Artillery batteries were furnished with mess kitchens. Meals were shared with infantry.

Afterwards, Defurio set off to investigate Charmaine. He observed informality as the standard mode of conduct. There wasn't any saluting of officers. In fact, the only officer above lieutenants was the company's captain, and he seldom strayed from his whiskey-stocked sanctuary. Defurio remembered yesterday inhaling his stale whiskey breath. Also absent from the premises were lifer sergeants. Sergeants in the field were young men promoted from the ranks.

Lieutenants were the workhorses of the officer corps. These non-lifer college boys provided leadership and administered to the needs of the men. They were trying to survive like the draftees. Unlike lifers, achieving rank wasn't a primary concern.

Charmaine was the Cadillac of frontline firebases. This curiously named place was a perfect entry point for Defurio to learn the ways of war in the central highlands. The company primarily did patrols and protected artillery and tactical operation command personnel. The company would be here for several weeks.

Firebases were larger, more established staging areas for field operations, often housing artillery batteries or other support elements. Landing zones, in comparison, only provided a place for helicopters to land. They may or may not have fixed sandbagged positions for defense. Firebases and landing zones were where troops were usually transported to conduct combat operations.

These were long days of adjustment and staving off boredom. Defurio helped unload and store mortar shells as they were air lifted in, and did maintenance and firing of the mortar. As an assistant gunner, he prepared rounds for firing and handed them to the gunner. Simple.

He had plenty of opportunity to explore the limited expanse of Charmaine; collecting information, evaluating, and making conclusions.

Charmaine had well-protected dug-in emplacements spaced in a circular line at the top of double hills. Infantry and mortarmen rotated guard duty at perimeter bunkers.

Charmaine stood as bastion in a string of firebases standing in the way of NVA trying to penetrate South Vietnam's heartland. They were nerve centers for patrols, combat assaults, sweeps, reconnaissance, and ambushes. The most active operations were short range patrols, usually consisting of four men. The goal of the SRPs (pronounced 'serps') was to detect, not engage, and to call in fire support to destroy the enemy. Good theory. In practice, SRPs were sometimes cut off, lost, ambushed, or victims of violent accidents.

Defurio felt for the bedraggled troopers coming in from patrols, bowed from exhaustion, wearing filthy, torn clothes, and bleeding from tiny cuts from sharp edged plants. He had been slated to be one of them. He still could be, since his MOS hadn't changed.

Charmaine had a tactical operation command. A TOC utilized radar to detect enemy movement and needed generators to run equipment. Defurio's squad happened to be bunkered near the TOC. Sgt. Colmes, demonstrating an innate wiliness, procured an electrical cord and a light bulb, and strung it to a TOC generator. For the privilege of allowing an electrical hook-up, the squad paid two cases of beer to the TOC team.

"What d'ya think, Jack? This light is pretty fucking nice, huh?" commented Couch. Usually GIs had nicknames or went by last names. His squad couldn't make anything out of "Defurio," so they simply called him Jack.

"It's a fucking miracle, Couch. I'm writing my wife about it as we speak." He didn't say Donna's name, her name being too personal to mention in casual conversation. The electrical lighting spurred a spate of nighttime letter writing to Donna, since there were too many interruptions during daytime, usually people wanting to talk.

Rumors flew. They went from top to bottom and bottom to top like a water wheel. Sgt. Colmes casually mentioned that the platoon would soon be receiving a trained mortar man. "Shit," Defurio thought. "I could be bumped from mortars."

"How definite is that?" he asked.

"I don't know. Lt. Duke mentioned it. Same shit, nobody knows for sure," answered Colmes.

Defurio worried. He anguished at the thought of being one of the pitiful souls dragging themselves in from patrols. Patrols weren't the worst of it. The bush held greater agonies.

Chapter 5

Big Jim Maloney

December 23. Kicking back. A hum drum day in Dnam. Daylight trickled in through a seam in the poncho. A massive form overwhelmed the opening, throwing the interior into darkness. A startled soldier twisted the naked light bulb to turn it on. Light fell on a hulking, square faced goliath squeezing through. The imposing visitor had a whitishness of skin as that seen on the underbelly of a fish.

"Is, eh, this where I'm supposed to be?" the giant blurted in a friendly east coast city accent, which seemed to emanate from his adenoids.

"You with Sgt. Colmes?" Jones asked.

"Colmes… that's it. I couldn't tell if they were saying 'cones' for ice cream, 'cums' for women, or something you run through your hair." This line, delivered with such wry wit, forced an unsuppressed giggle among squad members. In a flash, the big man had initiated the kind of affability afforded to playful panda bears. His intimating bulk became a secondary consideration.

"What's your name, man?" Jones asked. A newbie attracting this much attention was unprecedented.

"Jim Maloney."

"Where you from?" someone asked.

"New York City."

"No shit," crowed Jones. "Big Jim from New York City." The name stuck.

Big Jim was so entertaining, Defurio lost sight of the possibility that this character, an Army trained mortarman, could bump him from mortars. Tomorrow, Defurio could find himself in the line.

The next day, Sgt. Colmes and Lt. Duke didn't say anything to Defurio or Fox. The addition of Maloney had filled the platoon's roster. To higher-ups, the platoon was complete. They had overlooked the fact that two of the men on the roster didn't have job descriptions for mortars. For now, the Army had unofficially converted them to mortarmen.

Defurio and Maloney sat on sandbags eating breakfast. "How long you been in Nam?" Maloney inquired.

"About three weeks." Counting down the precise days would come much later. "How about you?"

"Three days. They bypassed orientation, took a couple of days to give us our shit, and sent us off." Jim shoveled in heaping amounts of food, contently chewing it. "Pretty good chow. Seen any action?"

"We have fire missions every night and sometimes during the day. We shoot off a lot of illum rounds in daylight to fix positions for patrols."

"Illuminations rounds?" Jim responded. "Hell, we never fired them in training."

"There goes one now" Jack said, pointing. "Watch, it'll explode high in the air, forming a sputtering ball of light for about five minutes. Sometimes we use them at night if we suspect possible dink movement."

"This is way different than I thought it was going to be. I thought they'd be shooting at me as soon as I got here. I thought I'd be sleeping in shit and eating it too," Jim said between chewing and swallowing.

"Were you drafted or join up?"

This was an important question posed by Defurio. It helped set parameters for a possible friendship. Anyone joining the Army came under suspicion.

"Nah, they drafted my ass. How about you?"

Jack told his story, and it visibly moved Maloney. "Those assholes must have been desperate to draft a twenty-six-year-old married college graduate."

"You look older than the usual draftee too," said Defurio.

"I'm twenty-three."

"What the fuck happened?'

"I kept getting 4-F'd because I weighed over three-hundred pounds. I wanted to do power weight lifting so I bulked up, then I stopped lifting, lost weight, and they fucking drafted me. I still weigh 275. Maybe weight restrictions were loosened. Too late to do anything about it now."

As long as Jim got enough to eat, nothing seemed to bother him. He had the basic loveable qualities of a sheep dog; feed him, don't kick him too hard, and he'd be happy in a pile of manure.

Jack and Jim hit it off. They sauntered back to their hooch.

"So, Jim, you were a weightlifter."

"Yep."

"What does it take to be a good weightlifter?" Jack expected a dissertation on training and technique.

"A severe complex," Jim answered.

"What do you mean?"

"When you think about it, it's kinda stupid to spend hours lifting heavy objects for no practical reason," Jim explained.

"How about a good physique?"

"Are you kidding?" Jim said jokingly. "I looked like a fucking Sumo wrestler. My clothes fit so tight they cut off my circulation. I felt like I was going to faint half the time and when I farted, it would damn near blow my shoes off."

Jim kept talking. "The real reason I started lifting was when I was sixteen, we moved to Harlem. I wanted to develop myself so nobody would fuck with me. I got carried away. People had already stopped fucking with me way earlier when I was at 225, which I reached when I was thirteen." Jim laughed. He had a laugh that stayed in his mouth. His eyes would dance and his head and shoulders bounce up and down. His quips were subtle, insightful, and frequent. He tended to be self-deprecating.

Jim was thick in his upper torso. When he went from place to place, his body followed his chest. Muscular pectorals were further amplified by a New York swagger, no doubt influenced by his exposure to Harlem's strutting male population.

Mortars were situated on flattened portions of hills to permit leveling of gun pits. Except for those, a hill had to be negotiated at a slant. To maintain some degree of style, attitude, and balance, Big Jim flung his arms in a distinctive motion when on the move. You'd think his flailing weightlifter arms were attached to swivels.

He couldn't help it—in word, deed, and action, Big Jim was naturally funny.

Jack and Jim's relationship adhered faster than quick drying glue. Overnight they established a bond based on mutual appreciation; by Jack for Jim's penchant for nuanced puns, by Jim for Jack's comic edged cynicism. They fit as closely as two hands folded in prayer. They became a team.

In the evening, Turner started it, wearing his anti-establishment purple hued granny glasses. A bowl was sparked, some tokes taken and passed on, man to man, spit to spit, black to white. Turner was hyper. He had a bulging lower lip hanging from a thin face. Whites below his pupils were prominent from angling his view over the rim of his granny glasses. He used those in unison to orchestrate his facial movement. In conjunction with two missing upper front teeth, they made his face a triumph of theatrical expression.

Ugliness of women was being discussed. "Fucking an ugly woman is the same as fucking a pretty one," he said, making it seem that at one time or another he had been with a pretty woman. Big Jim inhaling marijuana smoke when Turner finished, made a comment.

Jim had impeccable timing. He paused and pounced. "That means one thing, Turner. You must have gone with some pretty fucking ugly women." That brought a laugh from everyone.

Turner laughed too and acknowledged the retort, "you cold, Big Jim." Jim chuckled in marijuana-induced satisfaction.

Jack rested complacently on his rack, bypassing tokes, fairly pleased with his circumstances. A compatibility, an acceptance, and an easiness held together this mongrel group. Mostly he was grateful to be in a situation of relative comfort and security, however temporary.

A five foot long center aisle flanked by empty ammo boxes led to the hooch's single opening. Sleeping bags placed on the boxes kept them above sometimes soggy soil. These mortar ammo boxes weren't available to line soldiers. Taking his writing materials, Defurio would go inconspicuously from the aisle to a corner near the entrance. The rest of the men socialized at the back wall. Ammo boxes didn't leave enough room to sit upright. When not sleeping, everyone had to slouch against interior walls. Since there wasn't enough light or stability from his suspended bunk, Jack had to write sprawled on ammo boxes. Without head space, he laid in a prone position.

> *Dear Donna,*
>
> *I'm writing tonight from an enclosed plastic covered dirt box housing several trash talking teenagers. Oddly, we're listening to rhythm and blues, my favorite music. There is a haze of smoke similar in source and substance to that in a college dorm. So things can't be too bad. Oh, before I go further I want to let you know I've become fairly close to somebody who recently joined our squad; a big guy appropri-*

> *ately called "Big Jim" Maloney. He's from New York City...*

Defurio didn't mind his squad getting stoned. They were not in a perimeter bunker so being alert wasn't too much of an issue. However, although an established, relatively safe firebase, Charmaine as a fixed position could receive an attack at any time.

Christmas Day, 1968. Another in a long series of dreary days. Same frying pan heat, same lung sucking wet air, same pulverized earth everywhere, patrols going out and coming in, one or two fire missions, illumination rounds being shot off, the crash and thud of ordnance hitting in the hinterlands; the same crap over and over, day and night.

In the late afternoon, two Huey helicopters came in. Fly-ins from slicks were usually earlier. They weren't carrying troops or supplies. What's going on?

Off loaded were insulated containers of turkey, mashed potatoes, gravy, and rations of beer and gift packages. Score one for the Army. Hot food to a soldier is almost as good as hot sex, and warm beer better than no beer.

Food and beer helped, but it wasn't enough to break Defurio's dour mood. Being in this fucked up country at Christmas made him nearly inconsolable.

Inexplicably, he became incensed by his gift package. They had been distributed arbitrarily. His package contained packets of Woolite, a pocket knife, and a handwritten note from a couple asking the Lord to look after him. Fuck them! Using him to get themselves to heaven. He wadded up the note and stomped on it. What a fucking mockery. Goddamn Woolite and a pocket knife. What the fuck was he going to do with this worthless shit?

Angry and irritated, Defurio went by himself and sat on the rim of the gun pit. He baked in the sun. "This is stupid." He relocated to shade cast by an attached shelter where mortar shells were stored.

Half-drunk through his third beer—warm beer strikes fast—he saw big Jim chugging up. "I was looking for you, who you hiding from?" Jim chided. He plopped down beside him. The mere sight of his amiable buddy siphoned off a bit of Defurio's consternation. Jim, holding an overloaded mess tin, said, "Shit, I didn't think life here could be this good."

"What are you talking about?" Jack said, mystified, although confident Jim would have a provocative rejoinder.

Big Jim pocketed some food in his cheeks. "Well, where's the war? I thought I'd be eating mud and dodging AK-47 bullets. I didn't think I'd be on a mountain, sightseeing, eating turkey, and drinking beer."

Jack finished his can of Black Label and opened another. "I wonder who brews this shit."

"Probably a relative of the secretary of defense, passing himself off as a warm beer specialist."

Jack mulled over Jim's previous observation. "I know what you're saying about turkey, beer, and AK-47 bullets. Nothing adds up. It's a fucking upside down science fiction horror movie. You know demons are waiting in the cellar, and we could fall through any minute."

"I always wanted to be in movies. I…eh…didn't think I'd have to audition by standing on my head in a vat of Vietnamese shit."

Jim often used "eh" to hesitate for emphasis before finishing humorous statements.

Defurio enjoyed this exchange; two verbal swordsmen vanquishing lurking demons with jokes. His angst abated.

They got drunk and talked the way not done by men unless forced by extreme circumstances. Men cut off from family, friends, loved ones, and home, and constrained by fate.

Big Jim was half Irish, half Pollack; his father a longshoreman, his mother a housewife. His uncles were cops and firemen. An avid lover of animals, he particularly liked dogs, birds, and fish. He was a member of an aquarium club. Jim swooned when talking about the breeding and maintenance of guppies. He made his living as a draftsman.

"That's good, a drafted draftsman," Jack added.

Jack related his upbringing in Fresno. Happily, Jim learned Jack's initial major in college was zoology. As a result, of his empathetic description of her, Jim understood that Jack's universe centered on Donna. With touches of humor, both described stories of home, family, and personal interests.

Notwithstanding the intimate discussion, Big Jim couldn't help staying funny. He had a girlfriend, Louise. Jim believed she had been unfaithful to him. He wasn't sure, though getting clap from her when they met on his furlough was damning evidence. He prepared himself for the worst. He expected a "Dear John" letter any day. "Knowing Louise, she'll make it short. 'Yo, J.M., we're done.'" Jim did his head bouncing chuckle.

Chapter 6

Yellow Brick Road

Generally speaking, 4th Division Headquarters and 1st/14th Battalion Headquarters at Ennari were referred to as the Rear, the Rear Area, or the Rear Echelon. This is where men were processed in and out of the highlands. Various battalion headquarters were home to a myriad of support staff consisting of clerks and workers marshaling and maintaining goods and services necessary for the war effort.

For combat soldiers, a stopover in the Rear Area meant relative safety, hot meals, cold beer, sleeping quarters, clean clothes, showers, rotary fans, and so forth.

There was an encompassing element involved at 4th Division Headquarters broader than the term the Rear Area. This related to a black hole of decision making where 4th Division Commanders determined how, when, and where the war in the highlands was to be conducted. Frequently, these directives bore scant resemblance to conditions and problems at the site of execution.

Authorship of command orders were obscured by layers of bureaucracy. Decisions were handed down and signed off by mid-level officers. Unnamed generals or major-generals were correspondingly sheltered from blame or responsibility if anything went wrong. These filtered down orders were referred to as coming from higher higher. Unfortunately, higher higher decisions sometimes extended to everyday life on a firebase.

So it was a day after Christmas. Three master sergeants on temporary assignment were deposited on Charmaine. These were typical old-school safe duty pricks.

A company formation was called, and the who-gives-a-fuck troops were informed a high ranking English officer would be visiting Charmaine on a look-up-your-ass inspection tour. Preparations were put in the hands of these three nincompoop master sergeants. Having time-in grade, Master Sergeant Fullbright had been given responsibility for this prospective boondoggle. He had been given carte blanche authorization to utilize soldiers on Charmaine as he saw fit.

As if by magic, these sergeants garnered goods and resources thought to be unattainable. The first order of business involved installing flooring to accommodate a cozy briefing tent. A dip between the twin hills allowed some level land for such an out of place structure.

This busy work generated made-to-order barbs and quips from Big Jim and Jack. Looking from afar at troops sawing and hammering, Jack commented, "I wish they'd make up their minds. Are we killers or carpenters?"

"Good thing this isn't a visiting Bob Hope Show. They'd have to send in reinforcements," Jim said, alluding to the famous comedian's annual overseas Christmas show extravaganza.

The pair didn't linger. To stand there ogling invited unwanted attention. Work details were springing up everywhere. They ducked behind a bunker. "I'll be surprised if they don't arrange a fox hunt for this English fucker," Jim said, making his usual reference to animals whenever he could.

"I wouldn't mind tally hoeing this motherfucker to where he came from," countered Jack. Not wanting to be commandeered by the asshole master sergeants, Big Jim, Jack, and savvy squad mates made for their hooch.

Lt. Duke showed up there. He respected the privacy of his men and never went inside a squad's bunker without announcing himself. He really didn't want to know what was going on inside. "Hello," he said, and waited for them to snuff out their joints before parting the poncho liner and going inside. "Hi guys, we got a direct order to report to Master Sgt. Fullbright, ASAP," he announced unenthusiastically. This bullshit pissed him off too.

"Fullbright?" Defurio said. "The Army must have a special scholarship program rewarding weak minded master sergeants." Only Lt. Duke and Maloney got the reference to Fullbright academic scholarships.

Fullbright postured before the give-a-shit company and stiffened to his maximum height of 5'6", a measurement matched by his waistline. Coming directly from Ennari, he was freshly showered and resplendent in spic and span fatigues festooned with various insignias and Boy Scout type knick-knacks. He tingled with delight at a once in a lifetime opportunity to impress superiors with his leadership capabilities. He had an additional incentive—being at Charmaine would insure a combat infantryman's badge. The CIB was a coveted award given to those who had been in first hand combat. This fiction would be made possible because mortars would likely be on fire missions. With cronies in charge of the awards process, this would be enough to achieve the career enhancing award. For this prize, Master Sgt. Fullbright could sacrifice three days of fucking whores in Pleiku and guzzling beer at Ennari.

Inspired by what he considered a key responsibility, he hit on what he thought was a stroke of genius. He would kill two birds with one stone. One, he would have the men gather hundreds of rocks formed from hard packed earth when explosives were used to clear vegetation. This would give Charmaine an appearance of stateside military orderliness. Two, he would utilize collected stones to line pathways between bunkers, thus raising Charmaine to a level of parade ground excellence.

Breaking into a sweat and exerting considerable effort, Fullbright held up a rock about two fists wide. He pronounced it as the standard by which stones would be selected for placement. Positioning of properly proportioned rocks gave Fullbright, for a short while, an excuse to micromanage their arrangement. He strode confidently up and down paths as they took shape, were raked off (yes, with real rakes), and unsuitable rocks tossed to one side. Stoop labor by an infantry company. Fullbright had reduced B Company to a chain gang.

It reminded Defurio of field work in his youth. This kind of drudgery doesn't seem so bad when done by others, for instance when seeing fruit or vegetable pickers in 100 degree heat from the comfort of an air-conditioned vehicle while speeding down highways and byways of the Great San Joaquin Valley. Temperatures on Charmaine were above 115 degrees. Sitting in a rocking chair in such heat would be debilitating.

Sgt. Fullbright spent a majority of his day inside the newly erected briefing tent where he had an ample quantity of refrigerated beer and a rotary fan. He had delegated his two less time-in-grade sergeants to oversee his work program.

Naturally, Jack and Big Jim did not tolerate this state of affairs. Picking up rocks in a half ass manner, Jim grumbled to no one in particular, "What the fuck's next? Dress us up as maids, our asses hanging out so we can serve tea and crumpets to this English cocksucker?" Characteristically, Big Jim mixed sarcasm and humor. Unlike Defurio, Big Jim never really said anything in anger.

They carried a handful of rocks for show. When the sergeants were diverted, they lit out for an isolated bunker they had earmarked for such emergencies. The master sergeants didn't notice they were gone.

The following day, Fullbright outdid himself. Somewhere, somehow, he had procured gallons of gold paint and dozens of paint brushes.

The work crew painted "1st/14th" in large numbers on the landing pad. What to do with gallons of extra paint? Fullbright, feeling at the top of his game, had a brainstorm—paint the tops of rocks bordering completed pathways.

Peeping out from their hiding place, Jack and Big Jim scrutinized soldiers, backs curved frontwards, splashing paint on rocks. "Jesus, Jim, can you believe this shit?"

"No, but I believe I'd like to shove those gallons of paint up Fullbright's ass."

Captain Lowery spent most of his time sucking on fifths of Wild Turkey. He came out in mornings and evenings to piss and shit. Other than that, he stayed in his command post, drinking. His state of inebriation made him oblivious to Fullbright's path building project.

Morning came. Electric bolts of dawn revealed gleaming, winding yellow lined lanes running up, down, and all around Charmaine. Jack immediately dubbed the garish spectacle the yellow brick road. One could almost see Dorothy and her companions skipping towards Oz. Twitters broke out as the title spread from bunker to bunker.

There had been a problem of resupply. Helicopters were committed to support increased combat operations. Captain Lowery's stash of Wild Turkey had run out. Consequently, he became sober enough to become aware what had gone on. Arising for his morning piss and shit, he looked at the golden nuggets running everywhere.

Rubbing his eyes in disbelief, he yelled for Fullbright. "What the fuck is this, Disneyland? Goddammit, do something about those fucking piss-colored rocks!" Fullbright tripped over himself arranging hastily gathered work crews to turn over every painted rock.

Lowery recognized how vulgarly inappropriate it was to have pretty rows of yellow strands decorating a combat base where soldiers were subject to being killed or wounded. He was a drunk, but that didn't mean he was stupid.

Well, maybe semi-stupid. The garish numerals on the landing pad remained. It hadn't entered Captain Lowery's sodden brain that NVA spotters, zeroing-in mortar rounds, might appreciate golden numerals highlighting a target area.

When mentioning the yellow brick road, Jack and Jim discovered blacks didn't have any knowledge of "The Wizard of Oz," Judy Garland, Dorothy, or munchkins. This was fertile soil.

Big Jim and Jack, by some undefined natural talent exclusive to themselves, had an uncanny ability, without planning or forethought, to lead astray the unwary, and to do it so subtlety that victims didn't know they'd been had. There wasn't any real harm done. For them, this became a hobby, a tension relieving diversion.

For example, after completing the yellow brick road, squad members eased their exhaustion by smoking pot (which they would have done anyway). When they were sufficiently mellowed out, Big Jim posed a seemingly innocuous question. "Any of you guys know about the Wizard of Oz?" No, they didn't. Jack intervened in a seamless interplay off Big Jim's question. Jack recited a thumbnail sketch of the movie, emphasizing Judy Garland playing Dorothy. He concluded, "I heard stories Judy Garland loved to fuck munchkins."

"What's a munchkin?" said Jones.

Bingo!

"It's like an elf," Jim said, building on Defurio's hoax. Loveable Big Jim would make the story more believable. In his description of munchkins, Big Jim purposely didn't bother to differentiate munchkins from elves. When he drew to a close, someone in the spellbound audience asked excitedly, "Why did she want to do it with an elf?" Double bingo! In amused appreciation, Jack watched Big Jim's performance. "Because their dicks are twice as big as normal. Not only that, they can rotate their short bodies so that every inside inch and outside curly hair is taken care of. They say Dorothy couldn't get enough of elf dick." Jim deleted further reference to Judy Garland. He had successfully corrupted and distilled it down to Dorothy fucking elves. Jim paused, letting images of elves taking turns fucking Dorothy sink in.

Rucker, taken aback by talk of elves, spontaneously decided to rid himself of an ugly memory, one as distasteful as an unflushed crap-filled toilet. "I fucked a dwarf once. That's like an elf, isn't it?" Triple bingo!

"Tell us about it, Rucker," Jim coaxed in a confidential tone. This conversation had already expanded exponentially beyond usual soldier talk. Would Rucker spill out an engrossing, disgusting secret? He had the squad's rapt attention.

Rucker, an unappealing, non-descript person destined to live on life's bottom tier, had limitations in ability and appearance. He could never answer a question without getting confused. Average in height and weight, he had an unbalanced face and a crooked nose framed by a jaw bigger on one side than the other. He had a furry pelt for eyebrows, and puffy lips on a slanted mouth that only partially hid picket spaced teeth.

Rucker had never before been in the limelight. Big Jim gave him his chance. Jim's friendly encouragement gave Rucker an opportunity to shine.

Rucker eked out his tale. He had trouble completing sentences. Even so, his words were compelling. Ears adjusted to Rucker's country, mush mouthed rural dialect.

He came from a backwards mountain part of Tennessee. He had a cousin, a "squatty girl" with a big face, big teeth, and bushy hair. Because of her looks, she didn't have regular boyfriends.

Rucker said she had an insatiable appetite for sex. "She always gets her fucks in," he said. She had developed a method to lure men to satisfy her needs. She invited potential stud servers on a picnic, promising a fine meal washed down with her daddy's high grade moonshine. For a good meal and moonshine, a man can overlook a certain amount of ugliness and shortness of stature.

She extended an invitation to Rucker, and he accepted. She had a picnic table set up in the woods. As promised, she prepared a nice meal accompanied by plenty of moonshine. At dusk, she cleared the moonlit table.

She began to fondle him. By then, Rucker was moonshine drunk, which was apparently an elevated state of drunkenness. Rucker said his cousin didn't look half bad in moonlight. It might have been the same for her; Rucker wasn't any prize himself.

She stripped and reached into a tote bag, pulling out a rope attached to a crocheted harness, and had Rucker strip and lay back on the picnic table. She threw one end of the rope over an overhanging tree limb and climbed into the harness. She requested, no, demanded he hoist her up. She tucked her knees under her chin.

Rucker described looking up and seeing a glistening oyster crevice merging with an ass as firm and round as a melon. Rucker began dunking her on him like a donut in hot coffee. When his arms got too tired, he set her down and penetrated her to his pubic bone. She rocked and gyrated and listened to Rucker groan.

She increased her movement, violently thrusting her hips. "Turn! Turn! Turn!" She waved her left arm like a cowboy on a bucking bronco. Rucker got her message. He reached up, grabbed her narrow naked shoulders and pushed. He maintained tension on the rope. She began spinning rapidly as if on slippery ball bearings, furiously twisting and untwisting.

At this point, Rucker became unexpectedly eloquent. He related how his cousin made him feel as though he were in an electric chair with wires attached to his crotch. His cousin, demonstrating the agility of an acrobat, hopped off him and landed on her feet.

Rucker had become the latest of her satisfied stud servers. As for his cousin, she pranced home, merrily carrying a picnic basket containing her lariat of lust in a state of serenity at having found a way to cope with life's adversities.

If it hadn't been for Rucker's frequent hesitations and stammering, everyone would have had sustained erections. Even so, everyone had half hard-ons.

This is what passed for a successful day in Dnam. No one hurt, enough to eat and drink, and thanks to Big Jim, with assistance from Defurio, a spellbinding evening of provocative story telling.

His lordship—the reason behind the yellow brick road—failed to materialize. He had spent fifteen seconds buzzing over Charmaine in an observation helicopter. Typical Army fuck-up.

His no show came to light when fresh fatigues issued to troops the day before his expected arrival were removed and returned.

Chapter 7

Interlude

Helicopters weren't bringing food, water, or ammo. Ordinarily, they came daily to transport men and supplies. They were busy on combat missions. Radio chatter indicated the First Battalion 35th Infantry in the next sector and within mortar range of Charmaine was getting mauled. There had been a jump in nightly gunfights by other units in the AO. B-52 bombings were coming closer to Charmaine.

B Company was relatively inactive, restricted to guarding Charmaine, routine patrols, reconnaissance, and regular fire missions by mortars and artillery, often in support of other companies. No one kidded themselves; they knew they were about to be engaged in heavy combat.

Becoming increasingly touchy and agitated, Jack had gotten into a shoving match with a guy from third squad over whose turn it was for guard duty.

"You okay, Jack?" Jim had come across Jack brooding alone.

"Fucking Army. I haven't gotten a letter since I've been here. Those fucking incompetent postal clerk assholes could fuck up a wet dream."

Defurio had degenerated to saying some form of 'fuck' whenever he spoke.

"I know, Jack, we can't win." Defurio braced for Jim to present an interesting diversion.

"Did I tell you I got a Dear John letter from that cunt, Louise?"

"Nope."

Big Jim was a master of when and how to say something and had waited for the optimum moment to tell Jack.

"I told you I was expecting Louise to unload on me. Well, she did. At first I thought her letter was thoughtful and considerate." Wanting to drain away as much of Defurio's anxiety as possible, Jim deliberately dragged out the story. He stopped talking momentarily while they lit up cigarettes. Jack's jumpiness began to fade as he concentrated on the big man's monologue.

"Well anyway, she had the courtesy of writing why she was leaving me. My first impression was, what a classy bitch, going through the trouble of giving me an explanation."

"That does seem kind of unusual," Jack replied.

Then Jim landed the bombshell. "The reason she gave was that she was marrying, not engaged to, but marrying an East Indian psychiatrist."

"That's a cold shot, Jim, although you have to admit this guy is several levels higher than a grunt." Maybe Jim could take some comfort in that he had been cuckolded by an educated professional.

While contemplating this mysterious raghead cavorting with his ex-girlfriend, they inhaled deeply on their Army furnished filtered Kool cigarettes. To enjoy the complete benefit of this narration, Jack repositioned himself to face Big Jim. Without really trying to, Jim had an array of inflections, nods, and facial expressions used to good advantage when he spoke. With his shaggy hair, unshaven face, bear-shaped body, and New York slur, he could have been taken for a drunken wilderness guide telling tales to city slickers.

"Now why in the fuck would she go out of her way to tell me this asshole is an East Indian and a psychiatrist? I think she was dissing me and my family, insinuating an East Indian is better than a family of Paddy cops and Pollack firemen. What a cunt."

Jim tried to act mean by insulting Louise. "Maybe she'll give Mr. East Indian head shrinker motherfucker the clap." Jim undid any attempt at meanness by chuckling heartily.

"Mr. East Indian motherfucker probably gave it to you," Jack said.

Jim thought this over, arriving at the conclusion that his bout with the clap had assuredly come from Louise's East Indian paramour. "Sonofabitch, you're right, Jack. And I was thinking of marrying that bitch."

"Good thing you didn't," replied Jack. "Dr. Raghead probably saved you from years of living up to your eyebrows in shit."

Unlike Defurio, Big Jim accepted life's adversities philosophically. Any hurt inflicted by Louise only caused a skin deep, psychological flesh wound. Nothing permanent. His remorse concerning Louise's infidelity evaporated quickly.

"You know what would be cool, Jack? To get to New York, find Dr. Raghead, thank him for taking that bitch off my hands, yank off his fucking turban, and use it to shine my shoes in front of his dotted forehead."

Jack smilingly gave Jim a fist pound, one sideways fist coming down on Jim's. This greatly reduced the handshake popularized by blacks, a ritual representing brotherhood, agreement, understanding, and affirmation. The entire handshake involved one-potato, two-potato, followed by a series of steps, and finishing with crooked fingers clasping and pulling gently. Jack disliked sweaty fingers pulling on his. His modified version started and ended in a one-potato.

Big Jim had managed to dispel Jack's sour mood. Satisfied, he rumbled away with urgency unusual for him.

"What's the rush, Jim?"

"Shitter," he replied. It was Friday; horse-pill day. An intimidating pill as big as a bullet was given to prevent malaria. Ingested after breakfast, it caused diarrhea.

Shitters on Charmaine were deluxe models, preferable to emptying yourself in the wilderness and exposing your ass to being tickled or cut by sharp plants. Shitter-outhouses were made of plywood, the Army's favorite construction material. Inside was an elevated bench with a hole cut out. Waste dropped three feet into half of a fifty-gallon drum.

Medics were responsible for burning shit. On a regular basis, shit cans were removed, doused in gasoline, and lit. The resulting shit-fed smoke wasn't conducive to barbequing steaks or burgers. Everyone stayed indoors on shit burning days.

Plastic piss tubes were placed a healthful distance from bunkers. They stood four feet in length anchored in rocks and soil at a 45° angle. A mesh screen covered a five inch opening, insuring a fine mist back spray. Pungent ureic fumes funneling up through the tubes were merely another discomfort endured by soldiers who had to stand over them.

To conserve diminished supplies, patrols had been curtailed and the company put on restricted duty. With nothing else to do, Jack and Jim decided to investigate Charmaine's numerous nooks and crannies. Here and there, they paid short visits to line company guys. Men congregated inside squad bunkers, staying out of sight and out of the heat. Visitors were welcome, especially Jack and Jim, who brought with them a steady stream of anecdotes and rib-tickling repartee.

Spreading dollops of merriment as they went, Jack and Jim continued on their journey of exploration. Rounding a corner, Jack halted at the sight of an unsoldierly lieutenant smoking a cigarette. He had his shirt open, had a scraggily beard, and wore unlifer-like unlaced boots. Lt. Donleavy leaned cross legged, taking shade in a doorway of a convex. Jim's forward motion moved him past Jack, almost crashing into the lieutenant. "Oh, hello, sir. What are you doing...eh...guarding a shipment of condoms?"

"No, I'm a dentist. This is a dentist office."

"No shit," Jim responded, somewhat flustered.

He stimulated Jack's interest. "How do you do dental work without equipment?" he inquired.

"I'll show you, come on in." Lt. Donleavy flicked down his cigarette, pleased to have something to do. He showed them a completely outfitted modern dental facility within an 8' x 8' steel container. "If I have juice — meaning electric power — I can do anything here I do in the States—except pinch a dental assistant's ass. Do you boys need any work done?"

Jack had an upper filling fall out. It left an extremely annoying hole and was a site for potential dental problems. He had tried to get it fixed at Ennari, but officers had priority and he kept getting bumped.

"Right now?"

"Right now."

"Catch you later, Jim," said Jack, sitting on an overstuffed leather dental chair. Whoever manufactured this equipment didn't spare any taxpayer money.

"Okay, see you in a bit." Big Jim went in search of a home-sent snack.

Cooks had been serving limited meals. Stores of basic ingredients, canned and packaged foods were running low. Four days earlier, an observation helicopter managed to bring in a batch of mail and packages from home. These were shared and distributed when received. Packages were ripped open in hungry eagerness. Jim thought he might be able to beg for someone's uneaten Vienna sausages or sardines. Very doubtful.

Lt. Donleavy wasn't assigned to a specific platoon or company. Not having the benefit of regular companions, he welcomed intelligent conversation. While he worked, he freely exchanged banter with Defurio and indicated that he shared his intense dislike for Army regimen. It turned out they were Theta Chi fraternity brothers. He had become a member at Iowa State.

Lt. Donleavy was similar to a majority of lieutenants—good people adjusting to a bad situation. He seemed to be an excellent dentist. When he finished, Defurio thanked him. "Thanks, sir."

"Knock off the sir shit. It's Keith." They shook hands.

Jack caught up with Jim fruitlessly looking for food. They walked through camp taking stock of their situation. "Weird, isn't it, Jim? The horseshit we were given about VC hiding behind every tree, stuff about being impaled on punji stakes, being in fire fights day and night, danger of being bitten by poisonous snakes. What a lot of B.S. What gets me," Jim added, "is that we hardly know any of these guys." Jim referred to the one hundred or so men in the company.

"Yeah, what happened to that band of brothers shit?"

Companies were pasted together, and individual men came and went. Almost none of them had trained or entered the country together. Companies were composed of newbies coming in, replacing short-timers rotating out. Men were assigned to eight to ten man squads, with three to four squads to a platoon. Men were usually not that familiar with anyone outside their platoon.

Squads from B Company were distributed in the AO (area of operations). The term AO or "the field" referred to places in the countryside where there was active enemy involvement. Currently squads were in the AO on patrols, sweeps, reconnaissance, setting up positions, and ambushes throughout the region.

Unless on a fire mission, on patrol, or in an attack, life on a firebase moved at half pace. Why overheat your body by moving swiftly? They kept from view, rested, stayed cool, bullshitted, listened to music—blacks to Motown, whites to psychedelic rock—and got high.

Complete names were not generally known. Nicknames were common, first names uncommon, and last names the handiest reference. These men who shared quarters, food, hardships, and personal histories (of undetermined validity) could be described as intimate strangers.

Defurio's early morning hard-on, his silent alarm clock, initiated wakefulness. His right hand automatically inched downward. A masturbatory handshake launched a geyser forming two or three creamy pools. Spent sperm fertilized entrenched microbes already enriching an itchy pubic landscape.

He stirred. His fetid fatigues adhered to him. The brine stained clothes were never free from the smell and feel of wet mold.

When sleeping in the field, clothes, including socks, weren't removed. When shit hit the fan, no one wanted to scurry barefoot and bare assed looking for their wardrobe.

Boots were removed when sleeping in a rack. They were half-laced for comfort and ease of entry. Big Jim, ordinarily clumsy, displayed skill at sliding into his boots as though they were slippers.

Empty boots were routinely shaken out to dislodge spiders, scorpions, millipedes, vermin, and snakes. One morning, Defurio awakened to the repeated smashing of a boot. A scorpion had taken up residence inside a boot of Sgt. Colmes. He pounded it until its carapaced body became unrecognizable. Colmes, outwardly a calm, quiet guy, was nearing the end of his tour and this scorpion had touched off an unguarded moment of pent up stress.

Morning displeasures weren't restricted to bothersome erections, insects, and nocturnal intruders. Early risers were also greeted by the gagging odor of an unventilated roomful of infected groins.

Jungle rot was endemic. Everybody had it. Defurio's infection lodged on the underside of his scrotum, right on the ridge. An exquisite sensation came from grabbing squirmy folds on either side of the affected area and pinching with his thumb and forefinger.

Five days since Christmas. Still no fucking mail. Not hearing from Donna wore at his heart and mind. Big Jim took some of the edge off. "Got any cigarettes?" Jack asked.

"Just a minute, Jack, I have a family of bacteria I'm raising on my left nut. If I don't play with them, they get vicious." Jim plunged a hand down his pants, scratching vigorously.

In an Army where unusual occurrences are commonplace, it seemed unbelievable for a screen and projector to be set up for a night time movie. To maintain a straight line of sight between the screen and projector, they selected the highest point on Charmaine. It also happened to be the best place to monitor progress of the war.

That evening they showed *Hell is for Heroes*. Like everybody, Defurio maintained an explosive erection staring at Claudia Cardinale wiggle her tits, hips, and ass across the screen. The next night, *The Party* starring Peter Sellers was a limp dick affair.

Being outdoors watching Claudia Cardinale and Peter Sellers had been unexpectedly disturbing. Housed for hours inside a bunker, it had gone unnoticed how radically the AO had heated up. It happened overnight. In jungles surrounding Charmaine, numerous firefights were breaking out within eyesight. Sister companies were being hit regularly. Two hundred foot walls of trees blocked the sound of gunfire.

Nursing hard-ons thanks to Claudia Cardinale, Big Jim and Jack ruddered to their hooch. Jack's erectile condition didn't conceal his mounting concern. "Holy shit, Jim, what's going on?" They saw lines of tracers flashing on and off everywhere.

None of this troubling tracer activity had an effect on Big Jim. Although prone to emotional, over-the-top reactions to stressful situations, Jim wasn't a worrier. Shit had to actually happen before he reacted. "Who gives a fuck?" Jim responded. "As long as it's out there and not in here, I'm okay with it. Right now, I've got a date with Claudia. I got a blue ball special in my boxers that needs attention."

Two miles south, two Cobras mini-gunned and rocketed enemy positions. Early the next day a Chinook came in and carried a B Company platoon to where gunships had been attacking. Several unburied North Vietnamese Army soldiers were found. Dinks usually retrieve their dead. When lifting off, after depositing the men, several AK-47s opened up on the Chinook. A door gunner received a bullet to the head. A firefight ensued. Within an hour, twelve helicopters—Hueys, Cobras, and Chinooks—chewed up the area in a withering rain of fire. There wasn't any feedback as to whether the door gunner survived. By evening B Company had been extracted without further casualties.

Their luck held. However, feelings of disquiet and nervousness were developing. Two bamboo vipers were killed on Charmaine. Snakes usually don't dwell at inhabited sites. Patrols found tiger tracks. A nearby marine company reported a man dragged several feet by a tiger. B Company mortars dropped rounds on foraging monkeys mistakenly thought to be attacking NVA soldiers. A wild pig crashed across a trail in front of a scared-out-of-their-wits SRP team. A boa constrictor was hacked to death by another stressed-out patrol. Was something agitating these animals, flushing them in the open? Reconnaissance teams were finding NVA corpses in and around bunker complexes within mortar range of Charmaine; victims of air, mortar, and artillery strikes.

Waiting—for letters from home, for resupply of water and food, and for anticipated orders to embark on a major offensive or receive an NVA assault. The poisoned atmosphere dragged down spirits and attitudes. Men in B Company abandoned a "fuck it" mentality to one approaching Defurio's level of persistent irritability.

On New Year's Day, Terrible Earl and his skinny sidekick, Walker, were coming in from a rough three day SRP patrol. An NVA soldier had popped up shoulder high from a spider hole. Before he could get off a shot, Earl machine gunned him to ground meat.

An in-transit master sergeant passing through and temporarily stranded on Charmaine decided to hold a weapons inspection. He postured himself outside the mess tent entrance. Earl and Walker, filthy, hungry, and exhausted, dropped their packs and headed straight to the mess tent for whatever meager rations were available. Master Sergeant Asshole denied them entrance for not showing a clean weapon. Earl bristled. "Wait right here, motherfucker."

Earl, a rugged, flat faced black guy, featured a dangling gold earring to match two gold teeth hanging in his broad mouth. Under normal circumstances, he was a convivial jokester much beloved within the company.

Terrible Earl came by the name because of his fearsome reputation as a warrior. He had gotten his squad out of trouble more than once by his use of LAWs, a portable, disposable, plastic tube containing one rocket. Designed as an anti-tank weapon, Earl used it to kill people.

Not a man to be trifled with, and his blood already up from having blown away the sniper, Terrible Earl returned and stomped up to Master Sgt. Asshole. Earl had draped a belt of ammo across his broad shoulders. One end hung down to his M-60 machine gun. Asshole's back was turned when Earl slammed down the housing to lock and load his weapon.

Pandemonium. Men jumped chairs trying to flee. Tables were upended for protection. Men dove for whatever cover they could find. They didn't want to be hit by an errant bullet or bits and pieces of Sgt. Asshole.

When turning at the jarring sound of Earl chambering a round in his M-60, the sergeant's jaw dropped as if trying to yell "no", but couldn't. Earl shoved him aside, the tip of his machine gun barrel disappearing into the sergeant's abundant belly fat.

Walker grabbed two plates and slopped on some soupy rations. Earl and Walker calmly rejoined their squad, sat down, and ate. No one interrupted them.

There were several lieutenants present. They didn't intervene. Master Sgt. Asshole got what he deserved. In terms of value to B Company, the sergeant's credibility and usefulness rated a zero. In contrast, Terrible Earl had a reputation as a well-recognized asset.

Although a court martial offense, Terrible Earl's actions went justifiably unreported. However, his tantrum did represent an extreme to which tempers and patience had flared.

Rumors of a pending NVA offensive were rampant. Lt. Duke related that NVA forces were temporarily avoiding a confrontation. Sufficient troops and materials were being accumulated in preparation for an attempt to overrun this section of Vietnam. An expected prolonged pitched battle caused palpable tension.

An incident involving Fox exemplified a deterioration of equanimity on Charmaine. Coming from a shitter, Fox saw Defurio passing by. Fox had become a sullen pothead, part of a hard core subculture. He grabbed Defurio's left shoulder and unexpectedly stated, "Defurio, you think you're better than us because you went to college. College isn't going to stop a bullet." It wasn't true and didn't make sense. Furthermore, Defurio didn't let anybody rudely put their hands on him. He had fast hands and used them to punch hard on Fox's chest, breaking the hold on him. "I don't know what the fuck you're talking about. Why don't you crawl back in your hole and fuck yourself." Defurio set himself in anticipation of Fox coming at him. Fox was big, strong, and athletic. Defurio didn't give a shit. Fox turned around. "Fuck it." A fight would have delayed his drug fix. They wouldn't speak again. Too bad; Defurio had liked Fox.

"Jack, you're up, 0200 hours," Colmes said, announcing guard duty rotations. Shit! Two hours. Hundreds of seconds of staring at towering, formless masses of vegetation. Defurio committed himself to being vigilant. Lives, including his own, could depend on it. But nighttime guard duty was such a frustrating pain in the ass. Always a struggle. How to stay awake? A near impossibility. Self-talk, hollow whistling, pinching oneself, thinking of home, shifting positions, word games were losing efforts. Sleep usually won, mostly a kind of half sleep.

Flash dreams. Vignettes of his life with Donna. His chin dropped to his chest, waking him. How many seconds, minutes, had he been asleep? Enough of a lapse for dinks to have crept through undetected? "Goddamn it," he cussed to himself. His life was jeopardized because of fucking dreams. Was he asleep now? Was he asleep dreaming he was awake? What difference did it make anyway, asleep or awake. What good was it to look at a mass of sepia painted trees, shapeless underbrush, and swaying, creaking bamboo?

Defurio swished aside three dead flies. He scooped himself a half cup of brinish liquid. Charmaine had run out of water. Cooks saved what they had in pots.

A helicopter had brought cases of beer on New Year's Day. Nothing else, just beer. With water practically gone, beer had become a poor substitute. Couch's attempt to offset dehydration by drinking beer made his situation worse. He became thirstier, and really drunk. They had a fire mission. He wasn't in any condition to participate. Colmes told him to stand down. Couch scrunched up his face as through sucking a lemon. "Fuck you." He grabbed his M-16, pointed it at Colmes, and chambered a round. Couch—irascible to begin with and now dead drunk—became a monster. There wasn't any question he might pull the trigger.

There was a mad dash for the bunker opening. Couch sat spread legged at the opposite end. He kept his rifle trained on

Colmes. At this range, there wasn't a need to aim. Colmes moved slowly backwards.

Defurio hunched near Couch. He had been blocked from escaping by bodies converging at the doorway. Defurio maintained his composure. Couch's rifle pointed at Colmes, not him. "Take it easy, Couch. No sweat. Colmes is a good guy, put your rifle down." Couch ignored Defurio and kept an unwavering fix on Colmes.

Lt. Duke showed up, running to the bunker, when he'd heard Couch threaten to shoot Sgt. Colmes. Couch liked Lt. Duke. "C'mon, Couch. Y'all put down your weapon. We don't need you on this fire mission. Take a break. Don't worry, we'll need you later." Lt. Duke's voice was as delicate and comforting as a wet nurse's lullaby. Lt. Duke stood behind Colmes, and Couch didn't want to hurt him.

Muscles on Couch's face untightened, as did his hold on his M-16. Defurio leaned forward on his knees and carefully removed the rifle from Couch's loosened grip.

Crisis averted. Lt. Duke returned to his hooch. Nothing more said or done. Lt. Duke had a civilian mentality and a good heart, and recognized the situation for what it was. He wasn't interested in court martialing an impetuous, dehydrated, accidentally drunk teenager. He handled it as a family problem; outsiders, meaning higher-ups, needn't be involved. Couch never apologized. He didn't have to. No blood spilled. That's all anyone cared about.

Couch's flare up ended favorably—an unfortunate incident in a sequence of unfortunate incidents. Merely the end of another shitty day in Dnam. Worse days were coming.

Chapter 8

Smell of Blood

A Huey flew in at mid-morning with a desperately needed water tank strapped underneath. The one hundred gallon steel containers had two rubber tires on truck wheels and a trailer hitch for hauling them behind a truck or jeep. Water tanks were marked in big white stenciled letters, "POTABLE WATER." In a flurry of activity, water tanks were exchanged, empty for full.

Jack and Big Jim watched with bemused interest. Jack remarked, "Why in hell would they fly in water if it wasn't drinkable? Potable? Most of these guys don't know what that means, it's fucking redundant."

"Matter of fact," Jim said contemplatively, "every water container I've seen in Vietnam has 'potable' stamped on it. I've never seen 'non-potable' or 'don't drink this shit, its sewer water.'"

Jack said, "Is there a reason the Army would produce non-potable water?"

"Actually there is. Potable water isn't good for tropical fish." Jim's animal references again. "Probably some general didn't want to contaminate his aquarium of exotic fish."

"Probably an ambitious middle ranked officer bucking for a promotion came up with the idea, kinda like a self-advertisement, 'look at me, I know what potable means, and in case you missed it, I've ordered it printed on every fucking container in Vietnam.'"

Other helicopters arrived. Regular flights had resumed. Food, men, ammo, and equipment came pouring in. Two red bags came sailing from a chopper. Everyone looked forward to mail—their link to home. For Defurio, mail bags had held nothing but disappointment and vacant hopes.

Sgt. Colmes distributed the squad's mail. Colmes, wearing an infrequent smile on his usually impassive face, approached. "Here Jack, I believe you've been waiting for these," he said, handing Jack three letters. Silently, the squad had felt bad for Defurio not receiving mail.

Defurio sought an isolated bunker, wanting to be alone with her words, her touch of pen and paper. He could faintly detect her delicate smell on the paper. He read her pure, eloquent prose of everyday life, of her parents, two sisters, and older brother. He read of her heartfelt love and worry for him, of writing daily, reading his letters, knowing he wasn't receiving hers, of sent letters and a broken heart locket never received by him.

She ascertained her letters had been mistakenly sent to the wrong company. Why hadn't they been re-routed to Company B? Defurio blamed Army incompetence—clerks too uncaring or stoned to give a shit. Perhaps there was another explanation. There was. Many months would pass before he found out what.

Cases of beer had been brought in. He postponed drinking his allotment of it, wanting instead to gorge himself on her writings. Her artistic, evenly spaced script gave vitality to her words, like wildflowers blooming amidst rubble. Donna had a beauty in her touch and she had touched these pages.

He emerged from his sequester renewed. She had restored him. It was difficult to find a sober person. Crucial functions were relegated to a handful of teetotalers. His squad had fully indulged in drinking beer, intermixed with smoking pot. They joshed and laughed, forgetting temporarily sobering news from the AO. Defurio pondered the faces of these GIs. He had developed a genuine liking for them, their devil may care attitude and feistiness. Good to see them happy. Good to feel good.

Defurio chugged his beer and soon swooned in a reverie of private moments. "Ruby" by Ray Charles came on someone's tape player. He held her, dancing to it, kissing Donna's lips.

Giggling as he did when using weed, Jim got up and hulked over to Defurio. "Let's get some air." Outside, Jim patted Jack on the shoulder. "Everything fine with Donna?" he asked, smiling broadly.

Jack hadn't confided her name to anyone else. The big man had become teary when Jack described his and Donna's forced separation. "Yeah, thanks Jim. She asked me to say 'hello.'" Jack had mentioned Jim in a letter. Jim beamed, glad he didn't have to see his friend crushed from not receiving Donna's mail.

"She also asked me about Charmaine and how it got its name." Mentioning Jim and Charmaine were the only topics outside the boundaries of confidentiality. Most of the content of her letters referred to descriptions of love - emotional and physical. Her mentioning Charmaine opened an opportunity for Jack and Jim to go on one of their diversions.

Jack started it. "You know, I've been curious myself how they name these firebases. I mean, Charmaine seems like it belongs in France."

Jim offered a plausible explanation. "I'd guess it was named for Higgins's favorite whore in Saigon. I know it wasn't named for any whores in the highlands, otherwise this place would be called 'Butt Ugly.'" Higgins was currently the Lt. Colonel running battalion field operations.

"I've got another one." At this point, Jack and Jim were so drunk as to be almost incomprehensible. "Why do we call these diminutive," Jack stumbled badly over this word, "fuckers we're shooting at, dinks? For Christ sakes, that's a description for a stuffed toy. We should be calling them something a whole lot more insulting."

"That's true, Jack, we don't even call them gooks very often. Let's come up with a better name than dinks for these skinny assed motherfuckers."

They tried, but were too drunk to form coherent thoughts. They abandoned the effort, rejoined the squad, and continued to party. After a while, he wanted to sleep. Though seriously inebriated, Defurio, buoyed by Donna's letters, couldn't sleep.

By noon, a good many men had been dispatched on patrols. Consequently, Jim and Jack were stuck doing KP. It wasn't too bad. They had first choice of food and otherwise mostly goofed off.

They brewed coffee in huge urns. They had been directed to clean them. In between cleaning and chomping on tidbits of food, they engaged in their particular brand of small talk.

"Jim, you ever notice no matter how well we clean these things, there's always an iridescent film at the top when they're filled up."

Jim expanded this line of frivolous inquiry. "And it doesn't homogenize. It becomes an oil slick in everyone's coffee cup." Jim's mind started to drift. "Those oil spots have neat colors; yellow, greens, reds, blues. Reminds me of tropical fish." Another of Jim's animal references. Jack gave Jim the opportunity for a sure-to-be-funny close.

"Jim, what do you think the Army's official name is for a coffee maker?"

Sure enough, Big Jim didn't disappoint. "From our knowledge and experience, I'd say the name has to be 'potable iridescent stimulant dispenser.'" They snickered.

Lt. Duke frantically called for a fire mission, which were normally radioed-in routinely by patrols when they encountered enemy activity. But this one was different. The usually imperturbable, soft voiced Lt. Duke came running out, shouting as loud as he could. "Fire mission! Fire mission! All squads up!" Ordinarily, the three squads alternated fire missions. "All squads up! Hurry men, hurry!"

The entire platoon, recognizing the emergency, scrambled to their mortar pits. Inside five minutes, grid co-ordinates were given, mortar tubes sighted, and rounds fired off. The three gun pits were in action simultaneously.

At a fever pitch, protective canisters of cardboard, wax, and burlap material were stripped from high explosive rounds and prepped for shooting. Six powder bags of explosives were affixed to the bottom of mortar rounds. Some usually had to be torn off depending on distance. A twenty pound 81 mm shell dropped down the tube, slammed hard on a firing pin, setting off the powder and sending the round explosively on its way.

In late twilight, a patrol had spotted a bunker complex. NVA soldiers were seen moving about the entrenched position. When B Company mortars began landing, a steely nerved, keen eyed sergeant accurately radioed-in adjustments. He walked in rounds until they landed directly on target.

With the target zeroed in, Lt. Flack gave a fire-at-will command. There wasn't any further need to adjust fire. Rounds were thrown down as fast as possible. Due to slight variations in individual rounds, no two shells hit in exactly the same spot, but land yards apart in a tight pattern.

Radio communication from the patrol indicated the bunker complex and those in it were being blown to hell. The barrage halted after fifteen minutes. Hot, smoking mortar tubes needed rest. Roughly one hundred rounds had been expended.

Defurio didn't want it to stop. It was too thrilling. Killing was no longer an abstraction; they had eye witness proof NVA troops were being slaughtered. Nine dead were counted by the patrol. Many other dead and wounded had been dragged away. Defurio wished he could see the bodies, how they were contorted. He wanted to go through dead soldiers' pockets, find photos of their families, take souvenirs, trophies for what he had helped do.

Good for him. Fuck them. If it weren't for these fucking fanatical oriental bastards, he wouldn't be here.

The fire mission had occurred during a driving rain storm. Afterwards they hurried to dry bunkers. Mortar platoon bunkers were rain proofed. Mortar shells came wrapped in plastic sheets which were inserted between rows of sandbags in the ceilings, effectively keeping out the rain. Regular infantrymen didn't have this benefit. In a hard rain, their bunkers leaked, interiors becoming wet and muddy. It was another example of life's undeserved advantages and disadvantages.

When darkness came, mortar personnel guarded the entire half mile perimeter. Mortarmen were the sole combat soldiers remaining on Charmaine. The rest of the company was canvassing jungles below. Sweeps were being conducted to assess damage by artillery, mortar, and air bombardments, and to destroy surviving enemy troops.

Defurio maintained a solitary vigil behind a low sandbag wall. Sentinels were so thinly spaced, an NVA regiment could have walked through undetected. Rainfall drummed a steady beat on his helmet and equipment. Millions of drops hammered in ugly thoughts and feelings.

He thought of the fire-at-will mission. Something had happened to him. He submitted to remnants of joy persisting from the onslaught. He was curious as to why he had felt an almost orgasmic pleasure in it. He didn't have an answer. Perhaps, an undiscovered layer of primitive emotion had been exposed. This possibility did not perplex him. It felt too natural. Too good.

He did regret something about his Christmas gift package. He discovered his Boy Scout knife made an efficient tool for stripping coverings off mortar shells. He also figured out why he had been sent Woolite. The product could be used for washing socks. He had even come to appreciate the enclosed religious message, and regretted not keeping the address of the kindly religious couple so he could send a note of thanks. He felt ashamed for having consciously humiliated them.

Defurio annoyingly scanned his section of dripping jungle through a starlight scope. The high pitched mercury battery mimicked insects mating in his ears. The device magnified existing light a thousand fold. Faint star shine poked through occasional breaks in cloud cover, enough to provide decent, though confusing, visibility.

He saw a variegated wreckage of twisted plants cast in shades of chartreuse and black. Tiny alternating camera flashes from fireflies momentarily blinded him.

"Jesus!" "Fuck!" An electric jolt went through him. Thirty yards to his left, in front of an empty bunker, a tripped flare flashed neon red light on a section of jungle; leaves, tree limbs, stalks and trunks became hands, arms and legs of creatures from hell. Coiled strands of concertina wire extending from bunkers to the tree line became flaming tentacles of a supernatural monster.

Unthinkingly, he brought the starlight scope up to his face. He saw a sun. He saw white.

"Goddamn it!" Highly agitated by the blunder but not panicked, his senses remained focused. By feel, he loaded a fat shell in an M-79 grenade launcher. Firing his M-16 would give away his position. An M-79 doesn't have a muzzle flash. His vision cleared. He pumped three rounds immediately behind and three rounds ten yards back from the flare, thinking dinks would either drop flat or scramble rapidly backward. Three rounds hit low hanging tree limbs. Good. With luck, ricocheting shell fragments would shower downward, finding home in some dink's soft flesh. There wasn't any return fire.

The flare could have been tripped by animals, wind, or falling branches. Defurio chose to fantasize there were two or three NVA soldiers bleeding out, their life's blood being sucked into the matted muck where they lay.

He was elated thinking he had blown away slimy elusive sub-humans, to have removed them as threats. He would have liked to examine their bodies, to indulge in the pleasure of having exterminated them. He couldn't escape a feeling of exquisiteness for what he had done.

The flare died. He hunkered in the mud, alone, in the rain, in the returned charcoal of night, in the unrelenting jungle with his thoughts. His breathing stabilized and his inflamed nervous system returned to normal. He evaluated what had happened. Altogether, his confrontation hadn't been that distressing. Meting out death from a distance had to be qualitatively different than killing face to face.

Defurio's scattered thoughts settled on a blaring paradox. How could a reluctant soldier deigned as an unwilling cog in a man killing war machine, in a matter of minutes, feel possessed of such God-like power? Had he fulfilled a tenet of the nature of man—kill or be killed—with fruits of glory and triumph falling to the victor?

He became distracted. Earlier, when grabbing for his pocket knife, he had accidentally slashed his poncho liner. It leaked badly. He was getting soaked.

He mitigated his discomfort by thinking of Donna. He would write dismissively to her about shooting the grenade launcher. He didn't want to alarm her. Defurio would omit how pleased he had been with himself. He would refrain from telling her of his emergence as a willing taker of life, of an awakening of dormant animal instincts, of his transformation as a killer of men. It would be too worrisome for her to know and too shameful for him to have her know.

Chapter 9

Upside Down

Ragged, grim-faced men stooped by fatigue struggled in from patrols. Stories circulated, tales of finding clumps of dead NVA soldiers, hit and run fire fights; and a tragedy, one even hard-bitten, end-of-tour soldiers couldn't stomach. There had been a shooting, an incident absolutely searing, treacherous and indelible, irredeemable and irrevocable — because of an innocent victim — because it was unavoidable — because it was a fucking accident of war.

A ten man patrol had approached a village in a free fire zone, supposedly cleared of villagers. A VC sniper clad in traditional black silk clothing had taken a pot shot at the patrol, then ran to a hooch, dashed inside, and disappeared.

An M-60 machine gunner pulled to within ten yards of the hooch and emptied a belt of ammo, perforating every portion of the structure. Paper thin walls offered no resistance. Bullets went clean through.

The patrol gathered in a semi-circle in front of the hooch. Before entering, they waited for cindery splinters and pulverized debris to dissipate.

A woven mat hung over the doorway. It parted. A boy, less than two years old, walked out taking short, mechanical steps. His wide open eyes didn't hold tears, his wide open mouth didn't utter words. He held his hands at his belly button. They covered a bloody smear. A single bullet had breached his belly and hadn't stopped until it had splattered his guts on what was left of a back wall.

Either the toddler was in total shock or, more likely, the bullet had pierced tissue and fiber controlling his autonomous nervous system.

Sylvester, a black soldier having less than one month to go in-country, had younger brothers. He couldn't stand seeing the boy, plump with mother's milk, have life ooze out of him. From his hip, Sylvester leveled his M-16 and fired. The round hit the youngster's left temple, literally blowing out his brains. There wasn't a way to help the boy, his death was imminent. It was merciful to hasten it.

Be that as it may, merciful intentions wouldn't save these hard edged soldiers from having a piece of their humanity die. They would have a lasting reminder, a Vietnamese child's uncomprehending eyes would be staring at them for the rest of their days.

Guard duty again. Son of a bitch. Another night of fighting himself. Stay awake, Defurio, stay awake. There before him, as always, was a shadowy, monolithic profusion of softly shifting leaves, branches, stalks, and limbs.

His thoughts meandered back to the shooting of the Vietnamese child. The death bothered him as it did everyone. There was something about it, something different. The awfulness of war is often measured in cold exponential numbers of bombs dropped, objectives destroyed, and enemy killed. A single child gave a human face to a painful truth. As has been said, war causes a loss of innocence. It is a reason why combat veterans are never the same. Defurio remembered his uncle telling him of fighting the Japanese. His Uncle Gus had never really left the Pacific Islands. He continued to fight the Japanese in his nightmares.

Defurio recalled hardened WWII veterans in interviews, breaking down and crying over comrades killed sixty years prior.

Defurio's Vietnam contemporaries never referred to home as the States, the USA or America. They said "the world," like a separate reality, which in fact, it was, such as Couch saying he and Janey were planning on fucking their brains out when he got back to the world.

Trouble is, returning home, reality itself has changed. Inside a returning soldier's head is a tainted mindscape that will exist permanently. Janey may or may not fuck Couch's brains out. Probably not, because Couch would be different—in an unpleasant way. He'd have to readjust to civilization. Some do, some don't. Being so young and impressionable, Couch probably wouldn't.

In his mind game, Couch served as Defurio's prototype of a potentially emotionally damaged Vietnam vet. Couch, an immature, unsophisticated, uneducated, high strung teenager from a religious, upright rural farm family, would have a hard time coping. Blacks, Mexicans, and Puerto Ricans were better suited than Couch to adapting to life in the world. They were raised with low expectations, experienced at being fucked over by society. Couch wouldn't be prepared for the indifference and rejection he would receive when he returned home.

Defurio's two hours and fifteen minutes of guard duty were up. The last quarter hour seemed as long as the first two. He pressed a button. It lit up his watch, a durable Timex his father had given him for his twenty-sixth birthday. Two flimsy decorative coverings on an expandable band had snapped off. Its inner workings, however, were practically indestructible. Minutes seemed to have dragged by slower than usual. It dawned on him that he had entered his third month in Vietnam.

In a quirky change of weather, hot gusts of wind swept Charmaine. An updraft vacuumed thousands of insects from trees and bushes, showering them onto the firebase.

Witnessing this invasion so enthralled Big Jim, he became speechless. He snapped to attention, realizing he'd been presented a golden opportunity. He searched for containers or netting but couldn't find anything. In desperation, he grabbed his helmet, turned it upside down, and began shoveling technicolor specimens inside. Jim concentrated on catching butterflies. Most were reduced to molecular subparts yielding to Big Jim's ham-fisted handling. The blizzard of bugs lasted some five minutes.

Jim had guard duty that night. Forgetting about his insect collection, he plunked on his helmet. "Shit." Tickly butterfly parts sprinkled down his neck and shoulders. Coming off guard duty at dawn, Big Jim removed his helmet. Streaking each side of his blondish head were mucilaginous rainbows, colorful mementos from his suffocated insect friends.

To show support for Big Jim's bug collecting effort, Defurio had half-heartedly captured some specimens. He didn't snatch crushing handfuls like Jim. Consequently, he managed to capture, intact and unharmed, an unusual beetle.

It became their center of attention. Jim named it Homer, a reference to an intimidating weightlifter pal. Homer was 2" long and so deeply lacquered in purple he appeared black. A hooded head overlapped its thorax. Homer bore a striking resemblance to a triceratops. A single forked horn curved downwards from his forehead.

Jack transferred Homer from a sock to a jar obtained from mess cooks. Examining it, Jack came up with an idea. He broke off a 6" length of trip flare wire, attaching one end under Homer's hood, the other to his helmet band. Homer could move about, his wire tether invisible. Jack put on his helmet and strode casually through camp, lingering when he came to a group of GIs. Defurio's helmet attracted attention, since no one wore a helmet unless they had to. Homer moved jerkily around the helmet like a miniature Frankenstein.

"Hey man, you got a beetle on your pot."

"Yeah, I know. He's a pet. He goes wherever I go. His name is Homer. See you, fellas."

Jack moved on, trailed by Big Jim, his body bouncing up and down in subdued laughter. Jim rarely laughed openly.

Anything to break the tedium. Shenanigans such as showing off a captured bug helped push aside some of life's unpleasantness. Jack and Jim were masters at generating this kind of foolishness. However, hall of fame recognition would have to go to the indomitable Terrible Earl.

Defurio felt a fart welling up in his lower intestines, a precursor for a trip to the shitter. He let it go. Its impact was negligible in already befouled air of the bunker. His gas bubble wound up leading to a fortuitous meeting. On his way to the shitter, Defurio ran into Walker holding his stomach, sore from sustained laughter. His curiosity aroused, Defurio asked, "What the hell is going on?" Walker laughingly related what had occurred fifteen minutes earlier.

His squad had been partying inside their bunker. Earl supposedly had been sipping a Pepsi. He left it to take a piss. When he returned, it was gone. Earl demanded to know where his Pepsi was. He was met with a chorus of fuck yous. Earl went outside, saying he would return shortly. If his Pepsi wasn't produced, there'd be hell to pay.

"Go fuck yourself, Earl." Earl acted pissed-off and stormed out.

Coming back, his soda was nowhere in sight. "You goddamned motherfuckers. I'm taking a walk. If my Pepsi isn't here when I come back, I'm kicking your asses."

"Here, Earl, kick this." They cackled while flipping him off.

Earl motioned to Walker. They went outside. "Walker, that Pepsi be bullshit." It was a set up. Earl instructed Walker to remove the firing cap from a grenade and isolate it from the others. With the top screwed back on, the dummy grenade was indistinguishable from good ones. The procedure took less than a minute.

Grenades were strung by their handles on trip flare wire above a firing portal, an opening about 18" high and 4' wide. In the distractions of the bunker, it wasn't difficult for Walker to secretly deactivate a grenade and slide it away from the others.

Earl re-entered the bunker. He demanded his Pepsi. He was met by another round of fuck yous. In an apparent rage, Earl grabbed the deactivated grenade. Clearly a bluff. He would blow himself up too. Nevertheless, it was enough to get the revelers attention. After a momentary pause, taunting of Earl resumed. "Earl, maybe you accidentally sat on the Pepsi and stuck it up your ass." Earl pulled the pin, a preliminary move before activating it. A cotter pin locked down the handle. A grenade wouldn't go off unless the handle was released.

Earl poised to throw. He emphatically stated he wanted his Pepsi. If he didn't get it, he was blowing their asses to shit. Nobody believed him. Alfonso, a happy-go-lucky dude, had his shirt off. He had an immense beer belly and rich Puerto Rican accent. "Earl, maybe you no have Pepsi, maybe you have cola." The double meaning was clear; cola is Spanish slang for someone's ass. "Why don't you stick your grenade up that?"

Earl pretended to be enraged. "Motherfuckers." He pitched the grenade as if attempting to scare them by recklessly throwing it out through the portal. He purposely missed. The handle sprung off with a clang. The smooth surfaced fist sized explosive bounced off the wall into the middle of the hysterical Puerto Ricans.

Walker and Terrible Earl were in an eight man squad, six of whom were Puerto Ricans. Ordinarily blacks hung out with their own. Not in this squad. This band of merry men were seemingly as close as true brothers from having been tested, proven, and annealed under severe combat conditions. When not in combat, they kidded and joked at every turn. This playful group happened to be loaded with a plethora of pranksters. But this was too real.

It was every man for himself. Self-preservation overcame buddyhood. Puerto Ricans dove for the doorway, causing a wedge and plugging the exit. Former undying buddies pulled and clawed at one another trying to get out. Others were grabbing friends to use them as human shields.

The rotund Alfonso, sheathed in sweat, did a flying leap trying to elevate himself over the pyramid of packed bodies. He aimed for a 6" opening at the top of the mound of wiggling legs and torsos. He made it. It didn't do any good. There wasn't space to shove his face through.

The mayhem was brought to a halt when Earl's and Walker's raucous laughter filled the interior of the enclosure. Attempts at escape stopped. They realized that Earl had singlehandedly fucked them in the ass.

Even though it had been a contrived death trap, the Puerto Ricans were glad to be alive. Their response was to do what they usually did whenever they had an excuse. They celebrated.

Earl watched his friends rise to a louder, wilder level of revelry, freeing themselves from worries about alienation from life in the world, threats from dinks, and a general shitload of impending troubles. He was content. Satisfied. He was high. He was with his people, conscripted soldiers, shunned by society, forced to rely on cunning as a necessity for survival. This had become his world.

NVA forces continued to avoid open warfare in 4th Division's sector of operations. They were content to assume a defensive posture, biding time and accumulating troops and materials. A saturation point was being reached. NVA soldiers were being crowded inside bunkers and tunnel complexes. Chance hit and run encounters with itinerant troops were becoming increasingly common.

Red alert. These warnings of an imminent attack issued by battalion intelligence specialists had usually been ignored. They were seen as a ploy to keep troops from becoming complacent. Not now. Because of increasing enemy activity, red alerts were taken seriously. Three Hueys had been shot down in their vicinity. Villages could be seen burning here and there, set on fire by U.S. troops suspecting enemy sympathizers, some burned at the hands of NVA for similar reasons.

"Fuck, Jim, this place looks like a ghost town." All of B Company's line troops had been deployed on patrols. They were seeking concentrations of NVA. Three mortar squads of twenty-four men currently had responsibility for defending Charmaine.

Jack and Jim were stuck in separate positions on the firing line. Daytime guard duty sucked as much as night duty; tedious, odious work, no one to talk to, listening to the hypnotizing hum of insects, scrunched down in an unsheltered barricade, behind hot-to-the-touch plastic sand bags, under a boiling sun, in atmospheric conditions duplicating a steam bath.

In preparation for dealing with hours of nothing to do, Defurio gathered several skin magazines. Around 3:00 pm, underneath a punishing sun, Defurio focused on an unwaxed vagina smiling at him from a smutty magazine centerfold.

He had scooped out a shallow body-length hole. This provided cooler earth for him to nestle in. A voice rose from the tree line, startling him from the unnaturally pink vulva which had captured his attention. The voice, though provocative, wasn't threatening. Using binoculars, Defurio surveyed the tree line. Nothing. There it was again. "Uck, uck, uck," getting louder, then quiet. He couldn't see what it was. The serenade seemed to be over, then an expanded version; "Uck-u, uck-u, uck-u" in a single voice, clear as a bell. "I'll be damned," there is such a thing as a fuck-you lizard. Except for not pronouncing Fs, its enunciation was perfect; loud, clear, and unequivocal. Defurio imagined the lizard to be in the process of mating. He visualized a knee high, greenish reptile mounted on a smaller, helpless female held down by his front chicken-like claws, fervently pumping his lizard juices into her — his scaly lids half closed, contentedly concentrating on shooting his jizzum up her lizard cunt. "Hmm, I wonder what lizard pussy looks like," he thought. He came up with half a dozen possibilities. His imaginary lizard's vagina came down to a rubbery tube, greasy, something in the nature of an oily stem on an inner tube, her entrance enticingly beckoning via modified multi-colored, tightly curled scales. Defurio laughed at himself. This passed for fun in Dnam. How pathetic.

He developed a curious affinity for his projection of a copulating amphibian. This gunky quadruped was doing better than him. How bad can things be when you are outdone by a fornicating lizard? He laughed again. The Uck-u's lasted for twenty minutes. When his lizard seemed done, he said goodbye. He mentally wished his fuck-you lizard a fond farewell. He thanked him for putting on such a splendid show. This would be a one-time performance, he would never hear from this fuck-you lizard or his kind again. Like Walters, Vietnam had become a place for dead end farewells.

Startled awake, Big Jim leapt off his bunk. A gigantic caterpillar had gnawed through his sock. He threw it to the ground, hammering it with a boot. The segmented creature curled in a ball around its whiskery legs until its emulsified green slime body soaked into the dirt floor and disappeared.

Jim might have appeared foolish by his frenzied battering of this hairy insect. His outburst represented a general feeling of anxiety of something bad developing. There wasn't a man who didn't feel it, an increased presence of the unseen enemy. "Way to go, Big Jim," cheered the men.

Defurio hungered for Donna's letters. Men waited for early afternoons when Hueys, if they could make it, came in carrying supplies and mail. A Huey floated in, tilting in a final turn prior to landing. Seeing the red mail bag next to the door gunner brought a rush of excitement to those waiting on the landing pad. A cross wind made the copter lurch. Before it righted itself, the grommet top of the mail bag blew open. Hundreds of letters flew out, fluttering teasingly before disappearing into dark creases of thick overgrowth and lush underbrush. Defurio looked on in horror as the envelopes flapped earthward. He shook his head in disbelief. "Shit." Another torture. He consoled himself knowing Donna wouldn't stop writing.

On a dull afternoon, Defurio asked Big Jim to accompany him to a perimeter bunker to conduct an experiment. He had him pack marijuana in a pipe bowl. Jim lit it and handed it to Jack. Defurio toked repeatedly for an hour to no effect. They redid the experiment four hours later. "I don't feel anything, Jim." Jim hadn't indulged so he could objectively monitor Defurio's progress. "Damn, Jack, this is high grade stuff. I guess it's not your thing." Defurio never tried weed again.

At 6:00 am, Russell, a black trooper temporarily assigned to mortars and having less than thirty days remaining in-country, hopped and yelped like a kicked dog. To start his day, Russell had a habit of taking a shot of high alcohol cough syrup. This morning he sleepily reached under his air mattress for his bottle. He swallowed a mouthful, not knowing he had grabbed the wrong bottle. It held his ringworm medicine. He threw up for an hour. By the smell of it, ringworm medicine tasted like regurgitated fish.

Days passed. A Huey snuck in burgeoned with unexpected gifts; five letters from Donna, beer, underwear, and happily, a much anticipated Polaroid camera.

Hungrily, Defurio read Donna's passionate, earthy, straight-from-the-heart letters. He then examined his prize acquisition, a Polaroid 210 color picture camera.

Some weeks earlier, Defurio had borrowed thirty dollars from Big Jim to purchase the Polaroid and two rolls of color film. A Polaroid at $41.00 was the cheapest in the PX catalogue. Lt. Duke had promised to buy it when he went to Ennari on the company's business.

Defurio ripped open thick packaging encasing the treasured instrument. Big Jim could hardly contain himself. He planned on taking snapshots of Vietnam wildlife. Their joy couldn't be overstated. This camera gave a gigantic boost to their morale.

Jack and Jim hurried to take pictures before nightfall. They were schoolboys burning stored up energy at recess. Jack's fingers couldn't move fast enough, unfolding the 8" accordion fabric chamber. He excitedly loaded the film. Exhibiting dirty greasy hair, unshaved faces, and stained fatigues, they frantically struck dramatic poses. Unsuccessfully. A sandbag firing position didn't work as an interesting backdrop.

To themselves, they looked fine. This is the way they always looked (and smelled). Defurio and Maloney didn't appreciate that the sight of two filthy downtrodden GIs might be distressing to loved ones.

In their defense, Jack and Jim had taken the pictures in haste without an opportunity to clean up and prepare. Future efforts would be better.

Lovingly, Donna commented in a subsequent letter how overjoyed she was to see Jack's pictures. They were reassuring. She gently mentioned he looked tired, sickly, and undernourished. She started sending regular quantities of food.

Sixteen pictures had been taken, four each for Jack and Jim, eight for the rest of the squad. After taking the pictures, rejoicing squad members retired to the kid-cave coziness of their bunker. They drank beer and smoked pot. Jack drank until peacefully lapsing into wistful dreams of Donna. It was an enchanted close to a beautiful day.

An evening of intoxication and enthusiasm for a camera overshadowed daunting news. The next day, B Company would be moving off Charmaine to relieve ambushed remnants of two companies of the 1st /35th Infantry.

Dinks had begun their offensive.

Chapter 10

Terry

Defurio tried to get Big Jim's attention. It was nearly impossible to verbally communicate inside a bucking helicopter slashing through the air. Eight men in battle gear, crowded in an open-sided compartment, didn't make it any easier. Eventually, Jim saw Defurio waving at him and pointing downward.

A village crackling in flames receded in the distance far below. Jim turned his head away.

In hailing Big Jim, Jack had turned and met the face of a newbie twittering like a caged rabbit. He hated these fucking cherries. Everyone did. They were bad luck waiting to happen.

Infantry squads were like street gangs. You have to get beat up to gain full acceptance. Inside of two months, this quivering cherry would be roughed up and have the give-a-shit attitude of a reliable grunt. It would take a couple of patrols and seeing some action.

When motioning for Jim, Defurio noticed the Hispanics, heads bowed, lips moving in prayer. They did that on helicopter assaults because you never know what to expect. You could get a bullet in the throat or disembark to join a chow line for a hot meal.

Terry was supposed to be a hot LZ, meaning troops would be landing under fire. Struggling from the chopper like an overburdened Sherpa, Jack lugged himself as fast as he could for something to hide behind. He collapsed near a log. Not too bad. Sporadic small arms fire fell short. No sweat. Defurio sucked in a slug of oxygen and blew out a sigh of relief. Jim panted alongside him. Grinding mini-guns from circling Cobras kept dink harassment to a minimum.

Jack and Jim stood up, tilting under the weight of shifting equipment. Sweaty as whipped mules, they ran for better cover. Bouncing knots of grenades stuffed inside pockets, a bulky flak jacket, canteens of water, web gear, and bandoliers of ammo rubbed Defurio's skin raw as if he had been wrestling naked on a dirty carpet.

They ran to a clearing and dropped their packs. Jack rested on his knees. Taking a sip from his canteen, Big Jim took in the dismal setting and came to a descriptively blunt conclusion.

"It's like someone turned off the lights and we're stuck in a cold shower trying to keep our dongs warm." The setting sun behind uncut bamboo put the hastily prepared LZ in prison bars of shadows. A steady wind turned hot sweat cold.

Terry perched on the highest mountain of a prominent ridge. Its eastern side sloped for many miles before straightening to become flatlands. Stands of trees crowded Terry on three sides.

A high flying bird couldn't have a better 180° view of the central plateau. At evening time, barely discernible lights of Pleiko and Kontum could be seen through hanging mists. Cambodia was thirty miles to the west.

An uneven line of felled trees demarcated the perimeter. C-4 plastic explosives had been used to blow away trees to form an irregular oval with edges like torn cardboard. Terry had been set up as a temporary base from which to launch an effort to assist companies of the 1st /35th under attack on an adjacent mountain.

None of this information had reached the line troops. They didn't know why they were there. It didn't really make any difference to them what the purpose was. Immediate concerns were about keeping their asses safe on this unfortified sliver of land.

Sitting on dank soil smelling of spoiled spinach, they smoked cigarettes. Taking a break, Jack and Jim engaged in their particular brand of bullshit.

"Jim, you think Terry is named after a man or woman?"

"Are you kidding? Definitely a woman."

"Well," conjectured Jack, "it could be like Ennari, named after a dead lieutenant, or maybe it's named after a general's wife or kid."

"Sure, and tonight I'm going to get a blow job from Claudia Cardinale." Jim went further. "I'd guess some general named it for a nurse so he could get some free pussy."

Terry had five 105 mm cannons, soon to be beefed up by additional capability. Straining machines thundering up Terry's steep eastern side caused a ruckus. Seeming to defy the laws of physics, two tanks smashed up the severe, treeless incline, banging to a stop in the middle of the LZ. Clinging on top were ten terrified, dust covered replacements.

Artillery, tanks, replacements, this increased capacity caused worrisome speculation. For good reason. B Company had been given the upgraded responsibility for actually saving companies of the 1st /35th.

Terry's tanks and 105 mm cannons fusilladed a neighboring ridge, keeping NVA troops at bay while companies of the 1st/35th tried to find a way to escape. The companies had been caught in a vice with NVA above and below them. They had been chopped to shreds in an ambush. Gunships and jets were attacking from the other side. From this side, B Company's mortars couldn't reach the target area. During air and artillery attacks, dinks hid in extensive tunnel complexes.

Jack and Jim showed a passing interest in the outpouring of ordnance. They'd already become jaded by such displays of shooting and shelling and moved on to the practical business of building a bunker. Jack held while Jim shoveled dirt into a sandbag.

"Entrenching tool" is Army lingo for a short handled folding shovel. Jack noticed a discrepancy. "Jim, how come the Army doesn't have a fancy name for sandbags?"

Jim had removed his shirt, revealing prodigious glistening diamonds of sweat. "I don't know," he gasped. "But I do know I'd give my left nut for a long handled shovel." Jim never referred to giving up his right nut.

They switched positions.

Regaining normal respiration, Jim started to give Jack's question serious consideration. "It's hard to believe that some ass kissing mid-line officer hasn't designated an official name for sandbags. I guess it's up to us to invent one."

"I've got the perfect name." Jack halted. "Ouch, fuck." He'd hit a rock. Temporarily, his right arm took on the dull pain of a stubbed toe. Overcoming his pain, he quickly recovered his concentration. "You're going to love this. How about Hand Held Fabric Earth Containers," he said proudly.

Jim saw a flaw. "Is plastic a fabric?"

"Aw, shit." They dropped the subject.

Half of B Company had deployed to help the 1st /35th, resulting in mortars having to fill in on the perimeter. Defurio and four others in his squad had responsibility for a section of the defense line. Night was falling fast. He helped set up three claymores. He put reflective sides of gum wrappers on tree limbs in front of his position. If he had to throw a grenade, he could avoid a ricochet back into his lap. They weren't needed. As it turned out, there was a gorgeous full moon, reminding Defurio of a romantic lover's lane with enough light to see the hooks on your girlfriend's bra.

Other than sleeping on bare dirt in restless discomfort, the night passed smoothly for Defurio. Radio reports indicated his company had located and were not far from the stranded 1st /35th. Five squads had successfully air lifted in and established themselves fifty yards above NVA tunnel openings. Suppressive fire from M-16 rifles, M-60s, M-79s, and Terrible Earl's LAWS kept NVA soldiers hunkered down. This gave the 1st /35th a chance to fight its way through NVA positions on the lower side of the mountain.

Hueys brought in needed ammo as well as other goods. Lots of ammo was being shot off, both small arms and big guns. Renewed helicopter service also resulted in a resumption of mail delivery.

Defurio received a bonanza of sixteen letters, fifteen from Donna and another from his mother. Many letters were out of sequence, having gone to Company A. Some would never be recovered.

Donna's letters lifted him. Reading her words alleviated the pain of separation. They acted as healing medicine. He read his mother's letter last in an anti-climactic conclusion to Donna's soul soothing feast of correspondence.

Mrs. Carmen Defurio's letter was typical of her. Words ran across the pages, written in impatient, exuberant, wildly curlicued handwriting. It was tender, yet written as if she had other matters to attend to.

Defurio warmed reading her lines. They reminded him of his mother's upbringing. She had been raised in poverty. The Adamo family consisting of her parents and eight children had scratched a subsistence living on alternate sides of the Mexico-USA border, traveling back and forth from Chihuahua at a time of bloody revolution. They went to Texas, New Mexico, and finally to the Central Valley of California. Two children died from disease by age five. At times, the family had gone hungry. Hunger and the humiliation of it had left a mental scar on his mother. She did not send him many letters. She did send him numerous packages of food, in which she sometimes put hastily written messages. Self-centered and suspicious in nature, she constantly questioned the motives and actions of others, including her own son. Why did he worry her so much by being in Vietnam?

In many ways, Mrs. Carmen Defurio was radically unlike the traditional Mexican women of her generation. Irrepressible and independent, she also possessed a gift of musical ability, playing guitar and singing professionally throughout her high school years. A dark haired beauty, slender, shapely, and theatrically outgoing, she continued to play and sing to the present day. Despite these attributes, she remained trapped in an old-fashioned male dominated culture. She fought an oppressive culture but could not escape it.

Mother Defurio put her stamp on her son early. If gym classes were any indication, Jack may have been the only circumcised Mexican in the San Joaquin Valley. His mother asserted herself when and where she could.

In personality, he was a mirror image of his mother, although not matching her flamboyance. She taught him that life is brutal. She told many stories of treachery, hunger, and hardship. *"You must do whatever is necessary to survive."* She was a survivor, and so was he.

Big Jim and Jack established an "Office of Bullshit Dissemination," or OBD. They spent five minutes formulating its purpose. The aim was to invent or promote rumors. Rumors circulated through camp faster than outbreaks of foot fungus. Increased enemy contact had stirred stories of impending misfortune. A persistent rumor had B Company mortars disbanded and dissolved into the line company. Men in mortars would be reassigned as ordinary humping, patrolling, and perimeter guarding infantrymen. This couldn't be true. Mortars were too valuable for the function and protection of the company. Defurio and Maloney took advantage of the tendency of soldiers to exaggerate circumstances.

They leaked a rumor and monitored its effects. Men were working on building bunkers. Jack waited for a line sergeant to wander by. He hailed a likely candidate, a straight up, non-lifer good guy. This sergeant had the stature to give Jack's communication an aura of authenticity. "Yo, Sarge," Jack called loudly to reach as many lollygaggers as possible, "is it true we're linking up at Cacatum and joining elements of the 1st /35th?" The sergeant, shrugging his shoulders, ignored the question. He could give a fuck about unsubstantiated crap coming from an unseasoned private.

In less than half an hour, they overheard a recruit saying, "Cactum has become a staging area for a regiment of NVA. B-52s will be carpet-bombing the site. The 1st /14th will be moving in with other units on a large scale search and destroy mission. Heavy casualties expected."

Jack and Jim didn't bother to disclose their fabrication or dispel extensive revisions of it. They preferred to be amused and fascinated by imaginative soldiers fussing and fretting about an upcoming invasion. There would be confusion and relief when the action failed to materialize. In fact, there wasn't any such place as Cacatum.

Shot-up personnel from the 1st /35th trickled in by helicopter. They had managed to fight their way down to a river, where they were evacuated. It had gone badly. Defurio recognized a bunkmate from Ft. Lewis named Prosser. He remembered him as a tranquil, genial fellow. Defurio's squad listened attentively as Prosser spoke. He couldn't stop talking. He kept repeating himself as if it would purge the events of the last two days from his mind.

A major, needing a combat infantrymen badge to increase his chances for promotion, had assigned himself to Prosser's company for a couple of weeks. Companies are normally led by a captain. Officers above that rank were extremely rare in the AO.

On a patrol, two snipers showed themselves, fired, and fled. A classic move. The major went for the bait and ordered pursuit of the supposed NVA assassins. Everyone but him knew it was a trap. An initial volley cut down a quarter of Prosser's company, survivors had no way out, dinks were above and below them. Steep cliffs and impassable groves of bamboo blocked their flanks. Dinks had let the company run through an opening in their lower line, then sealed it shut.

Thanks to cover fire from B Company's assault team, Prosser's group busted through the NVA trap, incurring extensive casualties. The major had been wounded badly. Prosser carried him on his back. Gurgling from the major's throat made Prosser's stomach turn. The major didn't survive.

The major had bullet holes in his back. Prosser suspected guys in his company had shot him. They held the dumb-ass major responsible for the ambush. "Good riddance, the motherfucker had become dead weight," Prosser said with a demonic laugh.

He couldn't stop talking about the dying officer's swelled lips leaking red sludge, eye lids jerking erratically, head dangling like a dead chicken's, and his face turning purple. He recounted how a rescue helicopter was blown apart while lifting from the river. A B-40 rocket killed everyone aboard.

Defurio had some beers saved, buried to keep them cool. He attempted to get them below the temperature of warm piss, and maybe he did by a couple of degrees. He gave one to Prosser. Slurping beer interrupted the man's manic monologue. The alcohol calmed him. He stopped blathering and grew silent. Without warning, he curled up and began weeping in unremitting, sorrowful, wrenching sobs.

It was disturbing to see a man cry. Prosser aroused in Defurio a sympathy contravened by repulsion, perhaps a response to an echoed paraphrase of his mother's teaching. *Be a man, life is brutal, never give up or give in. Otherwise, the brutality will defeat you.*

Homer was failing. His lacquered coat drained of color. Jack and Jim couldn't solve the problem of what to feed him. What do beetles eat? Never at a loss for ideas, they decided to make the best of the situation. Before Homer died, they wanted to immortalize him on film.

Jim's sophisticated camera had a zoom lens. Utilizing rocks imitating boulders, as well as twigs, branches, pulled grass, leaves, and wet soil to simulate a primordial landscape, they snapped close-ups of Homer. He appeared as a dinosaur negotiating a Jurassic terrain. Homer crawled over and under obstacles manipulated by the trip flare wire still attached to his neck.

Shortly thereafter, Homer died. It happened amazingly fast. He became fragile and overnight dried up and began to disintegrate. When Defurio tried to pick him up, he fell apart in a crunchy, weightless pile.

The NVA had suspended its offensive thrust. They withdrew, having taken sizable casualties. It would be a temporary respite. Meanwhile, mortars prepared to rejoin the company. After packing equipment, there wasn't much to do but wait for transportation. While Defurio and his platoon waited to be airlifted, a lone Huey arrived, bringing in mail. Defurio received twelve letters; ten from Donna, one from his sister, and one from his father.

Perfect. With nothing happening, he could read in private, in broad daylight, without interruptions. He sat at the base of a shady tree reading his too-good-to-be-true stack of letters.

He read Donna's letters first, enjoying the opportunity to relish each word, undistracted by poor lighting, visitors, chatter, and bluesy Motown. His father's letter was strained, neatly and unemotionally penned in the format of a short business letter. He tried feebly once or twice to convey a sense of caring for his son in Vietnam. He confined his missive to a factual account of everyday doings of the family, and in a stretch, their family dog, Chiqui. Defurio could hear his mother pestering his dad to write in the first place. Defurio enjoyed the letter, even its tortured sentimentality, its familiarity, and its predictable tone. It brought Defurio closer to home.

His younger and only sibling was studying to be a school teacher and addressed him by his family nickname of "Jay," as did his mother and father. It derived from the first letter of his name. Katherine Defurio was a nicely featured woman. For unclear reasons, she had a tendency to be insecure and reticent. Her letter didn't rise much above the level of her father's. Personality-wise, she followed in the conservative, constrained footsteps of their father. She wrote in the same rigid, forced style. It was difficult for her to express anything personal and emotional. She tried. Defurio appreciated her effort.

Behind the correspondence from his family, as infrequent and bland as it was, Defurio sensed an ulterior motive. He hated to think this way. However, these thoughts did not eat at him. This is how he saw and accepted life. He hadn't ever relied on his family for emotional or material support. They were an ungenerous group. Understanding, sympathy, and caring were doled out in limited or token amounts. If you were sick or injured it was because you hadn't taken care of yourself; if you needed money you were a spendthrift; if you became a victim of circumstances beyond your control. That's life. Deal with it.

Feelings were about how events affected *them*.

Shaped by this negative view of his family, Defurio couldn't escape a troubling conclusion. Letters from his mother, father, and sister were not intended to provide him solace. They were for relieving their guilt if he were killed.

He had been in Vietnam for three months. Already in letters to Donna, he mentioned meeting her in Hawaii. He would qualify for an R&R in three months, sometime in June. For some reason, almost everyone went on R&R in the last three months of their tour. Not Defurio. He wanted to see Donna as soon as he could.

"Pack up, we're leaving!" Lt. Duke gave the command to get ready. Defurio stopped daydreaming. Wearing his helmet and flak jacket, he lifted on his rucksack. Carrying his M-16, he edged closer to the landing pad. Choppers lined up to take them out. Defurio boarded and they flew toward Cambodia, the staging area for NVA coming off the Ho Chi Minh Trail. They were already near the border, but how close, he didn't know. It could be a half mile or twenty. Cambodia brought visions of a forbidden zone, a killing field, legendary battles, a slaughterhouse for companies of GIs. Defurio cringed before taking hold of himself. He checked his equipment.

He sat stolidly. Onward they flew. It's interesting how the mind works, how emotions get convoluted. He thought of Donna, and his thoughts became sensual. The rhythmic vibrations of the chopper stimulated his loins, and he became erect.

Would this formation of Hueys land Defurio in the middle of a maelstrom? He kept control of his emotions. No need to psyche yourself out. Keep your wits about you. In this game, hesitation and self-doubt was for fools. Within a half hour, his Huey slowed and circled behind a nearby mountain. The line of Hueys formed a landing pattern. Defurio strengthened his grip on his M-16, rechecking it for readiness. He adjusted his bandoliers in an X across his chest as an extra precaution to deflect shrapnel or a bullet.

This was unnecessary. While in the air, the company had been diverted from its original destination. They had circled back to secure a hastily prepared LZ, and from there to collect dead GIs from the 1st/35th who were scattered and decomposing on a neighboring mountain.

Reports indicated that several companies of dug-in NVA soldiers remained in the area.

Chapter 11

Tiffany

This LZ jutted high above a river gorge. Looking like a craggy face, it pointed a sharp upturned nose inward toward other mountains. Its opposite side fell precipitously for miles.

There were three ways to get to Tiffany; by helicopter, scaling a sheer escarpment rising from the river, or by a trail hedged in by overlapping trees and quilted underbrush.

Defurio took stock of the area. "Shit, Jim, a group of grandmothers could overrun this place." It didn't have bunkers or dug in positions, and didn't have any tanks, artillery, or heavy caliber machine guns. It had a clearing for a landing pad and room for three 81 mm mortar pits. Mortars aren't effective for close in firing. Mortar rounds require a high arc to hit a target and so they're limited for warding off ground assaults.

Tiffany had its advantages. The narrow land approach would squeeze attackers into a convenient killing zone, easy targets for defenders and aerial gunships. Because of its altitude, they were out of range from most enemy mortars.

Tiffany had a penetrating steady wind vibrating through it, worse than Terry. Forget about amenities such as shitters and piss tubes. On the other hand, it had a stunning view of flat countryside to the east. On a clear night, lights of Kontum six or seven miles to the northeast could be seen. At sunset, a hard rain replaced a warming sun. The LZ, exposed to a harsh wind, became frigid.

They had to build a shelter. Due to conditions, it would have to be above ground.

"So long, Jack, see ya later." Jim temporarily reported to a different squad. Lt. Duke shifted personnel according to need. Defurio was stuck with a squabbling pair of bozos from the line company.

Mud prevented digging a hole or building any kind of sandbag structure. Defurio ignored his bickering companions and set to work constructing a shelter. He cut saplings to make poles and rods. He made an A-frame and threw on plastic sheets to make a tent. The three crowded inside. The hooch leaked badly and did poorly deflecting wind. It couldn't be sealed. The floor became a swamp. Defurio spent a sleepless night. Cocooning within a poncho didn't prevent goo from entering and irritating body crevices. Rubbing against skin, mud is like sandpaper. Defurio's testicles rolling on his thighs became shrunken bags of pain. By morning, beset by shaking, Defurio had a fever and a dripping faucet for a nose.

Before the rain hit, half of B Company had deployed by helicopter to the adjoining mountain to pick up dead GIs from the 1st /35th. This required the mortar platoon to fill gaps in the defensive perimeter. Positions were set in a line on either side of the trail abutting Tiffany.

That night, Defurio did his turn at guard duty. Sitting in refrigerated mud didn't do him any good. By morning, the rain stopped.

That afternoon Defurio began feeling better. He gave a heads-up to guys on the perimeter. "Don't shoot. I'm going to take a Sierra." This meant 'S' in the phonetic alphabet and often referred to taking a shit.

He forced his way through tangled underbrush. Hooked and bladed plants nibbled at his clothing. He came across a smooth limb hanging laterally just above the jungle floor. How lucky could he be? A waist high throne invited him to sit a spell.

He put down his flak jacket, helmet, bandolier, and rifle and unhitched his pants. Weighted by grenades, they dropped heavily to his ankles. He cushioned his butt on the mossy, crumbly bark. Shaded from midday heat, he shit in relative comfort with waste falling quietly on a bed of decayed leaves.

He couldn't see clearly past ten feet, although occasional deeper slivers of vision squeaked through the density of leaves and limbs.

Smoking a cigarette, Defurio rested on his branch. Thumping boots and cracking branches interrupted his reverie. Storming up the trail thirty-yards away strobed in peek-a-boo lighting were Terrible Earl and Walker. They were running from a listening post fifty yards down trail. Startled, Defurio yelled, "What the fuck's up, Earl?" Earl didn't slow down, didn't look left or right, didn't heed where the voice came from. "Dinks, dinks!" he responded.

"Fuck!" Defurio perceived an NVA ground attack to be underway. As Earl and Walker approached the summit, he heard their trailing voices shouting, "Friendly, friendly," notifying the guards not to shoot them.

Defurio slid his unwiped ass off the limb, tugging furiously at his pant legs. "Cocksucking motherfuckers." His grenaded pants had become a bola wrapped around his ankles. Putting on his flak jacket and helmet, holding his M-16 and bandolier in one hand, and partially pulling up his pants with the other, he shuffled for the perimeter like a convict in leg irons.

"Motherfucker!" A goddamned fan-leafed plant hooked his pant legs. "How much more fucked up can things get?" he thought, half pissed off and half struck by the absurdity of his situation. "I'm about to get shot in the ass trying to shit in this toilet bowl of a country." He freed his pants and made it to the perimeter.

Earl and Walker had spied two NVA soldiers on the trail. They could have been scouts or point men for a company of troops. B Company mortars trained fire on hundreds of yards of trail. There wasn't any counter response. In the uproar, Defurio never did get a chance to clean his ass.

Three successive days of strafing and bombing occurred on the other side of the next mountain a half mile away. A synchronized pair of F-100s conducted the attack. On diving runs, they came screaming in low over Tiffany, one followed by the other, banking to the left, straightening, and shooting rockets and dropping bombs on the target. After releasing, they nosed down through the river gorge, gained altitude, and repeated the exercise. Jack had some color film available. He loaded his Polaroid and perfectly timed a pass by an F-100 streaking overhead, so close it seemed he could jump up and touch it. What a disappointment. The strafing jets became blurry dots in the photograph. Defurio wasted two pictures discovering his Polaroid wasn't good for taking photographs at long range. Another agitation in a long list.

"What's the matter, Jack?" Jim asked, seeing his buddy in a funk.

"Everything," Jack replied, scratching the inflamed ridge of his scrotum. Not getting Donna's letters particularly sent him into a deep hole. They hadn't received mail or supplies for two weeks. The company had gone without water for three days. Only the poorest quality C-rations such as inedible lima beans were available. Defurio had lost weight.

The unsettling turbulence on the next hill, lack of mail and supplies, and the ghoulish business of collecting American corpses had gotten under everyone's skin. Having to gather open mouthed bodies frozen in a death laugh, misshapen, discolored, and fattened by bacterial gasses, depressed the entire camp. Temperaments, especially Defurio's from not hearing from Donna, were running thin.

Jim's inquiry distracted Defurio. I'm okay, Jim." He decided then and there for the sake of his mental well-being to take action. He reached in his ruck and removed an Army issued towel. He ripped an inch wide piece from the cloth and tied it around his head. "Look at this, Jim. I'm a bad ass savage motherfucker. A fuckin' barbarian." The headband had the practical purpose of keeping sweat from dripping in his eyes. More than that, the dirty green cloth identified him as to what he had become, a man stripped of normal comforts and rules of society, a man coerced and committed to destroying fellow human beings. Is this not a savage? This concession, this clarification, this declaration of truth cleared his mind and renewed his spirits. Big Jim's eyes glinted in approval.

Two unsure young men came by for a visit, unsure of themselves because Jack and Jim teased them unmercifully. Fowler and P.A. had come in-country shortly after Defurio. Both had tried to attach themselves to Big Jim and Jack. They hadn't come close to making the grade. Defurio and Maloney got to know Fowler on Charmaine. Fowler had presented himself as a cocky young man pretentiously proclaiming he hailed from La Crosse, Wisconsin. From then on, Defurio referred to him as La Crosse Boy.

One day, La Crosse Boy boldly approached Big Jim and Jack lounging outside their hooch. Displaying confidence and style, he wore a red kerchief tied around his neck, had his shirt off, and a cigarette waggling from his lips.

As his main justification for attempting to join them as an equal, La Crosse Boy offered up his sexual experience, thinking this made him uniquely qualified to belong in the company of worldly men. Defurio subtly elicited details. Fowler confidently and eagerly expounded on how frequently and in what ways he fucked his girlfriend in La Crosse. Routine stuff. He concluded by lighting up a cigarette with a flourish, forming and blowing rings of smoke through his lips.

"You done?" Jim asked pleasantly.

"Yep," replied Fowler, completely pleased.

"Sounds like you've got a really sexy girlfriend. Eh, Fowler, mind if I ask you a question?" Jack waited for Jim's trap to spring. Big Jim continued, "Eh, how's your girlfriend at hum jobs?"

The question confused Fowler. "What do you mean?" he asked hesitantly. "What's a hum job?"

Jim did his chuckle. "You know, eh, when your girlfriend is giving you a blow job, you, eh, have her hum."

Fowler wasn't exactly sure what a blow job entailed. Big Jim's explanation included having Fowler's girlfriend suck and hum simultaneously, the humming to provide vibration. La Crosse Boy became discombobulated. His bravado deflating rapidly, he slumped in bewilderment his upturned cigarette wilting over his lower lip. Befuddled, he wandered away not saying anything. It's not that they disliked Fowler. He merely presented an easy target for their ego destroying kind of humor.

Several days subsequent to dismantling La Crosse Boy, P.A. decided to make a run at Defurio and Maloney. A big baby-faced white boy in a baby fat body, they called him P.A. in deference to his Pennsylvania roots. Upbeat, friendly, and knowingly overmatched, P.A. nonetheless subjected himself to good natured joshing by Jack and Jim. He visited them often.

Squads sent out to pick up dead bodies of the 1st/35th had accomplished the task. The remainder of the line soldiers in B Company helicoptered from Tiffany to rejoin the rest of the company at the base of the adjoining mountain, the one ravaged by F-100 jets. The place that had become a death trap for the 1st/35th. Mortars alone defended Tiffany.

Helicopters transporting B Company troops had brought in food, water, and mail. Defurio received five letters from Donna. This made him happy but didn't detract from the fact the mortar platoon was an almost defenseless target. If the NVA knew of

Tiffany's vulnerability, a sneak attack would bring them twenty easy kills.

Defurio sat in his mud shit hovel reading Donna's messages of love, and for a while he escaped. Jim came to visit. He had received a letter from his father. In it, his father sent a photograph of a drawing he'd made, a touching pair of combat boots. Jim commented light heartedly regarding the disparity between his father as a talented artist and his occupation as a longshoreman. Jim joked about the content of the drawing. Jack suspected Big Jim didn't want to submit to the sentimentality and sensitivity of the drawing, fearing that it might break him. Both Big Jim and Jack had a habit of hiding behind humor to keep their heads together.

Jack changed the subject. "We're joining the line company tomorrow. What do you think we're getting into?" This question gave Jim an opportunity to defer sad thoughts concerning his father.

Jim returned to his usual optimism. "I don't know, Jack. For now we're a hell of a lot better off not picking up dead GIs or hunting live dinks."

Cigarettes were abundant thanks to resupply. They smoked and let Jim's remarks resonate. They weren't too concerned. From their standpoint, that's to say, standing in ignorance, the situation seemed okay. There couldn't possibly be many NVA alive on the next mountain. Not after the sacrifice of the 1st /35th; and barrages by artillery, bombs, rockets, and napalm delivered by the pair of F-100s. This should be an easy mop-up operation.

As an afterthought, Jack inquired, "By the way, Jim, did you get the name of this mountain we're going to, the one we've been blowing the shit out of?" Jim, sitting on an ammo crate, tried to keep his ass out of the mud. He dug at a can of C-ration pears, one of the tastier of C-rats.

"I saw Lt. Duke coming out of the CP.," he said, slurping pear juice. "He looked worried. Lt. Flack walked beside him not saying anything. He mumbled something about a shit storm." Jim took a bite of a pear. "Since he was right there, I asked him, 'Sir, do you know the name of that mountain?'" Jim pointed at it.

"Chu Pa," came Lt. Duke's curt reply.

Chapter 12

Chu Pa

War is a cruel chess master. He prefers to take life in increments; a leg, an arm, a functioning part of your body or mind. Lose big and you forfeit your life. It's exhilarating. The ultimate game. He determines the rules, time, place and opponent. False moves are made. What seems real, isn't. What seems unreal, isn't.

Defurio's stomach hung in the air when the Huey hit an air pocket dipping towards the LZ. Apprehension ran through the troops, as it always did on these combat assaults. Two soldiers dry heaved.

They experienced a smooth landing, with nothing but the ordinary ear-splitting, eye-searing irritation caused by rapidly turning helicopter blades. They did not come under fire. The absence of shooting allowed Defurio's stomach to relax. This sense of well-being lasted until the storm of dust cleared.

Striped in shades of black from trees blocking sunlight at its edges, the LZ appeared as a jagged rip in a hideous jungle tapestry. Defurio looked about him. What a fucking mess. Splintered logs littered an ill-defined kidney shaped space fifty to one hundred yards in diameter. This clutter of wood and dirt sat at the foot of a mountain, the sides of which rose steadily until forming a rounded pustule dominating the area. Its cool, aloof majesty gave Dufurio a shiver knowing so many lives had been given up beneath its crown. This is where the 1st /35th met its fate. The LZ didn't have a name and was simply referred to by its location on a map, a mountain called Chu Pa.

"Take care," a vacant faced soldier in A Company said to Defurio in a dull monotone. "They turned the claymores around on us last night."

By turning claymores, the directional mines could explode back on U.S. soldiers. The ploy succeeded when a jittery sentry, usually a cherry responding to a noise, triggered a mine, blowing himself up.

Maloney and Defurio climbed off the helicopter together. Defurio exchanged his spot with the frazzled A Company soldier.

Several squads of A Company had broken off contact and returned to the LZ after attempting to rescue the 1st /35th. In the process, they had received a crippling number of causalities. B Company now replaced them.

The words "turned the claymores" stung Defurio's ears. "Jesus, Jim, what the hell is this? How can these dink fuckers, under fire from us, artillery, and gunships, crawl through this pile of shit, find our lines, and sabotage our defenses?" Big Jim didn't answer. His mouth gaped open, his first showing of true fear.

The next morning, B Company's line soldiers moved out in a solemn procession. On a trail leading from the LZ, they entered a mawing jungle and were swallowed up one by one. A sense of abandonment and defenselessness swept Defurio as he watched the last man shrink from view.

A short time later, Defurio discerned spidery objects emerge on a bald strip two hundred yards long below Chu Pa's peak, which had been bombed free of vegetation. A one hundred man column, dauntless as a line of ants, surmounted the summit and vanished to the other side.

Emptied of line company soldiers, the LZ became still. Two Hueys broke the solitude. They came swooping in, dropping off cases of C-rations and a mailbag. The bright red bag reminded Defurio of Christmas.

He received two letters from Donna, and worries about him showed through. She had a bladder infection. Infections and stomach upsets plagued her since he'd left for Vietnam. On an up note, she had enrolled in a stock market class at a local community college. Donna liked numbers and the dynamics of finance and he felt better knowing her thoughts and activities.

Images went by of them together in San Francisco, her favorite place in the world. She shared the city's vibrancy. It energized her. She had been transferred to a main Safeway on Mission Street. Picking her up there in his '56 Chevy after work, she'd invariably ask him to stop at the mom and pop ice cream parlor adjoining the store. She'd order a double scoop of banana nut in a cone. She would slide next to him and lick her ice cream, the happiest creature on earth. She had a way of holding the cone, rotating her wrist, taking a lick one at a time. Her head moved from side to side as he drove, taking in scenes of the city. She spoke breathlessly of the affairs of the day; what happened in the store, of her friends and family.

He drove her to the showplace house on Twin Peaks she shared with childhood friend, Denise, whose father Reynaldo, a nightclub owner, rented to them at minimal cost. Denise liked dressing eccentrically, often in loud, flowing clothes and gaudy jewelry, making her look like a gypsy. Characters from go-go dancers to country club acquaintances of Reynaldo's might drop in for visits.

The house had an oriental motif. Reynaldo had been raised in Hawaii. Donna occasionally took advantage of Reynaldo's well-stocked bar to make Jack a drink of warmed Sake. A cushy rattan couch became a favorite place for prolonged sessions of passion. Jack eventually would have to get in his car and descend Mission Street until it entered a slum near St. Joseph's church at 10th Street. His Aunt Mary maintained a claustrophobic one and a half bedroom apartment located in an alleyway behind the church. Defurio stayed in the half bedroom located off the service porch.

She'd fallen asleep inside his '56 Chevy parked on Mission when he'd gone to fetch a pizza at Little Joe's Pizzeria. Although her head flopped to the side, her mouth open, she still looked cute. Wrapping his knuckles raw on his windshield in winter cold, he finally awakened her. Reynaldo gave them free drinks at his nightclub, the Zanzibar. They danced to juke box music. She caught him gawking at a semi-nude go-go dancer undulating on a platform above the bar. Always they returned to that rattan couch where they gave vent to their passion.

Lieutenants Duke and Flack monitored a PRC-25 radio, labeled Prick-25, as they were notoriously fickle. A radioman had set it in the middle of the compound.

About 4:00 pm, a stress ridden voice coming from a lieutenant in B Company radioed in a scratchy report. They'd been hit. Two dead; a lieutenant cut in half by a B-40 rocket and his radioman killed by the same rocket. Wounded would be reported when identified. News about the company knocked Defurio from his dream state. When he heard of the radiomen's death, he made a vow to himself to never hump a radio, a preferred target of NVA gunners.

A peculiar detachment took hold of the mortar platoon. They were remarkably unempathetic concerning the death of the two soldiers, instead displaying more relief at not being there. Besides, they didn't know the dead men.

Shortly after the disturbing broadcast, platoon members descended on recently arrived C-rations, avoiding lima beans, suet disguised as beef stew, and other unfavorable selections. Defurio picked through the bounty, finding some of his favorites; pears, peaches, fruit cocktail, scrambled eggs and ham, crackers and cheese. He had a pang of guilt. These rations had been requisitioned for an entire company, one fighting for its life less than an hour walk from the LZ. Shouldn't he save some choice items for survivors? This altruistic urge passed quickly.

GIs are criminally heartless and avaricious when it comes to seizing personal advantages. Acquired benefits and opportunities are jealously guarded and greedily indulged. Defurio recalled his theft of LRP rations at St. George. Men in mortars fed as shamelessly as vultures while their brothers on Chu Pa were dying.

Cobras and Hueys filled the sky above the far side of Chu Pa. They lay blankets of mini-gun and rocket fire in support of B Company's harried soldiers. Defurio's platoon watched worriedly from three quarters of a mile.

Nightfall brought a slowing of combat action on Chu Pa. Patchy radio transmissions from B Company received earlier ceased. So far, sixteen had been reported wounded, six severely, and no others killed. Darkness, danger from ground fire, and no cleared landing space prevented extraction of wounded by medevacs.

Defurio had guiltlessly enjoyed this day. He ate well, had received cherished letters from Donna, and by sheer luck had stayed safe. Never mind that he was stranded on an LZ defended by a handful of men at a site probed and violated by dinks the night before. He'd take the good of the day and deal with the bad of the night if and when it happened.

Lt. Duke set up defenses for a long night. He distributed men three to four to a position strung along an uneven, indistinct, unfortified perimeter.

Initially, Jack and Jim were inserted at the tip of an inverted V. This tumor of land extended thirty yards from the main line of defense. Two illusory lines of the triangle connected at 45° angles to the defense line behind them. The upside down V knifed into a grove of sparse bamboo. The bamboo spread outward for some thirty yards before surrendering to mature jungle. The trail to Chu Pa's summit lay seventy- five yards to Defurio's left.

Sizing up his situation, an ache developed in Defurio's neck and shoulders. His flanks were completely unprotected. He also disliked exposure to trigger happy cherries situated thirty yards above him on the main defense line.

"Jack where do you want us to put our stuff?" Breaking the norm, Fowler and P.A. addressed Jack by his first name. "Fuck!" Jack thought to himself. If things weren't bad enough, now he was stuck with these two. Calling him Jack, showed they still had hope of a fraternal friendship.

Evidently, Lt. Duke decided Fowler and P.A. were better off under his and Jim's tutelage than somebody else, which was probably an error in judgment. What a hand to draw into.

He doubted his loveable but over reactive friend, Maloney, could find his ass in a crisis. He guessed Fowler and P.A. would probably shit their pants in a firefight. Defurio would have preferred a couple of tough ghetto or barrio types to help him defend this fucked up position.

Defurio became de facto leader of this four man post. He instructed them to set up claymores, booby traps, and flares in a semi-circle at the tip of the inverted V, a configuration reminding him of the circled pyramid on a one dollar bill.

Big Jim, demonstrating dexterity of a three year old, strung a line for a trip flare. He tied a flare to a stump. Good thing it wasn't a grenade.

Defurio, busily constructing a makeshift hooch reacted to a flash, a bang, and a "whoa!" He seized his M-16 and whirled in Jim's direction, prepared to shoot. Ordinarily, he would have gone to the ground. However, something made him want to protect Jim.

From what? There stood Big Jim. He had tripped his own flare. Instead of jumping back, Big Jim froze, his right leg raised on an incline as if impersonating Washington crossing the Delaware. His ankles were showered in orange-pink light and sparks, which reflected off his pasty, shocked face. Fortunately, he didn't stand close enough to get burned. But his stubble, moustache, eyebrows, and hairline were singed, leaving a scent of baked hair in the wind.

"You okay, Jim?"

"Yeah. Fuck that was intense," he retorted, his eyebrows crisping.

They threw together a hooch similar to Defurio's on Tiffany, with plastic sheeting and bamboo offering some protection from weather but not bullets or shrapnel.

They turned in for the night. Fowler had first watch. To better survey territory in front of the position, he placed himself on a rise four yards behind the hooch.

Inside the shoddy structure, Defurio had the middle slot, sandwiched between Big Jim and P.A. This least preferred spot inhibited Defurio's maneuverability and response time. He would have to wait for either of these two slow moving behemoths to get out of his way before he could reach his M-16 or seek protection.

Watching the night close in on him, he lay there on his back feeling the touch of moist heat coming from the heavy bodies packed on either side of him. Dusk soon gave up the last of its light, leaving an unlit, unseeable jungle. A last vestige of treetop skyline took shape broken by the profile of Chu Pa, under whose heights a company of American soldiers fought to stay alive. Although he did not know any of them well, Defurio had compassion for his stricken comrades. Lying there sleeplessly, he began to realize he shared an edge of the same battlefield. He thought of what they were going through right at this moment. Whatever happened to them would likely happen to him.

He was confined within a caged jungle. Generally, Defurio avoided self-doubt in favor of practical action. Exposed and unprotected, he could do nothing but wait and hope. Isolation, worry, exhaustion, and the lonely hollowness of a deathly night can blur the line between conscious thought and dreams. Time, sound, and perceptions become distorted. From the bamboo, he perceived a dark figure coming at them.

He became highly sensitized and alert. He rolled on his stomach trying to find Fowler. If anyone could see someone coming, it should be Fowler. Defurio saw him sitting motionless. In the light of a falling flare, Fowler showed a mask of abject fear. "What's the matter?" Defurio asked urgently, keeping his voice low.

"I'm opening up, I'm opening up!" Fowler panted hysterically as he pointed his rifle laterally down line to his left. He sat, his rifle butt awkwardly pressed to his lower belly, barrel sticking through his bent knees.

Defurio had risen to his knees and elbows. "Don't shoot, don't shoot," he pleaded, crawling past P.A.'s head. The two slumbering giants remained oblivious. Defurio reached the freaked out adolescent, not wanting to spook him, to have him pull the trigger. "What's wrong, Fowler?"

"Voices. Over there!"

Defurio listened and heard hushed words carried on a fragile current of wind. "I hear them. Whatever you do, don't shoot. They have to be our guys. Dinks wouldn't be holding conversations on our perimeter."

Defurio's plain, irrefutable conclusion crushed the air from Fowler. "Oh, shit. Oh, shit. Oh, shit," he whimpered while wiping away tears, thinking he could have killed GIs.

"Don't worry about it." Defurio slid his arm along the boy's shoulder and gave him a reassuring squeeze. "You okay, Fowler?"

"I'm alright," Fowler said through tears beginning to dry. "Thanks, Jack."

Defurio returned to his air mattress, wedging himself between the hibernating bears. They had remained dormant throughout the incident. Their lack of awareness bothered Defurio.

He couldn't sleep. Worries about strange voices, the probing of the LZ, his company in jeopardy, and defending an indefensible position were grinding him down. He concentrated on looking and listening. He heard bamboo bending and leaves rattling in the wind and possible movement of nocturnal animals. Scratching, shifting fifteen or twenty yards in the bamboo initially was not too alarming. Noises travel at night, but this persisted.

He thought the scratching might be a distortion from one of their boots nervously rubbing an air mattress. When it didn't stop, Defurio asked under his breath, "Jim, is that you?"

"Oh, shit. I thought that was you," came the panicked reply.

P.A. said, "Oh, fuck." The foreign disturbance had penetrated the narcoleptic sleep of both him and Maloney.

P.A. and Big Jim tried to flee. "Hold it," Defurio said sharply while simultaneously grabbing their shirtsleeves. "Don't make targets of yourselves." They stopped floundering. "Jim, you go first. Get to the logs and give us protective fire if we need it." Logs were scattered above them near the main defense line. "Then P.A., you go. Both of you can cover me."

"Okay," they agreed shakily.

Big Jim promptly fell into a garbage pit of C-ration cans, causing a racket similar to cans dragging behind the car of newlyweds. This panicked P.A., who stood up, adding to the chaos by lifting up half the hooch. Defurio gasped, thinking these two clowns were going to get him killed.

Defurio joined the rush to the perimeter. Blindly they scooped up rifles, equipment, helmets, and flak jackets.

Fowler jumped up in a state of confusion. He had fallen asleep.

Defurio hurrying past, grabbed Fowler's shirt collar, and said aggressively, "Come on."

Responding to the commotion, B Company mortars put up illumination rounds, spotlighting the retreating soldiers as if they were escapees on a prison break.

They saw themselves. They were ridiculous; helmets on backwards, equipment dragging the ground, P.A. carrying his M-16 upside down, dumb-ass expressions, bent forward in a half assed attempt at stealth. Exposure and the comic sight of themselves released tension that had reached a breaking point. It spurred them to action.

Flares revealed a wood barricade, an eight foot span of fallen timber laying perpendicular to their line of flight. They ran for it, assaulted its top, and dropped to the other side in a heap. Safe. No shots fired.

Being behind something solid gave Defurio a chance to collect himself. He lifted to his knees, surveying their path of escape. Falling waves of flares could have been Chinese lanterns decoratively highlighting the landscape. No sign of human activity.

Relieved, Defurio sat propping his back to the log. Gulping in air to relieve heaving chests, the four absconders rested momentarily, too shaken to speak. When they regained wind, P.A. inarticulately but accurately spoke, as he usually did, as though his tongue were swollen. "Fuck, I thought we were going to get killed."

Defurio never did find out what caused the scratching. For all he knew, it could have been a foraging fuck-you lizard. Neither he nor his companions ever discussed it. It could have been a trick of mind or hysteria. Such unknowable matters were better left alone. No use driving yourself crazy over unknowns.

The four transplanted soldiers stayed where they were for half an hour. Then Fowler piped up. "I thought we had orders…" as if they should return to their abandoned post.

"Fuck orders," Defurio said, incredulous at Fowler's statement. "You can go down there and pound your meat if you want to. We're staying here." This got through to Fowler. He resumed his watch from the security of the tree trunk. None could sleep.

"Eggs, eggs" came from an invisible Lt. Duke tip-toeing through the redarkened LZ. "Bacon," called Defurio in an infrequent exchange of passwords. Conditions weren't usually this fucked up to require passwords.

"We heard talking so we came up here," Defurio said, fictionalizing his account to avoid possible disciplinary repercussions, although he doubted Lt. Duke cared about punishing them for anything.

"Yeah, a squad from A Company made it off Chu Pa two hours ago. They're set up about forty yards from you," he said.

Fowler's face drained of color knowing he'd come within an eyelash of shooting them. Defurio remained silent. No one else would ever know what had almost happened.

"It's good you moved, you're better off here." Lt. Duke decided not to let his ego disturb the fact it had been his orders that had endangered them.

Lt. Duke shifted Fowler and P.A. twenty yards down the line to fill in between A Company's squad and their present location. Jack and Jim stayed. The lieutenant left them a PRC-25. "Stay on your toes. Report any movement to CP. This mountain is full of dinks."

Lt. Duke continued his rounds. "Eggs, eggs," drifted back as if he were a short order cook calling to a waitress to pick up her order.

Jack could see Jim beginning to doze. "I'll take first watch."

Jim nodded gratefully while releasing himself to the turf. Concern etched Jack's face as his gentle friend sank into a deep sleep. Defurio knew they were in serious trouble, and that Big Jim wouldn't be much help.

Being from New York City, it seemed impossible that Jim hadn't acquired better survival skills. He'd been able to rely on his size and good nature to avert confrontations. In a crisis, Jim's reaction time, decision making, physical coordination, and emotional resilience were sorely lacking. He had the temperament of a Koala bear, whereas, in a critical situation, Defurio needed someone having instincts of a badger.

Defurio raised his head to the bridge of his nose, trying to discern the tree line. His eyes couldn't penetrate the blackness. Hearing became his main means for detecting intruders. So he listened, listened.

Nearly 3:00 am, the darkest part of night. No incoming or outgoing. Chu Pa rested. Silence crept down from the mountain. The hammering of guns had stopped.

Tall trees framed the grove of bamboo in front of their demolished hooch. Off in the trees, forty yards beyond, came a twitching of leaves. An animal or the wind?

Defurio had several grenades planted next to him. He readied one, holding it firmly in his right hand. Forefingers clasped the handle, his thumb in back.

His senses became as fixed and tensed as a coiled snake. Five minutes passed. There again, a stirring of leaves to his left front. In his mind this is where dinks would probe, coming off the trail to his left. Five more minutes. A crunch of leaves. The spot had moved ten to fifteen feet to the right. Eyes and ears working in unison estimated distance and direction.

Another five minutes went by. Then cat steps, ten to fifteen feet back to the left. The direction of travel, shifting, zig zagging, continued to move in five minute intervals.

Defurio bent down. He jiggled Jim. "Jim," he said in an urgent whisper, "we've got movement." Jim, in a high state of alarm, had trouble understanding. He staggered to his feet. They squatted shoulder to shoulder, their noses set to the top edge of the log. "Listen," Jack pointed. He'd predicted the time and course of movement; a foot, hand or knee ever so slightly disrupting leaves.

"Fuck!" Jim almost jumped out of his skin. He stopped short of hyperventilation.

"Jim, call CP. Tell them we have movement and if I hear it again, I'm throwing a grenade."

Maloney keyed the radio, hearing the usual short rasp of static. He informed the lieutenant on the other end about the movement, stating excitedly that there were people, "double timing in front of our position." Unable to suppress a quick smile, Defurio's anxiety subsided for a brief second.

"Yes sir," Jim clicked off the receiver. "CP said, don't do anything. Monitor the situation. If anything happens, report back."

"Fuck him," Defurio said, relying on his own evaluation of the crises. "If that motherfucking dink moves again, I'm blowing him up. What does that stupid ass lieutenant want us to do, wait until the son of a bitch sticks an AK-47 up our ass?"

They resumed their position at the log, not speaking, concentrating totally on what might happen. They could have been two expectant teenagers in a darkened theater waiting for a horror movie to start.

There it was, right on schedule, a footfall as delicate to the ear and deliberate as the turn of a page. Defurio had his grenade ready. Its steel oblong smoothness fit comfortably in his hand. Handling it gave him a sense of control. As a simple killing device, it wasn't far removed from a Neanderthal's hand thrown rock.

Having retained a mental picture of the tree line, he pulled the pin, cocked his right arm, and threw the compact metal explosive, attempting a throw of fifty to sixty yards.

Defurio heard a hollow knock. Oh no! He grimaced as a wave of nervous heat surged through him. His grenade had hit high in a tree and could land back in his lap.

An eight foot fan of flame accompanied by a WHUMP lit up a portion of jungle. Fortunately, the grenade had landed where he intended.

From his vantage behind the log, Defurio kept attention on his picture of the tree line. "Jim, I think I got him. Did you see where it went off?" he asked without turning. No response. He turned around. Starlight provided the skimpy lighting of a barroom and for a second, he had trouble finding Maloney.

"Jesus." The oath slipped through an involuntary grin. Four feet away, Maloney lay on his stomach, rigidly prostrate, his head sideways in dirt, his right knee sharply bent. Except for his hands squeezing fistfuls of soil and his eyes squeezed to watery slits, he resembled the chalk outline of a homicide victim.

Jim's eyes fluttered open. Swathed in a coating of dust, he got up, prying himself from the ground. "Sorry, Jack, I thought that grenade was going to kick our ass."

"It's alright," Jack said exuberantly as though he'd scored a winning touchdown. "Come up here. Let's check this out. I'm sure I got that little fucker."

From the log, they listened intently for an hour. The leaves remained undisturbed. Defurio listened for a groan. None. Good. Maybe he'd killed the gook outright.

Daybreak. The morning sun steadily washed away the grime of night. Defurio couldn't wait to confirm his kill.

"Jim, put your M-16 on automatic. Steady it on the log. If I yell, I'll drop and you open up. Go through a minimum of three clips. Aim for the bottom of the tree line." Defurio didn't worry about getting shot by Maloney. Hyper soldiers shoot high.

Trotting fifty yards to the tree line, he parted a thin screen of vines and stringy plants saturated in morning dew. An ambient dread overtook him.

He groped to where he thought his grenade had gone off and searched hurriedly through clumps of soggy five foot multi-bladed plants. Seeking a blast site, a body, a blood trail, or discarded equipment, he found nothing but overlays of green mucous colored plant life.

Finding himself inside a darkened space surrounded by walls of trees and moist long leafed plants, a chilling fright seized him. He became disoriented. The plants became green monsters blocking his path to the LZ.

The green things fell upon him. Fronded appendages strapped themselves to his legs, dragging him down. He kicked at them violently with the desperation of a man being buried alive. He wrenched lose from their slimy tendrils and fled.

Managing to see a shaft of light cutting through oblique tangles of vegetation, he detected the jumble of logs hiding Big Jim and struggled toward the opening.

The sight of a terror stricken Defurio coming at him, running for his life, transformed Maloney into a quaking bulk of anxiety. He had never seen Defurio not in control of himself. Maloney hesitated. Should he shoot? Defurio hadn't given him a signal. What to shoot at? He couldn't see what was chasing him.

Defurio hurled himself sideways, scraping his knees and elbows on the tree trunk. Dripping in sweat, he crumpled beside Big Jim and expelled a hot, dry choking gasp as if awakened from a horrible dream.

Not knowing what else to do, Maloney emptied three clips into the trees, as had been instructed by Defurio. Shooting aimlessly into trees seemed rational and in a real way therapeutic.

When he stopped firing, Maloney, finding his voice, asked "Jack, what happened?"

"Don't ask, Jim. Don't ever ask." Jack's words were resolute, deliberate, and solemn, as if he were a priest ending a sermon.

The finality of Defurio's response would forever close the subject between them.

Defurio lay grappling with himself. "Don't give in or give up or the world will defeat you." His mother's words came to him. "You have to be mentally strong."

He forced himself to banish his irrational thoughts that he had been attacked by plants. Necessity required returning to normal, whatever that meant. Put a sane man in an insane situation and he'll tend to act insane. A soldier pulling a trigger on command unimpeded by psychic distortions is normal in war. What about the dead dink? Probably eaten by plants. A capitulation to the insanity of war is a man returning to normal simply by pressing a mental button eliminating the existence of carnivorous plants. He did so.

"What are ya'll shooting at?" Lt. Duke inquired anxiously as he came running up, bent forward at the waist, thinking maybe sappers had been spotted.

"Nothing, Lieutenant. I think I stirred up an animal outside the perimeter."

"Okay. Heads up. The line guys are getting a lot of causalities. Other companies are coming in to try to get them out."

Jack sat up. He lit a cigarette, put his elbows on his knees, and clasped his hands together, holding the cigarette in the fingers of his right hand. He unclasped his hands and touched the cigarette to his mouth, sucking in a quantity of nicotine. A transient thought went through his head. What is normal?

Jim plunked alongside him puffing on a Lucky Strike. There were plenty of cigarettes available due to resupply of an absent company. They didn't talk. Jack sat smoking, comforted by the presence of his complacent, faithful friend.

Big Jim tilted his head back and inhaled slowly. Jack's attention fixed on the end of Jim's cigarette flickering and brightening before turning to ash. Defurio got to his feet, thinking he'd better make a last raid on the stack of resupply. He wanted to get his hands on as many cigarettes and preferred meals as he could before the other companies arrived. Thoughts of voracious plants receded to far reaches of his mind. Back to the business of getting through another day in Dnam.

Helicopters bringing in C and D companies also brought in mail. He received four letters. Defurio hadn't realized it until he read Donna's letters and card that it was February 14, Valentine's Day.

The new arrivals were deployed by noon, as soon as they could be assembled and briefed. In less than an hour, they were making the climb up Chu Pa.

Sullen old-timers and scared newbies fell in line to go up the mountain. Defurio chose to stand at a distance from them, avoiding eye contact, knowing some wouldn't be returning. Poor fuckers. He was glad he wasn't among them, although he had his own problems. Ever since Charmaine, a pattern had developed. Line troops gathering, then dispersing, leaving three squads of the mortar platoon abandoned and nearly defenseless.

As yet, the chess master hadn't swept from the board any of the mortarmen. For the moment, he preferred taking line soldiers.

The arriving companies hadn't had enough time to put a dint in the resupply stockpile. Defurio indulged in a surfeit of cigarettes and choice meals.

Throughout the day, radio reports clacked on, listing B company causalities, names anonymous, until they reported a man by the name of Reed. Goddamn it! Defurio knew Reed. He remembered a pleasant, soft spoken, older, round featured black guy who wore a puka shell necklace for good luck. He didn't talk much, and mostly came by to listen in on Jack and Big Jim's jam sessions. Jack and Jim hadn't fucked with Reed, mainly because he didn't try to put on airs, wasn't boastful, or given to self-serving bullshit. He was a genuinely nice fellow.

Reed wasn't a close friend to Defurio—he didn't have any except for Maloney. However, he knew Reed, knew him by name. "Fuck," Defurio said, disgustedly throwing down and crushing a cigarette beneath his boot. Fuck it. There wasn't anything he could do about Reed.

Finding the shade and solitude of an isolated log, he re-read Donna's letters and came up with an idea. Taking his Boy Scout knife, he carved the shape of a heart from a C-ration carton. In block letters, he stenciled "I love you" and then collected gum wrappers, placing them shiny side up to show through the letters. Borrowing a felt tip pen, he outlined the letters and edges of the heart in red and on the back, in red, wrote "Donna, Happy Valentine's Day. I'll love you always, Jack."

On February 15, Company B was rescued. In stilted military language, an after action report submitted by the battalion commander read, in part, as follows:

> *"Having been unable to line up on the 14th, the Golden Dragons were determined to reach their surrounded comrades on the 15th of February. Both Company D and Company C fired extensive artillery preparation to their front as they moved and walked the artillery down the ridges to their front.*
>
> *Additionally, they employed large amounts of small arms so at no time was it endangered by friendly fires. The artillery fire was walked down the finger until one round actually fell between the perimeters of Company B and the 1st Platoon of Company D. At that time, the fires were shifted. By noon, Company C had linked up with Company B; company D had secured the higher ridge to the north to protect that flank of Company B and Company C. The Battalion Commanding officer was overhead during the entire operation and by the use of smoke grenades, was able to keep all units informed of all friendly locations. The lead platoon of Company C had radio on Company B's frequency and was able to communicate the 1st platoon of Company D. When the elements got within voice range of Company B, the Battalion Commander had them make contact with each other by shouting. Thus positive identification was made and the units did not engage each other by fire. After the link up with the 1st platoon of Company D, Company C swept forward and linked up with the other element of the surrounded company.*

> *At this point, the commanding Officer of Company B said he could kiss these six men whom he saw first from Company C."*

So ended the day.

Chapter 13

Mary Lou

B Company had been hit hard. Sixty-one functioning troops remained of one hundred thirty. Those remaining were air lifted to Pleiko Air Base and put on trucks.

Defurio wearily crowded onto a deuce and a half. The worn troops sat side by side, not speaking. Going along a rutted road, a majority of them nodded off, heads rocking lazily as drivers shifted and swerved to avoid potholes.

Defurio sat near the tailgate. To him, soldiers on the truck looked like a musty set of wood dolls, a broken geometry of right angles sitting on shelves, a hodgepodge of unevenly spaced feet, bent backs and awkwardly crooked heads.

As they traveled further, ruthless humidity and road dust attacked his respiratory system. From a towel, Defurio made a bandit's mask. It partially relieved intrusion of moisture and airborne dirt. A steaminess arising inside the trifolded kerchief inhibited his breathing. Heated vapor gathered at his shielded nostrils, causing a suggestion of suffocation. Small price to pay for having survived Chu Pa.

Day passed to evening. After some hours, the truck rounded a bend and entered a well-fortified camp. Free standing lights turned night to day. From his seat on the truck, now moving at a crawl, Defurio approximated the base's dimensions somewhere between Ennari and St. George. MPs at its entrance indicated a top level, relatively secure facility. MPs were only found at the military's largest facilities.

Defurio's company was deposited near a row of billets. They received fresh underwear, socks, and fatigues and were directed to a building with gym-type hot water showers.

Defurio strode to a spot in the middle of ten or so men. Thousands of rubber knobs on a long mat tickled his feet. He twisted a handle and stuck his head under a spray of warm water. He let it run down the back of his head and neck. He saw his milky white feet gleam in a false cleanliness, having been sweat soaked for three uninterrupted months inside unchanged socks. His feet had also gotten frequent rinsing from rainwater, turned coffee brown from mud, saturating through his fabric sided jungle boots.

From a bank of shower heads, water drained down to a trough at the foot of a plastic sheathed portion of wall. Some men didn't have any inhibition about pissing while they showered.

Maloney joined Defurio. Soaping up, he put his head under a stream of water pasting his sandy blond hair to his forehead. Noticing the plastic walls, he laughingly blubbered, "What is this shit, why isn't this motherfucker tiled?"

Defurio washed away a three month layer of bacterial crud, paying special attention to his reeking crotch, crusty butt crack, and inflamed pee hole.

Doing bodily functions in a jungle environment is inconvenient, although not intolerable. Various sores, infections, and filthiness are something you adjust to, like how a sickly derelict adjusts to peeing, vomiting, and shitting in back alleys.

A mess hall prepared hot food. The meals would provide a greasy barrier of protection for the abuse of alcohol to follow.

Beer drinking and bullshitting swamped the billet.

Psychedelic rock gave way to down to the bone soul music. Racially mixed strands of men linked arms and shoulders, swaying and singing. They rejoiced in life, chugging cold beer, enjoying the feel of clean clothes and dry cots.

They drank.

Jim's big shoulders bounced uncontrollably in giggles fueled by beer and drags of marijuana. Defurio viewed these happy soldiers and shared their happiness. They had developed a kinship. They were strays united by hardship. They had been tested, branded, and fused by what had happened on Chu Pa. It was a small battle in a big war. They knew Vietnam wasn't finished with them.

For now, they were safe. Fuck tomorrow. Defurio crushed his empty can and opened another.

The circus of activity receded as he drank, his attention constricting in concentric circles before dissolving into a montage of her: Donna's faultless face, her high cheek bones, strong forehead, mouth, nose, jaw line, deep set aqua eyes arranged in perfect harmony. Her mouth opened. An emphatic, slightly high pitched voice, clear and pleasing to the ear, called to him.

Someone broke the spell.

"Hi," came a friendly but intruding salutation from a line soldier. Donna's fragile image floated away, like a balloon slipping from a child's hand. Defurio became foggily reaware of the boisterousness inside the billet.

"Hey," Jack acknowledged, disheartened by losing his vision of her. Jack and Jim were sitting apart from the hard core partiers. This seemed to attract the soldier. He'd been drinking heavily.

"You guys from mortars?"

"Yep," replied Jim to the fair skinned, handsome, older than average soldier. Jim asked his name.

"Dennis Sinksen."

"Where you from?"

"Clinton, Iowa."

"Pull up a chair."

Sinksen slid a metal folding chair in front of Jim and Jack and sat down. They made introductory comments. Gauging him,

Defurio was intrigued by his singular presence. He showed sensitivity, awareness, and seriousness.

Sinksen had a pencil thin silent movie star moustache, a wide mouth, firm jaw, and the alert eyes of a hunter. Soft spoken, he seemed to be on the shy side, out of place, too together, and although drunk, too intelligent. Starting a conversation seemed out of character for him. His speech and mannerisms indicated middle class.

Finally, Jim asked pointedly, "How the fuck did you get in the Army?" Jack and Jim were thinking the same thing, this guy is sophisticated, like them.

"I was attending Iowa State. In my sophomore year, they revoked my student exemption and reclassified me 1A. Probably the same call up that got you guys. My draft board of WWII vets thought it a duty and honor to serve."

"What were you studying?" Jack asked.

"Engineering."

"Boy, did you get it in the ass," Jim said. "I guess from your part of the country they didn't have enough blacks, browns, or poor-ass whites to fuck with."

Jack and Jim let Sinksen know they sympathized, although he didn't give any indication of feeling sorry for himself. "Same shit happened to us," Jack related. "Different dildo, same results." They gently slapped him on the back. He laughed along with them.

The trio cracked open more cold beers, wanting to get wasted; wanting to deaden their painful isolation in this shit choked garbage can of Vietnam. As time passed joking about the stupidity of lifer non-coms and officers, and the overall stupidity of the Army, a sadness showed through in Sinksen. Something ate at him, something that happened on Chu Pa. It was about Reed.

Sinksen had had a sufficient amount of alcohol to overcome an inclination to be reserved and private. His intoxication and unexpected rapport with Jack and Jim had given him an outlet, a means to unburden something that tore at him.

"Did you guys know Reed?" Defurio related that they did, that Reed had visited them often.

"Do you know how he got killed?"

"We didn't get any details," Jack responded. "We know they couldn't get to him for three or four days."

"Let me tell you what happened," Sinksen said in a steady voice. "Reed was in a lead squad scouting the bottom of a ravine about one hundred yards below the rest of the company. We were above them ready to lay down cover fire if they encountered anything. Trouble was, the dinks had firing positions hidden in bamboo. The initial burst caught the lieutenant and his radioman."

"We heard it reported right after they were hit," Jim informed him.

Sinksen nodded. "There were seven guys in that squad. Reed got hit in both legs. The four others were able to run to the top of the ridge where we were. We laid a shit load of fire around Reed. He was laying in the open."

"Was he conscious?" Jack asked.

"That was the problem. The son of a bitch kept yelling for help. It was getting dark. We tried to get to him. We couldn't. Fucking dinks opened up on us every time we moved." Sinksen paused. "They might not have known he was there or alive except for him yelling his fucking head off. We shouted for him to shut the fuck up. Either he couldn't hear us or was too scared to stop." Sinksen's voice lowered a bit. "He kept this shit up for an hour, 'help…I'm okay I just can't walk…help!' He must have screamed help a hundred times, until his voice gave out. It turned into a whimper. He may have been crying. A flare popped above him. We saw two dinks holding AK-47s run at him from the bamboo. We got one. The other blew the top of Reed's head off and disappeared." Sinksen displayed a twinge of resentment as if Reed had brought it on himself, which he probably had. "And that wasn't the worst part, we couldn't get to him for four days. When we did, he was a fucking mess."

Defurio's stomach tightened. By then he had seen days old NVA corpses decaying, becoming purple-black grotesquely bloated lumps. He had tried to forget the sight of stretched uniforms holding together expanding bodies like skins of sausages.

Sinksen volunteered to retrieve Reed. He was one of four white soldiers accepting the task of extracting the dead black man.

Climbing a considerable distance up a rocky incline carrying 180 pounds of shifting rotting meat, for this is what Reed had become, was gruesome work. Sinksen described Reed's swollen, sewer smelling, vermin infested corpse continually slipping off a poncho slickened by leaking fluids. Spare boot laces tied around him didn't prevent him from rolling in his own juices, shedding skin and exposing body parts. Sinksen expressed revulsion at seeing maggots in the pulp of Reed's head.

Sinksen's voice stayed steady, but as he went deeper in his narration, muscles in his face formed crinkles at his brow and corner of his mouth and eyes, especially when he mentioned the flies. Thirsty flies. He described them buzzing from Reed's decomposing carcass to the eyes and mouths of the body carriers, distaining sweat for the sweeter refreshment of eye moisture and drying saliva. Sinksen and the others fought for air between retching.

"The fucking bloods didn't help." Sinksen pinched these words from his mouth. "They didn't look away either. They lined both sides of the ravine and gawked. Didn't say shit, didn't lift a finger." That the blacks, to a man, let four white soldiers throw up their guts to save a black man from further deterioration is what clearly ate at Sinksen.

A vague thought occurred to Defurio. Maybe they were traumatized by old myths from the deep south. Maybe the black troopers saw through the moving shadows and haze of suspended smoke and dust, the ghostly images of confederate soldiers risen from the grave to carry a black man to his doom.

He let this rationalization recede to nothingness as he refocused on Sinksen. This man from Clinton, Iowa, was made of sturdy stuff. Once he got the incident off his chest, he let it go, a purposely diminished scrap tossed in the dust bin of memory. He put a beer to his lips, taking a long pull, letting the liquid flush out remaining dregs of bitterness or spite. Cold beer can dull a lot of pain.

Sinksen seemed incapable of hatred or vengefulness. Defurio, never easily impressed, thought what a fine model of rectitude displayed by this modest, remarkable man.

Patterson, in third squad mortars, an all-American happy-go-lucky kid, came by, shit faced, soliciting cans of beer. He had been at Mary Lou before and knew of a hut maintained by whores located on the opposite side of a banana plantation across from the main gate. He needed beers to bribe the MPs. Every GI in the company donated a beer, adding up to several cases. Everyone became infused in the spirit of the adventure, thinking vicariously, they too would be getting a piece of ass.

Having escaped Chu Pa, Patterson and four of his friends figured they deserved a shot at some Vietnamese, probably infected, pussy. So, wearing "What me worry?" grins, Patterson and his buddies, after paying off guards, dirtied clean fatigues low crawling through barbed wire and disappearing into a fringe of banana trees. They planned to move along the edge of the plantation so as not to lose their bearings.

Five Anglo-Saxon males, progeny of proud American parents, were on their way to getting themselves fucked silly by Montagnard harlots considered low class even by Vietnam standards. Watching them slither from view, Defurio thought there were a lot of ways this exercise could go wrong.

Fearless GI resolve won out. Hours later, a gleeful band of sex satiated soldiers returned, ostensibly unscathed. Symptoms of V.D. wouldn't show for a while. V.D. would be a bonus, requiring removal from the field for treatment.

Defurio celebrated their success by drinking. He drank. And drank. He drank to remember and forget; to forget jungle rot, whores, Reed, Mary Lou, Chu Pa, the central highlands—Vietnam. He drank to lose himself in sweet recollections of Donna; her laugh, the turn of her head as she walked, the flash of her eyes, her self-conscious embarrassment in response to compliments on her beauty.

He held his beer between his legs, elbows on his knees. Hanging his head, Defurio concentrated on the circle formed by the top of the can. A chunk was missing where the tab had been torn off. His life had been reduced to this, holding onto a fucking beer can for comfort at a place he couldn't find on a map, a way station called Mary Lou in the highlands of central Vietnam.

Helplessness filled him, but he didn't let it stand. He put the can to his lips. "Fuck this shit," he said, as if someone were listening. No one heard him or cared. He battled for control. Feeling sorry for himself wasn't going to bring Donna any nearer. He straightened his spine. His mother's words eked through the alcoholic haze: "If you're weak, the world will defeat you." He wasn't going to let that happen. Donna appeared in his mind as she always did when he was troubled. He made an unequivocal, precise vow to her, knowing that she would become aware of it or feel it or sense it in the intuitive way she had regarding him. "I'll make it back to you, babe."

Defurio felt strengthened, renewed, relieved, as if he'd said a prayer to the Virgin Mary and she had answered.

Any references to the Virgin Mary were allegorical. Defurio was not a religious man.

Chapter 14

Poliekleng

Morning wake up. Defurio constricted the flap under his tongue, permitting him to unstick it from the roof of his mouth. He undid a film of dry plaque and stale beer. Cottony congestion extended from his upper throat to congealed knots in the front lobes of his forehead. He couldn't remember draining his last beer, only a vague recollection of drowning in it. Two oily cups of thick, scalding mess hall coffee revived him.

Colmes relayed bad news. Assemble at 0900 to board trucks for Poliekleng. Back to the shit. Not enough time to write Donna. She would be scared out of her mind not hearing from him for so long. He hadn't heard from her either. He had expected mail to reach him at Mary Lou. The action on Chu Pa had fucked up delivery.

Nothing he could do about it. He readjusted his thinking. "Hey Colmes, do you know anything about Poliekleng?"

"It's a special forces camp. Green Berets, I think."

"What are we doing there? Shouldn't they be doing something to save us?" Colmes shrugged. Nobody ever knew what was going on. No one knew where this place was or how far away. It must be a geographic location since it didn't have a bullshit made up name.

Defurio set himself for a lengthy, dusty ride in an open truck. Not unfamiliar. He'd eaten a mountain of dust riding in the back of flatbeds in the vegetable and fruit fields of the San Joaquin. Worse would be a ride in the rain. Swift, warm, hit and run deluges had been racing through the highlands since Charmaine, auditioning for monsoons yet to come.

Ten young recruits joined the company at Mary Lou. Big help—they would be a detriment for a month. The convoy gunned onto a dirt road. A rough surface of gouged pits from mines and mortars and hard clumps of earth and rocks gave the sensation of bumping over railroad ties. Bumps were cushioned primarily by a man's butt cheeks since truck shock absorbers had been pounded to uselessness. Except for wired up rookies, B Company assumed normal give-a-shit attitudes, content to doze and savor the frivolity of the past two days—to hell with compounded spines and what might happen next.

He tried to picture Donna, but the pitch, roll, and knock of the truck didn't permit it. Defurio gave up.

A taste of bile lingered on his tongue and throat. The presence of undeveloped regurgitants didn't keep him from grabbing some sleep. His body adjusted to the truck's motion, autonomously limbering to adjust for its erratic movement. Restlessly, he had anguished dreams of bloody body parts soaking in a tub of greenish brew, limbs and organs rising to the surface in a disgusting replay.

Miles rolled by. Defurio slipped into an infantryman's trance, alert to sharp or subtle variances like the whoosh of a rocket propelled grenade or AK-47 gunfire, but in a stage of sleep. Eventually the convoy geared down and ground to a halt near the center of a bleak, forlorn outpost.

The place aroused serious concerns. Poliekleng lay on flat ground. Nearby foothills escalated to banks of mountains extending to Cambodia. It presented an easy target. NVA troops splintering off the Ho Chi Minh trail could reach it in a three day hump.

Green Berets occupying Poliekleng had deployed on an emergency mission, and B Company had been brought in to provide security for six dug-in tanks acting as artillery.

Stiff from sitting in a confined space for many hours, Defurio got down and stretched. He saw pieces of rockets lying around and multiple rips in sandbagged walls of bunkers. "Jeez," he said to Jim. "Doesn't this shit ever stop? Now we have to deal with rockets?"

Though not causing any serious damage, three seven foot 122mm rockets had penetrated the camp's interior the previous evening. Shards of ceramic plating large enough to show red soviet markings lay scattered as though gigantic unglazed pots had been hurled at the camp.

Camps, landing zones, and firebases all had individual characteristics. Poliekleng appeared as an old west frontier town on a plain tucked between a wide river and open land to its west. Shorn of vegetation, it appeared lonely and desolate.

Bunkers were empty. Jack and Jim commandeered one with eight bunks. Jack searched through personal belongings, finding a single mold steel ax, which he confiscated. Acquiring it made his day. A stolen ax; it's pitiful what a slim bone of satisfaction can be thrown to a grunt.

Jack and Jim went exploring, but they didn't go far. Wilting under a withering sun, they sought relief in the shade of a bunker wall. Using a two finger can opener contained in C-ration packets, Jim opened two cans of pears scoured from a concealed Green Beret stash. Munching on pears, they sprawled as leisurely as tomcats fresh from raiding a garbage can. They scanned the area.

Except for bunkers, Poliekleng was bare of manmade or natural structures. Its isolation was noticeable but not readily defined.

Jack put his finger on it. "Jim, notice how quiet it is here? Where are the helicopters, artillery, mortars?" B Company wasn't running patrols. No need for illum rounds or protective fire, not with tanks available. Who knows why helicopters weren't running. "What do you think?"

"I guess we're off the beaten path."

"It's weird," Jack said. "Dinks blow the shit out of these places at night, then during the day, nothing. You could have a picnic out here right now."

"If it wasn't so freaking hot," Jim replied.

Shifting from time to time to air out pockets of accumulating sweat, they could have been farm boys taking a break from the harvest. Their attention was drawn to a file of GIs moseying to and from a location down the river. Some locals from a village somewhere in the vicinity also strolled along the river.

Avoiding stagnant air in the bunker, they decided to stay in the open. "C'mon Jim, let's see what's going on." Villagers trekking in the open indicated that whatever the business being conducted downstream wasn't subject to interference by the enemy. Jack and Big Jim slung on M-16s and made off down river. They weren't used to sustained exposure to raw sunlight, and soon dizziness almost buckled Defurio. He temporarily reeled in the 120° heat.

"Jesus, Jim," Jack said. "This fucking sun is turning my ball sack to boiled eggs."

"I'd give up one of mine for an umbrella," Jim whispered, his cheeks reddening.

They passed a man on a motor bike negotiating a shallow place in the river. Seated side saddle behind him, a female passenger wearing a traditional conical straw hat had her silk covered legs demurely crossed. The motorbike went ahead of them, stopping at a junction of river and jungle. His passenger slid off, joining fifteen other women selling trinkets and themselves.

"Can you believe this?"

"No," Jim said, visibly energized. They had arrived at a thriving bazaar of self-employed prostitutes. Other than GIs, there weren't any males present.

Women were leading men behind a screen of high grass. Under their arms, they carried rolled up clear plastic sheets. "You see that, Jack?" Jim asked in astonishment. "They're using wrapping from our mortar crates to fuck on."

Women returned from the high grass to the water's edge, impassively pulling pants to mid-calf, squatting, and splashing water on themselves. Creamy blobs dripped down, catching the current before submerging. "Look at that!" Jim continued to be amazed. "Millions of microscopic tadpoles becoming fish food," he said, reverting to his fondness for animal references.

The women had uniformly smooth, hairless, girlish legs crowned at the top by a wispy slit.

Vietnam pussy. Such a delicate organ in such seemingly delicate bodies; an organ designed to produce babies, a moldable instrument corrupted to endure hours of abuse by GI phalluses, big and small. The women didn't seem concerned about pregnancy. Evidently, paddling water on themselves wasn't for purposes of birth control or hygiene but to remove messiness from GI ejaculations. Did these women know some oriental trick preventing insemination? Probably not. Unwanted fetuses were an occupational hazard that were promptly excised.

This meat market of female flesh both stimulated and repulsed him. Initially, Defurio experienced a surge of sexual sensation. However, his commitment to and feelings for Donna overrode carnal instinct. His urges converted to a curiosity and crude analysis of what was happening.

"Jim, can you imagine how many of these women get knocked-up? I mean, most of that shit stays inside them. This place must be riddled with shallow holes containing baby newts."

Defurio purposely made an animal reference for Jim's benefit.

His friend chortled a reply. "Dinks are being killed before they're born by them, and by us after they're born. Doesn't seem there'd be any of them left."

After that, Big Jim sort of went into a zone. Defurio recognized the signs of when a man fixes on a woman. He becomes a hunter separating his quarry from the herd. The sight of women squatting, showing scanty hirsute cunts and semen splattered buttocks proved too much for Big Jim. He selected a candidate debatably less ugly than the rest. A walnut faced, cum drenched young strumpet had become irresistible. Presumably young; Montagnard women, young and old, appeared toothless. They had a nauseating habit of chewing beetle nut, which turned their teeth black.

It didn't matter. At this point, Big Jim's testosterone engorged brain couldn't resist an unsightly Montagnard's putrid pussy any more than a starving man could resist tainted meat.

Jack waited patiently, titillated by visualizing Big Jim humping the petite Montagnard. She would have to sufficiently gird her loins to withstand such a vigorous attack on her pubic region. Like a pent up, snorting, breeding stallion, Jim should have finished in seconds. Instead, fifteen minutes passed. Finally, he emerged, picking his way through underbrush while hitching up his pants, his lips drawn in a taunt grimace. Trailing behind him, his liaison, without a gesture of goodbye, blandly turned and headed to the river to prepare for her next customer.

"How was it?" Jack said, expecting a glowing report.

"Let's go," Jim said, brushing past Defurio. Jack didn't inquire further. Clearly, it had not gone well. Jack rushed to catch Jim. The big man's iron jaw remained locked in silence. This was a side of Maloney Jack had never seen before.

Trudging along, Jim started to relax aided by the calming melody coming from the eddying and lapping of the slow moving river. Half way between the prostitute encampment and Poliekleng, they encountered an enormous boulder bordering the river.

Naked GIs were jumping fifteen feet to the water below. Each bore similar markings of white torsos and limbs (there were no blacks) topped by tan faces, and in the middle, fungal ridden, lobster colored groins.

Spontaneously, Jack and Jim scaled the easily climbable rock like gung ho commandos. Laying down their M-16s, they stripped and joined the passel of rollicking GIs.

Defurio wasn't inclined to go naked in public, however, at this stage he didn't care if passing female villagers looked on. Locals didn't pay attention anyway, preferring to rivet attention on whatever tasks they were performing. A brutal sun made the river an inviting diversion. The seventy-five foot wide muddy waterway wasn't deep enough to support commercial boat traffic. In some places during the dry period, it could be walked across.

Jack and Jim joyfully flung themselves off the rock, hairy unbound gonads swinging freely. Crashing butt first resulted in impacted fecal matter being pleasantly dislodged. Cooling water embraced them. Jim's mighty body smashing through water knocked free his anger. When he surfaced, he was his old self.

"I'm glad to get that bitch's shit off me," he said. In a short while, Jim would amplify this remark.

Sweaty, salty T-shirts starched by the sun served as scratchy towels. Refreshed, the two friends headed for camp.

"Jack, I would have been better off fucking a tree stump." He launched into a recap of his Montagnard misadventure.

"What was the problem, Jim? Pussy is pussy."

"Jack, you can't believe how bad it was."

Jim began to frame the encounter.

"First thing, you had to go around or over a bunch of naked-assed, groaning GIs. She didn't want to walk far, she tried to lie down and squeeze in between them. She wanted to finish fast."

"How many do you think there were?"

"I don't know; a whole field, maybe fifteen or twenty couples before, during, and after humping—plus more trying to find a place and those leaving."

"No shit! Fucking in plain sight."

"Yeah, we had to hike a couple of city blocks to find a private spot. She wasn't happy."

"Did she play around with you beforehand, you know, to get you ready?"

"I wish. I didn't even see her tits. She laid flat, pulled her pants down a few inches and that was it. She didn't look at me."

"She put a beetle nut in her mouth and looked sideways. She didn't talk. She pointed at her pussy trying to hurry me." Jim shook his head, recalling his exasperation. "Fucking thing looked like it was leaking my mother's hand lotion."

"Were you able to get a hard-on?"

"Yeah, but I don't know how, I just wanted to shoot my wad and get it over with. Jack, I might as well stuck my rod in the ocean." Jim was finding his tempo. "I couldn't find top nor bottom nor sides; it was like I was fucking a bowl of oatmeal. She was so slippery and widened out I couldn't get any traction."

He saved the ickiest part for last. "I almost threw up when she spit beetle juice. I was on top of her pumping like a madman when she did it. I stepped on a grasshopper once and its guts are the same color. I'll tell you, Jack, that shit smells like soy sauce gone bad." Jim laughed at this final detail. Catharsis completed.

Big Jim cranked up his New York stride. His sunny disposition had returned.

Chapter 15

Roundbottom

They'd been airborne for an hour. Defurio scratched at a two day growth of stubble. He didn't have a chance to shave. They were ordered to get ready ASAP, then waited five hours at the helipad.

A covey of thundering Chinooks had come for them. The massive double-rotor Chinooks were impressive compared to the much smaller Hueys.

The company landed safely at an LZ, having the usual barren appearance of a place cleared by explosives. The LZ was the highest of three in the area. This region's mountains broke into individual peaks rather than ridges.

Jack hurried to find an abode. He returned for Jim safeguarding their gear. "C'mon, Jim. I found a place." Jack gathered his equipment. "Do you know the name of this LZ?"

"Uh, uh," Jim couldn't care less.

"Think of a piece of ass." This raised Jim's interest. "We can congratulate ourselves, we've landed on a giant replica of the lt. colonel's girlfriend's butt." This loosened Jim's impassivity further. Jack drew out the pronunciation, "R-o-u-n-d-b-o-t-t-o-m." Jim's raised eyebrows would have been imperceptible to anyone but Jack.

Jack suggested they establish a two-man bunker. He discovered a suitable dwelling near to where platoon mortars were being placed. Using nails and the blunt end of his ax for a hammer and wood from ammo boxes, the duo built a table, shelving, and recliners for lounging. When finished, they tested their handiwork. Leaning back inside an uncrowded, noiseless, candle lit room puffing cigarettes, leafing through skin magazines, the war seemed far away.

February 20, 1969. A helicopter came in bringing overdue mail. Defurio received six letters from Donna plus a package from her containing Polaroid film, food, and a battery operated razor. Jack liked to read Donna's letters alone. Jim, respecting his privacy, departed for the main bunker.

Her latest letter bore the date February 7, 1969.

> *Jack,*
>
> *I'm so worried. Mama was watching Walter Cronkite when she called me. She said, "Donna, isn't that Jack's company he's talking about?" News reports were saying the 4th Division in the central highlands was involved in large battles with lots of causalities. Mama doesn't know the difference between a company and a division. I'm not sure myself.*
>
> *Jack, I know you don't tell me everything so I won't worry, but right now, I'm so afraid of what might happen to you. I'm always worried. Except now, it's like I know you're in more danger. I can't explain it. I don't know what I would do if something happened to you. I could never again be truly happy. Please, please, please come back to me, Jack. I love you with all my heart and will forever.*
>
> *Jack, yesterday mama and I went to the store and I bought you Spaghettio's, sardines, Vienna sausage,*

> *etc. a razor, and film for your camera. Hope they got there o.k. I love you, Jack. Please come home to me.*

On his first day at Roundbottom, Defurio felt secure. Donna's letter had forecast his peril even though she couldn't have yet known of Chu Pa. Did her misgivings still hold? Distressingly, B Company had returned to the matrix of mountains that included Chu Pa. Reportedly, a regiment of NVA troops remained firmly entrenched throughout the sector.

As at Charmaine, B Company provided security for an artillery battery and TOC unit. However, the company had also been tasked to actively find the enemy. Ten and fifteen man patrols were on scouting missions. At night, L-shaped ambushes were being set up on trails near Roundbottom.

In an L-shaped ambush, men lay hidden on one side of a likely path of enemy travel. A smaller number of men cut off the path at the foot of the L. When sprung, enemy soldiers are decimated in a cross fire.

Colmes had derosed at Mary Lou. There wasn't any fanfare at these departures. Ordinarily a helicopter returning from a mission heeded a call to transport a derosing soldier. Chopper pilots went to great lengths to extract these soldiers. Pick-ups relied on availability of a helicopter and the discretion of its pilot. Otherwise, soldiers had to rely on the uncertain arrival of supply helicopters. In either instance, a soldier had a matter of minutes to gather his gear, shake some hands, go to the landing pad, get on the chopper, and give a big wave to people to whom he would likely never see again.

Thorpe, a non-career sergeant, had transferred in from another company. He had two months left in-country. Jack introduced himself. "Thorpe, how'd you get the honor of taking this squad?'

"I'm short and they promoted a guy to take my place," he said quietly. "It freed me up to fill in until you guys get a full time replacement."

Squads were busy setting up the platoon's mortars. Under Thorpe's direction, 1st squad set, leveled, and sighted its mortar. Observation aircraft were already calling for fire missions. "God-damn, Jim, we haven't had a chance to scratch our asses and they're calling for fire missions." It was a bad omen.

First squad unleashed a series of high explosive rounds, and an hour later they let loose another bevy. Thorpe had calmly and efficiently carried out the instructions of Lt. Flack, the platoon's fire control officer.

Satisfied with Thorpe's competency but otherwise not giving a shit, Defurio and Maloney scampered to their hideaway, anxious to delve through Donna's care package.

A corner of the poncho covering the doorway lifted. "Hi guys."

It was Sgt. Thorpe. Shit. Jack quickly closed the cardboard flaps on Donna's package. He wasn't about to give hand-outs to an uninvited guest.

The plumpish sergeant shoe-horned his way inside. Thorpe stood about three inches shorter than Jack. His presence and girth appreciably diminished space in the room. He was similar to Colmes in the mildness of his voice and manner, although Colmes would never have invited himself to someone else's hooch. Thorpe's red-blond moustache matched color with his badly cut hair. Bad haircuts were a common malady for troops in the field. Dull scissors in the hands of give-a-fuck medics made for reckless hair-dos. Medics, because they possessed scissors, were untrained barbers for infantrymen, and haircuts were mandatory.

"What's up?" Jack said unenthusiastically.

Thorpe droned on about army shit. Jack and Jim found Thorpe to be a nice guy, but incredibly boring. They soon hinted for him to leave; they were tired, sleepy, had letters to write, etc.

"I guess I'll go," Thorpe said reluctantly. "See you guys." He returned to his squad.

Jack and Jim descended on Donna's package.

The next morning, Jack and Jim were cheerfully munching on Vienna Sausages. "Hi guys." Damn, Thorpe again.

"Hi there, Thorpe, come on in and have a sausage." Defurio didn't have a choice, the sausages were in plain view. Thorpe presented some weak pretext for visiting, something about loads of ammo coming in or some shit. Jack thought, "So what?"

Taking a sausage, Thorpe parked on the edge of Jim's bunk, four feet from Jack's. Defurio decided to make the best of Thorpe's unwelcomed presence and asked the obligatory question. "Where you from, Thorpe?"

"New Jersey."

Hmmm. Maybe they had underestimated him.

"Marry a local girl?" Jack asked, noticing a wedding ring.

"Nah, I married a Puerto Rican." Jack and Jim glanced at Thorpe.

"How'd you meet a Puerto Rican in the back woods of New Jersey?" Jack intended to mine this rich source of inquiry.

"I didn't, I met her in New York City. I have an aunt there. I met Maria on summer vacation."

"No shit, can you believe this? Jim is from New York and is married to a Puerto Rican." Jack conveniently omitted Big Jim's divorce or annulment (Jim was vague as to which).

"Let me tell you guys about bedding Puerto Rican women in New York," Jim said, regressing to a happier time. He held up his big mitts as though hushing a crowd. "It's difficult where they live, too many pesky little brothers and sisters. If the weather is good, city parks are the best." Jim went into detail, getting excited by his own rhetoric. In the middle of his soliloquy, he made a gesture.

"Whoa, Jim, go back." Jack requested clarification.

Big Jim repeated the motion—a side-to-side, hitch-hiking movement of his hand. Jim kept talking.

"Hold on, Jim, you mean…?"Jack mimicked the motion. Jim nodded. "You used your thumb to finger fuck your girlfriends?"

"You bet."

Jim pointed to the base of his thumb. "More circumference."

WHUMP! Further discussion concerning thumb penetration would have to wait.

Mortar attacks had occurred daily the three days they'd been at Roundbottom. Until now, the rounds had been inaccurate, hitting far from the LZ. Not today. Rounds were falling right on target.

Fortunately, accompanying ground assaults seldom happened in daylight. The company was reasonably safe. A 61mm dink mortar shell couldn't penetrate a decently built bunker. No sweat.

WHUMP! WHUMP! WHUMP! WHUMP! A series of four or five shells came in, interrupted by a pause of a minute or two before the next sequence.

"FIRE MISSION! FIRE MISSION! FIRE MISSION!" Defurio's platoon was being called to man its guns. "What the fuck?" Defurio threw up his hands. "Why are they calling a fire mission when the dinks have us zeroed in?"

A direct order had come from Flack for the platoon to return fire. To do so, the three mortar squads would have to place themselves directly under where the shells were landing.

"GO! GO! GO!" Holding his helmet down with his hand, Lt. Duke ducked and ran from squad to squad, flushing the platoon from the safety of bunkers.

From unprotected gun pits, the platoon collectively shot off fifteen rounds before having to pancake themselves to avoid being perforated by incoming. An up and down pattern developed, the squads springing up to fire a series of rounds and a longer period groveling in dirt when enemy mortars answered.

WHUMP! WHUMP! Defurio hugged the open ground of the gun pit.

"Fuck this." He ran to a shelter containing stacked mortar shells. Tumbling inside, he slammed into Ward. They sat face to face. There wasn't room to lay flat. Shells were landing close, very close. "Shit, Ward," Defurio yelled. "I don't know if we made things better or worse." He grabbed his knees and buried his face between them.

Ward did the same.

The above ground shelter had a sandbagged roof, three sandbagged walls, and an open side. It contained forty to fifty high explosives and willie peter, or white phosphorous, rounds ready for firing. They huddled next to these shells. A well placed round would obliterate them.

WHUMP! WHUMP! High velocity pieces of metal slammed an outside wall. WHUMP! WHUMP! Accelerated smoke and dust smacked Defurio's face. He coughed on a powdery chunk of phlegm. He raised his head, and so did Ward. Squinting through the haze, he gave Ward a smile and shouted above the clamor, "One thing, Ward, if this motherfucker blows up, we ain't going to feel anything."

Ward nodded. Although twisted in fear, his face maintained a frozen half smile. He may have been thinking the same thing as Defurio: this was as good a way to die as any. Falling rounds drifted to another part of the LZ before decreasing and discontinuing altogether. The platoon resumed firing until Flack gave the order to desist.

A hush fell over the hill. A pall of smoke lifted from the LZ. Shaken squad members returned slowly to their bunkers. Defurio, mentally drained, had the bent shoulders and gait of an old man. He crashed on his bunk, and Maloney did likewise. Initially they were too overwrought to talk, but young men recover quickly. "How many dinks do you think we killed, Jim?"

"None. We didn't kill them, they ran out of ammo."

"You're probably right. They'll get re-supplied by tonight or tomorrow." Jack lit a cigarette. "I hope they don't get re-supplied any time soon." He flicked ashes on the floor. "The son of a bitches had us dead on."

"What gets me is that they have shitloads of these mortar squads active in this area." This seemed to be true. Mortars had been pitched at them from every direction. Jim light heartedly expanded this thought. "Fucking dinks probably have contests to see who can drop the most rounds inside our perimeter."

They heard a tramping of boots across the compound. Jack ventured waist high from the door of the hooch to see what was happening. "James, come here, you gotta see this." Jim joined Jack.

Their upturned faces reflected orange light. They were slapped by waves of heat. Thirty yards uphill, at its peak, Roundbottom was ablaze.

A mortar had started a slow burn of some trash. It reached a store of fuel cans, causing a chain reaction. Flames twenty feet high were stabbing the sky. "Jim, this is spectacular." Color film for three pictures remained in his Polaroid. Jack anticipated three fantastic pictures.

He wrestled the camera from his rucksack, which was on the ground next to the bunker. He had to hurry, daylight was almost gone.

He fiddled anxiously readying the clumsy device. He extended its fabric accordion body and pointed the ponderous instrument in the direction of the unfolding drama. He was thinking that these pictures should make up for those disappearing jets in photos taken at Tiffany.

He didn't have to budge from his hooch. From there he had a great upward angle. A fluttering American flag attached to a bunker in the foreground would add a further dramatic touch.

He aimed and clicked.

Defurio pulled free the plastic square and impatiently waited for the picture to develop. The oily square stayed a slimy gray. He discarded it and snapped again, and again. Same results, blanks. In angry frustration, he inspected the camera. Not that it would do any good; he'd run out of film. He tilted the Polaroid sideways.

Gravely shrapnel spilled out through a hole. That's when Defurio observed numerous shrapnel holes in his ruck sack.

Defurio threw the camera down. "Jesus, goddamn it, Jim. Can't we ever get a fucking break?"

"Better in your camera than your ass," Jim said drolly.

The disappointed soldiers didn't stay long watching the fire. They didn't want to get roped into helping extinguish it. They hurried back inside the hooch.

Chapter 16

The Short Range Patrol

"You guys in there?" Lt. Duke gave his customary warning. He brought bad news. Robertson in 3rd squad had been seriously wounded and awaited a medevac. Worse news followed. "Sorry, Jack," he said gently, "you'll have to go tomorrow on a four-day SRP patrol."

Defurio protested vociferously. "Why me, Lieutenant? I'm not in shape to hump these mountains, I'd be a liability."

"I didn't want to send you, but the line is short of men and the other 11B40 guy in the platoon has done one already." Lt. Duke gave Defurio a brotherly tap on the knee. "It's your turn. You'll do okay. Be ready at 0800." Defurio tried hard not to like Lt. Duke, but couldn't.

Turning to leave, the lieutenant hesitated. "Oh," he said brightly, trying to say something positive, even though he knew they wouldn't give a shit. "For today's action, Captain Lowry is recommending us for a Meritorious Service Medal with a V for valor."

Lt. Duke let hang the reference to the Meritorious Service award as he vacated the bunker.

Jack, upset about the patrol duty, tried to get his mind off it. "Jim, do you know anything about this medal?"

"Nah," Jim answered apathetically while reaching for a can of sardines. "This SRP thing is fucked. You know, though, none of them have run into any shit lately." They both knew that since arriving at Roundbottom, SRP patrols had been playing Russian roulette with NVA troops. Steady mortar barrages were a sure sign of the enemy's presence.

Jack persisted in talking about medals. "I ignored that shit about medals and ribbons in training."

"Me too," Jim said, opening the can of sardines. Jim was scared for Jack, and eating was his way of coping.

"I recognize the CIB, Purple Heart, Bronze and Silver Stars, but that's about it. And I don't know where any of that shit goes on the uniform." Jack stopped talking, momentarily distracted by Jim plowing through the sardines. He regained his concentration. "You have to admit it, Jim, V for valor sounds pretty fucking impressive."

"What they ought to give us," Jim said dryly, finishing the sardines, "is a big silver S for stupidity."

Shit! What was he doing? He had to write Donna. He wouldn't be able to write for four days. She would be worried sick. He wrote a lengthy letter describing the past days' events, downplaying the danger, writing that he was at a secure outpost defended by artillery. This wasn't true; artillery is an offensive weapon. He also described the SRP mission as routine.

After finishing his letter, Jack went to visit Robertson, a six foot Georgian with crooked teeth. He lay on his stomach inside a bunker. His wounds extended from head to foot. Blood seeped through his fatigues from dozens of razor sharp cuts. Defurio had expected to see large gashes. Robertson was standing fifteen yards from where the first mortar had struck.

"How you doin', Robertson?"

Robertson managed a pained smile. "I'm okay. I don't think it's too bad." Through pain and shock, he spoke hesitantly. Robertson couldn't see the extent of his wounds.

"They got you pretty good. Good enough, looks like, to get you back to the world. I'll tell you, though, your wounds don't look deep." Indeed they didn't.

A medevac neared the landing pad and medics hurried in to take Robertson. "Good luck, buddy. Say hello to the girls back home." Defurio didn't have any idea if Robertson's wounds warranted a trip home. Medics placed Robertson on a stretcher. He bent down to awkwardly shake Robertson's dangling left hand as he was carried out.

Weary from the day's activities, Defurio needed rest. He wouldn't get it. Mortarmen were doing guard duty due to the shortage of men in the line. His turn came at 1:00am. At his solitary post on the perimeter, he immediately fought to stay awake and alert. Intel reports indicated a ground attack was imminent. So-called intelligence reports were hardly ever accurate. Just the same, daily mortar attacks and reports of enemy movement by patrols indicated heavy concentrations of dinks near Roundbottom. He couldn't stay awake though, and slipped into a restless consciousness, suspended somewhere between wakefulness and sleep. He woke briefly but was unable to sustain it. Incoherent pictures formed: scenes of confusion, doubt and concern, incoming…dinks ... SRP patrol … Robertson …fire … Donna…the SRP patrol ... the SRP patrol.

He sank further. He heard a voice inside his head calling to him to wake up. The voice faded as he began to drift through his subconscious. What elements of cosmic destiny, human history, his history, had led him to be a soldier at this time in this place, to circumstances so bizarre that even now he didn't know if he were dreaming?

Wake up, Defurio! Was he awake? He strained to see through the blackness. Blobs of bamboo, trees, and shrubs began to take shape. Did he really see something? Blind-folded by the night, how could he see?

A spark showed through the darkness. A firefly? An illusion? It grew larger. The image floated towards him. It took form; a thin, cylindrical object, a forearm in length, hovered before him. It was as though the object were awaiting his assent to proceed. Yes, yes. He wanted to know its secrets, even if it foretold his destruction. He would take the chance. Would this portend life, death, or something else? This was an adventure beyond comprehension. He sensed a positive prediction for the future. Yes, he wanted to know. The cylinder turned slowly on its axis. It was a scroll. On it were words written in calligraphic ornateness. The words had an orderly cadence:

"All wars are different, all wars are the same." The paper or cloth on which the lines unfurled, glimmered in a greenish light. *"Does it make a difference if one goes to battle on the back of a beast or the belly of a helicopter? A soldier is a soldier however he becomes so. Ultimately, a soldier, any soldier, faces similar challenges of climate, terrain, deprivation, and terror. Uncomprehendingly, he marches, runs, rides, or claws his way forward, drawn to the Siren's Song, beckoned by the Furies."*

The words had a ring of truth. A soldier's life is ruled by ungovernable laws of nature. Rules of rationality don't apply.

Defurio imagined or dreamed he could influence the scroll's message. By inclination, he vulgarized its meaning. His interpolation made perfect sense to him. "Fuck it" and "don't mean nothing" were true expressions of the scroll's meaning. They conveyed hopefulness. Realistically, the odds were in Defurio's favor. Not that many GIs, relatively speaking, were being killed or physically injured in Vietnam. This was a satisfying realization. If he survived one year, he would have a ticket home. Fuck you, Sirens and Furies. One year was doable.

He had to make it one year. One year. One year.

A hand tapped his shoulder. "Get some sleep, Jack, it's my turn." Big Jim spoke under his breath, everyone did on the perimeter.

Jack and Jim were having C-ration coffee. Jim stayed up to keep Jack company while he got ready for the patrol. Jack had managed maybe two or three hours of sleep.

Suddenly a man came in unannounced. He had three black chevrons on his shoulder. "You Defurio?"

"Yeah."

"I'm Smith. I'll be leading this motherfucker today."

Smith appeared surprisingly upbeat and apparently chafing to depart the LZ. The sergeant probably didn't have a say-so, nevertheless, Defurio registered a feeble protest.

"Shit, Sarge, I haven't fired my M-16 since it was issued to me. I'm not in shape to hump." The bouncy sergeant disregarded Defurio's pleas.

"Don't worry about it. It's better in the bush than being around these dickhead lieutenants and captains. Take some magazines. This will be a grunt style R & R."

Defurio thought, "As long as we don't hit any shit." Anyhow, he liked the positive attitude of the sergeant, a straight forward, wiry white dude of average height. "We're linking up at the east end of the LZ by the concertina. 0800 sharp." Defurio glanced at his watch. It was 7:15.

Packing four days' rations made his ruck weigh a ton. Moreover, he had stuffed twenty grenades in his side pockets and pack. He also carried five bandoliers of ammo. He wobbled across the LZ to the rendezvous point. He met the other two members of the ad hoc squad, a Latino and a white kid, both young. He didn't know them and he didn't catch their names clearly. They weren't friendly or unfriendly. They were mostly busy with the last minute details of getting ready, tying down pant legs and adjusting equipment. Leaving the perimeter, there wasn't any chit-chat. The white kid had point, and behind him, the sergeant trailed by his radioman. Last was Defurio. No one had solicited his input.

They humped in silence on a rough trail. Defurio tried to identify possible dangers. This lasted about fifteen minutes. A ubiquitous array of plants barricaded the trail. Visual penetration extended fifteen to twenty feet at best. A gorilla could be standing by the trail and not be seen. Nothing was as expected. The jungle presented a panoply of drab browns, blacks, and greens. Except for the whine of insects, it was deadly still.

Signs of fatigue came early. Shortly, heated globs of excretions claimed every surface of skin. Humidity coated his nasal passages, throat, and lungs. Going uphill called for his body to double its work. Bending to balance his pack, his upper body came near the ground, his face a couple of feet from the surface. Lungs pumped painfully. His mouth turned to parchment.

He lifted his gaze every so often to locate the radioman. To become separated from the squad would put him in deadly jeopardy. Without a compass, map, or radio he would become disoriented; easy prey for enemy gunners or a slow demise from thirst, hunger, and the elements.

He didn't expect how rapidly fatigue would overtake him. It didn't take long for it to infuse his lungs, tendons, joints, and muscles. He reached a threshold of pain and pushed through it. The physical distress wasn't going to subside, but at this stage it was manageable. He was glad Sgt. Smith had told him not to wear a helmet. He had also told Defurio to tie boot laces around his pant legs to prevent snagging on plants.

In two hours, they reached the supposed destination. The map showed it as one click from the LZ. It should have taken an hour to get there. However, Sgt. Smith could tell the map was in obvious error. It displayed false distances and terrain features. Relying on his experience and intuition, the sergeant advanced the squad another three-fourths of a click to a location reasonably resembling what should have been the place to set up an observation post, the purpose of the mission.

The hump had tested the limits of the squad's endurance. Defurio's extra twenty-five pounds of grenades had punished him severely. Dropping his pack, he fumbled for his canteen. He sat back on his pack, using it as cushion. He cocked his head forward and drank greedily. He dampened a towel and wiped his face. Blood rushed to fill capillaries squashed flat by the pressure from his pack where half inch indentions had grooved into the skin of his shoulders.

Sgt. Smith called for illumination rounds to verify the squad's location. The rounds popped low, a bad sign. Smith radioed in the azimuths. Sure enough, Lt. Flack radioed that the squad wasn't anywhere near its objective. Fuck! The map was a total aberration. Smith relayed this fact to Flack. A captain newly assigned and taking command of the company that day gave an order through Flack that the squad was to proceed to the objective shown on the map, a location which in reality did not exist.

From what Sgt. Smith could determine, they were half way from where the captain wanted them to be. The squad had better get there before dark or be stranded in the middle of nowhere. Defurio couldn't believe it.

"I've got a better idea, let's stay here. Fuck this asshole captain," he said. There wasn't any discussion. It was as if he hadn't opened his mouth. He didn't have any standing or credibility with these soldiers.

Smith said, "Let's go, saddle up. Koonce, you're still at point."

"Koonce!" Defurio now knew the name of the point man.

As soon as he got to his feet, the pack resumed its torture. To reach the objective by nightfall, the squad took the risk of venturing from the trail to cut cross country through a treacherous landscape. They slipped and slid through rotting underbrush. Rough, sharp edged plants clawed at them. Small cuts and slashes were aggravated by stinging rivulets of sweat. They had to backtrack and circle impenetrable stands of bamboo. The heat and humidity were insufferable. Breathing the muggy air dried out, scorched, and rubbed raw the lining of his mouth, throat, and chest. Insects screeched non-stop. From his ears to his feet, every cell in Defurio's body hurt. He pressed on.

It had taken two hours to make it to the presumed objective. Reaching the destination had required a final debilitating climb.

Defurio was spent and came down hard on his knees. He pulled his arms free from his tormenting rucksack and rolled onto his back, letting sensation return to his extremities. In a short while, he recouped and helped secure the area. Dusk had come.

Sgt. Smith attempted to radio for illum rounds. "Goddamn motherfuckers" were part of a string of expletives by the sergeant. They had gone beyond radio range of Roundbottom.

Defurio was too tired and inexperienced to grasp how precarious their situation was. Without radio communication, they couldn't call for mortar, artillery, or air support. They were alone, like being a helpless stranger in a bad neighborhood.

To Defurio, the situation didn't seem so bad. The clearing seemed like a favorable venue. A treeless expanse thirty-yards wide had been cleared by someone at sometime. Two easily defended trails dead-ended into it from the north and east.

Mainly he rested, pleased to have found a sleeping place not quite so uneven, a difficult task in hilly terrain. He didn't miss the tumult of the LZ, and the coming of dusk had quieted the bugs. Sleeping in the open jungle might be quite restful. Bedding down, his body jerked involuntarily at abrupt reverberations from a dink mortar tube. FUMP! FUMP! FUMP! It fired within half a mile.

Sgt. Smith had been trying various frequencies in an effort to contact any U.S. unit in the vicinity. He'd almost given up when a staticy voice came on. The PRC 25 rattled to life. "Red One, this is Big Bad Howie." Howie's unmilitary call sign had to be a violation of radio protocol. "Your company's been trying to locate you guys. You okay?" They'd gotten ahold of an artillery battery. "We've done better." Smith gave an estimate of the squad's grid co-ordinates.

"Howie, are you or Roundbottom receiving mortar rounds?"

"We're not, wait one." Howie's radioman contacted Roundbottom.

"Affirmative, Red One." Howie used the squad's call sign. "Roundbottom is receiving mortars."

During the give and take between Sgt. Smith and Howie, Defurio opened a can of spaghetti and meatballs. Eating his meal, he observed the sergeant, impressed by his adroitness and aplomb. Sergeant Smith guess reckoned a fire mission for Big Bad Howie.

Soon, six 105mm artillery shells bashed in at or near enough to silence the dink mortar. Sgt. Smith had an incredible sense of distance and direction. "Right on. Fantastic job, Howie. Red One, out." Good. Now maybe they could get some sleep.

Not yet. The radio came back on. Smith keyed the handset. B Company patched through a message via Big Bad Howie. The patrol wasn't at its proper location. "No shit," Smith said cryptically. The new captain had ordered the squad to move out at daylight to a mountaintop supposedly a click from the present location. "What?" Sgt. Smith gasped. "Doesn't this asshole know distances on his pin board aren't worth shit?" Calling the captain an asshole was a court martial offense. Bad Ass Howie communicated to Roundbottom a cleaned up version. "Ranger says you have your orders." Howie used the captain's call sign. "Sorry, Red One. We'll be looking out for you. Good luck. Out."

"That fucking cocksucker! He doesn't even know where we are. He's fucking out of his mind."

Defurio sat in dismay, his spaghetti and meatballs forming an indigestible lump in his stomach. They'd been ordered further east, he'd barely made it this far.

He calmed himself. He needed to relax, to rest, to physically and mentally prepare for tomorrow. This is when he discovered he'd made a terrible mistake. He'd forgotten his air mattress. Damp, lumpy soil and matted plants kneaded his spine throughout the night.

He twitched his lips, silently speaking to Donna, thinking that somehow she could hear him. He knew he was in extreme danger. "Oh, Donna, if anything happens to me, please go on and have a good life." He repeated sleepy variations of this until dawn.

They got underway early. Shit. The hurt hadn't lessened. Straps on his rucksack reoccupied indented tissue between bone and skin above his clavicles. Muscles and nerves in his neck and back tensed in rebellion to the pull of a sixty-pound pack.

Physically, it helped tremendously that they were descending a heavily traveled trail. Tough, leathery roots ridging the pathway had been rubbed to a sheen by Vietnamese troops wearing rubber sandals—dubbed Ho Chi Minhs by the Americans.

Defurio didn't waver, although he ached everywhere. Dehydration became a problem. He had to ration his water. They hadn't crossed any streams. The map, the fucking map, had showed an abundance of blue lines. If they had known of the absence of streams, they could have packed extra canteens. Daytime heat and humidity were unrelenting. Shrieking insects were a maddening irritation.

Layers of branches and limbs several stories high blocked the sky. The patrol traveled undaunted through the shadowy recesses.

Defurio was busy cussing the never-ending wail of insects when he heard something that made his blood run cold.

"WOO, WOO, WOO, WOO." For a moment, he went numb as though energy had been sucked out through his skin. "WOO, WOO, WOO." His mind struggled in a futile attempt to identify the hellish moans.

The squad didn't break stride. They didn't speak. Whatever it was, it wasn't shooting at them. "WOO, WOO, WOO." They pushed on, even as the WOOING increased.

The patrol passed under a break in the canopy. Above them to the left, a green fringed hole revealed blue sky. Effortlessly gliding across the opening were a pair of very large birds plumed in feathers of blue and black. They had elongated flamingo necks, black curved beaks, and majestic wings. Each powerful down stroke caused a loud WHOOSH of displaced air.

Defurio's fear turned to awe. He watched jealously as the beautiful creatures floated high above his misery. He smiled. At least he wouldn't be troubled to the end of his days not knowing what had caused the unholy howling on this day in the highlands of Vietnam.

Descending the hill, high trees began to give way to solid stands of giant bamboo. The trail went due east for perhaps seventy-five yards before hooking five or six yards to the right, then straightening and dropping through a path cut in the bamboo.

Somewhere below the crook in the trail, ranks of tall trees relinquished to the onslaught of bamboo. Sgt. Smith decided to abandon the trail. His intuition had put him on alert. He passed word that he thought he could find a short cut. He also had a feeling they were about to collide with a sizeable number of dinks.

After some hard humping, the patrol came to a ravine. Its sharp inclines would make it difficult to cross. It was too lengthy to circumvent. Slender young bamboo lined its banks. On impulse, Koonce jumped on top of one of the saplings. It bent in a gentle arc, depositing him fifteen feet below. He jumped on another, then another, until he disappeared. Smith, Hernandez, and Defurio followed suit. Defurio hopped on successive bamboo stalks, leapfrogging to the ravine's bottom.

They began to ascend the nearly vertical wall. Wiggling the front of his boots to dig in toe holes, Defurio continually slipped as dirt gave way. Tenuously, his outstretched fingers clasping thin bamboo stalks kept him from falling. While reaching and grappling for something to hold onto the weight of his body, equipment, and pack stretched apart his joints and tendons. Each hanging, jerking motion was as if needles were being ruthlessly jabbed through connective tissue holding together his arms and shoulders. Squeezed veins in his upper joints numbed his hands and arms. The striated green bamboo fibers tore off skin. His hands became bloody, the handles of bamboo slippery. He advanced upwards in half arm lengths. He couldn't see to the top of the several stories high embankment. The sides of his face roughly slid and bumped along the coarse matting of soil and vegetation tumbling away loose dirt as he went. Each kicking, wriggling, thrusting effort to grab the next handhold forced a low grunt from the bottom of his throat. The sound of rasping gulps of air was exaggerated by the closed in acoustics of the creviced den of rock, earth, and plants. Occasionally, a clod of dirt got into his mouth, blocking part of his breathing passage. The clods crumbled, combining with his spit to form a bolus of sludge, flavored with foul tasting jungle microbes.

He was only partially successful in spitting out the gummy mess, which formed a thick drool. Although much of it hung from corners of his mouth, he was able to expectorate enough of the spittle to unblock most of his windpipe. The stuff had the taste of decay, as if he were licking a corpse.

It was pull or die. He could see himself falling to the bottom of this unfindable fissure of earth. After the animals got through with him, there would only be scattered bones to bear witness to his horrible death.

Fighting to maintain himself, he went to her. "Donna," he said to himself, actually shouting to her in his mind. "Babe, I'm not going to let that happen. I am not dying like this, not here, not now."

Erratically, his fevered mind shifted emphasis. As was his habit, he became an aggressor. "You fucking cocksucker, I'm not letting you get me!" His tentative hold on life had taken on a new dimension. Death had become a miniaturized being, a half human half demon sitting on his left shoulder, taunting and teasing him. Defurio could see him and talk to him and challenge him. "Fuck you, you fucking bastard! You're not getting me, not now!" He returned to Donna. "Don't worry, babe, I'm not giving up. I'm not giving up." With tears pulsing from his eyes, he stammered out loud, "Pull! Pull! Pull!" Frantically twisting and turning, he lunged again and again, pulling himself up, his hands sliding in blood, digging in, holding on. However, he was weakening and couldn't last much longer.

The bamboo saved him. Half way up, bigger, stronger, denser stands of trees formed in pockets where the ravine had become less sheer. He straddled the base of a sturdy trunk and rested. He reached a dirty, bloody forefinger in his mouth and scooped out its contents, clearing his windpipe. Savagely, he took in large amounts of unrestricted air. His panicked brain also cleared. After several minutes, he continued his climb. He could hear the others noisily thrashing about out of sight off to his right and above him.

Steadily, he made his way up accompanied by the same ripping, tearing sensation to his fingers, wrists, elbows, and shoulders, except now knowing he could make it.

Death's presence stayed with him. He would remain Defurio's constant companion; a respected adversary who, this time, would wait to claim him. Thereafter, in strenuous times, they would hold heated communications, usually Defurio defying and cussing him. They seemed to have an understanding. No hard feelings. After all, Death always won, it was merely a matter of when. These were one way verbalizations. Death never spoke, he just grinned.

At short intervals, all four men rolled over the rim within eyesight of one another. Defurio was last. They laid on their backs, struggling for air while regular quantities of blood resumed flowing to arms and legs. They only had strength to nod in acknowledgement as each man came over the top. After resting a short time, they drank thirstily from their near empty canteens. The men, being young and toughened by numerous jungle patrols, recovered quickly—except for Defurio.

Conquering the ravine had a devastating impact on him. The effort left him severely weakened. He willed himself to go on. He tried to think of Donna. Pain invaded his every thought. Unable to form or maintain cogent thoughts, he applied his total mental and physical energy to the sole task of maintaining function of his lungs and legs.

The physically depleted soldiers finally halted for a breather. Each man battled his individual pain. They assessed the situation. The foremost problem was they were practically out of water. "I'd like to find the cocksucker who made this map and personally shove his head further up his ass," said the normally even tempered Koonce.

Hernandez reiterated his favorite phrase, "Jive-ass motherfuckers." Defurio was too bone-weary to say anything.

By late afternoon, the mountain they were seeking was nowhere in sight. The map's inaccuracies had worsened the farther they'd gone. Smith aborted the mission. It didn't have any strategic value anyway. None whatsoever. They were not intended as a reconnaissance or combat assault team. SRPs were charged with being the eyes and ears of the company. Nothing more.

The dilemma confronting the patrol became simple survival. It would take a great deal of luck and perseverance to make it to Roundbottom alive.

The squad sought a place to set up for the night. They came upon a rolling hill. On its slopes, enormous trees were set relatively far apart. The trunks formed magnificent columns supporting an intricate limbed ceiling of such ethereal beauty as to remind Defurio of the interior of a cathedral.

The patrol nestled itself at the base of a stand of mature bamboo two hundred yards up a gentle incline from the trail. Sgt. Smith gave the rotation for guard duty. Defurio's would be at 0100.

Defurio's poncho covered the moist ground. He unrolled his sleeping bag. No fucking air mattress. He slept fitfully. An animal crashed through above them, startling him awake. Defurio couldn't see. He couldn't discern any part of his body, including his fingers wiggling in front of his nose. Light didn't seem to exist.

Sgt. Smith was calling in a fire mission. He had maintained contact with Bad Ass Howie. Defurio sat possibly three feet from him and although he could hear him speaking in hushed tones, Sgt. Smith was invisible.

The distinctive FUMP of a dink mortar sounded like it came from somewhere on the other side of the trail. Smith relayed estimated co-ordinates, adjusting Howie's artillery until the mortar fell silent. How he could accurately guess grid co-ordinates, Defurio didn't know.

"You awake, Defurio?" Sgt. Smith asked.

"Yeah."

"Okay, go ahead and take watch. In two hours, wake up Hernandez. He's on the other side of me, you'll have to feel your way."

Did he say Resendez or Hernandez? Defurio remained unsure of the Latino's name.

Halfway through his watch, Defurio detected footsteps interrupting the mortuary stillness of the night. Leaves and sticks cracked and crumbled. He monitored the footfalls, striving to determine what could be causing them. They came from the direction of the trail. Tigers inhabited this part of the highlands. There were occasional incidents involving them. He dismissed this possibility and eased his finger off the trigger of his M-16. A stealthy hunter wouldn't be announcing his presence by stomping on dry leaves. He guessed an orangutan had alighted to investigate something near the trail. The threatening disturbance abruptly ceased, strengthening the likelihood that a prehensile animal had satisfied its curiosity and regained the heights. He also discounted the steps were made by enemy soldiers. Men would be careful and as noiseless as possible, attempting to find footing by means of filtered flashlights.

The threat passed and the velvet jungle returned to its secret doings. His shoulders sagged in relief. Slumping forward, he set his M-16 across his lap. "When is this fucking freak show ever going to end?" he said to himself.

He tore at a pack of cigarettes, fiddling impatiently, fingers trembling. He could feel the crinkling of dried blood. Cigarettes came four to a pack in C-rations. It was difficult pulling the last one from the humid cellophane. He lifted his shirt over his head, cloaking the flame from his lighter and hiding the ashy burn of his cigarette. His companions never stirred. He hadn't needed them. He had remained calm about the footsteps. He inhaled deeply from his bent, crumbly cigarette. Nicotine entered his blood stream, soothing him, giving an added sense of satisfaction.

He smiled smugly. Nicotine has a powerful effect on a deprived body. He became convinced he was a kick-ass soldier. By doing nothing, he had successfully diffused a potentially dangerous situation, proving that reason and rationality were prevailing influences in shaping events in the field. He persuaded himself he had these qualities. "I'm tired of getting fucked in the ass by this place. I won't stand for it," he bragged to himself defiantly. Defurio had come under the sway of a serious misperception.

They gathered themselves at daybreak for the dash to Roundbottom. "We've got to get there by nightfall or we'll be in deep shit," said Sgt. Smith, stating the obvious. The four men were exhausted, nearly out of water, and isolated in a dink-infested jungle. Having to hump double time in 120° heat in pressure cooker humidity didn't bode well for them.

The squad had a single favorable advantage: most of the way would be downhill. Unfortunately, there would be a major exception.

"Do or die, baby," Koonce pronounced, leading the way. They headed straight for the trail. Established trails were the easiest, fastest way to travel. And the most dangerous. The patrol would have to risk being ambushed.

Humping at this juncture was tolerable. They were going downhill and packs had been lightened by consumption of three days rations. Defurio had two cans of cheese and crackers and a fruit cocktail remaining. He had deliberately saved the fruit cocktail. The juice would be an emergency supply of liquid. Water was a critical concern. Defurio's canteen held perhaps three mouthfuls.

As before, Defurio trailed the squad. They were in relatively sparse jungle, an ideal setting for dink mortars. Dink 61mm mortars were similar to 60mm mortars used by U.S. Marines. They could be tripoded or used as a free standing weapon held against the ground by a soldier while another fed rounds down the open end. Spotters communicating by radio adjusted rounds. Many dinks were required to carry shells from place to place. The weapon itself was easily transported by two or three men.

Before long, they heard a dink mortar, its rounds landing in the distance. "This place is crawling in mortars," Defurio mumbled, knowing that Sgt. Smith had already eliminated two of them. There seemed to be an inexhaustible number of the lethal devices.

They began to climb. The jungle thickened as they gained elevation. Air became stifling as sultry vegetation closed in like bodies in an overcrowded sauna. Defurio's legs were cramping and losing feeling. "Shit!" His insides burned. "Think of Donna, think of Donna." He could see her as if he were watching a silent movie. Frame by frame she went by. He tried to get her attention. The film went blank. "Goddamn it." Pain spread through his body, concentrating in his legs.

The squad crested the incline and started descending its western side. This saved Defurio's legs. At an outcropping, Smith gave a low whistle. The patrol dropped in place for a break. They listened passively to the dink mortar. It had gotten louder.

Defurio reached for his fruit cocktail. Prior to opening it, he finished the meager amount of water in his canteen. The water had the same temperature as the atmosphere. Before drinking, he hadn't enough moisture in his mouth to spit. He dreaded the expenditure of energy needed to open the fruit cocktail. Weakly working the opener, he eagerly folded back the lid and gobbled its contents, careful not to spill the juice. Defurio licked the can clean, the syrupy juice giving him an immediate boost. Next, he ate the crackers and cheese. The salt would help retain fluids.

No one talked. Hernandez stood, ambled a ways, unfastened his pants, and playfully raked piss across a rotting log. Defurio couldn't remember anyone, until now, either urinating or defecating. Every substance taken in had been utilized.

Hernandez's high pressure stream began collapsing parts of the log. His piss started splashing off something green and shiny. A section of log fell away revealing an 18" triangular headed B-40 rocket. A dink had decided to lighten his load.

A smile creased Hernandez's usually expressionless face. He stuffed the wet rocket in his pack. What an odd thing to do. Why carry extra weight for no reason? Apparently, Hernandez felt hauling the rocket offered a real benefit—it couldn't be used to kill him.

The squad wearily got to its feet. Sgt. Smith attempted again to contact Roundbottom. No luck. "Shit, no fucking commo." The PRC 25 rested on the ground by Hernandez. Smith turned to Defurio. "You're up for radio." The thought of carrying additional weight repulsed Defurio. He also remembered the radioman that got killed on Chu Pa.

"I can't do it, Sarge, I'm too fucked up, and I've never used the radio in the field." Sgt. Smith knew this to be true.

Hernandez spoke up, "I'll carry it." The reed-thin Hernandez had been carrying it from the beginning. It was a practical matter. Assuming they reestablished commo, effective use of the radio could be critical.

Two thirds of the way to Roundbottom, the patrol came to a formidable hill, the one where they had spent the first night. Exhausted, they rested after having crawled through huge stands of bamboo. Defurio, near the end of his endurance, knew it would take everything he had to attain the summit.

The sun had tipped behind the peak. They were streaked in shadows. Bugs in the canopy were as incessant as ever. There wasn't a hint of a breeze. Moist heat seemed to radiate from the bamboo. The humidity was suffocating.

"Okay, let's go." Sgt. Smith gave the go-ahead. The patrol stayed in the original order; Koonce at point, followed by Sgt. Smith, Hernandez, and Defurio. He forced his weakened lungs and legs to respond. He hurt, but not as bad as before. The fruit cocktail, crackers and cheese, and short rest had revived him somewhat. Taking shaky steps, he leaned into the hill.

"Aaugh… Aaugh." Grunting to himself seemed to help. Relying on his standard distraction, he talked to Donna. "Hi, babe. Aaugh… it's tough… Aaugh… I'm doing alright… Aaugh… holding my own… Aaugh… pretty soon we should…" WHAM! A shell came crashing in behind him. Shrapnel cut through the bamboo. The smell and taste of burnt powder agitated his nostrils and throat.

Defurio and the others dropped to their stomachs. There wasn't anywhere to hide or seek cover. Arms covering heads offered paltry protection.

WHAM! WHAM! WHAM! Mortars fell on both sides and behind them. The dinks were firing blind. They had heard the patrol but didn't have visual contact. WHAM! WHAM! Metal fragments sprayed overhead. Splinters of wood and spent shrapnel sprinkled on to Defurio. He wiggled deeper into the dirt.

"Red Dog! Red Dog!" Sgt. Smith repeated Lt. Flack's call sign, trying to contact Roundbottom. The PRC 25 crackled to life. "I read you, Red One. This is Red Dog. Give me a sit rep. Over."

"We're getting the shit blown out of us by 61s! We're on the opposite slope from our first position. We need a fire mission to the top of the hill."

"Wait one, Red One." Flack checked his charts. "Negative, Red One. Say again, negative. Target is out of our mortar range and our arty's been pulled out."

Smith didn't answer. He threw the hand set in disgust and went to the ground as shells landed closer.

Five minutes later, the radio scratched on. "Red One, this is Ranger. Do you read? Over." Ranger was the captain's call sign. It's unusual for a CO to communicate directly with a patrol.

Smith pressed the handle of his hand set keying the radio. "We read you, Ranger. Over."

"Do you have any KIAs (killed in action) or WIAs (wounded in action)? Over."

"That's a negative, Ranger. No KIAs or WIAs. Over."

"Good. Red One, get to the top of that location and mark with smoke grenades. We'll get you an air strike. Over."

"Are you serious?" Smith sputtered, forgetting he was talking to his CO.

"Get your asses up there, Red One. Ranger out."

Smith threw the hand set, leaving it to dangle from its spiral cord. Hernandez grabbed the dangling phone. "Jive ass motherfuckers," he said tersely, hanging it up.

They had just been given a death sentence.

"We couldn't get commo when we were on top of this motherfucker. We get it now, and they use it to shit on us," Smith said in a fit of anger. The four men had been ordered to assault a platoon of dinks, maybe more, who were currently shooting at them from above. Because of thick jungle, the trail was the sole means of approach. Attempting to throw smoke grenades from a steep trail overhung with limbs was not only impossible, it was suicidal. Employing AK-47s, machine guns, grenades, and B-40 rockets, the dinks would cut them down as soon as they became exposed.

Aghast at the lunacy of the captain's order, Defurio asserted himself. "Fuck the captain. Let's go back down, circle around, and pick up the trail on the other side." He was ignored. They had received a direct order. That and the specter of dying piecemeal in a trackless wilderness caused the squad to dismiss Defurio out of hand. No one acknowledged or responded to him. Instead, they busied themselves checking gear and making sure M-16s were locked and loaded.

In a way, attacking the dinks represented a certain kind of crazy logic. The squad was cut off, out of rations, and physically depleted. To a fatalistic GI, it was better to die swiftly than bit by bit.

Smith motioned for Koonce to go. The squad lengthened out and snaked upward. As they went, Hernandez recited his mantra in a low monotone. "Jive-ass motherfuckers... Jive-ass motherfuckers... Jive-ass motherfuckers..."

Defurio's mind worked furiously. Not wanting to waste ammo shooting haphazardly, he clicked his M-16 to semi-automatic. He placed four magazines and two hand grenades in his waistband for easy access. He said good-bye to Donna. *"I love you, Babe. I can't think of you right now. I have to concentrate on what I'm doing. See if I can make it through this. Bye, Babe."* He tied a strip of towel across his forehead.

As they went upward, bamboo gave way to high reaching trees. Soon, the trail was framed by one-hundred foot giants, their trunks supporting tiers of bushy scum colored, vine wrapped limbs. The broiling temperature seemed to ignite the cries of millions of insects teeming in the heights.

Defurio became conscious of musky sweat pouring off him, of his heaving chest, of a whisper of wind, the flutter of leaves, the metallic feel of his trigger, the stink of decay. He became hypersensitive to everything he could see, hear, touch, or smell.

At one-hundred fifty yards from the summit, the shelling stopped. The squad came to a dog-leg bending to the left. Defurio riveted his attention on Koonce. He would get it first. Koonce approached the corner boldly, in a crouch, his M-16 at the ready. He rounded the corner, slipping from view. No shooting.

Same for Smith. Then Hernandez. Losing sight of Hernandez unnerved Defurio. Spikes of anxiety shot up his spine, settling in a sharp ache at the back of his neck and spreading to cords of his shoulders.

He hurried to catch Hernandez. He came to the corner expecting to see him carrying the radio on his back like a papoose.

An ear piercing blast rocked the hillside. He dropped. A wave of heat, smoke, and metal particles hurled past his lowered head. "What the fuck was that?" He made fast calculations; no shooting, no rockets, no shelling. Probably a booby trap.

He had decided he would flee at the first sign of trouble, retreat as rapidly as possible to save himself. He didn't. Aroused by the danger, he was drawn to it. He became elevated by an alertness he had never known. In a second, he rounded the corner.

"Fuck!" he couldn't see past the debris thrown up by the blast, so he ran through it. He was in a pink mist. His face parted warm, noodled strands. "Oh no! Fuck! No! No!" Defurio reacted as if a knife had been shoved his gut. Pieces of flesh, bone, cloth, boots, and equipment were plastered on plants scattered on the ground and hanging from trees. Hernandez had disintegrated. "Motherfuckers!" They had killed his brother! "Motherfuckers!" At this exact moment, the sum total of Defurio's existence, Hernandez had become his brother, more than his brother. He had become the manifestation of everything he held dear; his mother, father, sister, aunts, uncles, his unborn children…Donna.

Seeing and feeling the shredded remains of Hernandez triggered an unmitigated rage. He was overtaken by a fanatical need for revenge, to kill those who had killed Hernandez. From somewhere inside him came a primal urge so powerful as to vanquish his fatigue and fear and to nullify his ability to reason. He moved forward with the agility of a jungle cat. He ran to meet the enemy with the controlled fury of an attacking predator. He hopped over a gleaming projectile laying in the middle of the pathway. Hernandez's unexploded B-40 rocket.

Seconds had gone by since the last blast. Still no shooting. He weaved his way uphill, bobbing and dodging from one side of the trail to the other. More prey than predator, he closed in to meet the enemy.

Hearing an object bouncing in the upper canopy, Defurio hesitated. Distracted and confused, he fell to a prone firing position. The object came down leisurely, smacking limbs, slipping, sliding, rolling, and breaking through branches on its unhurried plunge. He heard a gentle thud as the object came to rest in leaves carpeting the jungle floor.

Scanning forward, Defurio detected Smith and Koonce camouflaged in the slime. The two were separated, straddling the trail. He could see them communicating by hand signals. Darting back and forth across the trail, he ran to join them.

Defurio jumped off the trail seeking brief refuge behind an upraised log. His right boot heel came down hard, crunching and squashing something beneath it.

"Oh, Jesus. No! No! No!" Defurio's stomach revolted. He vomited. He had landed on the right cheek of Hernandez's skinless face, caving it in. A bloody eye socket, exposed bone and teeth, and some hair was all that was left of Hernandez's severed head.

"Motherfuckers! Motherfuckers!" In rapid sideward kicks, he piled leaves on Hernandez's head, wanting to hide it from gloating dinks. This done, he raced to join his comrades.

Defurio dove headlong, bumping the soles of Smith's boots. Koonce, in the meantime, had barrel-rolled to Smith's location. The three soldiers perused the area ahead of them. There wasn't much to see, the ascending trail being undetectable in the jungle overgrowth.

In these last seconds, they didn't speak. Smith and Koonce knew Hernandez was dead and the radio destroyed. Fate dealt them this hand. There wasn't anything to do but finish it.

They were clustered fifty yards below the summit. No one looked at the other. They were alone and without hope. Fate would decide how the end would come.

Koonce was the first to go. He kissed the plastic cross hanging from his neck. If any of them believed in God, they made their peace. Koonce lifted and charged. Smith and Defurio, beguiled by the madness, did likewise.

Defurio was exultant. He wasn't thinking of God, family, or Donna. Consumed by a soul destroying hatred, he had a compulsion to kill the motherfuckers who had killed Hernandez. In his death throes, he wanted to kill as many dinks as he could while they were killing him — Defurio had gone to the edge of insanity.

The three ill-fated infantrymen loped madly straight at the rim of the hill. Approaching its outer edge, Defurio didn't know why the dinks hadn't fired upon them, probably they disbelieved there could only be three of them. Koonce breached the clearing. He stayed to his left, hugging the nearside tree line. Close behind were Smith and Defurio. By habit, they crouched to lower their profiles. Defurio braced for an impact of bullets. At any second, he expected dozens of rounds to punch through his body. He had re-set his M-16 to full automatic, making it, in effect, a machine gun. This would permit him to take down as many of his executioners as possible. His heart pounded like a jackhammer, his finger taut on the trigger. He twisted at the waist so his M-16 pointed at the opposite tree line, where he anticipated the firestorm to erupt.

Leaves tickled by a feint wind offered the only movement. Defurio listened for rifle barrels rubbing against brush as AK-47s and machine guns were being aimed.

The squad heard and saw nothing.

Creeping to the far side of the clearing, Koonce found the opening to the trail leading to Roundbottom. Doubting they were out of danger, he bolted down it. Smith did the same. Defurio, afraid he might be separated, shot, or captured, sprinted after them. The three soldiers, startled at being alive, ran as if chased by hounds from hell.

Defurio could hear and feel his boots scuff and scrape the earth as he ran. Occasionally his legs folded, then righted when he tripped on roots tentacled just above the soil. He wouldn't let himself go down, afraid that he wouldn't recover. His ability to reason had returned.

At the bottom, they fell like wounded animals; panting, gasping, and choking for air. Defurio's lungs had become heated bags that barely functioned. He needed air. He needed water. His body felt enfeebled and inflamed, as if the lining of his organs and tissues had been sucked dry.

"Dinks likely went down the north slope," Smith said in breathless, broken sentences. "Probably thought we called for an air strike or artillery." His face contorted from exertion. "Fuckers set a booby trap, a mine, I think, before they dee-dee'd," he said trying to avoid the anguish of saying Hernandez's name. "They didn't know there were only four of us." His voice trailed off. He faced the jungle and bit his lower lip.

Nothing needed to be said. Hernandez, who he was and how he died, would be forever etched in their minds. Although a solemn moment, they couldn't afford to wallow in despair. Smith redirected his attention to the situation at hand. It was imperative to reach Roundbottom by nightfall. Struggling to his feet, he led by example. "Let's go." They embarked on the last three clicks to Roundbottom. Defurio, as usual, trailed.

Physically wrecked, he had extreme difficulty getting his legs to respond. He willed them to move. They began a modest climb. After half-an-hour, he collapsed. His legs had become watery stumps.

The cumulative effect of carrying twenty-five pounds of grenades for four days had wreaked havoc on his body. It hadn't occurred to him to get rid of them, to toss them in the bush. He believed in his grenades, had faith in them. They were his protectors, his last means of defense, his tangible hand-held potential saviors.

Impassively, Koonce and Smith waited for him, showing neither impatience nor disapproval. They knew Defurio was doing his best, although they didn't know about the grenades.

He got to his feet. He went perhaps ten yards when his legs gave way again. After two minutes he arose, walked a few steps, and fell again. He repeated this sequence. At each interval, Koonce and Smith casually sat and allowed Defurio to recover. They didn't comment or complain.

Despite his deteriorated physical condition, his mind remained acute. Desperately trying to cope, he counted steps. Six steps. This became his goal. Do a minimum of six steps. On a descent, he could manage more.

Defurio disassociated himself from his failing body by playing mental games. He made observations, fantasized, constructed scenarios, made assessments.

He developed a system for falling. He cushioned his falls by going to his knees. He bent and set his left arm, keeping his hand downturned and rested his left cheek on his hand. This kept dirt off his face. His right hand clutched his M-16.

From this angle, every so often he saw openings along the path. Spider holes. He had heard stories of individual dinks taking pot shots at GIs, then disappearing. This is how they did it, by hiding in these holes. Defurio doubted his slowed reflexes would allow him to get off a shot if a dink emerged and came at him. Anyway, he concluded these were air vents. The openings were too small to contain a man. Likely, they were humping over an NVA tunnel complex. He jumped to another thought. He wouldn't mind being wounded—not permanently injured, but severely enough to be medevac'd. This was pure fantasy. They didn't have a radio to call for a medivac. Even if they did, a lifeline would be unable to penetrate the layered roof of jungle.

During one of his collapses, Defurio's attention wandered to the slumbering, haggard figures of Koonce and Smith. The two intrepid soldiers seemed amazingly unaffected by the shitty circumstances. These men were typical Vietnam GIs. Hernandez was of the same stripe; uneducated, small town throwaways. By some quirk of culture or upbringing, they made tough, resourceful, resolute soldiers.

Defurio's attitude toward his fellow soldiers had changed. Humbleness replaced arrogance; respect for cynicism. They, not he, had performed at a higher standard. They, not he, had shown greater courage, resilience, and fortitude. It was he who was the lesser man.

Although delayed by Defurio's collapses, the threesome forged ahead until dragging themselves to within eye-sight of Roundbottom.

The LZ had been denuded by explosives and gunfire. It was possible to see it from a distance of half a click.

Crippled by dehydration, hunger, and fatigue, but exhilarated at seeing the LZ, the three soldiers limped to its perimeter. They were undelayed by Defurio. Summoning a strength that seemed impossible, he pulled himself unaided to the perimeter.

They weren't expected. Shouting "friendly," the trio surprised a couple of pot puffing soldiers on guard duty. Nearly blinded from exhaustion, Defurio clumsily made his way through the rolls of concertina. Tiny blades studding the wire added final nicks and rips to his hands, arms, legs, and frayed fatigues.

Once through the wire, he continued his labored steps. Desperate for water, he separated from Koonce and Smith and headed for the water tank. His companions on the patrol went to rejoin their squads, where they would be given canteens.

Defurio slipped off his pack, dropping it next to his hooch. He stumble-walked to the steel water tank and knelt in mud below the spigot. He turned the handle, letting water flow onto his head, face, and into his mouth. Jesus, nothing ever tasted so good. He put water in his canteen, making it easier to drink. He alternated sips while dousing the back of his neck, crotch, and underarms. The taste and feel of the life-giving liquid rejuvenated him, instantly repairing much of the abuse his body had endured.

He didn't meet anyone on his return to the hooch. Tired, wet, and relieved, he eased inside. "Jack!" Jim sat up, stifling tears.

"Hi, Jim," Jack said, almost inaudibly. He went to his bunk. He was asleep before his upper body hit the air mattress, the one he'd failed to take on the patrol.

Jim centered Jack on the mattress and removed his boots. He patted Defurio's shoulder affectionately. The big man couldn't hold his tears. He thought Jack had been killed.

He awakened to the whistle and whump of incoming. Not seeing him, Jack supposed Jim was helping to return fire. He stayed put. Gradually, the incoming ceased. He peeked outside. Night had come. Jack couldn't believe how good he felt. He didn't seem to have suffered any physical damage from the previous day's events. However, he realized he was famished.

His face brightened at the arrival of Lt. Duke and Big Jim. Duke handed Jack a chicken and rice LRP ration. Perfect timing. "Where'd you steal this, Lieutenant?"

Lt. Duke grinned. He shoved aside the shock of hair continually draping his forehead. "Good to see you're okay, Jack. Too bad about Rodriguez."

Rodriguez? Goddamn it! Couldn't he get a reprieve from this fucking madhouse? Defurio hadn't even known the dead radioman's real name. He let the disturbing information pass. He wasn't in the mood to deal with it.

"Thanks, Lieutenant. How's everything here?" Jim got busy heating the LRP ration.

"Fine. No one else in the platoon hurt. We got word on Robertson. He had to have his bladder and a kidney removed. He's in Japan recovering." Lt. Duke's voice quavered. He coughed, covering his mouth in an effort to hide his emotion. Embarrassed, he turned away. "Take care. See you guys later."

Jack offered Jim half his chicken and rice. Jim refused. Jack wolfed it down. "Got any smokes, Jim?" His shrunken stomach satisfied, Jack lit a cigarette. Thoughts of Rodriguez came to him. How could he have not known his name?

Hernandez, Fernandez, Resendez, Rodriguez. What the fuck difference did it make? What was important was that his mother wouldn't know there wasn't enough left of her son to hold in the palm of her hand. What does the Army do in cases like that? Send home a coffin, pretending there's a body inside? Maybe scrape together some of the deceased's protoplasm, put it in an envelope, and throw it inside an otherwise empty box? He could see Rodriguez's family mourning over a metal box containing nothing but rocks.

How or why Rodriguez died didn't hold any meaning for Defurio. He was a good kid, and he was dead. Why dwell on it? Why relive the sickening awfulness of it? Defurio did his best to purge the radioman's grisly death from his mind.

"Where were you when those last mortars hit, Jim?"

"I was on my way to the shitter. I had to detour." Jim relaxed, reclining on his bunk, smoking a cigarette. "I had to dive in a line bunker. There were about ten of us crammed in there. We toked joints." This was leading to something. Jack could see Jim had regained his panache. "I'll tell you, Jack, my guts were ready to explode." Jim drew in smoke through a sly smile. "If those mortars hadn't stopped when they did, I would have turned into a human shit grenade."

Jack laughed.

Jack and Jim avoided the subject of the patrol. Everyone knew it had been bad. No one wanted to widen an unhealable wound. Defurio never discussed the patrol—then, or ever.

In an anticlimactic aftermath to the sad, grueling patrol, Sgt. Smith and Private First Class Koonce promptly reentered the sub life of their respective squads. They quietly became reabsorbed in the anonymity of the line company. Defurio would never see them again.

For him, Vietnam returned to normal.

Chapter 17
Alamo

Fox sweated profusely, shaking and smiling as he lay on the litter taking him to the medevac. He could look forward to a month of sham time in Cam Ranh Bay as he recuperated.

Cases of malaria were on the rise. They'd been at the Alamo for two days. It was part of a triad of LZs within 81 mm mortar range of each other. Why they were spaced so close, Defurio didn't know. Compared to Roundbottom, the LZ looked like the neglected child of a stepparent. It didn't have established bunkers, extra firepower, shitters, piss tubes, or any other amenities.

"What a lucky fucker," Jim observed, looking at Fox being carried to the chopper. There didn't seem to be any connection between those who became infected with malaria. Fox had become a hop head prick since coming in-country. A big, strong kid, he hadn't taken his anti-malaria pills like almost everyone else in the company. The company was rife with such pot heads. Why Fox?

"I don't get these fucking mosquitoes here," Jack said earnestly.

"What do you mean?" Jim asked, mildly interested.

They were sitting on a partially built bunker wall at high noon. Water soaked towels worn on their heads acted as an antidote to the spotlight of sun bouncing intense heat off their skulls. They had been building a bunker. They couldn't finish because the LZ had run out of sandbags. There was also a scarcity of logs and engineering stakes needed as underpinning for a roof.

"Well, in Fresno," Jack said, bullshitting as a way to distract from the scalding conditions, "as a kid, on hot summer evenings you'd get swarmed by hungry mosquitoes."

"Sounds pretty bad," Jim said.

"It's not like that now. They developed a mosquito abatement district, which pretty much eradicated them."

The wet towels muddied after becoming infused with dust from Fox's medevac powering off the LZ. Jack went on unperturbed. "I think the highlands have evolved a non-swarming, silent, sneaky breed of mosquito; so sneaky they have a bite that doesn't itch or leave a mark. You'd think all of us would have malaria." Jack touched a finger to his lips in thought, "or maybe the Army has developed a super secret mosquito abatement program."

Jim built on this. "New York could use this kind of program, only for rats. They could call it RAP—Rat Abatement Program."

This kind of inane conversation induced by high heat and listlessness provided thin gruel to satisfy their intellectual appetites. Allowing their brains to go dormant, they preferred saving their mental and physical energy by passively looking at the countryside.

In recent days, B-52s had bombed the area between the three LZs. This had the benefit of eliminating constant harassment from enemy mortars. B-52 strikes also increased the number of low grade grass fires. The night before, Jack and Jim had counted twenty fires. Dead circles representing bomb craters were visible from a distance of two or three miles.

This is where the company's line platoons were currently conducting sweeps.

A lone Huey winging in brought a welcome distraction from the brain baking temperature.

Hooray. Stacks of sandbags were delivered. Jack and Jim could finish the bunker and escape the heat. Best of all, the biggest prize, was a red mail bag.

Defurio received two packages and two letters from Donna. Her letters were difficult to read in the heat. Sweat from his hands slopped down his face, smudging the paper. News about Chu Pa had reached her from reports by the national media. Defurio's attempt to minimize the extent of the battle was refuted by reported facts. The Tet offensive was in full swing. Overall, the 4th Division operating in the central highlands had sustained horrendous causalities.

He had run a terrible risk by sending relatively cheerful letters, knowing that he might be dead when Donna received them. She didn't chastise him for diminishing his account of what happened on Chu Pa. She was so glad he was unhurt. Passionate avowals of love for him predominated her letters.

Damn. Jack wished that Donna hadn't become aware of how bad Chu Pa had been. He hated that she had to worry to her core about him. Now she'd be wary of his reassurances.

There wouldn't be any national news coverage concerning his SRP patrol. He would be successful in hiding this awful experience from her. He loved her so much. This is all he could offer her, to spare her additional restless days and sleepless nights. A sliver of satisfaction rippled through him. She would never know, and he would never tell her, what happened on that patrol. And she would never ask.

Jack folded the letters and placed them in the pockets of his fatigue pants. He would reread them until the next ones came. "Let's get this bunker done, Jim." Maloney had garnered a sufficient number of sandbags while Defurio was reading. They would open her packages in the privacy and coolness of their newly built quarters.

Boredom currently marked life in the mortar platoon. The line company tromped in the AO near Alamo and hadn't encountered the enemy. B-52 bombings had, for the time being, forced the NVA to stay underground. There wasn't a need for fire missions.

Defurio and Maloney became the chief loafers-in-residence. During this interim, Jack and Jim would make for the first squad's bunker and hold court. Many from the second and third squads would join in; oftentimes fifteen to twenty men milled in and outside the bunker.

It was a racially diverse group. When a newcomer came to the platoon from the rural south, Jack and Jim deferred to the blacks in the platoon. They were particularly adept at pillorying white newbies. The blacks often initiated a discussion as if it were a formal debate. To a bewildered young southerner they might ask, "Yo, Arkansas, why do you white dudes like to eat pussy?" This would lead to a round of laughs by everyone, except for the recipient of the question.

For men in the field who weren't under fire or on patrol, conversation seldom strayed from allusions to sex. Young men are preoccupied with thoughts of sex, and young soldiers exposed to combat are obsessed by it. Raw, raunchy depictions of sex relates well to the business of combat. One act is designed to create life, the other to destroy it. It would seem the same elements of instinct and nature apply to both.

At these informal gatherings, the poncho flap would be lifted from time to time to release volumes of marijuana smoke. Defurio would choose these instances to steal away from the group.

His main outlet for holding on to his sanity was to get by himself, reread Donna's letters, write to her, and stare at her pictures. A recent letter mentioned that she planned to take a stock market class at Bakersfield City College. Donna loved numbers. She knew Jack had always been an investor and she explained how interesting it would be to join him in exploring the world of finance and investment.

For her, studying stocks would be a shared experience between them. She didn't need such an excuse. She had a naturally inquisitive mind and a curiosity about life, liked to learn, was adventurous, and had an affinity for facts and figures. Jack jokingly referred to her as an information ferret.

There hadn't been any significant enemy contact since arriving at Alamo. The line company remained deployed in the AO. Line company platoons rotated on and off the hill, coming in for supplies and short rests. Fire missions were infrequent.

A shipment of beer came in. How could beer be brought in and no mail? It had been five days since the last mail delivery. Beer and bottles of whiskey distributed by a platoon member returning from R & R and copious amounts of marijuana kept the party going day and night.

Hearing laughter and joking smoothed rough edges of dreary days. Defurio enjoyed getting wasted with these men. They had a kinship born of desperation and took satisfaction in burping warm beer together, in together numbing their misery, and sharing the smell of their unwashed bodies.

Chapter 18

Brillo Pad

Brillo Pad, another LZ named for a part of the lieutenant colonel's girlfriend's anatomy. Maloney and Defurio set forth to find a suitable site for a two man bunker.

"First Roundbottom, now this. Jesus Jim, I feel like a crab crawling through the lieutenant colonel's girlfriend's pubic hair."

Different hill, same shit. Dig a hole, use the dirt to fill sandbags, pile sandbags to make four walls, string logs, limbs, and engineering stakes across the top, and layer on rows of sandbags. Do it in unblocked sun and 115° heat. Do it while helicopters come and go, fouling the air with dust. Do it until you get used to living like a beetle in a pile of dung.

Tagging alongside Maloney and Defurio like a puppy was La Crosse Boy. Since almost shooting at A Company on Chu Pa, he had become subdued and therefore tolerable. He had received a letter from his girlfriend saying she was seven months pregnant. She had withheld the information pending issues with her family. Currently, La Crosse Boy was awaiting orders for his return home on a hardship leave.

The Army wasn't being beneficent. They wanted to avoid a public relations disaster should a hometown boy be killed while his baby was being born. La Crosse Boy had a mixed reaction to the pregnancy. At age eighteen, while glad to go home, he would be facing a forced marriage and premature daddyhood.

When La Crosse Boy finally left for his squad's bunker, Big Jim offered a hasty prognosis. "The marriage won't last a year." Sloppily shoveling as he usually did, Maloney suddenly rooted the entrenching tool in the dirt. He sat on the edge of the pit. "La Crosse Boy," he announced, "is too immature. He'll be overwhelmed by his role as the head of the household." He spoke from experience. While married to his Puerto Rican wife, they had had a baby aborted. "La Crosse Boy will also be fucked up by Vietnam."

Jack wholeheartedly agreed. They gave a one-potato fist bump in honor of Big Jim's prediction.

B-52 strikes tapered off. Although no contact had been made, patrols detected signs of enemy movement everywhere. Dinks were streaming out of their holes like ants after a rain. They were up to something.

SRP teams had been left on Alamo and Roundbottom, both within visual and mortar range of Brillo Pad. Sgt. Thorpe had been put in charge of the SRP team on Roundbottom. They occupied Defurio's mortar squad's old bunker, but Roundbottom had otherwise been abandoned.

The northern part of Roundbottom was exposed to Brillo Pad. First squad's former bunker, occupied by Thorpe's SRP team, sat back from the perimeter line but had nothing between them and the perimeter. It could be considered a part of the original defense line.

That evening Roundbottom reported movement. Lots of it. The three mortar squads went to work. Lt. Flack had to rely on information from Thorpe to deliver effective fire. Thorpe was unable to give it. He had become immobilized by fright.

Unless something was done quickly the SRP team would be overrun.

A voice came on the horn, feeding accurate information to Flack. P.A., the goofy kid from Philadelphia, had assumed leadership.

Dinks were in the wire in front of the northern bunkers. P.A. coolly called in rounds striking dead center among the advancing NVA troops. Methodically, he adjusted rounds down the hill, decimating successive waves of attackers.

It became apparent that the dinks intended to overrun Roundbottom. However, they had been fooled. B Company had flown off Roundbottom in a hurry, leaving bunkers standing. The camp looked occupied, but wasn't.

B Company had, by a fortuitous stroke, established themselves on Brillo Pad overlooking the enemies' line of approach to Roundbottom. Never in a soldier's dream had a target been so well presented.

At the opening salvo of mortars, the hillside became alive with flickering lights. Upon being discovered, the dinks began using flashlights to hurry themselves up the rugged hillside, which had already been laid bare by defoliates and explosives.

By what logic did they advance? It should have become clear that a horrible miscalculation had been made. The NVA were being systematically destroyed by mortar fire, and worse for them, an even more efficient source of killing power came into play.

By chance, that day a recoilless rifle team had set up on Brillo Pad. Recoilless rifle is a misnomer. A short range artillery piece, it's unique in that it fires in a straight line, not an arc. Dinks crawling up Roundbottom made a perfect target for this weapon.

Everything had gone wrong for the dinks. They had chosen to assault from the north side, permitting every shot from the recoilless rifle to be a direct hit. Aim was taken at the flickering lights.

The slaughter lasted half an hour, then stopped. A calm fell over both LZs. The north face of Roundbottom was lifeless. P.A. reported he couldn't hear anything other than limp bodies rising and falling. Orientals die quietly.

Defurio turned and gave a thumbs up to the recoilless rifle team. He observed that the base of the barrel had become red hot. White smoke lifted from its mouth.

GIs on Brillo Pad spontaneously cheered the blood bath.

In the morning, two platoons were sent to reconnoiter and canvass the battlefield. Across the chasm between LZs, pings from an M-16 or .45 cal. pistol indicated a wounded NVA soldier was being hastened to his demise. A platoon leader radioed that they had found a total of thirty-six corpses. Three to four times that many had likely been killed. Bodies were dragged to the center of the hillside. If bayonets had been issued, ears would have been shorn off to be worn as baubles on a necklace. Red Army buckles and Ho Chi Minhs would have to do for souvenirs. Gasoline had been flown in for burning the bodies. Black smoke arose from the lumpy pile of corpses.

Looking from afar at the dead soldiers being roasted to ashes, Maloney commented, "Jack, I don't get how those fanatical bastards can risk dragging away bodies. I know it's to deny us a body count, but hell, it doesn't seem worth it. A whole bunch of them got killed going after dead guys."

"You said it, Jim. Gooks are a bunch of fanatical assholes. They're lemmings. They'll jump off cliffs if told to." Jack opened a lone remaining beer. He offered Jim a sip. "These guys aren't like us. They can live like rats in tunnels for months." They alternated sips. "Can you imagine the stink from dead guys carried to a crowded tunnel?" Jack drained the can. "Shit, we smell bad enough alive."

B-52 bombings resumed. One mission came within a half mile of the LZ. At midday, without warning, parallel rows of grey-brown columns shot upwards for hundreds of yards, accompanied by trembling earth and followed by successive thunderclaps from exploded bombs. The B-52s were too high to be seen. Swimming pool sized craters were left in their wake.

R & R became a major topic of letters. Jack would be eligible in three months, sometime in June. R & R gave him and Donna something positive to write about, something to help lessen the pain of separation, but Jack was concerned.

"What's up, Jack? Looks like something's bothering you." Jack had just finished reading a letter from Donna. She was already making plans for Hawaii. Big Jim was in good humor, having come from a visit to the shitter. "Worried jungle rot is going to shrivel your dick before R & R?" Jim was a good student of Jack's moods.

"Something like that. I've lost a lot of weight since I've been in this shithole." Jack had lost about fifteen pounds. "I've gotten blacker than the ace of spades." This wasn't a big deal. Donna wouldn't care about that. "And I've got this fucking polyp growing on my lip." The growth wasn't very noticeable, but if it continued growing it would become unsightly. "By the time I take my R & R, I'm going to look like a fucking Ethiopian with a twig sticking out of my lip."

What worried Jack was his stamina. He didn't want a repeat of his failure to perform for the third time, like he did in Tacoma after basic training.

Big Jim brightened up. "Hell Jack, that growth is an advantage. If it gets bigger, they'll send you to Ennari for minor surgery. Good sham time." This possibility appeased Jack somewhat. Jim rubbed his hands. "Really what you need, Jack my man, is conditioning. I appoint myself as your super qualified personal trainer."

Jim hustled out of the bunker whistling happily. He returned shortly. Jim was upbeat and energized.

"What's going on?" Jack asked.

"You'll find out." Jim waited until dark. "Follow me, Jack." He followed Jim to an uninhabited bunker at the edge of the LZ.

Jim had set up a weight room. He made weights by packing dirt in empty M-60 machine gun ammo cans. They had carrying handles on top. Jim used a spare aiming stake for a bar, which he slid through the handles.

Relying on his experience as a former weightlifter, Jim knew how to pack on pounds and muscle. He set up a rigid eating and weightlifting program for Jack.

They both wrote letters home canvassing anyone they thought would send food. Jim was specific as to what people should send, a powder called Sustagen being high on his list.

As it so happened, hot food had come in insulated containers from cooks at none other than Bad Ass Howie. Because most of their infantry were in the AO, they had extra rations.

Each evening, Jim supervised repetitions of curls, knee bends, bench presses, and behind the neck arm lifts for triceps. Jack did push-ups using ammo boxes as hand rails. Jim stuffed him with food.

The company was still seriously under strength. Replacements trickled in almost daily. Big Jim liked to have fun with rookies and would select likely candidates as they got off the helicopter.

"Yo, troop.., where you from?"

"I'm from Nowhere, Alabama, sir."

"Sir? Don't insult me, I'm not an officer."

"Sorry."

Jim proceeded. "Nowhere. That sounds like a nice place."

"It's real nice, ah…"

"Maloney, my name's Maloney."

"Nice to meet you Maloney, my name is Dumbfuck." Do you know where I'm supposed to go?"

"Report to Lt. Flack." Referring the recruit to Flack had a doubly amusing benefit. Flack didn't have anything to do with receiving recruits, and being perpetually irritable, he would get incensed at intruding newbies and tell them to fuck off. This confounded the rookies further. "Before you see Lt. Flack, let me tell you something. Can you keep it confidential?"

"Con…fi…den…tial?" asked the rube.

"Keep a secret," Big Jim clarified.

"I think so."

Jim continued. "First of all, I'm doing this because you're a U.S. soldier and we're all in this together." The newbie listened appreciatively, grateful that he was receiving individualized attention. "Okay. The first thing is, you're going to get jungle rot, right where your mama told you not to touch yourself. Don't worry about it, everybody gets it, especially white boys like you. The deal is, sometimes the fungus transforms and becomes a microorganism with tiny feet." The mention of microorganism gave the story a touch of scientific authority. "Tiny feet" implanted the desired impression. "This stuff with little feet crawls around looking for a warm, wet place to lay its eggs. Do you know where that is?"

"Ah, no." The recruit was hanging on Maloney's every word.

"It's in your peehole. It climbs in, gets around the middle of your Johnson, and starts laying eggs. And do you know what the eggs use for food?"

"Ah, no."

"That would be the inside of your dick."

Blood drained from the rookie's face. "Holy Jesus!"

"Holy Jesus is right."

"How come the medical people didn't tell us anything about… about…?"

"It's called Black Peegawa." Jim paused for effect. "Because your dick turns black before it falls off."

The rookie was genuinely scared.

"The Army doesn't tell you because it's rare and they don't want to scare you or the folks back home." Jim pulled the youngster closer and lowered his voice. "So as one soldier to the other, I'm going to tell you what to do. Listen carefully. Get a bootlace and soak it in bug repellent, and tie it under the head of your dick." Jim pulled the rookie aside, and he and Jack would show him bootlaces tied around their penises. That was the clincher.

"Keep the bootlace there until you go home and don't let the insecticide dry out."

"And another thing," Jim said, "and this is important. Don't tell any of the other guys about this. The in-country dudes have taken bets on which of you newbies will have your dick fall off. It hasn't happened in a long time, thanks to me and Jack. There's $2,000 in the pot, so don't mention this to anyone. If you do, the guys will get pissed at me and Jack and beat the shit out of you for screwing them out of a chance for that $2,000."

In four or five days, the soaked bootlace would cause a nasty circular welt sensitive to the touch. Periodically, a wail would go up from one of the piss tubes. Bystanders would laugh before telling the rookie he'd been officially initiated into B Company, First Battalion, Fourteenth Infantry.

By the time the company abandoned Brillo Pad, Jack, thanks to Big Jim, had acquired several pounds of muscle. On the downside, his polyp had continued to enlarge.

Chapter 19

Roberts

If Salvador Dali had painted a dead zone, it would have looked like LZ Roberts. It had been hurriedly prepared and bunkers were chaotically distributed. Many trees had been left uncut. It had been overrun two days earlier. The place lay in ruins.

Defenders had called in napalm and artillery in an outrageous attempt to save themselves. Hanging everywhere were solidified white-gray drippings of jellied petroleum. Lifeless trees with tops blown off formed jagged peaks that seemed to scream at the sky. Dirty white ash covered everything.

A sickening aroma accompanied the picture of destruction. Swelling hulks of NVA soldiers lay here and there along the perimeter, some inside it. Flies were busy. Maggots feasted.

Why they were helicoptered here, Defurio had no idea. Exigency of circumstances required Lt. Duke to direct Defurio and Maloney to rejoin first squad. Building another two man bunker would have to be postponed.

They strode through papery ashes on their way. Beige ash gave a deathly pallor to the LZ. "I swear, Jim, this is the ugliest fucking place I've ever seen." Ripples of goosey flesh showed on Jim's neck. Dumbstruck by the nightmarishness of the place, Maloney didn't speak.

Defurio could not conceive of what had happened here; of the helplessness, and extreme fear, and quaking panic that must have occurred within these bunkers. He did not have any information about whether the defenders survived or not. Apparently they had, since bunkers were free from the scent of cadavers.

While inspecting this unhappy moonscape, a Huey landed, bringing a big package from Donna. Jack and Jim were near the landing pad and intercepted the cardboard container before the squad became aware of it.

Soldiers are selfish opportunists. Jack and Jim hid the gift, stowing it behind a bunker on the other side of the landing pad. Jim stayed with the package while Jack went to find an empty bunker where they could secretly select choice food items for themselves. They would parcel leftovers among the squad.

Jack found a bunker at the far end of the LZ, located on a flat finger of land. It had served as a listening post. This is where NVA had broken through. It had a drawback: a swelling dink was ripening one hundred feet from the bunker. He had dug a fighting hole, which now crowded him at the waist. There was another hour of sunlight, and there could be enough heat in the day to cause him to burst. Presently, he looked like a sitting Buddha.

Jack went to retrieve Jim. They skirted the main complex of bunkers. Approaching the vacant LP, Jim gagged. "Fuck, it smells worse than a shitter."

"Oh yeah, I forgot to tell you, there's a rotting dink nearby." Jack had traded the advantage of isolation for the disadvantage of odor from the decomposing Buddha.

Jack and Jim halted and ducked behind a pile of logs when another problem presented itself. A coterie of GIs had gathered to take pictures of the bulging Buddha. This would make it difficult for them to get to the LP without being seen. Fortunately, a debate distracted the group. It concerned whether the dink should be beheaded for more exciting pictures. The foremost proponent for beheading was that little prick, Couch. In any event,

Jim and Jack were able to smuggle themselves and the package inside the bunker without being detected.

Jack lit a candle. Some time ago, Donna had sent an incense candle and until now, he hadn't a need for it. Its dancing flame and projection of playful shadows gave a welcome distraction from the hellishness of the LZ. Its fragrant fumes worked wonderfully to alleviate the stench.

Jack placed the tightly wrapped carton on the dirt floor in anticipation of what surprises might be tucked inside. Even before opening them, Jack's heart beat faster when he received correspondence or goods from Donna. Whatever she sent him she did carefully, thoughtfully, and lovingly.

His heart accelerating, he pressed his Boy Scout knife to cleanly slice through the tightly bound scotch tape binding the box. He pried it open, and inside were neatly arranged cans of sardines, Vienna sausages, fruit cocktail, and pork and beans. Hormel tamales were wedged between packs of Polaroid film and an unexpected find, a package of Lipton soup.

Removing the soup encased in green foil with gold lettering and holding it in his hands, Defurio had a brainstorm. "Jim, let's make a stew."

"How?" Jim asked, baffled.

"Go get your helmet and fill it with water. While you're doing that I'll get some C4 and rocks and build a cooking station." For the sake of secrecy, they would have to cook within the confines of the L.P. They hustled to collect the needed materials.

C4 plastic explosives came in many forms. Most preferable were the narrow blocks used for demolition. A blasting cap made C4 explode. If lit by a match or lighter, it burned slowly. GIs used C4 for cooking and heating rations. Blocks of C4 were usually not available. Therefore, GIs tore apart claymore mines, which were packed with a wide strip of it. This disabled the claymore, but to a hungry GI, it was a price well worth paying.

Jack procured a spare claymore and had a fire going when Jim came in splashing water from his helmet. On his trip to the LP, he'd spilled half its contents.

Jack emptied contents from the green package into the helmet. The water became yellowish. They were captivated watching bits of herbs and spices toss and turn as the water began bubbling. Jack slopped in a can of fatty beef stew from C-rations. He then added crackers, crumbling them with less than clean fingers. This worked better than expected. Cracker crumbs adhered to the fat as a thickening agent. Defurio's mouth watered as the broth came to a boil, setting off a burst of aroma from the herbs and spices.

Jack and Jim were pleased.

"Hi guys, what are you up to?"

Goddamn it, Thorpe. How the fuck did he find them? It wasn't hard to guess. He had trailed Jim, who may as well have sounded an alarm bell by filling his helmet and carrying it away in front of the squad.

Dismay at having Thorpe present didn't have anything to do with his breakdown on Roundbottom. No one blamed him for that. Shit happens. They resented his presence because it meant they would have to share the stew.

"We're making soup," Jim said unenthusiastically, hoping Thorpe would leave.

"Mind if I help out?" It was a rhetorical question. Thorpe had already unfastened his flak jacket, revealing a vest showing a row of pouches on each side that held a variety of herbs, spices and condiments.

Jack and Jim were dumbfounded as Thorpe put in a pinch of this and a dash of that. This man knew what he was doing. He was relaxed, confident, and focused. Gone were the actions of a hesitant, misplaced NCO. He adjusted the flame and mixed in numerous ingredients. The aroma intensified, going from relatively bland to scrumptiously tantalizing.

Thorpe allowed the upgraded concoction to simmer so that its contents blended perfectly. He then ladled the reinforced stew into each man's cup.

When circumstances are bad, anything good seems better. But Thorpe's meal would have been good anywhere, anytime. It could never have been more appreciated. The stew was so flavorful and satisfying that it suspended for a brief moment the taint of war. The deliciousness of that meal, eaten in a napalm ash heap of unburied bodies, would for Defurio forever be a fond memory.

That night it was quiet. There was no activity in the AO. Napalm and artillery barrages had taken the fight out of the NVA. In daytime, they half-heartedly lobbed 122 mm rockets and 61 mm mortars for five to ten minutes, all which fell outside the compound.

After the sporadic shelling and before the afternoon heat set in, Jack and Jim decided to investigate the LZ. Ordinarily, they didn't give a shit about idiosyncrasies of an LZ, but Robert's was different. It was macabre; its severe appearance went beyond the ordinary, way beyond.

They came upon Lt. Duke and Lt. Flack firing a captured AK-47. They were pumping bullets into a deep ravine stretching from the western border of the LZ. "Y'all want to give it a try?" Lt. Duke said, handing the weapon to Defurio.

"No thanks." Defurio had heard dink ammo was unreliable, and he didn't want to take the chance of a round exploding in the chamber and ruining his face. "Lieutenant," he said, handing the rifle back to Lt. Duke, "let me ask you something. What's the story with these darts lying all over the place?" Defurio and Maloney couldn't help noticing that sections of Roberts were covered in metal flashettes about two inches long.

"When the NVA got inside the wire," Lt. Duke explained, "dynamite rounds were called in with the napalm." Defurio loved to hear Lt. Duke talk. No matter what the subject, his voice sounded like a lullaby.

"Dynamite rounds?" Defurio asked. Lt. Duke momentarily ignored the question.

"That captain," he said, "must have had balls this big." Lt. Duke formed his hands to the circumference of dinner plates. "It was his call and it saved him and his company." Whoever the captain was, he had overnight become a legend among the officer corps of the central highlands. Flack intervened, ordnance being his area of expertise. It was the first time Defurio had heard Flack speak other than shouting commands for fire missions. "Dynamites are artillery rounds that explode just above the ground. They have more explosive power that way. They spray thousands of high velocity darts. They'll go through flesh but not a solid set of sandbags." Lt. Duke jettisoned a magazine and reloaded, and waited for Flack to finish his explanation before firing. Defurio bent down and picked up one of the innocent looking finned projectiles. They looked so common Defurio didn't think to put two or three in his pocket for keepsakes.

Lt. Duke said, "You ought to see what the guys on patrol around here have seen."

"What's that, Lieutenant?" Jim asked.

"They've spotted dinks pinned to trees by these darts," Lt. Duke said matter-of-factly, a curious smile on his face.

The lieutenant resumed firing.

"Shit," Jim said earnestly. "How come we've never heard of dynamite rounds?"

"I don't know, maybe they're banned by the Geneva Convention."

"So's the .50 caliber machine gun and we're trained to fire those." Jack shrugged. He didn't want to waste mental energy thinking about contradictions; they were too common.

Another flat piece of ground extended from the northern side of the ravine. There, another part of the LZ had been penetrated. The area had been turned into a collection point and an array of communist weapons were on display. The chicom grenades were uncommon and reminded Defurio of WWII German potato mashers, only with wooden handles.

Line platoons combed hundreds of yards of surrounding jungle. They collected hardware and documents, leaving bodies where they lay. Once in a while a shot could be heard—a cautious GI, ensuring a suspicious dink stayed dead.

Thankfully, Hueys came for them on the third day. Roberts stood apart as being particularly hideous and vile in every respect. Defurio was never so happy to leave a place.

The chopper pilot seemed as anxious as Defurio to flee Roberts. Jack leaped aboard as the Huey hurriedly pulled away. The craft dove and skimmed just above the rooftop of jungle, catching and trailing a vine on one of its skids, an occurrence which wasn't that unusual. After attaining sufficient speed, it lifted and banked into a clear sky.

From his seat, legs hanging over the side, Defurio saw the pimply, milky face of Roberts constrict as the helicopter gained altitude. Wind rushing through the open fuselage watered his eyes. His nostrils pinched and flared, his lungs welcoming the rush of fresh air. It felt good not to have to breathe the smell of festering corpses.

Chapter 20

LZ Short

3/15/69

Dear Donna,

I am writing to you by flashlight. I'm under a poncho. We got here the day before yesterday. It's called LZ Short. We're about 1,000 meters south of Roundbottom. We're on a low hill with a landing pad, nothing else. No bunkers, concertina, or cleared fields of fire. We're fenced in by damn jungle. I'm sick of being trapped inside a green cage 24 hours a day. No units have occupied this hill in quite a while.

We set up our gun pits soon as we got here. Good thing. We fired all night. Lots and lots of movement on this hill. Don't worry. I'm o.k. There wasn't any return fire.

We're sleeping on open ground. We've scooped out single man sleeping areas. Funny, you'd think we'd be in foxholes. I've never built or seen one since I've been in Nam.

It's been raining. Hard to keep my writing materials from getting wet. I'm concerned about my pictures of you. I've wrapped everything in plastic. If seepage gets in, it'll kill me. Your pictures keep me going.

You're so darn pretty.

I'm so sleepy. I'd better get some sleep.

I love you

A SRP team on Alamo had been overrun and four men from A Company had been killed. Defurio met the news with detachment, glad he wasn't there, but also troubled that dinks had become so emboldened and were on the prowl.

Lt. Duke relayed the SRP team's misfortune. Because of the absence of bunkers, Lt. Duke became a more visible presence. He and Flack monitored a company radio, listening to traffic between companies and the battalion's day-to-day operations. Ordinarily, they listened to radio traffic in the privacy of a bunker, where Defurio suspected they also smoked pot. Lt. Duke and Flack's private business didn't concern him. What bothered him was that four men had been killed within pissing distance of LZ Short; yet another worry and feeling of powerlessness leading to a growing sense of desperation and despair at being in an inextricably fucked up situation; of being in a jungle ten thousand miles from home; of being at the mercy of the Army and circumstances beyond his control; by being removed from civilization; and by the irretrievable loss of hours, days, weeks, and months away from Donna.

"I hate this fucking mud," Defurio said, trying to suck up a shovel full of soaked earth and filling a sandbag held by Maloney. The work would get easier since the rain had stopped and the ground was beginning to dry.

"You sure you want to do this?" Jim asked, regarding Defurio's decision to build a one man bunker.

"Hell, yes. I've got some good ideas I want to try out." This project gave him an objective, it was practical and creative, and would give him a measure of independence. Suspension of the rain allowed him to make rapid progress. He worked feverishly, and a sense of accomplishment took hold as the bunker neared completion.

Defurio's 4' x 10' room was wildly spacious compared to the 2' x 7' compartment he would have had in the squad bunker. He also didn't have to contend with delays involving everyone's opinion of how it should be built.

Defurio set his walls a foot inside the rim of the pit, permitting space for shelving. He employed his ax and Boy Scout knife to splay empty sandbags for wainscoting. This gave some insulation from damp earth and also made the interior homey and stylish. His bunker was better than expected. He could enjoy privacy, write letters in peace and quiet, and hide food sent from home from squad members. There were a multitude of advantages and no disadvantages. His spirits soared.

There was a luxury yet to be enjoyed. Almost overlooked by the dreariness at Roberts and the commotion of moving to LZ Short was the battery operated razor sent to him by Donna. Shaving had become another small torture. No longer. Defurio emerged from his one man suite effortlessly clean shaven, while others in the company weren't so fortunate. In morning light, men could be seen sleepily bent forward, faces reflecting off propped up mirrors, tugging at dirty beards lathered in C-ration soap, using safety razors containing blades dulled by humidity.

A shipment of beer arrived, which led Defurio to have a grand opening. The commemoration consisted of two people: him and Big Jim. He lit a candle. Thanks to Donna, he had an adequate supply of candles. With light suffusing the interior, Jack handed Jim a relatively cold beer, having dug a hole in the corner to keep the cans cool. Rainwater and clammy earth made decent cooling agents. "Yeah!" Jim let out an exclamation of enjoyment.

They relaxed on ammo box lounges made by Jack, the construction of which had become a specialty of his. They didn't miss the competing blare of Motown and acid rock, of thick tongued jive and southern twangs, or the endless chatter of adolescents describing every nook and hair of imaginary girlfriends. "Here, Jim, have a cigarette." Jack didn't have to share the pack with a roomful of soldiers. What a breakthrough. Defurio had built a refuge, a place of escape, within a wilderness of despair.

11:00 pm. Because of enemy activity, the company remained on fifty percent alert. Two hours on, two hours off. Platoons rotated, occupying semi-completed bunkers on the perimeter. On his first shift, Defurio worried at being exposed to an open ribbon of land between him and the jungle. He also didn't like the large gaps between bunkers. An elephant could walk through undetected.

Although he imagined elephants stampeding through the defensive perimeter, nothing much happened on his watch.

He returned to his hooch and slept peacefully until awakened by gunfire. M-16s and M-60s opened up in a broadside on the LZ's eastern rim. Such small arms fire, disregarding muzzle flashes, indicated an extreme emergency. There wasn't anything on Short to deter a ground attack other than individual soldiers shooting to save their lives.

Defurio had his M-16, ammo, and grenades arranged for easy access. He felt for his M-16 and slammed in a magazine, locked and loaded. He clicked it off safe. He filled his side pockets with grenades and scrambled topside and crouched behind his bunker, utilizing it as a firing position.

There hadn't been time to send up illum rounds. However, fifty automatic weapons streaming hundreds of horizontal bright red flashes was dramatically colorful and ear splittingly deafening, a chaos of fire and sound. The tingly scent of burnt gunpowder completed the sensory overload.

Strangely, there wasn't any incoming. Nevertheless, Defurio set himself to shoot at anything running, crawling, or coming at him. There was nothing between him and the tree line. Erratic illumination from tracers reminded him of blinking light from a broken motel sign he'd once seen alongside Highway 99. He held his fire, waiting for something to show and remained cool. He had a knack for not panicking under fire.

"Cease fire! Cease fire!" Platoon leaders were running up and down the eastern perimeter. A pair of green eyes had been seen in the tree line. A tiger was suspected. A tiger? Do they have green eyes? Just as plausible were lightening bugs or a skittish soldier's imagination. However, tigers were a real and legitimate concern. This issue aside, B Company emptied two or three clips into the black walls of jungle, except for Defurio, who elected to save his ammo. Firing automatic weapons is a stress relieving palliative for edgy soldiers. However, it was enough for Defurio that this wasn't a ground assault—one of his worst fears. He drew in a deep breath, feeling muscles in his neck and shoulders loosen as he exhaled slowly. He pointed his M-16 up and expelled a chambered round, withdrew the magazine, and went to catch up on his sleep.

The following day, two packages arrived from Donna, one contained pictures of her in a blue robe. They were innocent, most likely taken by her younger sister, Cathy. Donna didn't like to pose for pictures. It wasn't that she was shy, she just didn't like being the center of attention. She was up-to-date stylish but at the same time unsupposing. It was an endearing quality. Defurio couldn't wait to see her on R & R. Thinking of her, he felt his lower lip and could feel his polyp had gotten bigger.

Defurio found a way to augment his living arrangement by rigging wire to hang his boots and socks. A field GI's boots seldom leave his feet. Defurio had his hanging by his bunk, his socks draped next to them, both easily reached in the dark. He lay on his bunk wiggling his dry toes. Dry boots, dry socks, dry toes—heaven for a foot soldier.

Sgt. Thorpe stuck his fleshy, serene face through the flap of Defurio's hooch. "Pack up, we're moving out," he said mildly, as if they were going on a camping trip. "Damn it," Defurio thought, just when he was getting comfortable. On the other hand, setting up another bunker might not be so bad. He was already thinking of architectural improvements, such as a stand-up aisle in the middle of his hooch.

Thorpe, seeing Defurio's accommodations, came in for a visit. There wasn't any hurry. Moving a company always involved waiting. He stretched on one of Defurio's chaise lounges.

"Do you know where we're going?" Defurio asked, handing him a beer. "Might as well finish these." Defurio didn't mind extending hospitality to Thorpe. The culinary masterpiece on Roberts had redeemed him. Thorpe twitched his auburn moustache, which showed orange in the candlelight.

"Chu Pa."

"Shit!" exclaimed Defurio.

"Yeah, I know," Thorpe said, drinking his beer, some foam attaching to his moustache. "It's not for sure though, just rumor."

Helicopters neared the LZ. Something had happened; they were arriving too soon. Defurio and Thorpe braved a blistering sun to find out what.

They ran into Lt. Duke. "What's going on, Lt?" he asked as the first helicopter landed, disgorging bedraggled troops. "A Company got shot up doing a sweep off Brillo Pad." Lt. Duke had to shout above the whir of helicopter engines and blades. A Company was the undisputed hard luck company in the battalion.

Defurio saw a soldier by the name of Ryker coming from a chopper. He knew Ryker from Ft. Lewis, not well, but he remembered him as a carefree teenager, a skinny, bony-faced kid from Concord, California.

"Ryker," Defurio called to him. The kid responded as if he were a zombie. Ryker walked stiffly toward Defurio. He put his hand on Ryker's arm and guided him to his hooch and gave him a beer. Ryker dropped his gear. He was filthy. Blankly, he looked at the hooch, the beer, and at Defurio and Thorpe. He tipped the beer, nearly finishing it in a single gulp.

Maloney came in. "How's it going, Jim?" Defurio asked. Jim's eyes fell on the unexpected presence of Ryker. Without thinking, he said, "Guys from the helicopter look like shit." Ryker didn't seem to hear or care. He finished his beer and Defurio gave him another.

"Ryker, how many guys did you lose?" Defurio asked.

The beer and blunt question shook Ryker from his apathy. "I think eight or nine, maybe more. Packs of them came out of nowhere. They'd get one or two of us before we got them." The words came hard. He seemed confused, expressionless, and distant, yet wanting to talk. "We had thirty or forty guys wounded, some pretty bad. I saw a bomb crater that had a ring of gray and red around it. No bodies, it must have been a direct B-52 hit on the dinks. Stuff was stuck to trees like lumpy spray paint."

Soldiers have a tendency to unload traumatic events on other soldiers—people they can relate to, trust, and who will understand. Usually, if expressed immediately, these horrific experiences don't do permanent damage. Usually.

Listening to Ryker, Defurio's favorite uncle came to mind. Uncle Gus had spent WWII in the Pacific as a rifleman. An Alamo scout, he went behind enemy lines to do reconnaissance, and had killed many Japanese. By all accounts, he had been a young man of great promise; handsome, intellectually gifted, personable, well-built, and athletic. He retained these attributes when he returned. However, he was a broken man, restless, erratic, unreasonably stubborn, and generous to a fault. He mastered many trades, including watchmaker, welder, gemologist, electrician, artisan, and restaurateur, but never stayed in any of them. His wife ran away with a professional wrestler, ending a brief marriage. He went from owning a late model Cadillac to wandering the streets. He was a tough man who died at age 89 in a head-on car accident.

Ryker couldn't get his mind off the bomb crater. "You couldn't see any bodies," he repeated. "But you could smell them. They stunk worse than an outhouse." Ryker finished his beer and left without saying goodbye or thank you. His mind wasn't in the present.

When he departed, no one spoke. Defurio, Maloney, and Thorpe were all thinking the same thing. Maloney broke the silence. "That should have been us," he said, referring to the fact that B Company had originally been ordered to do the sweep. The entire company had been fifty yards underway off Brillo Pad when they were called back and A Company flown in at the last minute to undertake the mission.

Defurio didn't know the reason for the exchange of companies, but he had a theory. Captain Lowery was too drunk to conduct the operation. He had retained command of the company. His automatic six-month rotation to safe duty had been rescinded when battalion headquarters discovered that his replacement, Captain Asshole, had needlessly endangered Defurio's SRP patrol, and had been summarily reassigned.

"You know something, you guys," Defurio said to Maloney and Thorpe, half seriously and half in jest. "This place is like a loony bin. Nothing fucking makes sense. We may have been spared because Lowery is a known drunk. Headquarters may have accidentally saved our asses because Lowery can't find his own."

Whatever the validity of Defurio's speculation, they were alive and well. The three returned to the business at hand. Thorpe went to round up his squad. He needed to oversee destruction of the squad's bunkers. They were being destroyed so nothing useful remained for the dinks.

A Company didn't exist any longer as a viable company. They would be withdrawn in a day or so. LZ Short was being abandoned.

Maloney stayed to assist Defurio dismantle his bunker. They methodically kicked in walls, careful not to work up unnecessary sweat. They whacked at the gathering mound of sandbags using foldable shovels, known officially as entrenching tools. Another fine example of elegant Army nomenclature. Swinging them enthusiastically, Jack and Jim derived an odd pleasure in splitting bags open and watching the ocher contents pour from them.

They lackadaisically hauled their gear to the landing pad, joining men informally arranged according to squad, platoon, or ethnicity. It was too hot for much talking when Defurio and Maloney flopped down near the first squad. They were exposed to an open sun. While reclining on hot soil, jungle fatigues clinging uncomfortably to his sweaty skin, Defurio pulled the bill of his fatigue cap to cover his eyes. Sleepily, Chu Pa went through his mind. Fuck Chu Pa. He'd worry about the damnable place if and when he returned there. Meanwhile, he'd sleep while he could.

Chapter 21

LZ Stud

The 18" gray monkey had a sorrowful face. Big Jim balanced it proudly on his muscular right forearm. He anxiously wanted to show his newly acquired prize to Jack and walked to where Defurio was bullshitting a fresh crop of rookies. The two irrepressible soldiers were engaged in their own way of celebrating the company's good luck in not returning to Chu Pa. Jim delayed his introduction, waiting for Jack to finish his presentation. He hid his giggles from the recruits.

Defurio was promoting one of his and Maloney's standard pranks. In fake seriousness, he described the importance of concealment, elaborating on the art of camouflage, stressing how critical blackened faces would be on patrols. His remarks were designed to entice naive rookies to buy shoe polish for the purpose. In practice, ordinary infantrymen didn't bother with camouflage.

He had a limited supply of the polish. Friends returning from the rear area, acting as couriers from Ennari's PX, couldn't keep up with demand. At five dollars a can, the waxy polish sold like hot cakes.

Defurio didn't like taking money from soldiers. However, in this instance, it was part of the joke. The best part was seeing newcomers coming in from patrols wearing the almost irremovable black make-up.

Within minutes, he sold out. When he did, Defurio dismissed the group. "See you fellas later," he told his happy customers, many disappointed that they were unable to make a purchase.

When the rookies disbanded, Maloney gave Jack a shout out, "Yo, Jack, look at this."

Jack, in fine fettle having hoodwinked another batch of recruits, laughed uproariously at seeing Big Jim's simian companion.

"Whoa, what'd you do, knock-up one of the local girls?"

"Nah," Jim said, laughing. "I paid twenty dollars for her from a guy in Arty who's leaving for the States."

"Tell me about it while I search for a new site for my hooch." Jim switched the chimp to his other arm. They walked forty or so yards, passing several black troopers, who eyed Mona apprehensively.

"Jeez Jim, we need to get out of this sun. Lt. Duke said that temperatures were averaging 120°." LZ Stud sat on a low hill with breezes blocked by higher mountains. Contours of terrain seemed to funnel heat onto them.

They sat in some shade. The monkey hopped off Jim's arm. Jim had her tethered to a 4' leash. It moved nervously and in the blink of an eye reached under the leaf of a scraggly bush. With a quick jerk, it withdrew a wiggly, hairy pupa. Twitchy, skeletal fingers held the larval insect, which in short vicious bites, she crunched and swallowed in a ferocious gobble. The creature was a bit frightening.

"Alright, Jim, how did you obtain Mighty Joe Young? Or maybe we should call her Mighty Jo Bitch?"

"Man," Jim said in a mild shock, "how did she know that bug was there… and the way she ate it." Jim's love of animals was being tested.

"Hell Jack, I've only owned her for an hour. The guy in Arty is gone. He said she was gentle."

"Did he say what you're supposed to feed her?"

"He told me she'd get most of her own food. I think he was right about that part."

The monkey, named Mona, was marginally tame. Obviously, the fidgety animal had a mean disposition. Walking through the compound, blacks in the company were understandably leery of her. She frequently bared her teeth at them. Maybe at one time or another a black trooper had teased her. Whatever, she showed an overt hostility toward them.

Jack found a suitable location for his one man hooch. "Jim, I've got an idea. Help me build this bunker and I'll explain it." Jim tied Mona to a tree and assisted Jack. It was near dusk when they finished.

During construction, Jack outlined his plan. "Is it possible to keep Mona on your arm or lap for ten minutes or so?"

"If I give her treats, I think she'll stay a lot longer than that."

"Great." Jack waited until dark. "Stay here, I'll be right back." Jack snuck to the location of the captain's CP and used his ax to chop 8' of thin rubber tubing feeding fuel to a generator, which powered a rotary fan in the CP. Of course, this disabled the captain's cooling system. So much the better, as far as Defurio was concerned. He skipped to his bunker and made large and small funnels from the wax packaging encasing mortar shells, and attached the funnels to either end of the rubber tubing.

Maloney looked on in fascination, and understood that Jack was building up the suspense for his benefit. Finally, he revealed his plan.

They rehearsed inside Jack's lodging, working on timing. There would be a minimum of dialogue. Their creative machinery was oiled by sipping from a bottle of Jack Daniels sent by Donna. They were having a good time. Jim giggled when high on pot or booze. Jack liked seeing him this way, as though he was borrowing some of Big Jim's happiness.

They chose breakfast time to unveil the performance, bringing out Mona while troops were leisurely shifting and sitting around eating C-rats. Jim stationed himself on a box by the entryway to Defurio's hooch. He kept a firm grip on Mona's leash. Defurio stayed inside. No one took too much notice at first. Jim didn't make a display of Mona, he presented her subtly. They bided their time.

Jones, a hulking black guy, wandered by. A perfect candidate. "Jones, come over here and say hello to Mona," Jim asked in a warm, friendly tone.

"No man, I ain't getting close to no mean monkey."

"Aw c'mon, Jones. She's not going to hurt a big guy like you. She's sensitive. You're hurting her feelings."

His manhood questioned, Jones cautiously came closer. Mona tensed up.

Jim strengthened his grip, holding onto a part of her leash attached behind her neck, next to the hidden wax funnel. Jones relaxed slightly. He could see that Mona couldn't move, and tentatively reached out his hand. Mona's eyes widened when Jones's forefingers made contact with her scalp. At that moment, Mona happened to open her mouth in a yawn. "Hi," said a squeaky voice.

Jones let out a "YEOW!" and jumped about three feet. He ran off.

Jim barreled into the hooch, dragging Mona and laughing his guttural laugh so hard he almost choked to death. Jack joined him in convulsions of laughter. This was beyond expectations.

They composed themselves for the next round. Jim gave Mona a mouthful of treats. Mona, her cheeks full of C-ration pears, resumed her place on Jim's lap outside Jack's doorway.

Sure enough, Jones appeared leading a skeptical parade of his buddies. "Hi, guys," Jim said cheerfully, inconspicuously holding firmly to Mona's tightening leash, careful not to dislodge the hidden speaking tube. Mona sat on Big Jim's right thigh. The monkey's similarity to a ventriloquist's dummy drew a knowing murmur from the crowd. The trick was obvious.

With nothing else to do, the black soldiers played along with what they thought was Maloney's transparent deception. "Jones said your monkey can talk," someone in the snickering crowd commented. The twittering halted when Mona bared her teeth. The hardened troops retreated when she lunged at them. She could only rise up two or three inches.

"I swear I heard her talk," Jones said, looking foolish.

Jim came to his rescue. "She can, but she's afraid of you guys. She'll speak if you can calm her down. You have to smile and talk baby-talk to her."

"Aw man, you're shittin' me. I ain't going to smile at no fucking monkey," one of them said contemptuously. "Fuck it. She looks like someone I know. Come to think of it, Jones, she looks like one of your sisters."

"No way," Jones countered. "This monkey is way better looking than any of my sisters." This rejoinder broke the impasse. Laughs and hoots swept the group. Joking and jiving revved up, and a party atmosphere developed. Mona attempted to twist and turn. Jim held her firmly. Apprehension concerning Mona dissipated.

They became cocky. The black soldiers outdid themselves taunting Mona. "Come on baby, talk to me." "You're so cute." "Whose your daddy?" "Would you like to go out with me?" "Me Tarzan, you Jane." "Do you have any sisters?" They mimicked kissing her and got closer. They enjoyed provoking her, seeing fur on her head stand on end. Jones, making up for his earlier embarrassment, boldly brought his face near to Mona's, pretending to kiss her. This instigated others to do the same, to leer, drivel, and mock the monkey. Finally, the audience of faces drew to within inches of Mona. She froze, snapped her mouth in anger, eyes blinking wildly. This is when a falsetto voice, coming from the monkey and plainly not from Maloney, simply said, "Fuck you guys."

As though collectively struck by lightning, the black soldiers hopped up and scattered. Jack pulled his head up to witness a comical agitation of flailing arms and legs as if the soldiers were being chased by the devil. From then on, a black trooper wouldn't come within twenty yards of Mona.

Defurio's letters to Donna were heavily accented in words of love for her. Accounts of sarcastic endeavors or cruel jokes promulgated by him and Maloney, because they might upset her, were deleted or minimized. That night he omitted any reference to the crude humor elicited at the expense of his black comrades.

He never highlighted these prevarications to her, and certainly not who the victims were of these escapades, or that anyone was fair game, including a highly agitated and overheated Captain Lowery. Defurio smiled, picturing Lowery sweating copiously, like everyone else, without the robust circulation provided by his now deactivated fan.

Captain Lowery deserved to be made uncomfortable. The night before, in a drunken rage, he had publicly berated a young lieutenant, calling him "a fucking incompetent." This incident represented another in a backlog of unseemly and irresponsible behavior by the unpopular captain. The incident increased the possibility of somebody collecting a $250 bounty. This is what guys in the line had ponied up if someone were willing to kill Lowery, although these bounties were more exaggerated soldier talk than serious considerations.

The Mad Medic, a name given to him by Defurio, was a colorful, powerfully built eccentric; a gnarled, gnome of a man who paraded through camp, helmet on backwards, spouting Shakespeare. A conscientious objector, he refused to carry a weapon. He had a reputation as an excellent medic.

One night the medic unexpectedly dropped by and told Jack and Jim his story. He was the son of circus aerialists. His father had died in a fall from the high wire. The funeral procession of circus folks extended for miles. His mother died of heartbreak soon afterwards. He spoke at length of his parents; how handsome his father, how beautiful his mother, and that he'd been raised by circus people.

Although questionable, as soldier's stories usually are, the medic's history made for an entertaining evening. Not surprisingly, he performed an unconventional good-bye. In slow, ungainly strides, he made for the doorway. On the way, he filled the room with sonorous Shakespearean verbiage. Reaching the doorway, he paused, bent down, and petted Mona. She happily accepted his hand, which was odd, considering she didn't let strangers touch her.

Exiting Defurio's hooch, the medic's voice boomed. Defurio and Maloney listened to his resounding elocution fade in the dense night air. They never had any further dialogue with the sad, misshapen man who seemed to have lived a life of psychic pain.

Listening posts were monitoring high levels of enemy activity. The company went on 100% alert. Platoon mortars fired throughout the evening.

First squad experienced a hang fire. Thorpe put a round in the tube, which didn't go off. It slid down the tube and stayed there. This caused a commotion, and no one knew quite what to do or how dangerous the situation was. The squad detached the tube from its tripod and upended it, causing the H & E round to fall harmlessly to the ground.

B-52 strikes had subdued hostile enemy action. The NVA moved about but were unwilling to engage the Americans. For the past ten days, B Company hadn't suffered any casualties. Defurio welcomed this period of relative calm and stability.

This was about to change. The platoon's mortars were disassembled and air lifted to an LZ called Bunker Hill. The mortarmen would be joining the line company as regular infantry in a sweep to be conducted between LZ Stud and Bunker Hill.

Jack and Jim loafed inside Jack's hooch. There wasn't any urgency; the company wouldn't be leaving for a couple of days. "I wish I knew what the fuck we're doing." Jack didn't expect an answer. As usual, the purpose of the mission was unknown. "Sweep" was a generic term. Whether the operation was a sweep, search and destroy, reconnaissance, a blocking maneuver, entrapment, who knew? Either way, it was going to involve the entire company on foot in the AO.

Lt. Duke logically concluded a four day operation, since four days rations had been issued. However, this wasn't determinative; resupplied by helicopter they could stay in the AO for weeks. What they knew for sure was that B Company would embark in two days.

Jim was getting tired of Mona. She was unaffectionate and her constant fidgeting was annoying. She became more and more short tempered. Jim suspected a brain disease. They were resting on Jack's lounges, smoking. Jack was contemplating Mona's fall from grace.

"Jim, how'd you like to get rid of her profitably?" Just then, Mona shit on Jack's floor. Digested bugs emit a foul odor.

"The sooner the better," Jim replied, crinkling his nose.

"How about this: we'll hold a raffle."

Jim re-set his eyebrows, a sure sign of serious interest.

"We can cut up paper for tickets, sell them for two dollars apiece. We ought to be able to sell twenty or thirty of them."

Jim lifted his eyebrows in a show of approval.

"Alright, but first we need to think of a come on, you know, like a benefit for a charity or a cause."

Jim sat up. "Cause we need the cash." He had a fast wit.

"I've got it. We'll take advantage of La Crosse Boy becoming a daddy. We can say X-rays show the baby has a zaboda and will need an operation when it's born."

"What's a zaboda?"

"It's nothing. I made it up."

Jim extinguished his cigarette butt on the dirt. "I like it," he chuckled.

Defurio and Maloney seemed to hatch these schemes like chicken eggs. They delayed implementation of the plan, deciding it was better to wait. Bunker Hill had an artillery and TOC Unit, and this would expand the pool of ticket buyers.

Jack and Jim ate up stored cans and packages of food. Jim continued to supervise Jack's work-outs and weight gaining program. Jack's muscle tone and weight improved. Defurio was more concerned about the growth on his lower lip. For the moment it looked like a pimple, however, its cells were multiplying.

Yippee! A package arrived from Donna. It contained the best present ever: a new Polaroid camera to replace the one destroyed at Roundbottom, along with color film. Jack and Jim cleaned up the best they could and hurried to a border of the LZ abutting a stand of brooding bamboo.

Jack placed Mona on his left shoulder, then his right. He wore a T-shirt. Steamy heat from Mona's unclean rump penetrated to his skin. Stalks of bamboo blocking a setting sun striped him and the monkey in smoky shades of black. Jack wanted unique action photos. Because of Mona's testiness, the pictures were taken quickly. Defurio was afraid she might chew off an ear. She didn't, and the pictures were surprisingly near perfect in color and composition.

This is how Defurio and Maloney prepared for entering a jungle full of enemy soldiers, by deriving a little pleasure from a recalcitrant, ill-tempered monkey.

Chapter 22

Bunker Hill

Maloney had improvised a sling from a T-shirt and tied it to his rucksack. Mona seemed content to ride inside, rocking to the motion of Jim's heavy footsteps. The company traveled on a flat trail, making for a relatively easy hike, not anything like the difficulty Defurio had faced on the SRP patrol. Seeing Big Jim's sizable butt in front of him waddling from side to side provided a meaty protective barrier of reassurance.

The problem was water. The company left LZ Stud with empty canteens due to the negligence of Capt. Lowery failing to call for resupply. Into the fourth hour of the patrol, they were hurting. Defurio licked his dry lips and tasted salt. A wretched thirst tore at everyone's throat.

They came to a wide river and pivoted north to follow its course. Its current moved swiftly. Fast flowing, bubbling water indicated it was drinkable. They shadowed the river on a trail fifty yards west and above the waterway. Glimpses of white capped rapids could be seen through gaps in the trees. Luxuriant jungle overhung the opposite bank. Seeing and hearing the river alleviated the dehydrated company's mounting desperation.

The trail stayed flat. The company went a click before halting for a rest. Soldiers frantically unleashed packs and in unison stormed the river to drink, splash, and fill canteens. They had become a mob. At river's edge, lieutenants prudently posted guards to protect the dehydrated soldiers from becoming targets of opportunity for roving NVA troops.

Parked on the other bank between outcroppings of jungle, they sighted seven outrigger skiffs. Were they fishing boats from a local village, or had they happened on an enemy supply route? They saw no activity so they adopted a "don't mean nothing" attitude. The boats were ignored. Of greater interest to Maloney, and by association to Defurio, were the fish.

Sleek scaled torpedoes placidly glided near the surface as they fed during the last light of day. The fish were dark brown and splotched in ovals of yellow and white. The biggest, a three foot beauty, slithered and slid on its back on top of a flat rock within arm's reach.

Defurio, on his knees filling canteens, looked up at Jim, who stood transfixed.

"They'll never believe me at the Aquarian Club," he repeated two or three times.

After satisfying their thirst and filling canteens, the company ambled back to where they'd dropped their packs and dispersed themselves on either side of the trail. Rain pelted them as they set up for the night.

Jim fastened Mona's leash to a young tree. Taking shelter under a leaf laden branch, she seemed unbothered by the rain. The two wet soldiers hastily erected a plastic lean-to. Mud, uneven ground, and roots made it impossible to find a comfortable sleeping position. They lay butt to butt. "Please don't fart, Jim."

"Don't worry. I'm too tired to fart."

They ate a C-ration breakfast. Defurio's back arched in reaction to the bitterness of the coffee. The brew jolted an undeveloped thought to the forefront. "Jim, what do you think if we caught a fish?"

"How?" Jim asked, always a willing conspirator.

"I'll make a fishing pole." Defurio was never at a loss to take advantage of opportunities, such as a friend's interest in a river brimming with fish.

Defurio and Maloney were in the middle of the single file of troops. There was minimal danger, visibility being good in this section of immature tree growth and the right flank secured by the river. Periodically, the company rested near the trail. At the first stop, Defurio noisily chopped down an eight-foot stalk of bamboo, much to the upset of a new in-country lieutenant. Defurio thought, "Fuck you, dinks would have to be deaf and blind not to know we're here." The bamboo's circumference was about that of a hoe handle. At the next break, Defurio attached to its top a five-foot fishing line made from boot laces. For a leader, he adapted a two-foot length of trip flare wire. His crowning achievement was a hook made from a safety pin.

The company advanced at a leisurely pace. While thinking of ways to barb his hook, word came they were being evacuated, which was normally good news. Damn, he probably wouldn't have an opportunity to hook a fish.

Sometimes there's an advantage to having a fuck-up for a leader. Capt. Lowery had been required to lead the patrol. He liked to drink, not hump. He usually found clever ways to avoid these personally intrusive assignments. Although Defurio detested Lowery, he realized the company often benefitted from his derelictions. He imagined the captain making fervent radio calls, falsely claiming to pencil pushers at Brigade that B Company was disastrously short of water, ignoring the fact that they were beside a rushing river.

The company congregated by a sand bar lying in ankle deep water five feet from shore. A formation of Hueys appeared, flying in a beaded chain and breaking off in sequence to extract them. The birds came screaming low over the water through a canyon of jungle, pulling up briefly and hovering above the sandbar while troops shinnied aboard.

The choppers ruined Defurio's chance of landing a fish. He tried anyway. He opened a can of beef stew. The greasy substance slid off the hook. Ferocious down drafts from whirling blades egg-beated an already turbulent river. He kept trying and went to pound cake. Prop wash knocked it free from the hook. The last slick came for them. He had to get on.

Unassisted by momentum diving from a hilltop, the Huey strained under its load, and in a swirl of sand, wind, and water droplets, grudgingly lifted and tilted southward.

This is when Defurio reluctantly flung his bamboo creation in the river. The green-gold segmented fishing pole circled in the current before submerging. The Huey accelerated, flying in a straight line just above the gurgling river. After gaining sufficient speed, the craft banked skyward, silhouetted in the orange afterglow of sunset.

Bunker Hill hid in darkness. Nighttime landings were rare. Flares placed around the landing pad made it seem troops were falling through a ring of fire.

Elements of First Battalion Twelfth Infantry (1st/12th) co-occupied the hill with an artillery battery. B Company had to double up in 1st/12th bunkers. Both companies were in-transit. Bunker Hill acted as a way station for infantry companies moving in and out of the AO.

Defurio and Maloney were attracted to lively activity coming from one bunker in particular. None of the bunkers had room to lay out sleeping bags, so men had to sit or stand inside, or stay outside in the mud…may as well stay inside a dry bunker that had some action.

The bunker had been converted to a gambling den. Commanding the game was a twenty-year old Kentuckian referred to as "Coondick." He had a way about him as smooth and warming as a sip of fine Kentucky whiskey. He dealt primarily black jack and five card stud, and had a witty comment for every card and hand played.

To an outsider "Coondick" had racial implications, Coon being a derogatory term for a black man. However, it was clear that in A Company, $1^{st}/12^{th}$, the nickname for this white boy had become an accepted part of the vernacular.

Limited space around the blanket on the floor restricted participants to five players. There were a dozen or so onlookers. As a player busted out, another took his place. Coondick didn't break players immediately. He wrung more cash by letting them play awhile. He put on a show, gently chiding players to bet prudently while at the same time fleecing them. Sucked in by the showmanship and unable to sleep anyway, Defurio bought in for the equivalent of twenty U.S. dollars. He waited an hour for the privilege. To reach Defurio, Coondick worked his way through a lineup, each player eventually falling victim to his honeyed words and magic fingers.

Defurio couldn't prevent the inevitable. He won a pot at the beginning. In the course of an hour, Coondick siphoned away his twenty dollars and the winnings from Defurio's single pot.

Maloney hadn't seen the carnage. He slept. Jim had his own skill, he could sleep sitting or standing.

Defurio returned to his status as onlooker, wedging himself between two of Coondick's squad mates. He asked them how Coondick acquired his name. "He wears one around his neck for good luck."

"What's it look like?" Defurio asked the natural question.

"We don't know."

"What?"

"He wears it under his shirt."

"So?"

"None of us have ever seen it. He says it would be bad luck."

Defurio laughed in appreciation of Coondick's devilish intelligence and flair. Apart from establishing a legend for never losing at poker, he had made himself memorable by planting a seed of curiosity not easily harvested from common experience. What exactly does a raccoon's penis look like?

Chapter 23

LZ 34

Couch clicked Defurio's camera, and even though he was loaded on vast amounts of beer and marijuana, the impish, freckle-faced delinquent retained an artist's eye for photography.

The picture showed a conglomeration of diverse characters. Whoever happened to be in the vicinity jumped in. There seemed to be a desire by these soldiers to memorialize, to show proof that they were hard-core grunts serving time in the highlands of Dnam and still alive.

Couch turned out to be an excellent photographer. Authoritatively waving his hands and arms, he vocalized instructions, maneuvering the unruly group, and was so irreverent and disregarding of rank, he didn't think twice about positioning Lt. Duke.

Couch, drunkenly taking into account distance, background, and lighting, had a natural eye for composition. He managed to take a studio quality photograph. The picture captured the unique attraction of opposites in a group of men.

The husky P.A., displaying attitude in dark glasses, stood looming over Lt. Duke and Arkansas standing in the foreground. Lt. Duke struck a gentlemanly pose, resting his helmet crossways at his waist. P.A. was wearing his helmet for the sole purpose of displaying the initials "P.A.". Arkansas, without a shirt, from second squad, casually held a beer in front of his pot belly.

Arkansas loved Big Jim like a brother, and frequently came looking for him. "Beeg Jeem, you in there?" He drew out Jim's name, squeezing an Arkie accent between two missing upper front teeth. Jim would sit inside, cringing at the mincemeat of English and low brow conversation he would have to endure.

Arkansas was the dentally challenged counterpart to Turner, first squad's resident marijuana fiend and V.D. aspirant. Turner wasn't in the picture because, as usual, the blacks congregated by themselves.

A non-white in the picture, Dong, a Vietnamese Kit Carson scout, was a friendly little guy who seemed harmless enough. Kit Carsons were members of the South Vietnamese Army attached to U.S. units. They had switched sides, formerly having fought with North Vietnamese forces. They were generally viewed with suspicion, Dong being an exception.

Thorpe didn't hold a beer. He drank whiskey from a cup. He could afford to be extravagant, knowing he could coast for a month before derosing for the States. Maloney had his arms thrown over the shoulders of P.A. and Defurio, and appeared to be his normal, sleepy eyed, friendly, scruffy self.

Two others joined the picture. Baxter, a fun-loving kid from third squad, had a boy-next-door likeability and next to him was Crenshaw, an expressionless pothead who had corrupted Fox into becoming a sullen misfit.

Defurio appeared as a broad shouldered, slender, laid back, some would say handsome, confident soldier. He held an upraised Falstaff in a salute to the fine accommodations at LZ 34.

LZ 34 rose as an isolated peak overlooking flatlands to the east. Low hills were to the west. Eastward, hamlets dotted fields of crops as far as the eye could see. The LZ housed an artillery group, which protected territory lying between Dak To in the south and Kontum to the north. Both cities could be seen hazily from the LZ.

B Company had been flown in five days earlier. LZ 34 was a showplace, the bunkers having been built by engineers. Wood beams supported ten-foot ceilings. Rooms measured ten feet square. Many apartments in Fresno didn't look this good, and they certainly beat ninety-five percent of houses in Pinedale, a farm workers community on the northern edge of Fresno. Shitters were nicely constructed of finished plywood and painted a semi-gloss brown. A brighter color might have presented a target. Partitions offered privacy for up to five defecators at a time.

It wasn't named for a girlfriend's erogenous zone or a manly attribute, so Defurio and Maloney surmised LZ 34 probably had a high minded meaning entirely unknown and irrelevant to them. The facility had been built two years prior, and this is where dignitaries were taken to show how well troops were taken care of in the 4th Division. Army general staff might falter in supplying drinking water to troops, but when it came to kissing ass, they were unsurpassed.

First squad claimed a mansionesque bunker. Big Jim pounced on a well-crafted Adirondack chair. Ward passed by. Jim, affecting an English accent, waved his hand at him as though Ward were a servant. "Light up my cigarette, my good man," he ordered snapping his fingers. "Then fetch me a dry martini, a Havana, and an English-speaking woman who'll fuck me blind. And, oh yes, draw a hot bath and lay out my smoking jacket and slippers." Even Ward laughed.

Having been on the move in the AO and in-transit at Bunker Hill, it had been impossible to send or receive correspondence. Donna didn't have any idea of the company's present good fortune. Also, bad weather had inhibited helicopter traffic since their insertion at LZ 34.

The weather broke, resulting in stored up supplies and mail pouring into the LZ. Men rushed the helipad for mail call. Defurio received two letters and two packages from Donna.

A shipment of beer fueled an already festive mood induced by the palatial bunkers, custom furniture made by an unknown craftsman, the unlikelihood of attack at the insular location, and hot food. Defurio opened a Falstaff, thankful not to have to force down another Black Label, and carried the two packages from Donna to a shady wall near the landing pad. He decided to open them immediately, in public, which he'd never done before. It was such a nice day. Winds cooled the LZ, chasing away remaining rain clouds. Employing his Boy Scout knife, he split the packages open and found among the cans and other food items, three packs of color film. This instigated the round of picture taking.

Maloney was passed over for promotion. Defurio consoled him. A promotion list had been posted and Jack was on it, but Jim wasn't.

Defurio didn't know and wasn't interested in knowing the designation of his improved rank, whether Pvt. 2nd Class or Spec. 3, "Spec" being an abbreviation for specialist. The importance of the promotion would be another $60.00 per month. Presently he was receiving $225.00 per month, including $40.00 combat pay. His allotment check to Donna would be increased to $265.00, with him keeping $20.00 for himself.

Privates and specialists were supposed to wear a stripe or special patch to designate rank, but no one did, even in the rear area. To combat soldiers, except for the designation of sergeant, these ranks didn't mean anything,

Defurio wasn't aware of the process of promotion. He hadn't requested a promotion or even knew he was being considered. Lt. Duke had probably taken into consideration that Defurio was married. Other than that, he hadn't done anything to distinguish himself. He and Jim had performed equally—doing what was minimally required.

Donna tried to stay busy. Her job helped, working as a part-time checker at a Safeway in Arvin, near Bakersfield. She joined a

Waiting Wives Club whose members were married primarily to officers. According to Donna, the wives were as jealous of rank as their husbands. She wasn't a very active member. On the other hand, a stock market class at City College proved challenging and rewarding. Numbers and dynamics of the stock market intrigued her. She maintained an A average.

At the urging of her card-playing father, Donna had reluctantly accompanied a cousin on what was intended to be a stress-relieving trip to Las Vegas. At the casino, she cashed an allotment check, exceedingly ashamed when asked, telling the clerk her husband was a soldier fighting in Vietnam.

A four-man Special Forces long range patrol team dropped in for an overnight stay. Jack and Jim engaged them in conversation. The LRPs said they were on their way to assassinate a village chieftain suspected of being a VC commander. While Jim talked to them, Jack snuck to where the LRPs had stowed their gear and stole six bags of their freeze-fried rations.

He reached to caress her. Poof! A dream. He awoke. Men shifted, coughed, snored. Emptiness overcame him. The luxuriousness of LZ 34 did nothing to appease his longing for her. He hated this fucking place, this miserable separation from Donna, this heartbreak, this longing, this purgatory of Vietnam. He rolled over in his bunk, swallowing his bitterness, trying to reclaim visions of her.

Chapter 24

Dak To

Defurio and Maloney were two of fifteen fortunate troopers accompanying equipment to Dak To. They flew an hour by helicopter while the rest of the company was trucked to Poliekleng. "Trout" was the Special Forces camp's new name. They'd been there before. Maloney's liaison with the beetle nut chewing Montagnard prostitute made Trout an easy association. Jim said when she pulled down her pants she had smelled like a dead fish.

Defurio and Maloney stunk. They'd been wearing the same fatigues and skivvies since Mary Lou. Disregarding their uncivilized condition, they went directly to an enlisted man's club and ordered a pitcher of beer. The place was almost empty. Indigenous personnel were in mess halls having lunch. A majority of B Company line guys had departed for known drug dens.

Dak To was home to an army base and air strip. Army bases had the amenities of Smalltown, USA, with billets for sleeping, hot food, showers, relative security, and cold beer. The effect of the chilled beer started with the touch of the mug to Defurio's lips, its contents spreading liquid pleasure throughout his body. They consumed two pitchers in rapid succession before sliding off their bar stools to investigate the area.

Exiting the club, the beers subdued the impact of a harsh sun. The rise and fall of straining aircraft engines met their ears.

Shading their eyes, they could see two WWII type single engine planes flying irregularly above the airstrip. They walked nearer to the airstrip to watch the show. Two Vietnamese pilots were clearly visible when they skimmed the airfield, practicing touch-and-go maneuvers. At first, Defurio thought they were performing stunts when he realized the pilots couldn't fly in a straight line if they had to. There wasn't any improvement as they made pass after pass. They never landed, and after wasting a lot of fuel, flew away.

A Cobra gunship alighted. The Plexiglas canopy flipped open and a lanky captain untangled himself from the narrow cockpit. Loosening his limbs, he strolled by where Jack and Jim were standing. They gave him a casual salute and he responded with one of his own. "Excuse me, sir, mind if I ask you a question?" A question had remained in Defurio's mind since Charmaine. The captain stopped, turned, and faced the grungy soldiers.

"Nope," he replied, displaying a friendly smile. Helicopter pilots were different from standard career officers. They didn't shit their rank on common soldiers. He addressed the captain as "sir," even through Defurio was the older man. He didn't mind talking to younger officers if they weren't overbearing assholes.

"Sir, can you tell us why a Huey flies at a treetop level when coming off a hill?"

"That's easy. RPMs, baby, RPMs. In other words, to gain speed." Not waiting or needing to be thanked, the captain wheeled and continued in the direction of the officer's club.

They came across a black GI in the company. Defurio had his Polaroid and the GI wanted a picture. He posed next to a pretty Vietnamese girl working on the base who wasn't a Montagnard. Defurio took the picture in trade for the soldier's boonie hat. These bush hats were wide brimmed, well-ventilated covers made of a cottony material that were sold by locals. The comfortable, practical green hats weren't authorized by the Army and weren't to be seen in the rear area. A black velvet headband on this one made it unique.

Defurio raked the hat forward to his brow and proudly paraded back and forth, sporting his stylish velvet banded sombrero.

Near the air field, they bumped into Couch drinking from a bottle of local rice wine. He offered it to Jack, and Big Jim snapped a picture. Jack, skin the color of burnt toast, was captured taking a swig from beneath the brim of his hat, his face almost invisible except for the whites of his teeth.

The fifteen vacationing soldiers regretfully boarded trucks on a convoy headed for Trout. Helmets were worn as protection from snipers. The convoy wound through rolling hills. This was farm country.

The trucks roared through a quaint farming village. None of the villagers could be seen, as they were out tilling the soil.

Some GIs can't help being assholes. Several felt compelled to toss smoke grenades from the uncovered bed of the deuce and a half. They targeted the open doorways and windows of the pristine huts bordering the roadway. Looking back at the scenic village, copious amounts of red, white and purple smoke billowed from doors and windows. Quite a few of the troops laughed. The Vietnamese would have another reason to hate Americans.

There was an urgency to the trip. The trucks carried reinforcements and a large quantity of ammo. LZ Trout had been receiving mortar fire and 122mm rockets. A ground assault was expected, but there was no way to tell the validity of the rumor. However, increased incoming oftentimes foretold of a coming ground attack.

They preferred to concentrate on the present. Jack saw that Jim didn't have Mona. "Jim, what the hell happened to Mona?" Jim grinned. He had pawned the brain damaged animal on an unsuspecting GI from A Company. Happy to be rid of her, he'd sold her for $30. Jim brightened further.

"Hey, Jack, maybe going to Trout is an omen. Maybe we can catch a fish." The exciting prospect blotted out Jim's unfortunate river experience with the Montagnard prostitute.

Chapter 25

Trout/Bass

The convoy arrived at Trout. Jumping off trucks, men expected to be deployed in defensive positions ready for action. Nothing was happening. Scattered troops were standing everywhere.

Platoons from various units had been cobbled together to form an emergency protective force. Shellings were occurring at night. During the day, troops were waiting shiftlessly for something to happen. Bunkers were overcrowded and soldiers gathered wherever they could find shade. Men in small groups were smoking and talking. LZ Trout could have been a factory town at quitting time.

Jack and Jim arbitrarily piled rucksacks next to a bunker. People were stuffed inside, so they stayed outdoors. If an attack ensued, they'd seek protection inside, crowding with whoever was in there.

Defurio was resting on top of a bunker when a Catholic chaplain came by. Without warning, he put a choke hold on Defurio, grabbing his bootlace necklace to which his dog tags were attached. The chaplain unceremoniously inspected his tags, which marked him as Catholic. He ordered Defurio to attend mass in ten minutes. It was Sunday, and the chaplain, a captain, walked on to scour the LZ for other Catholic sinners. Defurio didn't want to go to mass.

"Jim, you're Catholic, aren't you?"

"Yeah."

"Son of a bitch didn't inspect your dog tags. He checked me out because I'm Latino."

"A pretty goddamned dark Latino," said Jim. Never fair-skinned, Defurio had been further blackened by five months of basting in the rarefied altitudes of the central highlands.

The altar consisted of a rickety folding table set up in an isolated section of the LZ. It looked appropriate for the occasion. The chaplain had vestments covering his fatigues.

Defurio doubted a chaplain could legally order him to mass. Fuck it. It wouldn't hurt him and it would help the priest have a respectable turnout.

There were twenty souls in attendance. Defurio counted them when he was supposed to be praying. These temporarily reverent men, a preponderance of them Latinos, wanted a blessing in the worst way. They wore the frightened faces of the damned. The priest accommodated them in an abbreviated ceremony. It wasn't wise to stay away from the protection of the bunkers too long. Defurio snuck away before a wafer could be shoved in his mouth. He'd rather die honestly than as a hypocrite. There's no use trying to fool the presumed deity of the universe.

An attack didn't materialize. The expected invasion of Trout was based on faulty intelligence reports. The threat gone, B Company was transferred by helicopter to an unprepared LZ called Bass. Obviously, somewhere down the chain of command, a fisherman had replaced a sex monger as head of field operations for the battalion.

Maloney inveigled Defurio to build another two-man bunker, although he preferred going it alone. However, the project stimulated his imagination. He settled on a right angle configuration of equal wings joined by a common area where the sides connected. The equal sided L would provide semi-private quarters as well as a place for socializing. Defurio figured 4' x 10' sides would do it.

This would give them an approximately 4' x 4' cubby hole at the foot of their bunks for sitting, eating, and interacting.

Everyone set to work digging bunkers. Setting up an LZ is an unpleasant and irritating enterprise. People were on edge and men were rummy from so many moves, on top of recuperating from earlier losses of personnel. Replacements were arriving in bunches of two to five per week. The wearying effect of so many unknowledgeable recruits put a strain on everyone. Something sinister was in the air.

A bunker line formed twenty-five yards in from the jungle. They were on a low hill. Men were toiling like slaves in the 110° plus heat with heavy layers of humidity pressing down on them.

Ignoring the unpleasant conditions, Maloney and Defurio dug enthusiastically. The trenched outline of their dream hooch gave proof of an inspired design.

Taking turns shoveling, they were making good progress. Defurio was loosening ground using his entrenching tool as a chopping device, sweating furiously, and singing. *"I've been working on the railroad all the live longed days. I've been working on the railroad…"* Maloney snickered.

In mid-stroke a shout came from the landing pad. "Defurio, get your shit together, you're being transferred to Ennari." He dropped his shovel. Jack and Jim were shocked into silence. Defurio's mind became a cloud of confused thoughts. Was it a mistake? Was it temporary? What was the assignment? Fuck it. Even if it was a mistake, a day or two of sham time at Ennari would be welcomed.

Lt. Duke came to congratulate him. "Do you know what I'll be doing, Lieutenant?"

"Not exactly, battalion told us to get you ready, that you'd be filling a clerk position. They didn't say what."

Guys stopped digging to come and wish Defurio well. Many assumed he'd be taking over as company clerk, and some were requesting preferential treatment for R & R slots.

Maloney was shaken. Normally loquacious, Big Jim didn't say anything. Gradually his senses returned and he helped Jack take his gear to the landing pad. Half an hour elapsed in silence, neither knowing what to say.

"Jim, let's go back to the bunker. I'll help you build it while I'm here. A fucking chopper might not ever show up." Helicopter transport for individuals was hit or miss. There were higher priorities than giving a ride to a clerk.

Defurio was shoveling dirt into a sandbag when BLAM!!!, a close, unfamiliar explosion vibrated the ground. Its impact shook him. "Aw shit!" In a single motion, he flung his entrenching tool to the side, reached for his M-16, fell to his stomach, rolled to his back, chambered a round, and rolled again to his stomach, assuming a firing position. He stretched his arm to grab his bandoliers, which he had piled next to his M-16. Subconsciously, he patted his side pockets, reassuring himself that he had his grenades. His helmet was at the landing pad. He wished he had it on.

Maloney stumbled around, trying to figure out what was happening. He presented a fat target. "Get your ass down, Jim!" Reacting to Defurio's vehement urging, Maloney thudded to the ground. Ordinarily calm and cool, in an emergency, he became a deer caught in the headlights.

They scrunched belly down inside the half built bunker. Popping his head up and down to prevent being snipered, Defurio studied the jungle. "Par for the fucking course," he said, trying to calm Jim. "I'm on my way to a desk job and I get caught in a fucking ground attack."

Pursing his lips, Jack expended a ball of stagnant respiration. "Watch your side, Jim, and keep your head down." Defurio continued ducking his head up and down. This motion came straight from Jack's Uncle Gus. His uncle had perfected this technique as a scout fighting Japs in the Pacific. He had told Defurio of a young recruit who wanted to accompany him on a scouting mission. Uncle Gus didn't raise his head for more than two seconds to scan an area. This kid took three seconds and got a bullet in the throat.

"Okay, Jack." Jim regained control of himself.

Defurio did his mental calculations. No apparent casualties. So far, so good. They hadn't had time to set up claymores. Not so good. The company would have fifteen minutes to half an hour to hold off attackers. It would take that long for aircraft to get there. If they were in range of an artillery battery, the jungle could be lit up in minutes.

Inwardly he was prepared. Defurio was a realist and found it hard to believe he was going to the rear area anyway. Fuck it. He concentrated on what he had to do right here, right now.

He emptied his pockets of grenades and lined them up. There were twelve of them. He had a throwing range of fifty to sixty yards. His grenades would take a toll on advancing dinks. It was an advantage not to be inside a bunker, since it would become a death chamber if hit by a B-40 rocket. They had maneuverability and, if necessary, could run and seek safer firing positions.

There wasn't any shooting coming in or going out. No dinks showed themselves. Defurio and Maloney waited.

In a short while, word came down the bunker line that Dong, the Kit Carson Scout, had accidentally blown himself up when a pin had come loose from a grenade, not an entirely uncommon occurrence. Cotter pins locking down the handles sometimes became worn or corroded and broke off. Other times they snagged on something, pulling them loose.

What a relief. Jack and Jim leaned back and lit cigarettes. Dong's tragic death was incidental in the scheme of things, his value to the company being peripheral. More importantly, no Americans had been killed and there was no ground attack.

Defurio doubted he would be leaving that day. There were two hours of sunlight remaining, and helicopters didn't fly transport missions at night.

With the bunker walls almost finished, they were taking a break when a call went up from the padman. "Defurio, get your ass up here. Loach in five!" Loaches were bubble domed observation helicopters with a spare seat next to the pilot.

Defurio made for the landing pad accompanied by Big Jim. Men came to see him off. Defurio pounded out a round of one-potato fist bumps. He gave his hatchet to Couch. Despite Couch's obstreperousness, Defurio liked him; his independence, his entertaining orneriness. He tried to give away his cherished hand grenades. Nobody wanted them. Dong's mangled body remained smoldering on the bunker line. Defurio threw his grenades in the dirt.

The Loach would be announced by a distinctive buzz, an indicator of its quick, sharp pattern of flight. There! It zipped in as if it were a low flying water bug.

Defurio's heart pumped so fast his brain overloaded on oxygen. Elation! Each heartbeat seemed to call Donna's name. He framed his good fortune in relation to her. He could see her getting the news, her blue-gray eyes and silky soft lips open wide. Astonishment and relief. He would be one hundred times safer, and would be able to write rationally to her, not in fits and starts from inside dirt pits in bad lighting, between shootings, mortar attacks, patrols, visitors, translocations, and a bunch of other intrusions and distractions. His feelings centered on Donna, and this turn of events meant his chances of seeing her again would improve dramatically. At Ennari, he would be closer to her world, a civilized world of clean clothes, showers, hot meals, cold beer, beds, and roofed shelter—of death not being so menacing a presence.

Chapter 26

Ennari

He wrote two letters gushing in love to Donna on April 16, 1969. One was written in the morning on paper that had become dog eared, water stained, and smeared by moisture, dirt and rough movement. The second was written in the evening on unwrinkled, crisp, blue-bordered writing paper purchased at the spacious PX at Ennari.

Aided by soldiers in the company, Defurio had plunked himself on a canvass seat inside the incredibly noisy Loach. Even idling on the helipad, the craft emitted a high pitched whir. He had on his crisscrossed bandoliers, web gear, rucksack, helmet, and rifle. His equipment poked and rubbed against metal and plastic inside the confined cockpit. He was the fat lady holding packages from a fire sale who sits beside you on the bus.

The pilot, in flight suit and headgear, looked like a rocket man, his head encased in an unscuffed, enameled white helmet with a full-faced visor and built-in communication system. Defurio was unable to discern the man's features or voice.

The Loach whipped to a high volume, and with a thumbs up from the pilot, they rocketed into a brilliant sky. The small aircraft, much faster than a Huey, leveled off after a couple of minutes. Defurio had a bird's eye view of the highlands. From the safety of the heavens, the verdant topography seemed benign and tranquil. Defurio knew of the rot and savagery lying beneath its surface. A twinge of sympathy pulled at him for Big Jim and other GIs having to endure that awful jungle.

Defurio refocused. Nothing he could do about Big Jim and the others. He contemplated his future at Ennari. He didn't know what to expect. Whatever tribulations might be forthcoming, without doubt he could handle them. His emphasis shifted to curiosity and exuberant expectation. Anything would be better than what he had. What quiescent adventures were in store for him at Ennari?

An hour later, the Loach landed at Mary Lou, the firebase near Kontum. A double rotored Air Force helicopter had delayed its departure waiting for him. This must be an important damn job he was assuming.

A major and captain were inside, the captain acting as the major's aide de camp. "Wow," he thought. "I'm being escorted by two high-ranking officers."

Not exactly.

After a half assed mandatory salute by Defurio, the obsequious captain introduced him to Major Carrington, who had recently been transferred to the 1st/14th Infantry from the States and had chartered the helicopter to tour the battalion's area of operation. This was completely unnecessary. Defurio later learned Carrington didn't have any operational responsibilities for the battalion whatsoever.

At first blush, Major Carrington appeared as a typical senior officer flaunting his rank. Of this, there was no doubt: he was wasting taxpayer's money and military assets to go on a sightseeing trip just because he could. Yes, Major Carrington fit the mold of an archetypal rear echelon dilettante.

The rotundish, bespectacled major engaged Defurio in friendly man-to-man conversation. He didn't speak in regard to rank, and inquired of Defurio's education, where he grew up, and his infantry experience. Defurio reconsidered the man. He seemed to be a civilian at heart.

The Air Force helicopter had a sealed compartment that reduced engine noise, making a determined level of conversation possible. The major had a mouthful of overcrowded teeth and tended to spit when trying to make himself heard.

Major Carrington seemed to crave normal, non-military conversation. He and Defurio entered a lively discussion. Defurio asked the major where he had acquired his east coast accent. Carrington cheerfully acknowledged he had been born and raised in Boston and gave details of his upbringing. He had come from an upper crust military family that went back generations. This personal history solved the puzzle of how an egregiously unmilitary acting and looking Boston Brahmin could become a major in the U.S Army. Easy: family tradition and influence.

The smooth riding helicopter followed the road leading from Kontum running through Dak To to Pleiku. Passing Dak To, the demolished remains of LZ 34, which had overlooked this region, could be seen fading to the west.

Half way to Pleiku, the spirited dialogue between the major and Defurio came to a sudden stop. The chopper dipped low and circled a parked half-track, in front of which were five dead dinks. The dead were easily identifiable as VC because they wore what looked like delicate black sleepwear. NVA troops wore uniforms.

Major Carrington rapped his knuckles on the plastic window doorway separating the cockpit from the fuselage and pointed downward, wanting the pilot to land for a closer look.

Upon landing, the major and captain hastened to inspect the bodies. Not Defurio. He'd seen enough dead dinks and preferred joining the guys sitting in the shade of the half-track, smoking. They were stalling prior to dragging the bloody carcasses off the road, where they'd be soaked with gasoline and set afire. Two hours earlier, an alert member of the crew had spotted dinks sneaking up on them. The crew waited inside, watching the dinks until they were fully exposed. A sergeant stood up and ripped them apart by means of a mounted .50 caliber machine gun. Those bullets do horrific damage.

Major Carrington reverted to privileges of rank by putting on his asshole hat of authority. "You men," he addressed the seasoned kickass half-track crew. "I want you to clear this road in five minutes." He commanded them as if they were coolies. "If some deuce-and-a-half hits these bodies, they'll stink up the road for miles."

Defurio guessed Major Carrington would take some kind of credit for the successful defense of the half-track, thereby falsely earning a combat infantryman's badge. The CIB is a critical medal on the resume of an ambitious Army officer. And there is no officer in the military above a lieutenant who is not hungry for higher rank. Ironically, common infantrymen received CIBs routinely. For non-combat majors, it takes cunning and chicanery to achieve the award. Major Carrington needn't worry; his kiss-ass captain would be glad to make up a recommendation.

Near evening, the helicopter landed at the Air Force base at Pleiku. The base rivaled Bien Hoa in its dimensions. When the helicopter blades spun to a stop, normal hearing returned. A hollow rush of warm air invaded his ears. Defurio, his hearing accustomed to booms and blasts of ordnance and aircraft, discounted the routine protective sounds of war conducted at far extensions of the base.

He was in another world—a quiet, orderly world. He could have been in a sedate American town. There were some glaring differences: no women, every man in fatigues or uniform, and a scarcity of vehicular traffic.

The chopper had alighted in an asphalted landing zone near a chain link fence. The fence enclosed a baseball field with a pitcher's mound, back stop, base bags, and chalk lines. Men in baseball uniforms and cleats were taking hardball practice. A passing wave of incredulity went through him. Was this war? Was this Vietnam?

The major had called ahead for transportation, a jeep and driver awaited them. Defurio, marinated in field stink, crowded in the rear seat next to the revolted captain. Major Carrington, in the passenger seat, turned around. "Private Defurio, would you like a cold beer or a drink?"

"Yes sir, I would."

Carrington had taken a liking to the stray infantryman. He ordered the driver to take them to the nearest officer's club. The captain blanched.

To the relief of the captain, the officer's club was closed. Genuinely disappointed, the major rebounded. "Oh hell," he exclaimed, "we're putting the cart before the horse." Thereupon he ordered the driver to the mess hall. The jeep rode on paved streets between green lawned, two story dormitory style buildings. They approached a hangar operating twenty-four hours a day where hundreds at a time could eat.

As the trio entered, a buzz filled the hanger. Heads turned. Men gawked. These pansy-assed airmen had never seen a grunt come directly from the field. He was a creature from another planet. The fact that Defurio was hosted by a major and a captain added to the fascination.

Bent under his pack, carrying his dust covered rifle, wearing his badly scuffed helmet, torn flak jacket and filthy fatigues, Defurio knew he looked and smelled like shit. He didn't care. He thought to himself, "Yeah, you candy-ass motherfuckers, this is what a real life fucking grunt looks like."

Defurio couldn't eat half the food he placed on his plate. His stomach had adapted to parsimonious, tasteless field rations, not the tasty choice of plentiful meats, casseroles, vegetables, side dishes, and desserts set before him on steam tables and iced dessert trays.

Ennari was ten miles from the Pleiku Air Base, and Major Carrington wanted to get there before nightfall to lessen the chance of a VC ambush. The respective military bases were connected by a rough, unpaved road. Bumping through Pleiku, located half way between the air base and Ennari, Defurio's attention was drawn to schoolgirls walking at the side of the road, graceful and delicate as swaying willows. These elegant young ladies shyly refused to steal even a sideways glance at passing GIs.

They dropped Defurio off at the S-1 administration building, where all personnel matters in the battalion were overseen. Major Carrington offered a perfunctory goodbye to Defurio. "Take care of yourself, Private."

Major Carrington's abrupt good-bye would turn out not to be a show of indifference. He wasn't through with Defurio, not by a long shot.

Walking through the S-1 building, no one looked up from clattering vintage typewriters. It was after hours and half of the desks were empty. Thin wood planks spread on waist-high filing cabinets served as desks. Work stations were arranged haphazardly on both sides of a center aisle. Clerks wore ear phones, listening to music as they worked.

The forty by eighty foot building had a cement floor. Plywood walls framing the rectangular structure converted half way up to plastic sheeting. The building had a pitched corrugated tin roof. Gas fed generators provided electricity.

He got the attention of B Company's clerk. Sliding his earphones behind his neck, the clerk said, "Oh yeah, you're the battalion's new legal clerk." This is the first time Defurio heard his actual job title.

He signed in. Every company had its own clerk. Defurio would officially be carried on B Company's roster as though he were in the field. The B Company clerk looked to be in his teens. The friendly blond kid had a mismatched jaw, as if a jawbreaker were permanently lodged in his left cheek. He directed Defurio to supply.

The visually depressing layout of the grounds consisted of two rows of unpainted structures identical to the S-1 building. The rows were separated by a fifty-foot wide dirt road. Doorways fronted the road. The road ran for about a block before teeing off to other sections of Ennari. Buildings were approximately seventy feet apart. Supply was at the end of the block on the same side as S-1. Billets were on the opposite side of the road.

In falling darkness on the way to supply, as he did in the full light of day on his first days at Ennari, he didn't pay heed to a painted sign signifying the intriguing name of the battalion.

Staff Sgt. Perkins, a supply clerk from the Canary Islands, had the pleasing disposition and voice of a song bird. "Hello mista legal clerk," he sang in an accented alto voice.

Defurio surrendered his M-16 to Sgt. Perkins, where it would be placed in a locked rack in his barrack. "Make sure you put it in the right barrack." A soldier gets anxious when separated from his weapon. "Don't worry, mista legal clerk, I will," he responded, handing him five sets of boxers, socks, T-shirts, new boots, and two pairs of standard fatigues. The sergeant pointed him to the showers.

The showers were a two-man affair, located in a dimly lit hovel kitty-corner from the supply room. Defurio was by himself. He stripped and piled his rotten vegetable smelling socks, underwear, and fatigues on a shelf. Adjusting his vision, he detected a rope dangling from above and pulled it. A can tilted spilling water on him. Its coolness startled him. Sgt. Perkins had given him hand soap, wash cloths, and towels. Defurio lathered up and rinsed off layers of caked filth. His sweat-softened feet pressed gingerly on the shower's wooden slats.

He stepped into the night freshly washed and groomed, eager to start his rear echelon life. He looked down the road, trying to orient himself. Although low wattage street lamps helped, he had difficulty seeing anything clearly. There weren't any people around as he went down the row of billets looking for the number of his barracks.

Coming the other way, out of the dimness, a short, fat, sour-puss master sergeant appeared. He stopped, asked Defurio's name, and wrote it down on a clipboard.

He ordered Defurio to report for guard duty at 2000 hours. A soldier on guard duty had gotten sick and needed to be replaced. This didn't bother Defurio. He was in clean clothes, showered, and safe in the rear area. Guard duty in a fortified tower? No sweat. It was 7:00 pm. He asked the fat sergeant directions to the PX. Defurio wanted new stationery on which to write Donna. The pudgy sergeant ran through sketchy directions. Defurio could tell the sergeant resented helping him.

They happened to be standing in front of Defurio's assigned barrack. When he entered, it was empty of personnel, although mementos near bunks indicated occupancy. Defurio located a vacant bed. An actual bed! It had a thin mattress on top of woven wire, with a plywood locker at the foot of the bed. He'd set up the locker later. He reminded himself to buy a lock for it at the PX. He parted the mosquito netting and threw in his stuff.

The huge PX overflowed with an incredible variety of goods. He couldn't dilly-dally. It had taken a while for him to get there. The asshole sergeant's directions were insufficient, probably deliberately. Defurio purchased stationery and a lock for the trunk, and returned to S-1.

"Goddamn it, you were supposed to report to the guard tower at 8pm, not back here." Master Sgt. Buffano shouted apoplectically when Defurio reported to him. Personnel in the rear area had names printed on fatigues above the right pocket. In the better lighting, Defurio could decipher the name of the gruff sergeant. Defurio knew he was supposed to report directly to the guard towers, which were a 45 minute walk from battalion headquarters.

Defurio figured he could buy himself an extra forty-five minutes of freedom. "Oh, sorry Sergeant, I didn't hear you say that. I'll get right over there." Defurio stretched the forty-five minute walk to an hour and a half.

It wasn't a bad walk on a clear night. A zillion stars were on display. Defurio strolled, looking at the stars, thinking of Donna. He casually reported to his post at 9:30 pm.

Three men rotated guard, one in the tower, two others waiting in an adjoining above ground, cement floored reinforced bunker with four spring beds. Hell, Defurio had been in cheap motels that weren't this good. He said hello to a newbie soon on his way to the field. Poor bastard.

On a table lay a flashlight. Defurio brought out his writing materials. "Uh, sir, they told us it was a court martial offense to write a letter on guard duty."

"Why are you calling me sir?" Because of his age, rookies assumed Defurio was of higher rank. "Don't worry about it. At this location an officer would have to crawl a mile on open ground to catch me writing anything." The rookie hushed up. Defurio turned on the flashlight.

It soon went dead. Defurio had prepared for a dead battery, and pulled out a standard issue container of insect repellent. Using his Boy Scout knife, he cored out the plastic spray top and inserted some rolled-up toilet tissue from a C-ration pack. He lit the paper, which acted as a wick. The miniature torch lit up a corner of the bunker and lasted about twenty minutes. He had learned the trick three months ago from a guy in A Company. He had made a habit of raiding shipments of insect repellent. The men didn't mind, they wanted to get malaria so they could get a month of off for treatment.

Defurio wrote quickly and finished as the flame played out. Soon after, a jeep pulled up on the road behind the bunker and he heard his name called.

"Yo," he said as he emerged from the bunker.

"Get in."

"What the hell is going on?"

"I don't know. Sgt. Buffano is really pissed off. Some major called and ordered him to take you off the line."

From what Defurio gathered from the driver, Major Carrington had called to check up on him. When told he was on guard duty, Major Carrington unloaded on the prickly sergeant, asking him what the hell was he doing putting a man fresh from the AO on guard duty. From then on, men from the field were to be given a minimum of two days exemption from duty.

The driver took Defurio to the S-1 building. Inside, guys were drinking beer, some watching television and writing letters. Some were working. Two were playing chess. Defurio couldn't believe there was a TV.

He went in trying to find Woods, the legal clerk he'd talked to prior to leaving for the field. "You won't see him before morning," he was told by bemused clerks.

The clerks knew who Defurio was and they came up and introduced themselves. Cool guys. Defurio liked them instantly. An older guy, Conrad, suggested he go unwind at the beer hall. Defurio had seen the beer hall on his excursion to the PX.

"Good idea. I'll see you guys later." They sent him off with warm smiles. These men were birds of a feather. They'd been pulled from the field like Defurio and they knew what he'd been through.

Black troopers filled the beer hall. They were drunk and loud, hooting and hollering and making fun. On the juke box, of course, Motown ruled the night. Defurio joined a group at a round table. They welcomed him like a brother. These were grunts, many in the process of derosing. They were celebrating life. "Get a glass, man, get a glass." He went to the bar for a mug and a pitcher. They poured and poured, pitcher after pitcher. Blacks like to laugh and he loved their company. Defurio got drunk, seriously drunk. Happy drunk.

The special services sergeant in charge of the bar announced last call. Fifteen minutes until midnight closing. A last song. No one knew about it. It was a coincidence. Someone in this haven of soul music had made a mistake.

The song by a country and western singer, Bobby Bare, was called "Detroit City." The opening words instantly, and to the core, emotionally overpowered every grunt there. Tough, gritty men. They cried. Men got on tables, boots pounding time to the slow beat. They hugged and cried. Defurio, deep in the throes of drunkenness, didn't cry. He came close. Every nerve in his body screamed a yearning to be home, to be free from this place. The blacks hugged him. He hugged them back.

The words were sung in a rich baritone accompanied by a mournful guitar. *I want to go home, I want to go home. Oh, how I want to go home.* The song goes on to tell of a lonely man failing to make it in Detroit city. He dreams of returning home to the cotton fields of his youth, to his mother, father, brothers and sisters, and his lost love. *I want to go home, I want to go home. Oh, how I want to go home.* The simple words expressed the gut feeling and desire of every man there.

Leaving the beer hall in an ebullient stupor, Defurio went in the direction of his barrack. Under a half moon, Ennari was a stark, lonely place. He walked by himself. Negative thoughts flushed from his mind. He envisioned being safe, of not having to traipse through jungles, of not having to live like a mole in earthen burrows, of being clean and well-fed, of sleeping in a bed, of uninterrupted nights dreaming of Donna asleep in his arms.

He reached his barrack. Noisily he went to his bed and swept his possessions onto the floor. No one stirred. These field conditioned soldiers responded automatically to incoming, nothing else. He removed his boots. He didn't undress. He struggled to get through the mosquito netting. The bounce of the bed under his falling weight triggered a memory of home, of sleeping in a real bed. As slumber overtook him, Defurio repeated the same goodnights he had since being in Nam. *Goodnight, babe. Goodnight, Donna.*

Soon it was the 5:30 am wake up call. Defurio's mouth had the taste of a dead mouse. At 7:00 am formation the S-1 staff, soldiers going and returning from R & Rs, derosing GIs, medical referrals lined up across from Defurio's barrack. A day to day group of fifty or so men in five rows stood at ease on thinly applied, poor quality gravel. This was the end of the road for gravel dispersal in Vietnam. Defurio looked for Woods and didn't see him.

"Fuck". Glaring at them, his fat butt leaning on a wall of sand bags, was Master Sgt. Buffano. He was responsible for the roster and work assignments. A clipboard occupied his left hand. He checked off and wrote names. Once roll call started, he never looked up. He was interested in names, not faces.

For work details and guard duty, newbies were sacrificed first. S-1 personnel were selected sparingly due to the essential nature of their work. If necessary, newer appointees like Defurio were chosen.

Not wanting to incur Major Carrington's wrath, Buffano pointedly bypassed Defurio for extra duty. He would get to him sooner or later. Nothing personal. Somebody had to do these work assignments.

Before being dismissed for breakfast, the men formed a line to the north of the compound for the policing of the area ritual. Cigarette butts, gum wrappers, and other litter were to be picked up. Why not stick your hands in garbage before eating? In actuality, rookies harvested the debris. Everyone else faked it.

A common mess hall situated behind the barracks served the 1st/14th and an adjoining battalion. Meals were a notch above food served in field mess tents. The oily coffee was bitter, but would quickly become an acquired taste and a prerequisite to start the day. He didn't see Woods in the mess hall.

After chow, Defurio reported to S-1. Woods wasn't there either. Defurio sat on a swivel chair belonging to Woods. It had arm rests. Not bad. He rummaged through drawers, searching for pertinent items of interest, something he might study while waiting. He discovered a stack of porno magazines and other smut buried under legal documents. Paperwork lay in piles everywhere.

A clear plastic mat covered the green painted plywood desktop facing the aisle. Underneath the plastic were savagely funny caricatures of a legal clerk drawn in ink by a talented artist. One showed a Simon Legree character with slicked hair and a handlebar moustache holding the scales of justice. A hairy ball sack hung beneath his robe. Half of the scale tipped to the absolute bottom, and had on its tray the initials "UCMJ". Suspended at the top of the other tray was the word "you".

Woods wandered in. "Sorry Jack, rough night." Woods refrained from the military habit of using a last name. "I didn't forget about you, Jack." Woods had been responsible for pulling Defurio from the field.

"Don't worry, I'm not going to do to you what Scarpio did to me." Woods swore he intended to thoroughly train Defurio and simultaneously eliminate weeks of backlogged work.

Buffano came bursting in, extremely irritated that Woods had missed roll call. He had other complaints. "Goddam it, Woods, if you don't shave that Fu Manchu, I'm going to hold up your deros orders. And if you pass out at your desk one more time, I'm going to have you arrested by MPs." This seemed to be a legitimate concern, but easily resolved, as Buffano would find out. These were largely empty threats. Woods had two weeks left in-country and until then, he was in control the battalion's legal machinery. Unless he committed an overt illegal act, he was pretty much immune from judicial or administrative sanctions.

Seeing that his histrionics weren't having any impact, Buffano stormed out as pissed off as when he entered. Unperturbed as if he'd shooed away a gnat, Woods turned to Defurio.

"Dude, we gotta do something about your fatigues," he said while reaching inside a compact refrigerator sitting behind his chair. He handed Defurio a beer. Woods instructed Defurio to get extra pairs of fatigues from supply. "Place two sets in a bag at the foot of your bed. They'll be returned in the afternoon tailored, starched, and pressed. House dinks tailor and launder our fatigues for five bucks a month." Tailored fatigues were unauthorized, a rule uniformly ignored by the non-lifer clerks. Woods finished his beer. Defurio did likewise. It was 8:00 am.

"Let's get out of here." Pointing to mounds of paperwork, Woods said, "We'll get to this shit later."

They trekked to a distant bunker. Christmas tree lights decorated its interior. Wood's buddy, in dark glasses, was puffing on a seven foot bong made from beer cans and taped together sticks. Woods and his friend alternated hits. They offered the bong to Defurio. He declined. No problem. Jack had invisible credentials. Woods laughed, recalling stories he'd heard of Defurio's and Maloney's unmilitary exploits in the field. Woods puffed vigorously. Jack looked at his watch. 9:00 am.

By noontime, repeated tokes of opium laced marijuana had reduced Woods to a semi-catatonic state. His ability to walk, talk, and think diminished significantly. Interestingly, given his constant state of intoxication, Woods, when upright, managed to maintain an air of dignity. He held his chin up, never lowered his gaze, and stood ram rod straight. He and Defurio were the same height. Woods had narrow shoulders, looked undernourished, and had sallow skin. His dried stick appearance made him seem taller than Defurio.

They had lunch at the mess hall. Afterwards, Defurio accompanied Woods to his office. "Here," he said, "go over this. This is the Bible for everything we do." He opened a beer. Ask me any questions after you're through." He handed Defurio a copy of the Uniform Code of Military Justice. "Ah", Defurio thought, the UCMJ referred to in the cartoon.

His intestines groaned. Woods pointed Defurio in the direction of the battalion shitter. He walked to a nicely painted peak-roofed shed and opened the door to find a nice one-hole toilet seat. Privacy and toilet seats were unique. The high quality shitter had a magazine rack, and he unhurriedly read through a *TIME* magazine until he heard knocking.

"I'll be done in a minute," he responded. He exited, coming nose to nose with a bad tempered lieutenant.

"What the fuck you doing here?"

The lieutenant didn't let him answer. "This isn't yours. Yours is up there." He gestured irately. "If I catch you in here again, I'll Article 15 your ass." Easy to tell the lifer types.

Article 15? Defurio would get to know that term well.

Defurio's shitter troubles persisted. Later on, he found a squalid, splotched toilet that he discovered belonged to house dinks who squatted instead of sitting when going to the bathroom.

Eventually, a couple of days later, he made it to the enlisted men's shitter, an eight seater, the dead animal smell of which buckled knees of the unsuspecting. Locals hired for the purpose were supposed to burn the eight cans of waste daily. In practice, they went unattended for days. On his initial visit, gagging from the smell, Defurio placed himself over one of the bare plywood openings. He heard sloshing and looked between his legs. Two feet below roiled a colony of hungry shit and piss coated maggots. Sinking wads of toilet tissue were mixing in to help form a brown, lumpy sludge.

He spent two days studying the UCMJ, a well presented, clear set of legal codes and procedures that corresponded well with Defurio's criminal law background and legal training.

Defurio couldn't ask questions because he could never find Woods, who had followed Sgt. Buffano's order not to pass out at his desk. He didn't, he passed out outdoors. Defurio spotted him one morning at 8:00 am asleep in a drainage ditch at the side of the S-1 building. That was the last he saw of Woods.

Woods was a sergeant, and he must have done a hell of a job before burning out. Even in his present downtrodden condition, he maintained a certain respect from his colleagues. Maybe experiences in the field had caught up to him. Whatever. It didn't make any difference. Woods was a saint in the eyes of Defurio. He had done what a draft board, congressmen, the most decorated officer in the military, personnel clerks at the Presidio, and others had been unable or unwilling to do. Woods had saved his ass. How this drug addicted man rescued him seemed an impossibility. His effort would have involved an intricate knowledge and manipulation of protocols and procedures governing the personnel operations of the battalion.

After handing him the UCMJ, Woods disappeared. He never cleaned out his desk, bequeathing to Defurio his collection of pornography and months of unfinished work. His drug pals saw to it that he made it to the plane at Pleiko Air Base in time for him to deros home.

Chapter 27

Battalion Legal Clerk

Defurio received a sad letter dated April 18, 1969. Donna worried about R & R. They were planning for June, the earliest date he would be eligible, but she had been seriously sick. Because of the upcoming R & R date, she couldn't conceal her condition any longer. She had been ill since his deployment to Vietnam. She had contracted a series of stress related rashes and infections, culminating in an ulcerated bladder. She had written cheerful letters, not wanting her health problems to add to his worries. Defurio had done the same for her. However, letters underplaying his circumstances couldn't overcome the crush of media coverage highlighting casualty rates that were the highest of the war. Hundreds of GIs were being killed monthly. Donna lived tormented that Defurio would become a casualty.

He slumped in Wood's chair. Her letter slipped from his fingers, falling to the floor. He hesitated picking it up. He looked hard at the delicate curves of her writing. "Fucking Army, fucking, fucking Army!" His letters informing her of his transfer to Ennari wouldn't arrive for days. Anxiety concerning Donna's medical condition caused Defurio to reflexively feel his lip. He had to see a doctor about his sprouting growth. It hadn't become too ugly, but could soon. His trivial cosmetic problem didn't compare to Donna's health problems. She wouldn't care how he looked. However, if this growth went untreated, the sight of it would send her into an additional turmoil of worry. He needed to see a doctor.

Easier said than done. A medical appointment would have to be postponed. Woods had left months of untouched work. Defurio had to address this problem first. He got to work and stayed at it until 2 or 3 am every night. Within a week, he'd acquired the basics to do the job.

He consulted the legal clerk in the neighboring battalion, who was another teenage GI. He had become a clerk the hard way, having had a testicle shot off by an AK-47 round. He wasn't a legal scholar, but he gave Defurio a good foundation regarding forms and timelines for filing documents. Battalion legal actions had to be approved by Division. Defurio immediately determined prerequisites and specifications for filing legal charges. He easily grasped the technicalities involved in the job. However, he wasn't a proficient typist, and the ancient Underwood typewriter didn't make it any easier. It had a thick rubber band attached to the carriage, the other end tacked to the wall. This gave enough tension for the defective carriage to slide from one side to the other. Even so, he steadily made headway through the mountainous backlog. If he hadn't been exposed to daily shit in the AO, he would have thought his clerking responsibilities untenable. Now, wrapping his fingers around a cold beer in between shuffling paperwork, Defurio considered his job a blessing.

He learned that no one in the battalion knew shit about legal processes. Officers came by wanting to file actions that didn't have any legal validity. Based on his general knowledge, he could tell if complaints were legally sufficient or not, and explain why. He acquired an understanding of legal documents and requirements within two weeks. By the second week, he knew more about legal protocol than all officers in the battalion combined. Even though he was a low ranking private, Defurio had instantly acquired status, respect, prestige, and influence from being the battalion legal clerk.

The S-1 building hummed with activity until midnight. Keeping track of over a thousand men kept clerks busy. They worked independently, juggling hours as needed. Work days of twelve to sixteen hours were common. Clerks were assigned to each of four companies: alpha, bravo, charlie, and delta. In addition, there were specialty positions such as R & R and awards clerks. Like Defurio, most of them had served in the field as infantrymen.

Two career staff sergeants, specializing in personnel matters, oversaw the work of the clerks. Both were married. Sgt. Jewell followed in the tradition of able, responsible men running affairs of the personnel. A six foot, lean, sad-looking, hatched-faced chain smoker of moderate temperament, Sgt. Jewell exemplified competence. Defurio guessed his age at thirty-five. His partner, Sgt. Garinger, displayed a sharp intelligence when sober. Unfortunately, he fell into the category of a lifer drunk. After 5:00 pm., the official end of the work day, Garinger would sit at his desk and drink hard liquor, becoming soused by 9:00 pm. He finished each day by listening to recordings of his seven and eight year-old daughters, who shared their schoolgirl activities sprinkling, "I love you, Daddy" throughout the narrative. "We miss you, honey," came from his wife at the finish of the recording. Night after night, he degenerated into a slobbering inebriate while listening to his daughters and wife. His little girls' voices penetrated every corner of the S-1 building. He'd finally click off the recorder and stagger to the motor pool, where he'd check out a jeep and drive to Pleiku, where he lived with a local bar girl. Guys in S-1 said Sgt. Garinger seldom varied this pattern.

Article 15s, a term introduced by the bad tempered lieutenant protecting the sanctity of the officer's shitter, formed the bulk of Defurio's workload. They were so-called non-judicial punishments, meaning the alleged transgressor didn't have a right to a hearing.

Ordinarily, Article 15s were minor offenses referred by lifer sergeants and officers. They had to be signed off by the accused's ranking officer, most often a captain. Then they went to Division for approval and implementation of sanctions.

There were two grades of Article 15s; company grade, those filed by company clerks and subject to Defurio's approval, and battalion grade filed by Defurio. Company grade wasn't a problem. Punishments were restricted to extra duty and a reprimand. Battalion grade Article 15s, however, had serious repercussions, including an almost automatic reduction in rank and commensurate reduction in pay. Most were generated in the rear area. Commonly, intoxicated soldiers failed to salute officers, failed to carry out a minor order, cussed at sergeants or officers, disturbed the peace, or openly used marijuana. Defurio balked at filing papers against good soldiers. Often by the time paperwork was filed, many of the transgressors had returned to the field and were under fire. Reluctantly, captains in the field were compelled to sign the documents.

He realized that if paperwork didn't get referred to Division, no action would be formally taken or recorded, with nothing showing on the record. Defurio got in the habit of setting aside Article 15s, at least those he concluded were unjust. If no follow-up inquiries were made, he destroyed them. Everyone concerned assumed official action had been taken. Defurio never breathed a word to anyone about this. It didn't save him any work, he merely didn't forward them to Division. He supposed that many a soldier wondered why he never officially received a reduction in pay and rank, obtained regular promotions and why, when separating from the Army, his Article 15 and its punishments never showed on his record. Defurio had appointed himself judge and jury in the dispensation of justice. He loved his job.

The roomful of clerks respectfully gave him space, letting him find his comfort zone and giving him time to adjust to the daunting nature of his assignment. They knew about him. They had access to his records and knew his test scores, his education, his age, and that he was married. By general knowledge and word of mouth, they knew of his experience in the field and about Chu Pa. They had also heard of some of the shit that he and Maloney had pulled in the field. Unknown to him, Defurio had already acquired a measure of respect and stature.

"Defurio!" Sgt. Buffano shouted happily, appointing him to that night's guard duty roster.

"He's exempt, Sarge." The words came from the middle of the formation. They were spoken by Sgt. Dicicco, appointed as liaison between the personnel sergeants and staff clerks. Dicicco, a draftee, had a jolly disposition and a fine sense of humor, and didn't mind twisting a lifer's shorts in a knot whenever he could.

"What?" Sgt. Buffano said, highly agitated.

"Check your exempt roster. Captain Smith put him on it because of the shitload of work Woods left behind." Muttering cuss words, Sgt. Buffano disgustedly signed up some other poor slob for guard duty. At his signal, the formation aligned itself to police the grounds.

Clerks pretended to pick up trash. Defurio sidled up to Dicicco. "What was that about?"

"Sorry, my fault, I should have told you." Dicicco bent and brushed the top of his boot, giving the illusion of picking up trash. "It was a last minute thing. I knew you'd be up to your eyeballs in shit so I asked the captain to exempt you."

"Thanks."

"It's temporary. When you're caught up they'll put you on the duty roster again."

"If I can eliminate that pile of crap in my office, it'll be worth it." Defurio referred loosely to his unpartitioned confines as his office. "Let me ask you something, Sergeant."

"Forget 'sergeant.' Call me Louie. It's Louigi, but no one calls me that." Defurio noticed most everyone in S-1 went by their first name.

"Alright, Louie. Is it my imagination or is Sgt. Buffano out to get me?"

"Pleiku Fats? Don't worry about him. He's a joke. He's always like that. He's got a sharp stick permanently shoved up his ass."

Pleiku Fats uttered some form of misplaced, off the mark or incomprehensible ranting at every formation. His nickname had a humorous context in that it accurately described his portly physique. Fats never smiled, stayed agitated, and his smirk was irreversible. He didn't speak normally. He spat words. Fats reminded Defurio of Yosemite Sam, the cartoon character, minus the moustache.

B Company's clerk sat at his desk located across the aisle near the rear of the building. It was after hours and Defurio needed to talk to him about R & R. He didn't know what to expect. Defurio drank three beers in rapid succession. Seeing him approach, Johnson removed his headphones placing them by his recorder. Johnson, like the other clerks, was white, that's why psychedelic rock, not soul music, leaked from his headphones. *"Take a little piece of my heart now, baby."* Janis Joplin's voice escaped from his headset. *"If it makes you feel good..."* She sang in a drawn out, sexually charged way.

"Hi Fred, I want to ask about R & R for June."

"Sure. There are two available slots."

"I'd like to go at the earliest possible date."

"You got it." The youthful clerk jotted a note. "See Sine to cut your orders."

Sine's desk sat partially behind a mimeograph machine and some cabinets. Sine, the R & R and awards clerk, went by his last name. He didn't like his first name, Duane, and requested not to be called that. Sine had unhooded ice-blue eyes, a smiling mouth of white, even teeth, short cropped Julius Caesar style hair, and the wide hulking shoulders of an athlete. Defurio estimated his height at 5'10". He was second oldest of the staff clerks, behind

Defurio. He came from the Midwest and was married. Sine welcomed him, but made a point of not initiating the black power handshake that had been adopted by white troops. Sine wasn't especially fond of blacks. He approved Defurio's R & R request without hesitation. Unmarried applicants having more time in-country than Defurio would have to go elsewhere. Clerks gave each other preferential treatment.

Sine had another motive for not sending unmarried soldiers to Hawaii. He said they were often religious types who were virgins and, commendably, trying to take advantage of an opportunity to visit siblings, parents, and grandparents in a vacation paradise. According to Sine, this ran counter to natural instinct, so he did them a favor. He unilaterally directed them to the flesh pots of Asia, in particular, Bangkok. There, answering the call of hormonal needs and repressed lust, they easily surrendered to pent up carnal passion by getting their virgin brains fucked out.

Proof of Sine's success in fulfilling the wildest dreams of these sexual novices wasn't hard to come by. When returning to battalion, the former virgins invariably couldn't stop talking about how much fucking they'd done. Wanton fucking. When Sine finished telling of his contribution to mankind, he broke into a wide smile, which seemed to defrost his ice blue eyes. Defurio shared a good laugh with his new friend.

Pleiku Fats whistled for the 7:00 am formation and made a short, depressing announcement. Division personnel at Ennari were temporarily being converted to a reactionary force for the purpose of conducting a three day sweep of territory lying south of the city of Pleiku. Tomorrow at 9:00 am, ammo would be distributed and troops loaded on trucks for delivery of the reactionary force to the field.

The next day, the battalion assembled at 8:30 am for distribution of ammunition. They were marched in orderly fashion to ammo boxes. This was premature and manifestly stupid since troops had not yet been issued weapons and didn't know what ammo to draw. Heavy metal lockers of ammo had been hauled in for the occasion. Lifer sergeants in charge couldn't find keys.

Defurio and the whole troop broke into laughter and hoots. "Way to go, Sarge." "I smell a promotion." "You guys are the best." The assemblage rearranged themselves in loose clusters, smoking and bullshitting, waiting for the lifers to get organized.

Embarrassed, feeling harassed, and overwhelmed, Fats went directly to the captain's office located at the rear of an enclosed portion of the S-1 building. Captain Smith, a handsome, well-built, wholesome looking captain-of-the-football-team type, intensely disliked being disturbed by non-coms. Underneath his wholesome façade lurked the disposition of a rattlesnake. He could be overheard reaming Fats. "Why don't you guys get your fingers out of your asses and try using your heads for once?!"

His door flew open, loudly banging the side of the building. Fats, red-faced, slinked behind him. Captain Smith promptly put three non-career S-1 sergeants in charge, ordered them to pick squads on the spot, and mandated weapons be issued under direction of the sergeants, followed by distribution of ammo. If keys couldn't be found, the locks were to be busted open. That was it. Captain Smith huffily returned to his office, violently slamming the door and seriously damaging it. It hung precariously by a single hinge. The captain's irate display had completely captured the attention of the assembly. The distraction allowed Fats and his crew of incompetents to flee the premises unnoticed.

"Oh, bullshit," Dicicco said with a smile. He had assigned Defurio an M-60 machine gun, who had flatly refused to carry it. When Dicicco asked why, Defurio repeated the same excuse as when he had unsuccessfully tried to get out of the SRP patrol, but what had worked for him to get out of carrying the radio on that same patrol. "I'm inexperienced. I haven't fired an M-60 since basic."

"Fuck that. You're taking it." Defurio's excuse was indeed bullshit. He was a trained infantryman and knew how to load and fire the damn thing. Dicicco was a good guy and didn't begrudge the effort to avoid toting the heavy weapon. He gave Defurio a concession. He assigned him an in-transit newbie to be his personal ammo carrier.

Oversights are an inevitable part of every military operation. In Defurio's opinion, grander missions generated a disproportionate number of logistical and strategic fuck-ups. This was a division wide enterprise, and his thesis was sure to be tested.

The nature of this mission was different from the outset. There wasn't the sense of apprehension normally associated with an offensive action. Defurio couldn't determine if this was a real military operation, a training exercise, or the result of a wild hair up some general's ass. He suspected the latter.

Lifer sergeants were hardly ever in the field. In this operation, several battalion staff sergeants including Jewell and Garinger participated. And they didn't look at all worried. If there was something amiss, they would be aware of it.

Hundreds of clerks interspersed with rear guard infantry fanned out in multiple single files. There was an uncharacteristic casualness in conducting the sweep. They had the advantage of a flat plateau, so lumping the M-60 wasn't a problem. Harkening back to old Tarzan movies, Defurio had his ammo carrier call him Bwana. The unsophisticated white kid would ask, "Bwana, can we stop for a rest? Bwana, is it okay if I have a drink? Bwana, how long have you been in-country?" Defurio fed him lies of personal heroism. Newbies were so gullibly entertaining.

A surprisingly sprightly Sgt. Garinger, forcibly sober, passed him. "What do you think, Defurio?"

"It's great, Sarge. Let me ask you a question though. Is there a name for this campaign?"

"It's called operation Iron Hammer," he said happily, speeding past Defurio. Sgt. Garinger seemed relieved to be unchained from his desk and his compulsion to listen to the nightly hauntings of his daughters and wife.

Not so much as a rabbit sprang from the dry, weedy plateau fringed by family farms. Hours passed. In late afternoon, temperatures of 115° began taking a toll on the pampered clerks. The inevitable happened. How could goddamned senior staff idiots not prepare for delivering water to hundreds of troops trudging through a tropical hot box? The majority of clerks drained canteens before sundown. By habit, Defurio conserved his water, taking sips not full swallows.

Water flowed languidly in shallow, narrow irrigation ditches bordering cultivated vegetable fields. Foolishly, men drank from them and filled canteens with the slimy, brackish water.

Squads were directed to set up L-shaped ambushes. Defurio grabbed shade in some scattered banana trees. Two hours of sunlight remained. He told squad members not to drink the obviously contaminated water.

The benefit of an ambush is surprise. In this respect, squads wasted their time. The entire division was on open ground. Anyone could see an ambush being set-up. Montegnard villagers walked freely through them until nightfall.

The next morning, medevacs filled the sky. The encampment had become a sewer. Men, cramping, vomiting, and too sick to pull down pants, had diarrhea running into their boots. Potable water had come too late. Unable to function as a viable fighting force, the troops were being evacuated. Iron Hammer had come to a screeching halt a day after it started. The Army had brought about a stinging defeat of itself without having fired a shot.

Defurio completely rearranged his office, placing forms, documents, and legal manuals in logical order. He kept Wood's pornography, but separated it from legal paperwork. There were volumes of regulations and procedures for every legal action taken.

Battalion paperwork was forwarded to Division, and by them to the Adjutant General's Office. The Adjutant's Office had real lawyers and sharp legal clerks. Defurio established an excellent rapport with them. He had gone to Division, introduced himself, and asked them what pitfalls to avoid. It helped that clerks universally shared anti-Army views. They were basically civilians in Army clothes.

"Bring the guilty bastard in," the captain said, initiating guffaws from subservient lieutenants. A quorum of three officers, which had to include a presiding officer with a rank of captain or above, composed a special court martial.

Defurio acted as puppeteer in court martial proceedings. He pulled the strings, directing officers what to do according to a manual he understood and they didn't.

"Goddamn it, Sergeant, can't you get somebody else?" complained the captain. Defurio had appointed him as the presiding officer. Although requiring the S-1 captain's signature, it was Defurio who cut orders for special court martials. He named a panel from a roster of available officers, and the ones he appointed would invariably squeal in protest when notified to report for court martial duty. They called him sergeant presuming he held that rank. "Sorry, sir, you're it." Officers understandably detested being taken from leisurely pursuits to sit as ignorant judges.

Special court martials imposed sanctions beyond that of Article 15s but stopped short of incarceration, which could only be authorized by a general court martial conducted by lawyers at Division.

Special court martials were officially impartial. In practice, the accused's guilt was predetermined. It was an efficient system for delivering swift justice for outrageous breeches of conduct. An example would be a wrongdoer pointing an unloaded rifle at a non-com and saying, "I'm going to blow your head off." A general court martial would handle the matter if the accused actually shot at him.

Being so busy during the day distracted Defurio's loneliness from Donna to a certain extent. Evenings were slower, giving him an opportunity to sit in his office looking at her pictures, dreaming. "Two more months until R & R." He touched the loose sprig of flesh on his lip, feeling that it had branched. "Damn, I've got to see a doctor."

Big Jim sent a letter from Cam Ranh Bay hospital, where he was recovering from a bout of malaria. Good for him. A month of sham time. Naturally, he had a story to tell. No sooner had he gotten there than the hospital came under a rocket attack. While nurses and orderlies tended to bedridden patients, Jim ran for cover, taking refuge in an outside bunker. There weren't any injuries. He sent a picture of himself standing by the bunker in white boxers. Jim described resort-style living, sandy beaches, waterskiing, cold beer, and warm nurses.

Defurio had two other listed duties, casualty clerk and public information specialist. The latter job he didn't worry about. That duty had been totally neglected by Woods. Company clerks had assumed the responsibility by default. Hometown newspapers were regularly and efficiently notified by the dedicated clerks whenever soldiers were promoted, received awards, wounded, or killed.

Casualty clerk was an essential responsibility that entailed receiving radio reports of those killed or injured anywhere in the battalion at the time of occurrence. This initiated a process granting Purple Hearts and entry of data in Army records.

"Jack, you like to play ball?" Sine entered S-1 bouncing a basketball.

"Where'd you get that?"

"I bought it at the PX. Well?"

"Hell yes. It's second to sex on my list of hobbies." Sine flashed a toothy grin.

After dinner time, guys worked at a slower pace. Socializing increased.

"Jack, let's go take some shots." Sine headed for the rear side door of S-1. "I'll get a broom." Unbelievably, behind the S-1 building across a narrow road stood a concrete, dust covered half-length basketball court. An inconspicuous basketball pole and hoop had blended in with far off mountains. At some time or another, a high-ranking officer liked playing basketball. In recent times, the barren court had fallen into disuse.

Seeing Sine take a couple of jump shots improved Defurio's mood considerably. He tossed the ball to Jack, who made a layup and a jump shot. The feel of the pimpled ball on his palms and fingers transported Defurio home to Romaine playground, a teenager shooting hoops on a hot summer's day.

They engaged in a friendly but fierce feeling-out game, testing each other's ability. Sine drove to Defurio's right, expertly handling the ball with his left hand. Over Jack's outstretched right arm, he banked a ten foot half layup, half jump shot. He wouldn't have that shot again. Defurio would crowd space to Sine's left.

Sine missed an ensuing straight up fifteen-foot jump shot. Defurio's right elbow kissed his nose but not enough to call a foul.

Defurio got the rebound. He dribbled back to the free throw line (or where the free throw line would have been marked). He faked right, turned, and pivoted to his left, swishing his patented turn around jump shot. The ball dropped cleanly through the rotted net clinging to a side of the hoop. Sine took note. He would be prepared for that shot in the future.

Adapting to playing in jungle boots, both men faked and shifted dribbles from hand to hand, improvising moves to get away shots. They were evenly matched. Sine was a natural athlete,

Defurio a natural competitor. The man to man game fostered a mutual respect and cemented a growing friendship.

On a late afternoon shortly after assuming his new duties, Defurio was called to the commo shack, located in a reinforced bunker behind the barracks. Gobbler was in charge of monitoring radio traffic for the battalion. A burly, outgoing Mexican enlisted man, he could mimic a gobbling turkey perfectly. He pumped his Adam's apple loosely to affect a gobble indistinguishable from the real thing.

Defurio put on the head set. "Hello," he said, disregarding phone protocol. He spoke into a microphone sitting on a table. A low power light bulb hung from the ceiling giving an eeriness to the room.

"Dragon Slayer?" The lieutenant on the other end of the line said correctly, referring to Defurio's call sign. "Yeah," he responded, extending his abuse of protocol. The lieutenant spelled the name of a soldier who'd fallen off a footbridge and drowned in a river. His body wasn't recovered.

Defurio made entries on a simple one page casualty form, then forwarded the information immediately to Division. He hung up the phone.

A drowning? Perturbed by his inaugural transfer of information concerning a dead soldier, Defurio slowly walked toward his barrack. He gazed up at the beginnings of a starry sky, mulling over his role as casualty clerk and realizing he would be forced to take unwanted looks at tragedy.

Fucking Nam. It had found a new way to perplex him. He reached the barrack and opened the screen door, trying not to let it slam behind him. He adjusted his thinking, rationalizing like he always did when shit hit him in the face, thinking, "Fuck it, I'd rather be a chronicler than a victim of this fucked up place."

His initial recording of a soldier's death had drained him. He would get used to it; there would be many more. After parting the mosquito netting surrounding his bed and crashing onto the thin mattress, he said his nightly goodbyes to Donna. He laid the back of his head on the pillow and fell asleep instantly.

Chapter 28

R & R

Afternoon pickup games of three on three or four on four became routine. Sine and Defurio were the dominant players. They became good friends.

In another positive development, Dennis Sinksen was brought from the field to become B Company clerk. He quickly became one of the mainstay basketball players. Defurio had two close intelligent, mature, ball playing buddies to help him pass the hours and days. Another older clerk, Conrad, was teaching him to play chess. He had even set up weights in an unoccupied bunker so he could maintain Big Jim's exercise program.

"I hate to see a full grown man jump through his ass," Dicicco said, referring to a recently arrived lieutenant who had mistakenly reported to the wrong battalion. As a non-career sergeant supervising S-1, Dicicco had a talent for efficiency while maintaining a loose, relaxed working environment. He loved to poke fun at officers and lifers. An exception was Jewell and Garinger, who were off limits for derogatory comments. Even though Garinger was an afterhours drunk, both men had the respect of the clerks.

Defurio slid comfortably toward his R & R. Sine had given him the earliest possible date for which he was eligible, June 2. Guided by Donna's suggestions, he bought civilian clothes at the PX, purchasing pants and a swim suit to fit his thirty-inch waist, five loose fitting shirts, one for each day of R & R, and a Samsonite suitcase.

He established a comfortable balance between taking care of ongoing business and eroding heaps of work neglected by Woods. Defurio, at last, had an opportunity to see a doctor.

"Done." It had taken the doctor less than ten seconds to freeze dry the offending tissue. The branchy clump disappeared, barely leaving a mark. There wasn't a drop of blood. Defurio had expected a surgical procedure, and was greatly relieved that he wouldn't have unsightly and bothersome stitches in the way when he met Donna.

After living in shit for five months, he was having a miraculous run of good luck. He had a satisfying position of influence, was relatively safe, and his early R & R assured. He enjoyed the company of his peers, and thrived playing ball, lifting weights, eating hot meals, taking daily showers, wearing tailored fatigues, and in some instances, telling officers what to do. His work had become manageable and finally, his bottom lip was perfectly healed.

At midnight, Defurio was called to the commo shack. "Dragon Slayer" he said sleepily into the mike. Two soldiers at a listening post had been attacked by a tiger. One had been badly clawed, the other killed instantly, his head bitten through.

Casualty reports didn't require a lot of time. Defurio spent less than five minutes per report. Transmitting information to Division as soon as possible was the priority. If a man was shot in the face, he wouldn't know how badly; it could be a flesh wound, or part of a man's brain destroyed. He merely noted what part of the face or head was damaged.

Casualty reports came in sporadically day and night, a preponderance of them coming at night. They were often senseless, as when a soldier twirling a .45 caliber pistol cowboy-style shot himself in the neck.

Defurio didn't mention casualties to Donna. They would have saddened her too deeply. He put in sixteen-hour days, and the combination of work interspersed with playing basketball, drinking beer, bullshitting, and learning chess helped lessen the intensity of waiting to see Donna in four weeks.

On May 31, Defurio was driven by jeep to Pleiku air base. From there, a C-130 cargo plane would fly him to Cam Ranh Bay, where he would exchange military script for dollars and wait for his flight to Hawaii by commercial jet.

C-130s had an upswept tail section. A hydraulic ramp underneath the tail allowed for loading. As he went up the ramp, he felt a twinge under his right ankle bone. He'd twisted it when he began playing basketball and had sustained the injury on a driving layup. The cement court rose three inches above the ground and ended about a foot beyond the basketball pole. He folded an ankle coming down on the edge of the cement. This minor injury wouldn't prevent him from accompanying Donna wherever she wanted to go. He smiled, relieved and confident regarding his overall physical condition.

The twin propellers whined liked sirens when the craft ponderously bumped down the runway. C-130s were designed for short takeoffs, therefore, they required maximum power from a standing start.

Defurio and other troopers sat inside a naked fuselage. Wires overhead played tug of war when the pilot pressed or released pedals. Condensation dripped from exposed pipes in the ceiling. In a rattling hulk of vibration, the craft became airborne. There weren't windows to offer passing scenery to indicate lift off. "I hope this motherfucker can make it," Defurio jokingly shouted at a private packed next to him. The terrified private nodded.

Cam Ranh Bay had wide beaches and ocean inlets guarded by mountains and an adequately strengthened Army garrison. Occasional harassing rocket or mortar fire did minimal damage.

The spacious base acted as a transfer point for GIs leaving and coming from R & R or going home. Most GIs happily returning toted the latest model recorders, head sets, and tapes. A majority of them had less than two months to go in-country.

Poker games abounded. MPs participating as players, not policemen, controlled high stakes games. Many MPs stationed at the base had the skills of professional gamblers.

Defurio preferred sitting at the enlisted men's club satiating himself with thoughts of Donna. He repeatedly thumbed through his picture album of her. The battered album had survived rain, sweat, and mud. Until now, he had doubts he would ever see her again. He found a place in the corner, wanting to be by himself. Sipping beer, looking at her, his heart warmed thinking of the various tones she used pronouncing his name. Seeing a baby, she would gently grab his arm and say, "Jack, look at that." In a department store, she'd yell, "Jack" in a way that sounded like "Jock." "Jock look at this," she'd say, holding up a garment. When irritated by him she'd say, "Oh, Jack" or "Jeeze, Jack" in a mild reprimand.

She invoked subtle intonations when speaking, and had a knack for personalized inflections, giving everyone she talked to a sense of importance.

He could hear her calling him "babe." "Babe, what do you think about this? Babe, what do you think about that? Babe, look at this." He smiled and ordered another beer.

After setting down in Honolulu, Defurio and the other R & R soldiers were bused to Ft. DeRussy to meet loved ones waiting outside the gate. Through the ornamental iron gates could be seen rows of well maintained, nicely landscaped bungalows. By all accounts, Ft. DeRussy offered excellent accommodations for soldiers and their families. However, being an Army facility, Defurio wanted no part of it.

An excited throng of merging couples congregated on DeRussy's asphalt entryway. He met Donna with passionate kisses and hugs. God, she felt good. "I love you, babe, I love you, babe," they said in between kisses. A sergeant holding a clipboard signed him in. Free to go, they dashed for a cab. "Holiday Isle," he told the cabbie exuberantly. Donna had booked an inexpensive hotel two blocks from Waikiki.

Block after block of Japanese-owned high rises walled off Waikiki and the beach couldn't be seen from the cab.

They had five days. They would cling together as only desperate lovers can, catching the light and indulging in the white hot intensity of their passion until the inevitable longing and return to the unbearable loneliness of separation.

Reaching the hotel, they went to their room, fell on the bed, and didn't get up for hours. She touched him softly on the face, "I'm hungry," she said dreamily. Neither of them had eaten since breakfast. It was 6:00 pm. They showered and dressed. The sun hadn't gone down completely, and to her dismay, Jack brought out his Polaroid. She protested, but he insisted. If she hadn't loved him so much, she wouldn't have done it.

"Donna, put your arm up on the window frame."

"Oh, Jack."

"Tilt your head a little bit."

"Jack, this is silly." She had on a sleeveless sun dress.

In their room, she stood in front of a five by four foot window. They were on the seventh floor. Nearby hotel construction hadn't yet risen enough to block the light. Fading sunshine played on the contours of her bare shoulders and upraised arm. Sunlight followed the delicate curve of her neck. This would be the sole record of their five day stay at the Holiday Isle.

They ate at Gus's Steak House on the ground floor. Jack ordered prime rib. Delicious. "Why don't you order another, Jack?" He did, consuming it with equal relish. Two months ago, he wouldn't have had room in his stomach for four mouthfuls.

In daytime, they rented a car and went to isolated beaches on the other side of Oahu. They wanted to be by themselves. "Donna, pull up your skirt." She sat on a beach in her swimsuit. "Hold your knees and look at the ocean." Shyly, she did. Aggravated, she reluctantly complied while Jack excitedly busied his Polaroid.

They ate breakfast and dinners at Gus's. They reserved lunches for picnics somewhere on the opposite side of the island. Donna had on her sun dress; blue almost black, the hem line well above her knees. Giant centers of flowers were imprinted on the dress radiating oversized colored petals. She wore her sun glistened hair high in front and pulled back to the bottom of her shoulders.

He spent a day photographing her on Waikiki. Because of her discomfort posing for photos, he didn't insist that she smile. Two Hawaiian girls, sisters, about seven and eight were behind him playing. Donna stood in an unaffected statuesque stance, resignedly looking down the sun drenched beach, arms to her side, holding straps of a purse in her left hand. While pointing his camera at her, she suddenly smiled, fascinated by the two Hawaiian girls playing. Defurio happened to catch her unsolicited smile on camera. This would become his favorite picture of her.

On their last day, sunshine greeted them rather than the cold of a nighttime Alameda mist. They embraced. They kissed; warm, tender kisses, innocent kisses, tongues not leaving their mouths, desperate kisses of farewell, not the nighttime, hungry kisses of lovers; kisses of longing, of lips not wanting to part for fear of never touching again. He had to leave. He got on the bus. She cried, sobbing his name again and again.

The fierce pain of separation resumed — like a kind of dying, a kind of slow bleeding.

Chapter 29

Return to Ennari

After Donna and Hawaii, the sight of Ennari was revolting. In its drab, beaten down way, it could have been the distorted analogy to a thousand LZs. It occurred to him that before leaving for Hawaii, he'd gotten used to the depressing sameness of Ennari. It had represented a hint of civilization. What a joke. In the honest light of day, it was nothing but leveled dirt stripped bare of vegetation replaced by a monotony of hundreds of one story dirty white corrugated roofed boxes, a place of forced servitude by uniformed indentured servants.

Everyone welcomed Defurio with heartfelt hellos, especially Sine, who flashed his shiny smile. The clerks of S-1 went about their business, not wishing to intrude on Defurio's fresh memories of Hawaii. These men had a sensitivity peculiar to combat troops, an almost feminine awareness of another soldier's internal pain. After leaving Donna in Hawaii, Defurio hurt. He hurt badly and nothing they could say or do would help.

He signed in at B Company's desk, vaguely aware of tap, tap, tapping of typewriters, the spillover of music from ear phones, and the general hustle and bustle of S-1. He wasn't comforted by the old sights and sounds. "See you guys tomorrow," he said tiredly on his way out. As evening fell, Defurio fidgeted on his way to the barracks, his boots crushing dry ridges in the road. It had rained briefly. Monsoons would be here soon. In his pocket, he rubbed a small gold cross given to him by Donna in Hawaii. He'd never liked being away from her for even short periods. In the middle of thousands of men, he experienced an excruciating loneliness. Reaching his bunk, he sat on the edge in the dark, alone, thinking of her. Not to see, touch, hear, and hold her. Unrecoverable moments, gone forever. Why did he leave her? Why did he come back? From paradise to hell. He let go his hands, dropping them between his legs, fingers hanging loose. He shook his head, saying no to the dark. Please don't let them be apart. No. Please, no more. Anger came to his rescue. He always had his anger. Anger became rage. He mouthed profanities. "Fucking Nam, fucking, fucking Nam. Six more months of this shit. You motherfucker. I won't go down. I'll kick your ass." A street fighter mentality. "Hit me, I'm not going down. I can take it. I can take it."

Lifers infested Ennari. They were a necessary evil. Army installations depended on them to transmit procedures and policies coming from those above to those below. Those below were mostly privates. The predominant activity of lifers, a majority of them staff sergeants, consisted of calling roll and assigning duty assignments. This vacuous work in the 1st/14th rested primarily on the narrow shoulders of Pleiku Fats. Nimble thinking clerks made a hobby of outmaneuvering him.

Shortly after returning to Ennari, Defurio and Sine were throwing a football in front of S-1. Concentrating on the ball, Defurio nearly ran into someone jaywalking across the road. That someone happened to be a lieutenant colonel. Defurio made the catch, turned, and threw the ball back to Sine. Fats ran up to Defurio, berating him for not saluting an officer. By then the unconcerned colonel was at the end of the compound and out of earshot. "Sorry, Sarge, I didn't see he was an officer." Defurio played it up. He snapped off a salute to the lieutenant colonel's receding backside. "Sorry," he yelled. "I didn't see you were an officer, lieutenant colonel, sir." Fats fumed.

At 7:00 am formation, Fats called out, "Defurio you're on K.P." Formations had to do with issuing work assignments and giving out other unpleasant information. Disgruntled troops lined up at-ease eight abreast in a sloppy imitation of a military formation. Fats constantly blew his whistle to gain attention from the murmuring, marginally interested troopers who saw formations as an unwelcome stop on the way to breakfast, lunch, and dinner.

Sgt. Dicicco spoke up. "He's still on the exempt roster, Sergeant." Fats, his roly-poly body shaking like jello, his face thermometer red, charged up to Defurio, craning his neck to make eye contact. Even trivialities made Fats comically enraged.

"Are you shittin' me, Defurio?"

"No, Sergeant, I wouldn't shit on you." Fats didn't quite get the play on words.

Rocket attacks were occurring nightly. The 122mm rockets were notoriously inaccurate, rounds usually falling in the no man's land encircling Ennari. Inside sturdy high ceilinged bunkers, men drank beer and smoked. The attacks lasted fifteen minutes to half an hour. They triggered full alerts requiring available personnel, including clerks, to maintain all night vigils on the bunker-line. Sleep became a premium. Sixteen hour days, then guard duty at night. Sleepless days and nights were an inconvenience but not a severe hindrance. Defurio cat-napped in between grinding out Article 15s, special court martials, an occasional general court martial, casualty and investigation reports.

Investigation reports, called 15-6 investigations, were often cases of alleged negligence or misconduct by officers. In the $1^{st}/14^{th}$, they were conducted by none other than Major Carrington. The crafty major had invested well in Defurio. As it happened, he indulged a colossal laziness. The 15-6s were his responsibility. He signed them, but it was actually Defurio who did the investigations and wrote the reports. The major had satisfied himself as to Defurio's competence and judgment. Investigation reports held the serious possibility of ruining an officer's career or subjecting him to disciplinary proceedings. Defurio, in effect, determined their fate.

Big Jim came by, shit-faced. He'd been released from the hospital in Cam Ranh Bay and was temporarily reassigned to Ennari to receive a two week refresher course in mortars. He'd arrived that morning and was smashed by noon. He weighed less by twenty-five pounds so regular doses of marijuana and alcohol were having a greater effect on him.

As a trained, experienced mortarman, what training could Maloney receive that he didn't already know? Jim interpreted his two week training as a well-deserved vacation. Consequently, he didn't attend classes.

Although Maloney obviously didn't need it, Jack reached in his refrigerator and pulled out a frosty beer for him. He took a mighty swig. Wiping suds from his auburn moustache, the big guy was duly impressed. "Goddamned, Jack. Your own refrigerator. Cold beer at your fingertips. I'd give my left nut for this set up." Taking another swig, he did his chuckle.

A shortage of in-transit personnel, lack of seniority in S-1, and a significant reduction of Wood's backlog resulted in Defurio being dropped from the exempt roster. At the next day's 7:00 am formation, Big Jim and Jack were put on a work detail. They were to hoe weeds and do other maintenance at a bunker tower. They were to report for duty at 1:30 pm. Temperatures were in the 115° range. Jack gave a knowing look to Jim. Their internal radar clicked on. Fat chance. No way were they chopping weeds in the fiery heat of day.

Jack packed beers. On purpose, they went to the wrong bunker. In daytime, tower bunkers were usually unmanned. They chose a bunker where the efforts of their designated work crew could be monitored. Sipping beer, they occasionally sneaked a peak at the work crew toiling in the sun. These crews were composed almost entirely of newbies. Newbies hadn't acquired the moxie to avoid them.

A sergeant of the guard wrote names of men put on work details by Pleiku Fats. These were non-lifers finishing their tours. These hardened short-timers rotated in and out frequently. They could give a shit about Fat's duty roster. It was easy for Jim and Jack to say they'd been sent to the wrong bunker. Fine. The young sergeants would give them credit for a full day's work without Fats ever knowing the difference.

At a noontime formation, a deuce-and-a-half drove up. Defurio, Maloney, and others were loaded on the truck and taken to dismantle a Quonset hut. Temperatures hovered at 120°. Heavy equipment operators had reduced the metal structure to rubble. Their intuition operating in sync, Jim and Jack hopped off the truck, grabbed a girder, hoisted it to their shoulders, and earnestly walked away, fooling the lifer in charge into believing they were carrying out some kind of order. They weren't. The twosome carried the girder behind a barrack, tossed it aside, and went to the beer hall.

Off a ways on a dirt road connecting the bunker line, a single growing object in front of spiraling dust announced the coming of a vehicle. A jeep came to a stop at the guard tower where Jack and Jim were supposed to be working. A lieutenant colonel was inspecting the bunker line because two GIs had been killed the previous evening on the other side of Ennari. A sapper team had penetrated Ennari's defenses. The GIs had been inside a bunker hit by a B-40 rocket.

From their hideaway in a nearby bunker, Jim and Jack watched the scene unfold. The lifer supervising the work crew spotted the colonel approaching and spun to face the officer, puffing out his chest and offering a smart salute. In doing so, he tripped a wire attached to tear gas canisters. They had been set up as booby-traps to disable infiltrators. The work crew fled. The lieutenant colonel, tears streaking his cheeks, holding a handkerchief to his face, frantically waved to his driver to get the hell out of there.

Work details were sometimes interesting. On an unsupervised work detail, Jim, Jack, and other members of a crew were lying in shade when they spotted a five-foot black snake. Jim made an effort to get to it. Quick as lightning, it slipped under a sandbag. Big Jim removed his shirt, planning to use it to capture the reptile. Somebody kicked the sandbag off the snake and before Jim could throw his shirt on the creature, another soldier with a quick stab from a long handled shovel, cut off the snake's fist-sized head.

"Aww, why'd you do that?" Jim protested.

"I ain't dealing with no fuckin' snake," replied the decapitator. Watching the headless snake writhe in dirt as if it were angrily alive, Jim was heartbroken.

"Wake up, soldier." Defurio, sleeping by himself, having purposely gone to a wrong bunker to avoid a work detail, looked up to see a nice looking, trim, black lieutenant colonel. Defurio jumped up and gave the colonel a formal salute. The colonel asked in a moderate tone, "What are you doing here, private?"

"I'm here for work detail, sir. I got here early and I'm waiting for the rest of the guys to show up."

"Very good." He returned Defurio's salute, then went to his waiting jeep and sped off.

"Nice guy," Defurio thought.

And so it went. Work details were part of living in the rear area. They were easy to avoid or ameliorate for crafty rear echeloners. As new clerks come on board and he gained seniority, Defurio would avoid them altogether.

Sergeant Major Manfredo represented a textbook example of an old fashioned non-commissioned officer. Disciplined and straight laced, he didn't swear, smoke or drink. Tall, well-postured, and not fat, he looked to be about fifty years old. Colorless, humorless, and inflexible, to him, regulations and commands were infallible.

Sgt. Manfredo's professional pursuit of military principles gave him a measure of grudging respect by Defurio. The sergeant major's devotion to Army pomp and procedure, however, also elicited a thorough dislike for the man.

Lifer sergeants were a rarity in the field. Why Sgt. Manfredo, having the highest noncommissioned rank in the Army, had been dumped on B Company three months ago wasn't known to Defurio. Apparently, the Army didn't know what else to do with him. Too old for combat and too dull for duty requiring sophisticated thinking, knowledge, or decision making, B company's captain decided to utilize him as a liaison between field operations and the rear area. A glorified errand boy.

Division mortars were incensed that Big Jim hadn't attended training. They demanded B company take action. The captain gave this responsibility to Manfredo. Thus, it fell to Sgt. Major Manfredo to see to the prompt and proper punishment of Pvt. James Maloney.

Thereupon the sergeant major duly submitted to Defurio a request for a battalion grade Article 15. Over a period of days, Defurio typed it up, but deliberately took as much time as possible. Manfredo checked weekly on its progress. When finally completed, Manfredo hand carried the Article 15 to B company's captain for his required signature. Defurio ordinarily sent papers to the accused's captain by erratic helicopter delivery.

Having no tolerance for violators of Army rules, Manfredo relentlessly pursued Maloney's Article 15 and dogged Defurio to forward it to Division. After the sergeant major had returned the signed document, Defurio had put it in a filing cabinet to gather dust, thinking for sure he could outlast Manfredo.

Fucking Manfredo wouldn't stop checking, even though Defurio kept delaying him by offering numerous plausible excuses. Not having anything else to do, Manfredo spent a lot of time hanging around Defurio's desk. In a way, he felt sorry for him. A pathetically friendless relic, there wasn't anyone in the modern Army he could relate to. Manfredo mentioned being of Italian descent and from San Francisco. Defurio withheld any information that he had married, gone to school, and had family in San Francisco. He wanted Manfredo to go away.

In the end, Manfredo won. Defurio ran out of excuses and Big Jim got screwed. Besides a reduction in pay and rank, he also received informal punishment from B Company's captain, who put him in the line for a month of infantryman's duty.

Maloney wrote of his month of adventure in the line, and gave details of a casualty report Defurio had received. He was on a ten man patrol when two VC shot at them from tall grass. Before anyone could stop him, a recent in-country kid sprinted to where the assailants were hiding. In a deadly lapse of reason, the kid stupidly blurted a line from a cowboy movie, "come out with your hands up." For an answer, he received an AK-47 burst to his upper right arm. The bullets entered his ribcage, ricocheting off bones before gouging an exit hole in his back. The VC fell to a storm of bullets from the patrol. Jim wrote that every man in the patrol, angry and frustrated, filed past and emptied a magazine into the dead men. He said the dinks looked like two piles of bloody meat staining the high grass where they'd fallen.

Jim didn't give any indication of being particularly traumatized by the killings. Unloading a full clip into the dead VC effectively relieved any immediate distress. Jim accepted the situation for what it was, another unfortunate act in the drama of Vietnam. He didn't reveal as much emotion as when the five-foot snake was killed.

Captain Allen, the adjutant (the title for the officer in charge of administration) was doing his six month rear duty stint and followed in the footsteps of most career officers; willing to sell their mothers for a promotion. The gruff, handsome young adjutant and Defurio were natural enemies. The conceited adjutant didn't like being told by a lowly draftee what he could and couldn't do regarding legal matters.

The animosity began when Allen came to Defurio's desk and stated sarcastically that if he were absent again from guard duty, he'd be typing his own court martial papers. That day, Defurio had filed general court martial papers, which required lengthy, detailed, complicated pages of documentation. Captain Allen had personally exempted Defurio from guard duty when general court martial papers were due. Division had time limits for their submission. Defurio reminded the captain of the exemption he himself had authorized. Changing the subject, the aggressive captain accused Defurio of making a mistake in a legal proceeding. Jack showed the captain that he was referring to the wrong proceeding and that, in fact, no error had been made. "I'll let you know when I'm ready to be court martialed, sir," Defurio said cynically. He wasn't shy about rubbing the captain's nose in his own self-produced shit.

Allan gave his legal clerk a hard look. "You do that, Defurio." He turned and went to his office.

Alienating officers had become a bad habit. Defurio had trouble controlling a monumental arrogance. He hadn't yet suffered any repercussions. The captain, obviously peeved at his irreverent legal clerk, knew he needed Defurio for the smooth running of the unit. In addition, efforts at retribution would detract the captain from more productive activities such as kissing up to his superiors at Division.

The weather became as turbulent as his association with Captain Allen—cold and windy in the mornings, raining off and on in the afternoons, and gooey mud everywhere. Gray skies spread a dismal mood over the camp.

He finished a poorly written letter to Donna at 1:30 am. Exhaustion and sleep deprivation had followed him from the field. A presentable literary effort required clear headedness. Regardless, he wrote every day unless prevented from doing so by his duties. He described ordinary affairs of the day, but mostly he wrote, often clumsily, of his abiding love for her. He addressed mail to her parent's residence in Bakersfield. He'd post the letters in the morning with Satterhorn, another southerner and the battalion's mailroom clerk. Satterhorn had a thick droopy moustache that seemed to bend his short body forward with the weight of it. Though in his early twenties, Sattherhorn had an old man's body. However, he exhibited lively enthusiasm, and Defurio had the great advantage of giving mail directly to him, thereby bypassing the usual erratic mail service.

Mud sucked at his boots. The seventy-five feet from the S-1 building to his billet seemed longer. He stripped off his clothing down to his green boxers. He lifted the mosquito netting and crumpled on the trampoline spring bed and its wafer thin mattress. He put his head on the pillow, absently listening to the ever-present clatter of far off ordnance. The attenuated booming lulled him to sleep but not before he drowsily moved his lips. *"Goodnight, babe."*

Chapter 30

Dog Days

156 days until his deros date; nearing the point where he could call himself a short-timer, to begin counting days; the intensified awareness of which made each day seem longer.

Fats could be recognized from a distance. Being severely pigeon-toed made the lard in his ample butt and stubby legs shift violently from side to side when he stormed through the compound. Defurio saw him coming, but didn't take evasive action. Fats had accepted him as a veteran rear guard trooper, and he no longer targeted him as a newcomer providing raw meat for work details. Fats stopped in front of him. "Can you believe this shit, Defurio? While you were on R & R, I got fragged." Someone had tossed a grenade next to a wall of Fat's sleeping quarters, blowing a hole in it. Inside his lifer's cocoon, Fats seemed bewildered. "Who would want to frag me?" This wasn't an attempt to kill Fats, that could have been easily accomplished. He was disliked, not hated. Someone had decided to have some fun. Sine had already told Defurio about the fragging and they had shared a laugh about it, as did everyone in S-1.

"It's terrible, Sarge. If we find out who did it, I'll throw the book at the son of a bitch," Defurio lied, laughing inside.

The Fourth of July passed uneventfully, a day like any other. Afternoon basketball games offered a break from the grueling work schedule. At night, he talked regularly to Sine, Sinksen, and others in S-1. Sometimes darts were played. A dartboard hung on a wall by the doorway next to Defurio's desk. Care had to be taken not to spear someone coming through the door. He sometimes played chess but could never beat Hawkins. He always made time to have beers with anyone visiting from B Company. Defurio wrote Donna in late evenings when there were fewer distractions. This is when clerks drank beer, listened to music, wrote letters, or engaged in low volume conversation. For some reason, there wasn't card playing of any kind.

Two days before, three men were killed on Ennari's bunker line, another B-40 rocket. How could the little dink bastards penetrate a minefield, hidden booby traps, rows of concertina wire, and crawl unobserved across a quarter mile of cleared ground? The three GIs had been killed in a different sector so Defurio didn't have to do the casualty reports. This was the extent of his concern. He had acquired the impersonal detachment of a mortician regarding KIAs.

Sporadic rains of the past two months were replaced by constant downpours. By the middle of July, monsoons had struck with a vengeance. In the daytime, rains blotted the sun, falling warm and thick, and enfolding the highlands in cascades of crystalline light. Ennari sank in mud. Men fresh from experience in the AO would sometimes rush out to take advantage of the downpours, running naked from billets, soaping up as they went in anticipation of taking an infantryman's field shower. Monsoon rains stopped as quickly as they started, and at times naked men could be seen standing helplessly in ankle deep mud while an unexpected sun baked on a filmy skin of dried soap.

Hawkins, a slender, dapper, sophisticated black guy from Detroit, had street smarts and an accounting degree, training that he adapted to thrash Defurio regularly in chess. Hawkins shared Defurio's hatred of the Army. As a part time company clerk, he also split R & R duties with Sine. He was derosing soon.

Drinking beers late at night, listening to Defurio lamenting his absence from Donna, Hawkins was touched and inspired by his friend's love story.

"Jack, I've got a fantastic idea." Hawkins had spontaneously thought of a way for Defurio to see Donna on another R & R. He became animated describing the plan, explaining that he would be able to execute it just prior to his deros date. He beamed with satisfaction at having discovered a way to help his friend while screwing the Army at the same time.

A conjunction of factors made the plan feasible. Foremost, Captain Allan was rotating out of S-1, and a new adjutant would be unaware of Defurio's previous R & R. Close knit personnel in S-1, including staff sergeants Jewell and Garinger, would protect his interests and wouldn't raise questions. Hawkins would have to originate and submit orders in a precise sequence.

Hawkins initiated a request for a seven day leave. Normally, this would add seven days to his deros date. Hawkins omitted that part of the order. Captain Allan signed it. Officers almost always signed anything a clerk placed before them. Subsequent to obtaining Captain Allan's signature, Hawkins erased "leave" and substituted "vacation," which was the official designation for an R & R. He submitted the altered order to Division for approval. The order was signed off at Division and returned to S-1. The R & R order authorized Defurio's departure and his transportation to and from Hawaii. Hawkins would hold the modified order until Captain's Allan's transfer.

Defurio happily wrote to Donna about the likelihood of another R & R. They would have to wait for the actual dates, depending on when the new adjutant signed the order releasing Defurio from the battalion. This order had to be signed after the arrival of the new adjutant and before Hawkins derosed. There was a chance something could go wrong, so he and Donna would have to wait and see if the plan worked. Waiting, the bane of lovers; the maddening drip, drip, drip of time.

Snickers proliferated. A general order titled "Directive for the Designation of Tunnel Destruction Commandos" circulated through S-1. Defurio and the other clerks were listed on the order. Defurio had absolutely no training in destroying tunnels, and neither did anyone else in S-1. These kinds of orders came from the ethereal world of high command. No one knew from where in the hierarchal reaches of Army bureaucracy or government these kinds of orders originated. They could have been from the White House, Congress, the Pentagon, or a general's whim.

Sgt. Dicicco usually transported paperwork to Division. On this day, Defurio decided to deliver a general court martial request to Division himself. Taking advantage of a cessation in the rain and having a bit of free time, Defurio welcomed a break in the merciless work schedule. After arriving at Division headquarters, he had a friendly conversation with the legal clerks working there. He was on good terms and had an excellent reputation with them.

Out of curiosity on his return to S-1, he made a detour to see a section of Ennari set aside for the general staff. He was appalled. Air conditioners hummed on tops of a row of mobile homes. Sparse lawns bordered by two feet high white picket fences were an idiotic attempt to duplicate a hometown neighborhood. Soldiers were glumly mowing lawns and doing other yard maintenance. Not a general in sight. Why leave the hedonistic plushness of air conditioned housing? Why lose a drop of sweat when every need is being met indoors; personal toilets, showers, color TV, high class prostitutes, drinking from well-stocked liquor cabinets, and servants to serve you. Generals had personal attendants, U.S. soldiers of Filipino extraction, who were adept at mixing splendid drinks, laying out wardrobes, and running errands.

Generals' privileges are not what turned Defurio's stomach. In a war zone where soldiers were dying every day, seeing U.S. soldiers menially cutting a general's lawn made him want to puke.

"Fucking assholes," he said to himself, in re-affirmation of his disgust for senior officers.

"Jack," asked Sine, "weren't you at Roundbottom under Captain Lowery when it was hit by mortars and set on fire?" Sine, in his function as awards clerk, had received a Silver Star application on behalf of Captain Lowery. Sine continued, "I heard Lowery is a drunk. This application looks like bullshit."

"You're absolutely right, Sine." Defurio described the mortar attack, emphasizing that Lowery never showed himself.

"Fuckers," Sine replied.

Sine dutifully typed up the phony award application. "Guys, listen to this." Clerks stopped what they were doing while Sine read aloud the recommendation for the Silver Star word for word. In the standard language for awards, it began that on such and such date at such and such grid co-ordinates, then went on to fictitiously say Captain Lowery extracted two soldiers from a burning bunker who had been overcome by smoke. After presenting this qualifying information, the lieutenant, who'd been coerced into requesting the award, had cynically written the words "blah, blah, blah," leaving it to Sine to fill in the necessary bullshit. As customary, whenever a combat action could be conveniently misconstrued, a captain would automatically receive a custom made Silver Star. This was pursuant to an unwritten rule to enhance promotional opportunities for career officers. Lieutenants were pressured to request these awards. If a lieutenant refused to go along, he might find himself doing a one-man reconnaissance mission deep in enemy territory.

The incident in question occurred at LZ Roundbottom, where Defurio had attempted to take pictures with his disabled Polaroid. Fuel containers had been set on fire, not bunkers. Sine detested being a party to this farce. After finishing the paperwork, he motioned to Defurio.

"Fuck this, let's go to Division and play some ball." In the middle of the day, they left behind a heavy load of work. Defurio knew his friend had to get away.

They had been cleaning up on the battalion's basketball court. As a two man team, they were undefeated. In two on two games, they'd taken on any comers. Beers were bet. It wasn't a question of them winning, just by how much.

On a Sunday at the gigantic Division gymnasium, mostly black players were on the courts. Sine challenged winners of a game that was finishing up.

The tall black winners watched the average height white guy and skinny Latino take warm up shots. They could shoot. The black players weren't worried. Warm up shots don't reveal how a man performs under game conditions.

Defurio played ferocious defense, not letting his man get close to the basket. Sine had broad shoulders, strong arms, and his man couldn't get past him either. Sine penetrated to the basket, making lay ups, shooting, and dribbling with either hand. Defurio had quick moves, shooting and hitting jump shots from anywhere within sixteen feet. When they expected Sine or Defurio to shoot, they dribbled. If they expected them to dribble, they passed. They fed each other easy shots, smoked the stunned black players, and earned their respect. "You dudes are good."

"Thanks, we'll see you guys." They had to get back to battalion. Basketball was the closest thing to happiness Defurio could get in-country and good therapy for both him and Sine.

Half way back, the rains started again. Monsoon rains hit without warning, like suddenly being under upended buckets of water. They arrived at their barracks wet as baptized babies. They changed clothes and felt refreshed.

The exhilaration of basketball followed by the drenching of a cleansing monsoon rain made them temporarily forget the abuses of the officer corps. That night, Defurio and Sine got rip roaring drunk.

Chapter 31

Yamamoto

Captain Imu Yamamoto exhibited the crude, uncaring rudeness of a despicable man. The squatty captain introduced himself by hurling notebook paper on Defurio's plywood desktop. "Here, legal clerk," he said loudly. "File an Article 15 on this idiot and have it on my desk by 1400 hours." Yamamoto had a jowly face connected to a short, thick neck. A narrow topped skull looked as though the sides of his head had been put in a vice and mashed in at birth. A tuft of cropped bristled hair sat on a leathery tanned head. The writing was illegible.

"Sir, I can't read this." To the captain's irritation, Defurio had him read his writing aloud, repeatedly. Yamamoto relayed the information in almost unintelligible pidgin English.

"Where you from, sir?"

"Hawaii, why?"

"Just curious, sir." Defurio finally deciphered what the captain wanted.

"Sir, this isn't filable."

"Why not?"

"There isn't any evidence the substance tested for marijuana."

"Shit, legal clerk, everyone knows what marijuana is," Yamamoto said stupidly.

"The law doesn't unless you prove it," Defurio replied undiplomatically.

"Just file the fucking thing, Private."

It should have ended there.

Defurio's arrogance prevailed. "It will be a waste of time, sir. Division will laugh at this."

"I'm not telling you again, Private," his voice rising. "File this now or you'll be doing K.P. for a month."

Even though he couldn't win this argument, Defurio wanted to impose his superior knowledge on this repellent creep. "Okay, but you'll be making the battalion look bad at Division." This final jab at Yamamoto sealed an instant enmity.

Provoking a senior officer who has power to put you in harm's way wasn't wise. Defurio's impudence would have repercussions. For now, Yamamoto could bide his time. He needed him; Defurio controlled the entire legal system for the battalion. Battalion Article 15s were submitted to Division for approval. None of Defurio's referrals had ever been rejected. He attached a note to division clerks informing them he'd been forced to submit a legally insufficient charge. Division speedily rejected the captain's insupportable allegation. A division clerk, a friend of Defurio's, attached a return note. "Your new adjutant has shit for brains."

That night, compliments of "Yams," as the repugnant captain was being called, Defurio pulled guard duty. This violated a past order from Major Carrington excusing him from extra duty. Leaving for his guard post, Defurio passed Yams. He calmly ignored the captain's sneer.

"Gee, Captain," Defurio said with false innocence, "there must be a mistake. Major Carrington specifically excluded me from extra duty." Yamamoto didn't know of Carrington's former order or that it was now defunct. Actually, Defurio didn't mind this single night of guard duty. His workload had stabilized. Guard duty would give him a place of solitude to write and think without interruptions. Guard duty wasn't that bad if not attached to a nineteen hour work day.

Defurio's comment produced the intended effect. At the mention of Major Carrington, Yamamoto's eyelids fluttered uncontrollably. This physical affliction was one of many. The adjutant's body, in fact, hosted a collection of odd, herky, jerky tics.

He knew Yamamoto, as a typical kiss ass officer, would be worried shitless of running afoul of Major Carrington. Defurio would not have to worry about extra duty in the foreseeable future.

Monsoons were taking a short break clearing the sky for stars to put on a spangled display. Defurio moseyed along to his duty station in the manner of a carefree schoolboy reluctantly on his way to school. He recognized a form lumbering ahead of him. "Jim!" he called. The big man stopped and turned. Jim's slightly raised eyebrows revealed his trademark show of emotion.

"What the hell you doing here, Jim?"

"I got transferred to Division Mortars. I got in this afternoon. Before I could get my shit in order, Fats nailed me for guard duty." They exchanged pleasantries, avoiding a touchy subject.

"Listen, Jim," Jack gently grabbed his friend's left arm and patted him on the back. "Sorry about your Article 15, buddy. I couldn't get fucking Manfredo off my ass, he kept hounding me until I had to file it." Jim didn't blame Defurio. He, like everyone else, didn't know of Defurio's program of shit caning Article 15s.

"I know you couldn't help it, Jack. You actually did me a favor. Because he thought I got an unfair punishment, Lt. Duke transferred me to Ennari when this slot opened up."

Defurio clapped his hands. "What do you know? Instead of us, the Army ended up fucking itself in the ass this time." They arrived at the guard tower in high spirits. Waiting inside, a newbie sidetracked en route to his unit, sat uncertainly in the shadows. Without discussion Defurio told him, "You're going first. You're on from 7:00 to 11:00." In fact, as a newbie, they hardly acknowledged his presence.

"What do I do?" the young man asked.

"Nothing, you're a lookout. It's cowboys and Indians. You're protecting the fort, if you see anyone coming at the perimeter, yell 'Indians' real loud." Thinking he'd received knowledgeable information, the newbie seemed reassured.

"See you, guys," he said in a friendly voice, leaving the bunker to ascend the ladder up to the tower's crow's nest.

Jack inquired of the platoon. "Everyone's good, no one else hurt. Turner got his wish, fucking bottom-of-the-barrel whores paid off. He's got clap. He's here at Ennari receiving treatment."

Jack laughed. "He and those Montegnards—that's ugly on ugly. Remember when we were at Dak To, how we set him up with 'The Reamer'?" Jack retold the story. "That horny little bastard would fuck a dead skunk." Maloney would gag whenever Turner talked about how good Montegnard pussy was.

"I don't recall if you or me told him about the reamer, that she'd only charge half price for a blow job if you made out with her first."

"Poor old crazy, half blind, toothless thing just wanted some genuine affection," Jim said.

"For half price, Turner gladly accommodated the old crone." Jack continued. "He came back happy as hell."

"How'd you do, Turner?" someone asked.

"What the hell, for half price, I gave her a few kisses. I didn't use my tongue, though."

"Good thing," Couch said.

"Why?"

"Do you know why they call her the reamer?"

"No."

"Because, for an extra dollar, she'll lick your asshole. And she's busy doing that day and night."

"Oh, shit."

"Shit is right. You probably have some of me on your lips right now, Turner."

The platoon roared.

"Couch and Ward are short timers on limited duty waiting to go home. Thorpe should be coming through any day now on his way to the States," Maloney related. "P.A. constantly refers to us as his best friends, I don't know why."

"He's a good kid," Jack said sincerely. "Never stops smiling and talking like a punch drunk fighter. How's Lieutenant Duke?"

"He's rotating home soon, Flack too."

"You know, Jim, I think Lieutenant Duke probably saved our asses. I mean the whole damn platoon, but you and me specifically."

"I agree," Jim said thoughtfully. "He wanted to go home like us. He didn't give a damn about putting our asses on the chopping block for the sake of a promotion."

"I'll tell you, I'm glad he got me this transfer. That fucking ten men patrol scared the shit out of me."

Defurio hesitated, debating if he should broach a taboo subject. He decided to. "Jim, you think that kid getting killed will affect you in the future? I mean, the senselessness of it? '*Come out with your hands up.*' It's like committing suicide."

"I know, it got to all of us. But I don't think it's going to bother me. Shooting up those dead dinks got the whole fucking thing out of my system."

The death of GIs wasn't normally discussed. You try to forget or ignore such things. That's not really possible, but it helps not to bring it up. Defurio made an exception in talking to Jim about killing of the young GI. He wanted to console him if he needed it. Thankfully, he didn't.

Maloney possessed a deceptive toughness. His over the top displays of excitement were offset by a tendency to ward off destructive impressions, to stay physically prepared, and emotionally maintain a positive nature. A white guy who lives amiably on the mean streets of Harlem knows how to survive.

They eagerly BS'd until 11:00 pm, when Maloney relieved the rookie. Jim properly secured his helmet and flak jacket. His M-16 remained in the bunker. The tower had an M-79 grenade launcher and lots of ammo stacked next to the plywood barrier at the top. Jack accompanied Jim to the base of the tower. The air had gone from crisp to sultry. "Don't fall off, Jim." Maloney's awkwardness made his climb up the ladder precarious. Watching him, an image of King Kong scaling the Empire State Building came to Jack's mind.

At midnight, the radio clacked on, ruining a blissful sleep. Fumbling for the handle, Defurio answered it. He received a report of sniper fire in this section of the bunker line. No cause for alarm. They were well protected. Long range, imprecise harassing fire by lone VC gunmen was common, probably a cheap attempt at psychological warfare. However, such instances did call for caution.

Defurio groggily went to warn Jim. From the bottom of the tower, he could see the burn of a cigarette below the rim of the plywood parapet. "Jim?"

"Yo."

"Keeping awake?"

"Kinda."

"Listen up. Be careful, we're getting some sniper fire."

"Yo," Jim acknowledged.

Sleepily, Defurio returned to his bunk, folding himself up in it. Almost immediately, explosions muted by the thick sand bagged walls started going off somewhere in front of the bunkers. He awoke instantly. He shuddered at the possibility they were under attack. He lay motionless, assessing the situation. He realized the firing was outgoing. His infantryman's ears were well tuned to distinguish incoming from outgoing. Nothing to worry about. He rolled on to his back and resumed dreaming of Donna.

Goddamn it. No sooner had he drifted to sleep than the radio scratched on again. He groped for the handset. "Yeah?" Pop, pop, popping of flares had joined the nearby exploding of shells. Responding to the shooting, Division mortars were illuminating the perimeter. "I can't hear what the fuck you're saying." Defurio spoke grouchily and according to his habit, unmilitarily, totally disregarding radio protocol. So did persons on the other end. "Will you stop that cocksucker from shooting? Shrapnel is flying all over the fucking place!" Some hard bitten combat veterans forced to pull guard duty were highly pissed off that friendly fire was hitting their bunkers, and that the rounds were coming from Jim's tower. "Okay, okay, I'll find out what the fuck is happening." He clicked off the handset.

He paused to check the newbie. The kid lay in his bunk, cringing and jerking at the crash of each round. Unused to Vietnam's chaotic violence, he began trembling. Defurio didn't have time to deal with him. "Stay here. Don't touch your M-16 or anything else until I tell you to. I don't want an accidental shooting. Don't worry, kid, everything's fine. Calm down, I'm going out to investigate."

He emerged from the bunker. The evening air had become like a heavy wet blanket, and a breath robbing mugginess almost strangled him. He located Jim, only slightly visible in the unsteady light. Taking advantage of a modest breeze, Maloney had made himself naked from the waist up, piling his helmet, flak jacket, and shirt in a corner of the tower. Incandescence from the airborne flares reflecting off his sweating body made him appear on fire.

His legs spread and braced, Maloney furiously pumped M-79 grenade rounds in an 180° arc. His jaw was firmly set, his face a mask of indifference. Smoke from a bent cigarette hanging from a corner of his mouth narrowed his eyes. Paradoxically, his emotional overreactions never showed on his face.

"Jim! Stop firing! Stop firing! We're not under attack, you're hitting our own bunkers!"

Jim froze. He pivoted. Stunned, he peered down at Defurio and forced himself to ask a sickening question. "Did I hit anyone?"

"No, no one's hurt."

Realizing he could have killed GIs, Maloney sagged to his knees. On the brink of hyperventilation, he straightened upright, fixing his eyes on Defurio, his massive chest pumping in and out in short spasms. Jack had seen other soldiers melt down like this. He needed to divert Maloney's attention. "Jim, get rid of that fucking cigarette. You want your head blown off?" Dry spit had kept the cigarette attached to Maloney's lower lip.

"Oh, shit. Yeah, okay."

"Everything's cool, Jim. There's nothing out there but a trigger happy gook a quarter of a mile away. He could get lucky though if you make a Chinese lantern out of your face."

Jim struggled to focus. "Tell the guys I'm sorry."

"I will. It's okay, no harm done."

His breathing steadied.

"Sit down. Have a smoke, just don't stand up with it."

"Alright, Jack," he said evenly.

He could see Jim light a cigarette. He had gotten ahold of himself. "I'll relieve you in an hour." Jim waved okay. The crises ended.

Defurio brushed by the sandbag wall protecting the entrance to the bunker. There was no need to bend much to clear the six-foot doorway. In the darkness, he edged towards his rack.

With the danger and tension gone, the spectacle of seeing Big Jim turned fiery orange while shooting at imaginary enemy invaders brought a smile to Defurio's face. His smile became a silent laugh. Whatever the situation, Big Jim always managed to make him laugh.

He reached his bunk yearning to rest. Tiredly removing his boots, he became aware of muffled whimpering. Shimmering light from flares crept in through the gun portal and doorway. Across the room, he could see the rookie's bed cover quivering. "Aw, shit," he murmured to himself. "What's the use?" Sitting up, he placed his socked feet on the floor.

"You smoke, kid?"

Embarrassed, the boy uncovered his head and sat up to face Defurio. He had on his boots. He'd gotten under the covers to hide, not sleep.

"No, sir," he said through chattering teeth.

"Goddamn it, don't call me sir." Defurio chastised him mildly, trying to distract the youngster. "What's your name?"

"Bennington."

"Have the guys started calling you Benny?"

"Yes. How did you know that?"

"It's not unusual. Almost everyone here goes by a nickname." Bennington, a fresh faced white teenager, looked like every other fresh faced white teenager coming to Nam.

Defurio lit two cigarettes. He reversed one, giving it to Bennington. "Here, it'll help you. You'll be smoking more than this before leaving Dnam." Bennington sucked in some smoke. He choked and coughed, but continued puffing. He became light headed. He stopped shaking.

Yamamoto refrained from directly shoving formal punishment requests down Defurio's throat. He used intermediaries, lifer sergeants or lieutenants temporarily stationed at Ennari. This method avoided confrontations and possible intervention by Major Carrington on Defurio's behalf. Jack easily recognized trumped up charges coming from Yamamoto and dismissed them routinely. This kabuki dance, where both men performed without speaking, allowed Yams to protect his dignity. Defurio assumed his quashing of Yamamoto's requests for legal proceedings rankled the captain to an extreme degree. Fuck him.

It later became evident that Yamamoto waited patiently for an opportunity to wreak vengeance on his impudent legal clerk. He had in his favor an Oriental's stoic patience, an Army captain's power, and a limitless capacity for cruelty.

In an early afternoon of Yamamoto's second week in the battalion, a medical team soldier became deranged. He helped deliver medical services to villages near Ennari. Because of emotional problems, he'd been taken from combat duty and retrained as a medic. He had a reputation for delivering outstanding medical service to Vietnamese villagers. One day he came upon Yamamoto haranguing a soldier, and snapped. Crying and wailing, he told Yamamoto that officers like him were vicious cocksuckers. He kept crying and repeating that the volcanic tempered captain was a slant eyed cocksucker.

The medic had obviously undergone a mental collapse. Defurio witnessed the altercation and wondered what Yamamoto would do. The confrontation set off the captain's assortment of tics. Involuntarily squinting, he also had a weird habit of cocking and uncocking his left leg, cranking it to a 90° angle, then letting it down hard.

He called the medic a fucking coward, ordered him to do a month's guard duty, and confined him to barracks. Defurio would be getting a request for a general court martial.

A single pistol shot rang out at 2:00 am. Men came running from barracks to find the medic lying face down in the mud. It had been raining. A self-inflicted .45 caliber bullet had torn apart the right side of his head. Medics came for the body and cleaned up the mess as best they could. Defurio did the casualty report.

A somber 7:00 am formation broke up early. Fats skipped policing of the grounds. Yamamoto came by in a jaunty mood. The rain had stopped. Seeing drying specks of brains on walls and sandbags, Yamamoto made a joke. "Boy oh boy, makes you want to eat lunch, doesn't it? Ha, ha, ha, ha!"

Insensitive, insulting remarks and harsh punishment for trivial infractions had become standard fare for Yamamoto's treatment of troops. He patrolled battalion grounds, hunting candidates for punishment.

A bounty went up on Yamamoto's head. If an opportunity arose, he'd be killed in the field, preferably using a captured AK-47.

Yamamoto had volunteered for a fifth tour in Vietnam in order to gain rank. A further promotion wasn't going to happen. "How did this motherfucker become an officer, no less a captain?" Sine, struggling through a written communication from Yamamoto, spoke for everyone in S-1. Besides brutish behavior, Yams proved to be functionally illiterate. He couldn't write a complete sentence in English if his life depended on it.

There were various theories as to how Yamamoto had become an officer, some not so serious. At the beginning of the war, officers were in short supply. Standards were lowered. Somebody took tests for him. Family influence. He got plucked from a Hawaiian National Guard Unit. As a lieutenant, he may have done something impressive in the field. He received a lateral transfer from the Japanese Army.

Yamamoto didn't prey on S-1 personnel. He needed them. In conducting the business of S-1, of which he had no grasp, he tried avoiding Defurio altogether. Occasionally when they crossed paths, Yams, blinking wildly, would give Defurio a menacing smile. "Hello, legal clerk."

Chapter 32

Foreboding

Lopes typed solely using the forefinger of his right hand, although he did so with blazing speed. At the beginning of his tour, Lopes had mistakenly been put in a line company. It was easy to see why he'd been trained as a clerk and not an infantryman. He had eye glasses thicker than the bottom of a whiskey glass. Defurio asked how he'd fared in the AO. "Fine, they made me a point man." It sounded ridiculous. On second thought, 20-20 vision didn't necessarily help; you couldn't see shit anyway in the jungle.

The other Army trained clerk in S-1, Pvt. Teer, a horn rimmed, chipmunk cheeked Midwesterner for whom the term misfit could be considered an understatement, had teeth too big for his mouth and could talk a mile a minute. He had recently been transferred from another battalion headquarters.

Pvt. Teer started trouble the first day by not showing up for guard duty. On the same day, when he ignored a direct order by an officer, court martial papers were requested. When typing the allegations, Defurio realized Teer could probably beat the charges. Teer claimed his eye glasses were broken, making him unfit for duty. That he broke them himself would be unprovable.

Teer's transfer papers purposely omitted that he had been general court martialed for refusing orders and that during his subsequent incarceration at Long Binh Jail (commonly referred to as LBJ), he had willingly let inmates use him as a girl.

S-1 clerks followed Teer's day to day flaunting of orders as though watching a sports contest. Teer versus the Army. As an underdog, he'd squiggled out of every trap the Army had set for him. Troops rooted for him. In his second week, Teer seemed to have had an epiphany, showing up for his clerking duties early and leaving late. Working with impressive dedication for a week, he refrained from his usual jabbering and unexplained absences. Then he disappeared.

Two weeks went by. Hawkins, returning from R & R, casually mentioned to Sgt. Jewell that he had run into Teer at the airbase preparing to board a jet bound for the States. Jewell stopped in his tracks. Teer's outrageousness had offended Jewell's professional sense of order and fairness. He rushed to the phone placing a call to Pleiku airbase. MPs arrested Teer entering the jet's doorway. He had expertly forged documents and orders honorably discharging him from the Army. He had even arranged extra travel pay for himself.

Teer had become a celebrity outlaw. His escapades were becoming known throughout the highlands and beyond. His notoriety had risen to such a magnitude as to have come to the attention of the capricious Major Carrington. The major issued an order, probably illegal, to confine Teer in a locked tool shed pending further legal proceedings.

The windowless, five by five, seven-foot high turd brown shed sat in an isolated stretch of the compound. MPs removed his handcuffs when placing Teer in the cramped space. Neither Defurio nor anyone in S-1 liked seeing the hyperactive, freedom loving Teer locked up. Sadly, S-1 personnel returned to work.

He wasn't done. In the morning, the shed rested on its side. There wasn't a trace of Private Teer.

At 7:00 am formation, Fats announced the escape of Pvt. Teer. Cheers went up. "Way to go, Teer!" "You're da man!" "Go,baby, go!" "Don't let the bastards catch you!"

From that point onward, rumored sightings of him came from headquarters up and down South Vietnam. No one serving in the 1st/14th would ever know what happened to Pvt. Teer. Every infantryman in the battalion hoped he'd found his way home.

Daily monsoons were saturating the highlands. This forced Yamamoto indoors. His learning curve had flat lined. He didn't have the capacity to understand the basics of personnel administration. He liked to prowl. Stuck inside, Yams became a bellicose, interfering irritant to S-1 staff.

On August 22, he approached Defurio's desk, tossing at him a preliminary investigation report submitted by a lieutenant. It had been due six days earlier. "Get this done, legal clerk!"

"I can hear you, sir, you don't have to yell."

Yamamoto began blinking.

The lieutenant's report lacked critical elements of information. Defurio had to rewrite the entire thing to make it presentable to Division. Every fifteen minutes, Yamamoto would come by asking if he'd finished. After the third inquiry, Defurio told him, "I'd be finished if officers knew how to write reports, sir." Yamamoto's left leg shot up backward at the knee. Defurio smiled, ignoring the fact he was playing a dangerous game.

The monsoons eased and enemy contact increased significantly. Wounded and killed in action reports flowed in daily. Defurio needed to go in the AO to obtain depositions for a court martial. He welcomed the opportunity to get away from Yamamoto.

The convoy to St. George had the benefit of some general's latest brainchild. Jeeps modified to accommodate .50 caliber machine guns mounted on steel posts weaved enthusiastically in and out of the convoy. The jeeps had a driver, and behind him, standing in the middle of the vehicle, a machine gunner held on to the weapon's handles for balance. Helicopter escorts already provided effective support for convoys. Jeeps floating about were redundant. Obviously, the general watched TV. The flamboyant action of the jeeps exactly duplicated a show called "Rat Patrol".

Arriving at George, Defurio grabbed a bite to eat at the mess tent. He relaxed in the hooch of a friendly clerk. A generator supplied electricity for a light bulb. Comfortable surroundings. As a forward support firebase, St. George had strong defenses; .50 caliber machine guns on the perimeter, artillery, mortars, and wide booby-trapped fields of fire. Importantly, the base served as the lieutenant colonel's headquarters for conducting field operations, and as such, his staff included clerks. Defurio contemplated staying here. St. George offered a peaceful sanctuary compared to Yamamoto's chamber of horrors.

He sensed a show down coming between him and Yamamoto, and wanted to avoid it. He had no doubt the fat Jap would fuck him over badly if given the opportunity. He had entered his ninth month in-country, the zone of a short-timer. Riding out his time at St. George appealed to him.

While thinking of ways to manipulate the system so he could stay there, he hitched a last minute ride on a Huey delivering supplies and troops to LZ Tiffany, where he would be taking depositions from three soldiers in Charlie Company.

Coming in for a landing, the head of a soldier sitting beside him jerked violently to the side. A metallic ping rang Defurio's ears. A saucer-eyed soldier removed his helmet, revealing a two inch hole on its right side. "Wow!" Defurio exclaimed, referring to a bloodless groove in the soldier's scalp carved by an AK-47 bullet. "You lucky bastard." He gave the shocked soldier his one potato fist bump.

The depositions weren't finished until after dark. By then, choppers had stopped running. He'd have to stay overnight. Bunkers were at capacity so he ended up sleeping on muddy ground.

At mid evening, he picked up the whistling of incoming. His nerves and muscles reacted instantaneously. He flung himself into the nearest bunker, terrifying the soldiers inside. "Friendly, friendly," he yelled, calming them. Mortars peppered the LZ for half an hour.

On a Huey returning to St. George, Defurio reconsidered staying there. The mortar attack at Tiffany had made him think. The AO, including St. George, presented unreasonable risks. As a long standing fixed and exposed post, St. George would be subject to a major attack sooner or later.

Two other considerations compelled his return to Ennari. To accomplish his illicit R & R, he would have to co-ordinate efforts to steer the process around Yamamoto and any other potential hazards.

Another key factor was that B Company had an upcoming allocation for a promotion to sergeant. Before leaving for St. George, he had submitted his own recommendation for the promotion, which had been signed with approval by Sgt. Jewell. Since he showed on B Company's roster as an infantryman, justification for a promotion would have to appear as if it were based on his performance in the field. In actuality, Defurio hadn't done shit in the field. In writing the fabrication, he had a twinge of guilt. Attaining the higher rank meant screwing someone more deserving out of the promotion.

Hawkins did a beautiful job originating the order authorizing Defurio's R &R. He skillfully forged necessary signatures. To accommodate his request to depart at the earliest possible date, August 31, Hawkins had to arrange for Defurio to go standby, which ordinarily was not a problem.

At 5:00 pm on August 24, Fats notified the formation that standby flights were being cancelled due to maximized flight schedules. "Oh, shit!" Defurio broke formation, running to his desk to scribble a letter to Donna. He ran to the mail room, telling Satterhorn to please, please expedite sending it. If Donna were to arrive at Ft. DeRussy and not find him there, she would assume the worst. The trauma of expecting to meet the man she loved to find he was probably dead would ravage her emotions. She would be alone, falling through a black hole of doubt, confusion, and unimaginable grief.

It would take a week and a half by return correspondence to discover Donna had received Jack's letter in time to cancel her flight. Satterhorn deserved thanks. After hours, Defurio carried two six-packs to the musty and surprisingly dim mailroom. The isolated building at the far end of the compound served as Satterhorn's place of work and refuge. "Here, Satterhorn, I can't thank you enough."

"Oh good, Jack, I'm glad she got it. I hope you don't mind, I had to promote you to a colonel so it would get special couriered."

Satterhorn was perusing mail intended for the medic who had killed himself two weeks earlier. He expertly unsealed and resealed letters he thought might contain pornography or pictures of GIs naked girlfriends or wives. Sure enough. He and Defurio viewed with appreciation a curvaceous brunette sporting a prominent muff who turned out to be the dead medic's girlfriend.

"What happened to your R & R?" Satterhorn asked, not taking his eyes from the pictures.

"Hawkins has already arranged for a regular R & R on October 31."

"That's great, Jack," he responded, not looking up.

"Thanks again, I've got to go. Yams will be missing me."

Satterhorn rearranged angles of the sleazy pictures. He took his eyes off them for a moment. "Be careful, Jack, the captain's a weirdo. I hear other officers saying he's a sadistic, brainless, deviate."

"Nobody knows that better than me," Defurio acknowledged.

He opened the door and turned towards Satterhorn. "Thanks, buddy, for everything," he said. Rain drizzled in. "See ya, don't let that nasty brunette keep you up too late tonight." Slogging through mud, a light rain fell on him. The monsoons were weakening.

Days dragged; roll calls, meals, typing, taking casualty reports, drinking beer, small talk, basketball games, occasional darts and chess games, more typing. All the while, boorish behavior and caustic remarks by Yamamoto maintained an atmosphere of severe tension in the S-1 building.

Near the end of August, Defurio made sergeant. Skillful manipulation and guile had combined to allow him to become a non-commissioned officer in the U.S. Army. To ensure the final result, he had hopped on a convoy to St. George to personally obtain the signature of the lieutenant colonel.

At the end of a long day, he had handed the tired colonel a sheaf of orders and documents requiring his signature. Hidden among them was the order awarding his promotion to sergeant. Under a kerosene lantern, the colonel signed the order, only looking to see where to affix his signature. Less important signatures were forged by clerks, who were experts at signing for their COs. The kindly and knowledgeable Sgt. Jewell had given tacit approval for the elaborate subterfuge attending his promotion. He wanted to reward Defurio for the quality and quantity of his work.

Initially, Defurio did not wear sergeant's stripes. Not caring about status or privilege, he became an invisible NCO. Primarily, he was interested in sending an increase in pay allowance to Donna. He never bothered to go through the trouble of walking to the PX to pay a dollar for black sergeant's stripes. All insignias in a war zone are black.

The battalion's temporary sergeant of the guard was a tall, thin kid from rural Texas by the name of Elpidio. "Pete" was in the process of rotating to the States. He had the same last name as Jack. Pete came from A Company. Defurio had never met anyone with his same last name. Meeting him, it became clear why he hadn't received mail during his first months in-country. He looked to see if Donna's half-heart locket hung from Pete's neck. It didn't. Too embarrassed to admit it, Pete, a shy, humble kid, denied receiving Defurio's mail. He didn't pursue the matter; he liked Pete.

"Listen, Pete," Defurio said, changing the subject. "Can I have your fatigues, shirts, and cap when you leave?"

"Sure, Jack, I'll have them laundered and sent to you." Pete made good on his promise.

Fatigue shirts have a soldier's last name over the right pocket. Normally, names were stenciled. Defurio had scrawled his with an ink pen. Thanks to his namesake, he now wore proper identification. His name was stenciled in capitals, and he had three hard stripes sewn on his shoulders, meaning they were earned for performance in the field.

Defurio wondered if his scheme of moving up his deros date when signing in at Long Binh would work. If so, he had less than two months to go in-country. Nine months represented the start of the unofficial title of short-timer. They created imaginative calendars to mark off each day. Usually the last day ended in a pornographic display of a female crotch.

Responsibility for conducting special court martials moved to Division, resulting in a sharp drop in Defurio's workload. This permitted him to finish his labor within an eight hour work day. This didn't last long. In addition to his regular duties, he became a part-time jeep driver, running errands and hauling officers from place to place.

Yamamoto kept harassing clerks regarding administrative procedures, of which he had no comprehension. Witnessing these oxymoronic exchanges, Defurio's dislike for Yamamoto became a seething hatred.

Jack developed a new trick. When placed on extra duty, selected men reported to the sergeant of the guard, who signed them in. When selected, he would fall out of formation but didn't join the line reporting to the sergeant. Instead, he would join the line for those who had finished signing in. With his duty roster apparently completed, Fats would dismiss the formation, only to be told by the sergeant writing names that the roster was a man short. Fats easily corrected the apparent oversight by arbitrarily grabbing a soldier retiring from the formation. Off the hook, Defurio headed for the beer hall to drink a toast to the poor chap who had taken his place.

"Goddamn it, Sergeant, can't you do your fucking job?" Yamamoto was referring to an Article 15 disapproved of by Division. A colonel at Division had personally called Yamamoto to rebuke him for sending inappropriate referrals. Defurio had attached his standard note absolving himself from blame and placing it squarely on the head of Yams. Division clerks confidentially relayed this information to superiors.

"Don't yell at me, sir, I told you that Article 15 was a piece of shit and Division would throw it back at us. This kind of stuff is ruining our reputation at Division."

"Just do what you're fucking told, Sergeant."

Yamamoto had switched to calling Defurio by his upgraded rank. Previously he liked referring to him by the pejorative use of "legal clerk".

Yamamoto had absolutely no idea how Defurio had become a sergeant. He merely, dumbly, accepted it.

"I did do as I was told, and we got shit on by Division when you refused my advice, sir."

Foolishly, Defurio couldn't stop from getting in the last word. He let his distaste for Yamamoto overcome good sense. The captain fled to his office, his face breaking out in twitches.

When he finally boarded the plane for his illicitly arranged second R & R to Hawaii, Defurio had erased Yamamoto from his mind. What troubled him was that Donna may have been unable to reschedule her flight to coincide with his arrival. There hadn't been time to get verification by mail. Stepping off the bus at Ft. DeRussy, uncertainty occupied him. He had to see, hold, and hear her before he relaxed. She could have gotten hurt, sick, or otherwise missed her flight. Some family emergency could have delayed her. When he spotted her running towards him, elation rocketed through him. They embraced, kissing and hugging. He grabbed her hand, pulling her behind a building for privacy. "I love you, Donna. I love you, I love you." He said over and over again.

"I love you too, Jack," she repeated tearfully. "I love you too." They ignored the fifteen-minute orientation and hailed a cab.

They went to the Holiday Isle. In their room, he promptly shed his Army clothes and put on the pair of grey corduroy pants he'd bought at the PX. Donna gave him a loose fitting blue short-sleeve shirt. She'd brought him a shirt for each day. They went for dinner, kissing in the elevator all the way down to Gus's Steak House.

While he ate prime rib, Donna told him of her anxiety before leaving for Hawaii. Because of the last minute cancellation of his R & R in August, she had contacted the Red Cross to verify his status. Women in her Waiting Wives club, the wives of officers, informed her that in an emergency, the Red Cross could reach their husbands in Vietnam, most of whom were pilots carrying the rank of captain.

Donna talked to a haughty lady at the Red Cross. The woman denied Donna's application for assistance. When asked why, the lady bluntly told her, "Because your husband is not an officer."

"What difference does that make?" Donna said challenging the stupidity and unfairness of the policy. "He's a soldier. He doesn't want to be there. He's serving his country as much as any officer." The lady turned her away.

"Nothing new." Jack stopped chewing momentarily. "These elitist son of a bitches who run everything really don't care about anyone. They care about themselves and making themselves look good. Looks like the Red Cross is run by the same kind of kiss-asses as the Army."

Days were too short, the nights shorter. They stayed, as yearning lovers do, interlocked, loving through evenings and a good part of daytime. During the day, they escaped to the other side of Oahu, seeking the solitude of isolated beaches.

It came to the night before his return to Vietnam. "I'm afraid, Jack. I'm afraid that captain will hurt you."

"Don't worry, I have less than two months to go. The hard part is over. Yamamoto can't hurt me, he doesn't have enough time. I'm a short-timer, he has to leave me alone. Arranging to put me on work details is the worst he can do, and I know how to get out of those." Jack didn't exaggerate, he had prestige and standing in the battalion and Division as a highly regarded legal clerk. The entire S-1 staff had conspired to ensure him a promotion to sergeant, and they had helped him achieve a second R & R. His married status drew additional support and sympathy from administrative staff. NCOs Jewell and Garinger had actively protected him from the wrath of Yamamoto. Altogether, Defurio's short-timer status and protective circle of influential insiders gave him a concrete barrier insulating him from the vengeful hands of Yamamoto.

So he thought.

Chapter 33

Blow-Up

A mud splattered trooper from B Company came off the convoy from St. George. He opened the screen door wide, letting it slam shut behind him. It jarred Defurio from daydreaming of Donna, Fresno, having babies, and who they would look like. A short-timer can think of the future because he can foresee a future. "Yo, J.D., how you doin'?"

Smiling broadly, J.D. dropped his pack. Defurio, seated at his desk, reached behind him to fetch beers. He gave one to J.D. "Thanks." He had no idea why J.D. went by those initials. They weren't the initials of his name.

"Made sergeant, huh?" J.D. an older, sensible, reliable soldier noticed Defurio's stripes. "Good for you, but I'll outrank you in four days. I'll be a civilian. I'm ETSing out of this motherfucker." An ETSing soldier mustered from the Army upon returning home, whereas derosing soldiers had time left to serve. For Defurio, it was six months.

"That's fantastic, J.D. I'm glad for you." He gave him his one-potato fist bump.

The thought of six months dead time when he returned home irritated him. Everything irritated him. He'd been in a bad mood since Hawaii. Leaving Donna again exposed him to two impatient months of controlling a nearly uncontrollable hatred; two months of enduring the bile of Captain Imu Yamamoto.

October 7 came and went. If he were derosing early, November 7, his orders would have come by now. Cheating on his departure date at Long Binh hadn't worked. He would have to hang on until December.

At the beginning and at the end of a year in Vietnam, one day seemed like two. At the beginning, a man agonizes about his next long day in the bush. In the middle months, soldiers adapt to the lengthy days; there's an acceptance, and trying to stay alive becomes routine. Near the end, they became obsessed by time. They try to hasten it by devising short-timers calendars and falsely eliminating the last day by calling it a wake-up. A short-timer having thirty days left in-country would brag, "I got twenty-nine days in Dnam and a wake up."

Defurio scrawled an "x" through the previous day's date. This constituted his first meaningful act in the morning. He didn't have a short-timer's calendar, and wasn't inclined to count days by marking a sex queen's body parts. He marked a standard calendar he'd bought at the PX, and which hung on the wall next to the rubber band attached to his typewriter.

Yamamoto maintained his regular intrusions. He abandoned his previous pattern of avoiding Defurio. He'd deliberately walk by his desk, occasionally remarking behind a fake smile, "How you doing, Sergeant?"

"Fine, Captain." The smile would broaden. Defurio knew Yamamoto didn't give a shit how he was doing. He became leery of his growing boldness. He had become like a circling vulture.

One night around 1:00 am, a majority of S-1 clerks, having become sufficiently drunk and drowsy, made for their bunks. Defurio reached for his writing materials in a drunken but well-intentioned effort to complete a letter to Donna. Dennis Sinksen had stayed behind, wanting to talk. Defurio welcomed postponing his writing since his brain was fried anyway.

Private by nature, Sinksen didn't reveal his personal life unless he had too many beers. Then, he lamented about Margaret, his lost love, a divorced older Protestant woman, that he, a devout Catholic, couldn't marry outside his faith. Getting drunker, both drank to loss of love.

Sinksen abruptly changed the subject. Something bothered him. Beers and a freak moment by themselves, allowed him to vent an inner turmoil. "I'm going to hell, Jack." Defurio could see an immense sadness in the face of his deeply religious friend. "I saw my bullets hitting the dinks who killed Reed." He referred to the killing of Reed at Chu Pa. They'd had already discussed the horrible circumstances of Reed's death and the difficulty in extracting his body. "The dink I shot went down and didn't get up. I killed him."

Sinksen had serious hidden worries about damage to his soul. "I don't think you're going to hell, Dennis. You weren't alone, five or six guys opened up."

"I know that, I also know I nailed the dink I shot at." Sinksen didn't have any doubt.

"So you killed him, so what? You're a soldier, you were trying to save Reed. This is war. Go to confession, get forgiven."

"I went to confession. It didn't seem enough."

"Dennis, I've helped fire off hundreds of mortars, killing and maiming a lot of people. I'm not religious, if there's a hell, I'm going. There'll be no forgiveness for me." By making his situation worse than Sinksen's, Defurio hoped to give his friend some relief. "Keep doing confession. You're a good man. I don't think angels will close the gates of heaven to a beat up soldier like you." They laughed. Jack opened them another beer. He'd have to finish Donna's letter tomorrow.

Yamamoto clearly wanted to make Defurio's remaining days in Vietnam miserable. He side stepped directly confronting him, trying not to be verbally humiliated by his impudent legal clerk.

He resorted to a cultural imperative; a sneak attack, a modern day personal Pearl Harbor.

It wasn't an accident Defurio's name came up at every roll call for guard and work duty. Fats followed orders. His orders from Yamamoto were to put Defurio on extra duty.

"Be cool, Jack. Don't let Yams get to you," said Sergeant Jewell.

It had become an open secret Yamamoto had targeted Defurio for special treatment. Jewell wanted to protect him. Defurio knew how to escape extra duty. Yamamoto didn't know this or that his devious attempts to punish him were obvious to everyone.

Yamamoto's punitive efforts didn't have the desired effect. However, his shamelessness had the major consequence of stoking Defurio's hatred for the fat Jap.

"Defurio," bleated Fats at 5:00 pm formation. "You're on Division patrol. Report to Division 0900 tomorrow."

"What?"

Yamamoto was flagrantly violating an unwritten cardinal rule of Vietnam honored by officers and non-coms alike. You don't unnecessarily put a man having less than ninety days in-country in harm's way. Defurio had less than forty-five.

That night, having given the order to put him on Division patrol, Yamamoto dawdled in front of Defurio's desk. The Jap's grin went from ear to ear. He wasn't hiding his animosity any longer. Without saying a word, he announced his message loud and clear.

"I'm fucking you, legal clerk, and there's nothing you can do about it."

Witnessing this display disgusted everyone in S-1. Though tight lipped with frustration and anger, they didn't stop working, but did so noticeably slower. There was nothing anyone could do. After Yamamoto had triumphantly departed, Dicicco stepped up. "Jack, don't worry about it, I've been on these Division patrols. They're like a two day R & R. You'll see, take plenty of beer."

Dicicco looked in the direction Yamamoto had gone from the building. "Somebody's going to kill that sawed-off motherfucker."

Defurio didn't respond. "Fuck you, Yamamoto," he thought. "I can take anything you can dish out."

He followed Dicicco's advice and stuffed twenty beers in his ruck. He requisitioned his standard number of grenades and bandoliers of ammo. He decided to wear his bush hat. The rains had stopped and he expected a strong sun. About half the twelve men in the truck wore helmets, the others had bush hats and head bands.

These were hardcore infantry guys. Each had over nine month's in-country. They'd been intercepted for this patrol while on the way to their companies from R & R. Fine with them. They considered Division patrols way better than the crappy conditions in the AO.

"What happened to you, get caught fucking the general's daughter?" a trooper asked jokingly. Defurio stood out as the only clerk on board. For rear guard personnel, patrols were considered a means of punishment.

He and his companions were deposited at a trailhead fifteen miles southwest of Ennari in a landscape of flat ground and thick woods. The sergeant in charge, a white scruffy street fighter type, gathered up the men. Defurio noticed something different and realized there weren't any blacks, Puerto Ricans, or other Mexicans. He didn't know why. The sergeant produced a map protected from possible rain by a clear plastic overlay. He pointed to a spot on it.

"We're supposed to go here." He designated a place about five miles down trail. "Fuck that, we're going here." His forefinger jabbed a place on the map indicating a mile from where they were. "I talked to guys who have been here before," he explained. "There's a friendly village less than two clicks from here and a half of a click from the main trail. We're holing up in that village. We'll camp by the trail and set up in the village at sunset."

The plan entailed calling in phony grid co-ordinates. Periodic radio checks would appear to Division as though the patrol was progressing to the objective.

They embarked on a well-defined trail. Forty-five minutes later, they established a resting place prior to heading for the village. Before breaking up in search of individual locations in which to lounge, Defurio asked the pugnacious-looking sergeant a question. "Let me ask you something out of curiosity. What's the purpose of this mission?"

The sergeant gave a concise answer. "Fuck if I know."

Defurio asked, "I mean, what do they expect us to do, turn back an NVA regiment getting ready to attack Ennari?"

"It's pure bullshit," replied the sergeant. "NVA aren't active here. This is considered a pacified sector. Local VC are passive, and they don't want to fuck up the local economy. These local dinks depend on doing business and working at Ennari and the airbase. Hell, I walked dead drunk in downtown Saigon. No one touched me. Same thing. Locals don't want to do anything that's bad for business. It's economics."

"What about B-40 and 122 attacks at Ennari and the Air Force base?" Defurio asked.

"That's for show. Psychological warfare. They believe in that shit. Those attacks don't accomplish a goddamn thing."

The men formed a sloppy, uneven perimeter as they separated together in twos and threes to relax and bullshit. Soldiers wouldn't do this in the AO. They'd space themselves ten to fifteen yards apart, not wanting to set an attractive target for a bunch of them to get killed by a single grenade, mortar, rocket, or AK-47 burst.

Soon the pungent aroma of marijuana permeated the site. The smell of freedom. Relaxing in the countryside beat the hell out of the restrictions at Ennari. Marijuana smoke dissuaded the presence of flying insects. Hours passed leisurely. Every two hours, the PRC-25 scratched on. The sergeant called in the false grid co-ordinates. Defurio drank five beers before dozing by himself below a jumble of rocks rising twenty feet high. The air sizzled in a high heat. Vaguely, he perceived an absence of birds chirping or squawking. Invisible insects maintained a persistent screech. Men lay lazily strewn about talking, sleeping, smoking, or drinking.

Then, blam! The sharp crack from a rifle broke the calm.

The men reacted instinctively; fielding weapons, diving, falling on bellies, taking fighting positions wherever they could find cover. Defurio threw himself behind a log, not feeling scratches and bruises from rough edged nubs of rotten branches. He had good protection with a log in front and rocks behind him, but had the serious problem of being separated from the main body of the patrol.

An M-60 machine gun opened up in the direction of the rocks. Twenty feet behind him, bullets sparked like struck matches off the rocks. The rifle shot had come from the direction of the rocks.

"Friendly, goddamn it, friendly." He strained his throat, trying to be heard above the blasting machine gun. He waved the barrel of his M-16 in the air and the shooting stopped.

At that same moment, three villagers came out from behind the rocks. They were hard to detect in the profusion of underbrush. "No shoot, no shoot," they shouted, hands upraised. By hand gestures, the patrol determined the men had been hunting. Smiles, relief, and a small celebration broke out.

The hunters were given beers. At night, these guys were probably VC. At this minute, man to man, possibly soldier to soldier, they offered them no harm.

The M-60 machine gunner, a big man, grasped Defurio's hand, glad he hadn't blown off his head. "Sorry, man."

"Good thing you can't shoot for shit," Defurio said joshingly, his adrenaline rush subsiding. The big guy smiled underneath a helmet that seemed too small for him. Defurio looked down to see an eight inch tear in his fatigue pants above his right knee.

He had multiple bruises and scratches but no bleeding. He didn't know how the tear happened or when his bush hat had fallen off. He retrieved it lying in front of the log, and smacked it on his leg to shake the dirt loose. They followed the hunters to the village.

By his actions, Yamamoto became increasingly frustrated. Defurio hadn't shown any ill effects from the campaign of harassment. On the contrary, he had become adept at reversing Yamamoto's aggressiveness and having fun in the process. Frequently, he came to Defurio wanting him to file trumped up Article 15s or court martial charges. Defurio would explain specifically why Division would reject them. Yamamoto had an officer's lap dog mentality, wanting to please his masters, and he balked at the prospect of official chastisement by Division. His promotional opportunities, hopeless to everyone but him, might be jeopardized. Defurio wielded this hammer of Division rebuke to good effect on Yamamoto. Many times, he bluffed him from following through on legitimate cases. However, the stubborn son of a bitch persisted in bringing case after stupid case of unwarranted charges.

Yams never learned. He never deviated from a set course of action. Defurio used this trait for his amusement, although it pushed him dangerously close to the edge of catastrophe.

He made a game of offending the repulsive captain. Jack would wait for him. Storming from his office, he never varied his line of approach. Defurio would spring from his chair to meet him in the aisle. Standing button to belly, Yamamoto had to severely angle his short neck to make eye contact. While doing so, Defurio would seize the initiative, putting Yams on the defensive, asking him if he understood the charges. He would mention how Division was a stickler for evidence to substantiate allegations. Not understanding, the captain would struggle to answer, rushing his words. Defurio piled on complicated, largely irrelevant, legal terminology. Yamamoto would lose his train of thought, his words becoming unintelligible gibberish. Stopping mid-sentence, he would spin and beat a retreat to his office. This scenario happened fairly often.

Defurio marked his calendar. Thirty-eight days to go. Sgt. Jewell approached him.

"Jack, Yamamoto wants me to take you to his office."

"Fuck, what a way to start the day. What's up?"

"I don't know. Looks like he's ready to jump in your shit with both boots."

"Jesus, how many times does he have to use his boots to shovel his own shit?"

"Be careful, Jack, don't give the bastard a reason to fuck you. I think he wants me there to testify against you if anything happens."

"Hell, Sarge, the stupid ass doesn't realize you're my best insurance from getting fucked over."

Defurio hadn't been in Yamamoto's office before. Its sterile interior could have been a prison cell. An impersonal green file cabinet sitting on the floor and an indistinct upright photograph on his desk failed to alleviate the bleakness of the space. Yamamoto sat behind a big green metal desk, which made him look even squattier than he already was. "Why the hell wasn't this investigation report filed on time to Division?"

"I'll be damned," Defurio thought. Yamamoto, barricaded behind his desk, had accidentally discovered a way to confront Defurio without humiliating himself, by not having to degradingly crane his head to face his towering rival. This wasn't the result of planned strategy; the Jap didn't operate at that high a level of mental sophistication.

Yamamoto began a high volume obscenity laced castigation of Defurio. Throwing down the investigation report, he accidentally knocked over the picture frame on his desk. Jack picked it up, taking the time to examine it. It contained the photograph of a hideously ugly woman. She could have been a World War

II propaganda cartoon. The slope-eyed woman wore large oval metal rimmed glasses and an unfortunate smile showing a fierce overbite of rounded teeth. She wore a black helmet of straight, unstylishly cut hair.

"This your wife, sir?" Defurio asked innocently.

"Yes!"

Defurio's aside temporarily threw Yams off stride. He rectified his confusion and relaunched his diatribe.

While Yamamoto yapped, Defurio reviewed the documents. Quickly, he saw the problem. "Sir, this report is late because the captain signing it did so in the wrong place. I had to send it back for a proper signature." This unassailable explanation didn't penetrate Yamamoto's thick skull.

"I'm tired of your fucking excuses, Sergeant," he screamed, his face turning purple, his voice hiking to a falsetto. "It's your job to see these forms are completed on time."

"What am I supposed to do, sir, personally go to the AO and hold the captain's wrist so he signs in the right place?" Yamamoto looked like he'd been struck between the eyes with a sledgehammer. This fucking clerk had turned the tables on him again. He stammered in a hapless effort to say something substantial. Defurio pressed his advantage. He spread his arms in mock frustration.

"He's a captain, he's supposed to know where to sign documents. That's why he is a captain," he said, as if lecturing an adolescent.

Because he thought himself an invulnerable short-timer, Defurio made a decision to make Yamamoto pay for fucking with him, and do it in a way that wasn't officially actionable. "I'm not responsible for captains, they're responsible for me. If he's too stupid to know where to sign a document, then maybe he shouldn't be a captain." Sgt. Jewell's perpetually lit, unfiltered cigarette fell from his mouth.

Yamamoto understood the unsubtle insult. "Get the fuck out of here!" he sputtered in a rage. Sgt. Jewell followed Defurio to the doorway.

"Jesus, Jack," he whispered, "I'm worried what the crazy son of a bitch will do."

In a final insult, Defurio departed without a salute to the captain. He had been at ease when Yamamoto ordered him to leave. Defurio executed the order immediately, turning and exiting the room. Yamamoto, broiling in anger, realized he hadn't given his clerk a chance to give him a required salute. He would not repeat this mistake.

The captain's tirade had resounded throughout the building. When leaving Yamamoto's office, a step behind Defurio, Sgt. Jewell motioned to the staff that Jack had won. There weren't any cheers, only relief. Typewriters resumed clacking. Experienced soldiers don't display emotion concerning incidentals, anything not resulting in the letting of a soldier's blood. A powerless clerk standing up to a deviant captain deserved silent acknowledgement and respect, not accolades. Defurio went straight to his desk and buried himself in his work. No one congratulated him, and he didn't expect it. In a war zone, office politics don't rise to a level of serious importance.

Days settled into a dull routine. Yamamoto returned to his policy of avoiding Defurio. He also suspended his regular travels through S-1. Jack didn't consider Yamamoto a threat any longer. Monsoons were sputtering to a close. Moods brightened.

"Joey, where you goin?" Defurio asked Joe Lopes, C Company's one finger typing phenomenon. At midmorning, men usually didn't go through the front door, they exited through the side door on their way to the shitter. Lopes had to direct his whisky bottomed lenses at Defurio to see him. His eyes magnified to twice their normal aperture. "I'm on my way to the hospital, a buddy of mine got hurt."

"Nothing serious I hope," Defurio said.

"I don't know. A piece of casing from an illum round fell on him." A ceramic material encasing illumination rounds spun to the ground when they burst. A danger of giving false grid coordinates on patrols was that someone grossly out of position could be struck by falling pieces. It was extremely rare. Defurio had never heard of this actually happening until now.

Sometime later, Lopes returned stone faced. "How's your guy doing?" Defurio inquired, expecting Lope's friend to be enjoying some rear area sham time.

"They amputated his leg." Without further comment, Lopes went to his desk and went about furiously pounding his typewriter.

Yamamoto persisted in lambasting troops and requesting outlandish legal actions. He transmitted requests through Sgt. Jewell to avoid humiliating confrontations with his legal clerk. A majority of Yamamoto's referrals were summarily rejected by Defurio. Sgt. Jewell informed Jack that with each rejection, Yamamoto would angrily exclaim, "that fucking legal clerk."

Defurio tried to stay occupied. During the monsoon season, playing darts had become a regular activity. The games carried through October and November. Nightly contests were hotly pursued. Sine and Defurio vied for best player status. One early evening, a less gifted player threw a dart, missing the board completely, and hit a soldier entering the door. The dart stuck in his left bicep. It hung in the fabric of the soldier's shirt like a dead wingless insect. More startled than hurt, the soldier pulled the dart free and pretended to hurl it at the offending dart thrower. The offender almost killed himself trying to get out of the way.

Defurio maintained Maloney's workout schedule. About 8:00 pm, he'd interrupt his beer drinking and dart throwing to go to an abandoned bunker and lift improvised weights made from metal ammo containers. Jack saw Maloney about once a week. When they were a team, Jim fell in easily with Defurio's mischievous ways. In his present life, the winds of change bent the big man in the direction of cannabis induced mellowness. Jim had joined a social pot smoking group at Division mortars and cheerfully stayed loaded most of the time. His relationship to Defurio had changed. Maloney had become more like a favorite cousin than a brother. In his relationships and attitude, Jim took the path of least resistance.

November 1 marked Defurio's last month in Vietnam. This date arrived along with Pvt. Jacob Symanski, "Jake", an infantryman from C Company and Defurio's replacement as battalion legal clerk. He hailed from Rochester, New York, and presented himself as a likeable, smart, confident kid, not overwhelmed by his upcoming responsibilities, and not awestruck by Defurio's status as reigning legal expert in the battalion. Hardened infantrymen are generally not easily overwhelmed or impressed. The young man had a pale, skeletal, sharp featured Ichabod Crane look about him, with stooped shoulders and a prominent Adam's apple. Symanski could afford to be confident; he wouldn't be inheriting months, or even a day of unfinished work.

Defurio identified relevant portions of the UCMJ, which Symanski studied determinedly. Using Yamamoto's constant flow of referrals, he instructed Jake on the difference between suitable and unsuitable charges. He'd explain each day's referrals and then disappear for the day. Defurio checked his work in the evening. Symanski learned more in one day about legal procedures than Yamamoto had since being appointed in August.

Not wanting to encounter Yams, Defurio stayed away from battalion headquarters. He bought another Samsonite suitcase and civilian clothing at the PX. He frequented the Division beer hall, taking an isolated table to write upbeat letters to Donna. His moodiness subsided. Optimism filled his letters. Since Hawaii, he envisioned life as a normal civilian, uncrippled and unmarked. He mentally prepared himself for leaving the obscenity of Vietnam, the Army, and the madness of Captain Yamamoto.

In the early morning on November fourth, Yamamoto broke his pattern. He brought a referral directly to Defurio, bypassing Sgt. Jewell. Jack, instructing Symanski, hadn't seen him coming.

"Sergeant I want you to file general court martial charges on these three men. Have the charges on my desk before 5:00 pm formation." Yamamoto displayed unusual confidence. He didn't nervously stumble and stammer as he usually did when addressing Defurio. Remarkably, he didn't raise his voice.

Jack reviewed a single witness statement submitted by a master sergeant. He also examined Yamamoto's childlike statement, replete with misspellings and pidgin English, requesting legal action. Basically, the master sergeant reported three drunken soldiers from the battalion had disrespected him and, more importantly, failed to salute a lieutenant colonel.

"Jake, read this. He expects us to draft general court martial papers based on this shit." Symanski had trouble deciphering the writing, not because of illegibility, but for the simplistic nature of the contents. Trying to make sense of it, he read Yamamoto's statement haltingly to Defurio.

"Soldiers… no… salute a Lt. Colonel… in U.S. Army. Soldier… drunk. They flip-off… Masta Sergeant… and say fuck you to him."

There weren't any dates, places, times, or corroborative evidence submitted. In his statement, the master sergeant let it slip that the lieutenant colonel was too intoxicated to make or sign a witness statement. Defurio pieced together that the incident had occurred somewhere between Division and battalion headquarters about midnight after the closing of the beer halls.

Defurio could see what had inspired Yamamoto's confidence. The master sergeant's statement mentioned a lieutenant colonel, which in the stunted mindset of Yamamoto presented an opportunity to gain points at Division. Yamamoto didn't have an appreciation that this kind of inept referral would enhance his reputation as a complete idiot.

"Jake, the main thing here is that there is not a single piece of evidence that the lieutenant colonel knew of the existence of the three soldiers. On a dark night, in poor lighting, he was drunk, and so were the three soldiers. There isn't any evidence they saw one another. You can't salute what you can't see." What we have here, Jake, is a minor offense, soldiers being disrespectful; using obscene gestures and abusive language to a master sergeant. It's not a serious offense because they didn't disobey a direct order or endanger anyone.

He paused, letting Symanski digest this information. "What I'm about to tell you is extremely important, something asshole officers like Yamamoto never get. General court martials are reserved for the severest offences because they impose the harshest levels of punishment, including, in the annals of history, death by firing squad."

"Listen, these guys could have pissed on the lieutenant colonel's boots and it wouldn't merit a general court martial. Get ready, Yamamoto is likely to shit his pants when he sees this."

Yamamoto wasn't in his office at 3:00 pm. Defurio put a note on his desk saying he referred the case of the three drunken infantrymen to B Company's clerk for filing of a company grade Article 15. A court martial or battalion Article 15 wasn't actionable or warranted. While there, he turned Yamamoto's wife's picture around. Pulling at his crotch, he sucked in his lower lip to form an overbite and squinted at the innocent woman who substituted for the object of his hate.

At 4:00 pm, Yamamoto returned. Defurio watched and waited. Shortly, Yams catapulted from his office in a furious state of upset. Jack arose, prepared for a fight. They clashed in the middle of the building like jousting knights.

"What the fuck is this, Sergeant?" The captain waved Defurio's note in his face.

"It's an efficient, appropriate resolution of the case, sir, one that won't embarrass us at Division."

Yamamoto had reached his limit. His tics were setting a record. With every spastic beat of his eyelids, his head jerked in unison. His leg cocking spread to his right leg, alternating one to the other.

"It's shit, Sergeant. Don't you understand English? I asked for a court martial." He went to his falsetto.

"A court martial isn't justified, sir," Defurio said, calmly staring down at the runtish captain.

"Goddamn it, I'll tell you what's justified!"

"It's not up to you, sir, it's up to Division. I'm trying to save us time, trouble, and embarrassment."

"We're not at Division, Sergeant, we're here. I want you to file the fucking court martial papers and I want you to do it now! I'm giving you half an hour!"

"Sir, it'll take me a minimum of four hours to type separate quintriplicate copies required by Division. Carbon paper doesn't work for that many copies and we don't have a copying machine."

"I don't give a shit. Just do it or I'll get somebody who will!" With that, the captain stomped to his office.

Defurio went to his chair. "Fuck him." He sat and did nothing. Clerks held their collective breath, waiting to see what was going to happen. Jack brooded, conjuring Yamamoto sitting confidently counting the minutes. The captain knew how to exercise power, and had his legal clerk right where he wanted him, with his back to the wall.

At precisely 4:40 pm, Yamamoto appeared, buoyant in apparent anticipation of humiliating his insolent legal clerk. They danced the same dance, Defurio intercepting him in the middle of S-1. "Where are the court martial papers, Sergeant?"

"They're nowhere, sir."

Initially unnerved, Yamamoto hesitated. Summoning the power of his rank, he reasserted his forcefulness. "What the fuck do you mean?"

"You said if I didn't file the charges, you'd get someone who would. Go ahead, sir."

"You're being insubordinate!"

"No, I'm not, I'm being honest. I have witnesses, sir. Everyone in S-1 heard you."

Conceding that point, Yamamoto strived to regain his momentum. Speaking measuredly, loudly, and clearly, he issued the ultimate threat. "Sergeant, I want you to file those court martial charges now or you can get your ass back to the field!"

Defurio abruptly turned and headed for the door.

"Where the fuck you think you're going, Sergeant?"

"I'm getting my shit and going to the field, like you suggested." This wasn't as flippant as it sounded. Defurio had made a snap judgment that he could lay over until his deros date in the relative comfort and safety of St. George, the battalion's well-defended forward support firebase.

"Get your ass back here, Sergeant!" Defurio returned and stood casually in front of Yamamoto. "You click your heels when talking to an officer, Sergeant!" Defurio came to attention. Yamamoto had retaken command of the situation. "Sergeant, you're the worse fucking excuse for a soldier I've ever seen. Your fucking mother had an abortion that went wrong." He launched a tired litany of drill-sergeant style insults. Yamamoto's voice went mute, drowned out by silent "fuck yous" Defurio shouted inside his head. He could see Yamamoto's flapping lips and spastically beating eyelids. He choked on musky fumes set off by the captain's agitated state, and could see him sneering like a man enjoying the smell of his own excrement.

Watching Yamamoto, he fantasized cutting off the fat Jap's head and sticking it high on a pike. Food for flies. Would his eyelids continue fluttering? Yes! Yes! This vision completed, Defurio reengaged in time to hear Yamamoto end his vulgar recitation. The captain finished by saying, "I'm giving you a direct order, sergeant." He maintained his sneer. "Have these court martial papers done by 0800 tomorrow." He capped his admonition sarcastically. "I have witnesses."

"Okay, sir." Defurio, still standing at attention, saluted. Yamamoto returned a victory salute. His mouth gaped in a smile, revealing two rows of yellowed teeth and releasing the revolting odor of rancid soy sauce.

Defurio refrained from saying, "Don't blame me when Division sticks these court martial papers up your ass."

After Yamamoto returned his salute, Defurio turned and went directly to his desk. Seated next to him, Symanski had the shocked expression of an onlooker having watched a circus performer fall from the high wire.

"Go get some beer, Jake." Defurio didn't want to talk.

"I'll get three six packs."

"That'll be fine." Defurio went to work. For the second time in two weeks, the building had fallen silent. Slowly, clicking and clacking of typewriters, low level conversations, and hushed refrains of psychedelic rock refilled the room. No one approached him.

Chapter 34

Final Days

Sometimes unknowable forces combine to promote evil. The death of eight men gave Yamamoto his chance to destroy Defurio.

At 1:00 am on November 7, exactly one month from his deros date, a call came from forward support firebase St. George, where three days earlier Defurio had contemplated hiding.

"Dragon Slayer."

"Yeah Lieutenant, I'm here."

"We're under attack! Sappers got in the wire. A B-40 rocket blew away a bunker. Eight guys dead."

"Jesus. Any more dinks get in?"

"I don't think so. We killed a shitload of them." The lieutenant crashed sentences together, making him difficult to understand.

"Slow down, Lieutenant. Do you have a list of guys that were in that bunker?"

"Yes."

"Alright, give them to me slowly. Go ahead."

He reported two. Then, "Shit, too many rounds coming in. I'll get back to you."

He and Gobbler waited. "Gobbler, what did you find out when you got the call?"

"They were being hit by mortars, small arms, and B-40s. Except for that one sapper team, it didn't look like any other dinks got through the wire. Looks like hitting that bunker started the attack."

Defurio offered an assessment. "If they can get through the first half hour, air cover will get there. The worst should be over."

"Goddamn, I hope you're right."

Defurio's rationalizing didn't deter from the obvious. Dinks must have a sizeable force and well-planned strategy for taking a firebase as well-defended as St. George. A half hour elapsed.

"It's not good they haven't got back to us," Gobbler said, worried.

Defurio tried to put a good face on it. "Radios are hard to find in the dark. There's dust, smoke, guys running around, incoming, shooting. It's chaotic." They came up with theories and excuses why there wasn't a call back. Gobbler, being a radioman, settled on the possibility that available radios were concentrated on contacting and coordinating artillery and Huey gunships. Defurio waited two hours. "Listen Gobbler, I'm getting my poncho, I'll rack here tonight."

He spread his poncho on the dirt floor near the radio equipment. Thinking of so many guys killed, Defurio had trouble sleeping. If there were eight known dead, there were many more wounded. Worry occupied him. He couldn't get rid of seeing eight dead U.S. soldiers. His imposed shell of indifference had cracked. In his imagination, the eight were lined up naked on the ground, faces and genitals charred beyond recognition. His insides churned. For eleven months, he had maintained a wall to shield his emotions, preserve his sanity. Now in his twelfth month, he couldn't stand the thought of GIs killed or hurt. He didn't know the dead men. Nothing had changed. The veneer of civilization had early on been stripped away. Teachings of family, being kind to others, the Bible, thou shall not kill, and respecting the lives and property of others had long since been supervened by the venality of war, by the loss of compassion and morality derived from the numbing deprivations and depravity forced upon a combat soldier. Why did these eight men disturb him? Nothing had changed, other than an accumulation of eleven months of witnessing young men die for nothing. Absolutely nothing.

The commo shack had a multitude of luminous dials. The distracting green lights were annoying. They penetrated his mind so that the skin of the dead men radiated a fluorescent green. He dreamt of the radiating corpses until daybreak.

Morning formation. Defurio stood sleepily at ease. Fats informed them that St. George had been attacked, and that the firebase had incurred substantial casualties. Of course, Defurio already knew that. He and Gobbler had had the battalion's only direct contact with the embattled firebase. Other information had also drifted down from Division and Brigade through an informal network of lifer non-coms. This actually produced solid information. The firebase had held firm, repelling a massive ground attack. Dinks didn't appear to have abandoned the effort, and mortars were still coming in along with sporadic small arms fire. Dinks were observed retrieving dead and wounded. St. George expected another attack that night.

Fats announced a convoy would try to break through to bring in a team of medics, infantrymen, ammo, radios, radio batteries, and claymores. Other than ineffective sniper fire, since Defurio had been in the battalion, a convoy had never been attacked. However, to him this convoy, scheduled to leave in an hour, looked extremely dangerous. Dinks could easily shift personnel to set an ambush.

Because of unstable conditions at St. George, Defurio's secondary role as casualty clerk became pre-eminent. Sitting beside Gobbler at the mess hall, he ate his breakfast vigorously. Not sleeping well had made him hungry. "Any news?"

"Nope. I think they're holding together okay. My guess is they're saving radio batteries to call in support fire and medevacs. We'll reestablish contact when they receive the new radio batteries."

Defurio carried a cup of coffee to his work station. "Morning, Jake."

"Hi, Jack." Defurio laid out the day's legal work for Symanski.

Yamamoto came at them, his sneer wider than ever. "Shit, what does this fucking asshole want now?" Defurio murmured.

"What is it, Captain?" he said dismissively, not bothering to stand up.

"I want you on that convoy, Sergeant."

"Why?"

"Because we need those casualty reports."

"They're taking radios and batteries. They'll call in casualties right after the convoy arrives."

"We don't know that, Sergeant."

"They're still under fire, sir."

"So what? You're an infantryman, aren't you?"

"Yeah and I'm also short. I'm due to leave in a month, sir."

"Tough shit, Sergeant. I want you on that convoy. That's an order."

"My replacement is here, send him." This wasn't a breach of ethics. Every grunt picks up the slack for short timers. Symanski wasn't offended, he knew the rules. He would get the same consideration when his turn came.

"I'm sending you, Sergeant. Get your ass on that fucking convoy." Yamamoto's nervous misfires became displays of a sick happiness. His left leg cocked enthusiastically. His face pulsated around a sneer, broadening to a rapacious smile.

Yamamoto had driven a final nail into the coffin of his career. To endanger Defurio, he was violating tenets of conduct and responsibility expected of an officer for the welfare of his men. He had sacrificed any last remaining hope of promotion in a maniacal attempt to harm Defurio, and possibly subject himself to disciplinary action for conduct unbecoming an officer.

Jack reported to Division, where trucks rumbled expectantly. He suspected Yamamoto had called ahead for them to wait. Defurio pulled rank, ordering a private to sit in the rear. He perched within the added safety of the steel boxed cab. He'd ridden shotgun before, and it all seemed so familiar. However, he didn't dwell on nostalgia. He concentrated on the present and getting though this hassle. He permitted himself a reflection—any way he cut it, dead or alive, this would be his last chauffeured trip in Vietnam.

The grinding deuce and a half stuffed with men and supplies joined the middle of ten trucks speeding through the gates of Ennari. They were in flat, oven baked country. Monsoons were gone, and skies were clear. The convoy traveled on a road reduced to powder by cavalcades of trucks, tanks, and half-tracks. He had two choices: crack the window for a whiff of steamy air thickened by dust, or marinate in a sweatbox of humidity. He alternated.

Defurio watched contortions of the boy behind the wheel. He didn't look big or strong enough to control this roaring high-suspension vehicle. Why were these drivers so young and scrawny? A bag of pills sat by his side. Swallowing handfuls of stimulants fueled his hyperactivity. He bounced up and down on a sandbag under his butt and another under his feet. These would protect him should the truck detonate a pressure release mine.

He changed his mind about the Rat Patrol. He liked the idea of additional security. He honestly didn't believe in the validity of the Rat Patrol, however, at this stage, he'd take any extra precaution he could get. Trailing white silk scarves waving from the necks of rat patrollers made them look like huge flightless birds running about aimlessly.

Waiting to hear from St. George the night before, Defurio had managed to scrawl a tired, fractured letter to Donna. He told her of the trouble at St. George and related objectively what he knew, not knowing then he'd be thrown in the middle of it. He constantly worried about her worrying about him. In her last letter, she admitted she had started smoking again. She had smoked before they met, but began again after he left for Vietnam. She'd been too ashamed to tell him. She stopped in anticipation of his returning home. If Donna knew of this dangerous journey to St. George, her emotions would come close to the breaking point. Defurio's face flushed. Thoughts of her became contaminated by the sneering face of Yamamoto. As he'd done before, he mollified his hatred by imagining killing the fat lizard. He visualized emptying a clip into the pudgy Jap starting, at his fresh dog shit soft belly, and stitching a line of rounds upwards. He'd finish by placing the final bullet square between his reptilian blinking eyes. Or maybe he would decapitate him, putting the rounded mound on a stump and shooting to pieces his jack o' lantern pumpkin head. These imaginings preoccupied him until they reached St. George.

Dark smoke lifted from a bunker near the gate. Defurio jumped from the truck and sought the lieutenant colonel's personal clerk, Pvt. Rollins, who had the trademark appearance of a majority of clerks—tall, studious, frail looking, bespectacled, and white. He had completed one and a half years of graduate work in political science. He greeted Defurio warmly. "You can bunk with me."

Pvt. Rollins had a comfy eight by five foot stand-up tent featuring a raised plywood floor. A typewriter rested on the table. Next to it, a sophisticated tape recorder blared rock music. Defurio found it odd the tent wasn't located near the lieutenant colonel's CP. The tent sat about fifteen yards behind a perimeter bunker, uncomfortably close to no man's land. Rollins verified the burning bunker had contained the eight dead soldiers. "What happened to the bodies?"

"I'll tell you, Jack, the guys weren't going to let them burn. They risked their asses to pull them out. They tied ropes around them to do it."

"How long since you had incoming?"

"Not since morning."

Defurio surveyed the eighty yards between perimeter bunkers and jungle line. Dead dinks riddled the ground. They were definitely dead; GIs had used them for target practice.

"Here, I save this for special occasions." Defurio took a pull from a bottle of Wild Turkey and handed it back to Rollins. "From the colonel's private stock. He let me have a bottle. He's a pretty good guy."

Rollins lifted the bottle. "Here's to you, man. It's a fuckin honor to have a drink with you."

"Oh yeah, why?"

"You're a fuckin legend. Everyone knows the shit you take from Yamamoto. The guys know you're looking out for them. We've even heard some of the shit you pulled way back with Maloney."

Legend?

None of this made much of an impression on Defurio. He considered his conflict with Yamamoto a personal fight.

Rollins had prepared a list of the dead men along with thirty-one WIAs. Medevac's were still coming in. Conditions at St. George looked favorable. It wasn't reasonable for dinks to launch another attack. Firebase mortars and artillery were resighted for close fire. A ton of ammo had been brought in. Gunships at Ennari and Pleiku were on ready alert. An abundance of claymores ringed the perimeter. Every perimeter bunker had a starlight scope. Clear skies made them very effective. The base would be on full alert. The dinks were certainly aware of all this. Defurio settled in Rollin's tent prepared to sip whiskey, get a good night's, rest and get the hell back to Ennari on tomorrow's convoy.

That afternoon the men were called to formation. Goddamn it, more bullshit. He didn't want to do this. Why stand in the smothering heat of day? He just wanted to get his business done and get the hell out of there. Less than forty yards to his left front, thinning black plumes continued to rise from the bunker that had become a crypt.

"Ten hut!" The fatigued soldiers came to attention. Coming from his CP, the lieutenant colonel walked solemnly to the front of the formation. "Shit. Goddamn it, goddamn it," Jack repeated to himself. "Now I have to listen to a fucking speech."

The lieutenant colonel didn't say a word. He did an about face. His right hand went crisply to his brow. He held the salute. That's when Defurio saw them. Eight pairs of scuffed, unlaced boots. They were lined up on the ground facing the formation unadorned by anything but surrounding dirt.

"Oh, shit." The dead soldiers' boots. Defurio swallowed hard. He hadn't expected this. He wasn't prepared. He had no warning.

"Ta ta taa."

"What's that? How did they do this? No! No!"

"Ta ta taa."

Taps.

"Ta ta ta ta ta ta taa."

"No, please stop." Each sorrowful note ripped through him. Defurio struggled to steady himself. His head raged. "Motherfucker, Stop! Stop! Stop!" His knees turned to mush.

"Ta ta taa." What did these young boys look like? "Ta ta taa."

"No, don't think." He bit his tongue. "Don't go down, take the blows." He fought back tears. He didn't want to submit, didn't want to cry. "Don't give in to weakness," the voice of his mother. "Ta ta taa." He couldn't escape the shrill sadness of the bugle, its notes pierced his soul. "Ta ta taa." Eight pairs of empty boots. "Motherfucker." He bit harder. "Don't give in, don't cry." The mournful refrain finally ended. He sighed in relief. His knees regained strength. He'd been shaken but had held firm. He hadn't been defeated. No tears. He had maintained his pride, no tears… not on the outside…on the inside, his blood had become a river of tears.

Sometime near midnight. Boom! Boom! Boom! Incoming. "Oh, fuck, not again." Did he have to see and hear the lightning and thunder of battle again? A thousand demons pounding drums. An eruption of M-16s and machine guns answered AK-47s, automatic weapons fire and B-40 rockets. The rockets weren't accurate from the tree line. Sappers couldn't get closer. The heart of the firebase received zeroed in mortars and stray B-40 rockets. Rollins twisted into a spider hole on the side of his hooch. "Jack, run for the middle of the LZ, there's a pit there."

Defurio lay on the plywood floor throwing on his cross of bandoliers and tying one around his waist. He put on his flak jacket, not taking time to cinch up the front. He slapped on his helmet and rolled onto the ground, holding his M-16 in his right hand. He locked and loaded, taking it off safe. He'd pre-set it for semi-automatic fire. His grenades were bunched in his side pockets. He laid prone, his head toward the interior of the base.

He couldn't see shit. He wanted to get away from the brunt of the attack, away from the perimeter. Green tracers crisscrossed overhead. He weighed his options; they ranged from bad to none. He couldn't stay in the open, mortars were pounding the center of the firebase. He made a decision. He'd try to find the pit. He rose to his knees and bolted, knuckling the ground with his free hand, and skittering across the ground like a hell bent ape. He came to the pit laying thirty yards behind the southern section of perimeter bunkers. He could have kissed Rollins. He slid inside, hugging the security of its banks. The hole was eight feet deep and twenty wide.

Defurio couldn't ascertain the purpose of the pit and didn't care. Its sides sloped at a forty-five degree angle. A mortar would practically have to land on his head to injure him. Great. He would wait out the attack, get on the convoy in the morning, and get the fuck out of here. St. George's mortars came on line, putting up a barrage of H and E and illum rounds.

Descending flares flashed fluttering patches of light and shadows across the landscape. To assess his situation, he ventured a visual surveillance, careful not to expose his head longer than necessary. He didn't want his face to become a resting place for flying shrapnel or an AK-47 round. Between bunkers, he could see motionless dinks spread in front of the perimeter. Others were squirming in agony, some crawling, vainly seeking a place to hide. Reflected pools of blood and mounds of guts constricted in the dirt like living things. He couldn't understand dinks. It was the same as the annihilation on Roundbottom; the element of surprise was gone. Why press the attack? Why commit suicide? Within fifteen minutes, helicopter gunships would turn the jungle into a dink graveyard. There wasn't any way they were getting inside the wire. Relieved, Defurio rested.

Gunships began circling St. George, concentrating a chain of rocket and mini-gun fire on the eastern and southern sides of the jungle. Defurio's location was to the south. His tension eased. He'd stay there until the dinks gave up the attack. They foolishly persisted in trying to overrun the base.

A lieutenant shepherding a flock of eight newbies crashed into the pit. He exhibited the nervous anxiety of a greenhorn. Seeing Defurio's stripes, he lit up. "Sergeant, I'm putting you in charge of these men. I want you to assist in defending this section of the perimeter." In a flurry of legs and arms, the lieutenant departed, leaving Defurio to babysit the shit-assed newcomers. These cherubs were breathing harder than a virgin bride, and just as scared. They leaned forward in fish-eyed wonderment, as if Defurio were about to deliver a sermon from the mount. Fuck it. He resigned himself to the situation.

"Listen up, I'm splitting you in two man teams. Set up behind a bunker. Each of you take a corner." There were four perimeter bunkers to the south of his position. "I don't want any of you fuckers to fire a shot unless you get a signal from me. Use hand signals. Flares will give enough light. Let the guys inside the bunkers do the shooting. You got that?"

"Yes, sir." Newbies and their yes-sirs. Defurio didn't want them doing what newbies were famous for: shooting other GIs. He arbitrarily selected two. "Form a tripod using your free arm, knees and lower legs. Dig hard with your boots, don't rise higher than your waist. If you hear a whistling sound, stop and lay flat. When the round hits, take off again. If I see one of you son of a bitches not flatten out, I'll shoot you myself." He patted the helmets of the first two. "GO!" They made it safely. He assigned bunkers from left to right. "Okay, you two. GO!" Shortly, he had them distributed and out of his hair.

A dragon ship joined the Hueys. In lazy sweeps, hundreds of thousands of rounds poured from mini-guns, hitting along the jungle line and working back some distance from it. A medevac barreled in low, braving green tracers. A bunker had been hit on the eastern side, taking casualties. Symanski would get his baptism as casualty clerk. Everything under control, Defurio fell asleep on the pillowy shoulders of his pit.

An additional Huey escorted the convoy. When the ten truck procession broke into the open, Defurio celebrated by lighting up a cigarette. He rolled down the window. Not much dust. They were the lead truck. Rat patrollers jockeyed through the pack. Machine gunners swaying behind .50 calibers hung on to them. Wearing goggles and WWII pilot's headgear, they flashed gloved peace signs when dashing past. For Defurio, this signaled the end of his war in Vietnam. That should do it. Fuck you, Yamamoto, you had your chance and didn't get me.

He'd underestimated the baseness and tenacity of his adversary.

Returning to Ennari, he drank some cold beers, showered, and put on fresh fatigues prior to 5:00 pm formation. Fats made the usual announcements and completed the battalion's duty roster.

At the end of the briefing, Fats personally approached Defurio. Reluctantly, he informed him he'd been placed on another Division patrol. He'd have to report to Division the next morning. Fats didn't like doing Yamamoto's dirty work. At this point, he hated Yams as much as anyone. Division patrols were generally regarded as a windfall, a two day pleasure fest for infantrymen, a bonus. Everybody in the battalion knew that wasn't the issue. Yamamoto's unpardonable sin was that you don't put a soldier, no less a married one, having less than ninety days in-country in a situation of possible peril. Period. Defurio had less than thirty. "Sorry, Defurio." Fats showed genuine disgust at the unfairness being done.

"It's okay, Sarge. I know it's not you."

Yamamoto's abuse compounded in its effect on Donna. Defurio would write her that night glossing over his experience at St. George. There would be a three day gap in receiving his letter. Donna perceived nuances. She suspected something was terribly wrong when Jack had unexpectedly been dispatched to St. George. She agonized whenever she felt he was exposed to increased danger. These prescient concerns caused Donna a series of stress related ailments and sleepless nights. To alleviate her concern, he'd have to admit his participation in tomorrow's patrol. He would describe the two day affair in the mildest of terms. Despite his efforts, she'd worry herself sick.

Defurio lazed in a clearing drinking beer. He rested on a bed of crushed underbrush. They had traveled the exact route as his previous Division patrol. As before, they intended to stay overnight in the village. As before, bullshit grid co-ordinates were radioed in. Defurio vaguely recalled Joey Lopes' buddy having his leg amputated. He'd been injured by a mortar casing because his patrol had given false grid co-ordinates. Defurio dismissed the possibility; the chance of that happening twice was one in a million. He failed to recollect two GIs in B Company and a third on his recent return to Tiffany having scalps grooved inside their helmets by AK-47 bullets. What were the odds of that?

"Saddle up," announced the sergeant leading the patrol. The homogenous, carefree patrolmen casually grabbed weapons and slung on packs. Defurio noticed, as on the previous Division patrol, there weren't any blacks, browns, or clerks except, of course, for him. He didn't know why. He guessed prejudice by the white people who put together these superfluous luxury patrols.

In high spirits, the patrol welcomed an early daylight visit to the village. It amounted to fun, recreation, and a change of pace. Nothing seemed out of the ordinary; birds chirped, insects buzzed. Defurio would have ample opportunity to explore village life. He'd write Donna about it. They formed up, ready to get under way.

Then it came, that bone chilling pop of close in small arms fire. "Bruump!"

"Goddamn it!" Anger was always Defurio's initial reaction to conflict. A four round burst had come from his left. On the way down, locking and loading, the men flattened in a single move. Defurio reached for a grenade, placing it by his right throwing hand. He could feel his thumping heart beat the earth, yet he felt a strange calm. His normal instinctual response to violence of war—a drastic hormonal jump and an electric triggering of his nervous system—brought him a certain calmness and clarity. Life was reduced to its harshest and simplest terms, an uncomplicated, unambiguous single ambition. A total devotion to kill or die trying.

Within seconds, a voice came from the direction of the fired rounds. "Accidental fire, accidental fire, it's okay, accidental fire!"

"Sorry, sorry." A soldier got to his feet, giving embarrassed apologies.

"What the fuck happened?" someone yelled.

"My rifle slipped." In an act of extreme carelessness, the soldier had leaned his M-16 on a tree, on automatic, off safe. When the stock struck the ground, it set off the rounds.

"You mean I shit my pants for nothing?" This broke the ice. The patrol renewed its spirit of joviality. They reassembled on the trail and headed for the village. Someone could have easily been killed—another sad, foolish casualty. There wasn't any anger directed toward the veteran trooper. What had happened, happened. No one hurt. Fuck it.

The village, a peaceful, orderly small town of thatched huts, didn't seem to inhabit a war zone. Villagers went about their business, not taking much stock of the big Americans. An Army medical unit had a clinic here. This is where the medical assistant who committed suicide had been attached. He must have had other problems. Living here was Shangri-La compared to the AO, or for that matter, Ennari.

Defurio visited the medical clinic and observed the staff of four dispense medical care. The medics had pride in what they were doing. They weren't administering lethal doses of bullets and bombs, the work of infantrymen. Defurio's comrades sought more profane endeavors, mainly procuring high quality dope and making arrangements for female companionship. He had seen villages at a distance but not up close. The bucolic setting gave him safe haven, away from Yamamoto, turmoil in the AO, and the sadness of recording casualties. However, appreciation of Vietnamese culture or village life didn't hold any appeal for him. He longed for a reminder of home. Buying a pineapple seemed as civilized a thing as he could do. He nearly cut through his thumb when he tried to slice it with a machete. Its hard surface deflected the blade when he swung to chop it in half. The flat side of the blade struck his finger. Enough of the edge caught to make a nasty gash. A medic applied an antibiotic.

"Thanks."

"No problem. How long y'all going to be here?" the friendly southerner asked.

"Overnight, I think. Mind if I crash here until we bed down?"

"Hell no, nice to have some round-eyed company."

"You guys seem to get along with the locals."

"They're simple, hard-working folks. If we'd get the hell out of here and leave them alone, they'd do fine. They don't give a shit about politics. They want to grow fruits, vegetables, and raise their goats and pigs."

"What about at night? These guys are VC."

"They have to be. In another sector, I saw what they did to a village chief who didn't cooperate. They tied him to a tree, cut off his genitals, and stuffed them in his mouth."

"No shit, I thought those stories were propaganda."

"They're not, man, it's fucking gruesome, and I'm used to that kind of shit. These villagers do what they have to do to survive. Basically, they're good people."

Defurio developed an instant liking for these medics. They had maturity, seriousness, and a sincere desire to mend broken bodies and help the sick and injured. These reasonable, dedicated men reminded him of home; a semblance of normalcy.

In his final months, Defurio had actively begun a process of disconnecting himself from Vietnam. He had never subscribed to military life. Its rigidity repelled him. Nor had he become bound to the seductive lust of warfare. It became an easy transition for him to think in terms of being a civilian, a civilized person—a status which, for the most part, he had never mentally relinquished.

"I see you're married," the southerner noted.

"Yeah, I am."

"How long?"

"A little over two years."

"What a fucking bummer. How much longer in Dnam?"

"Three weeks."

The medic clasped Defurio's hand to his chest in an improvised handshake. "Good for you, man, you're going to make it out of this shithole."

"Thanks, that's if I can get this fucking captain off my back."

"Yamamoto?"

"Yeah."

"We know. Everybody knows about that asshole. We heard the joke he made when Rodgers shot himself." Defurio had forgotten the dead man's name. "If that son of a bitch ever comes here and gets shot, I'll let him bleed to death."

"You'd have my blessing. Alright, man, I've got to get going." It was starting to get dark. "I have a letter to write. Take care."

In late afternoon, no one occupied the schoolroom. His letters in November were about the future. He wrote of mundane items that two people in love discuss when planning to resume a life together.

Finishing his letter, he bought a cold six pack of bottled Tiger beer from a peddler. 'Tiger' aptly described the Vietnamese brand, since the foamy green tinted substance tasted as if it may have been brewed from the piss of tigers.

The next day, the squad trudged a mile to a smaller village. Defurio didn't know immediately why. A thin walled structure with a woven mat floor housed the schoolroom. The patrol set up there. Schoolrooms made for convenient sleeping quarters since they were bare of students at night. There weren't any desks. Students sat on the floor and did schoolwork on blackboard-type tablets. Depositing gear, not rifles or ammo, the soldiers went in search of recreation. They returned early. The village didn't have evening entertainment for wandering U.S. soldiers. Saturated on booze and drugs, sleep came easily.

At about 7:00 am, the putt, putt, putt of motorbikes broke the morning quiet. Fifteen minutes later, he heard squishing noises. Defurio slept at the end of a row of sleeping bags arranged on the floor. He turned on his side to see three Montagnard women mounted on GIs. The impassive women pumped mechanically, like unsynchronized pistons interrupted occasionally when switching from one GI to another. The expressionless Montagnards spit beetle nut juice in Tiger beer bottles as they worked. Smooth baby skin of exposed flanks didn't counteract the mottled roughness of their blunt features. The allure of unblemished porcelain legs didn't suffice to alleviate Defurio's revulsion at the ugliness of the scene. He shifted to his other side, preferring to look at the blankness of a rice paper wall. This, however, didn't hide his ears from the hydraulic squishing of fluids.

Defurio returned to Ennari in the afternoon of November 12. His orders for departure, payroll allotment, and travel vouchers were waiting for him. He would leave at 10 pm on December 6 from Pleiku airbase to Ft. Lewis, Washington. He was to report to Ft. Carson, Colorado, on January 11, 1970. His orders were handed to him by staff Sgt. Jewell. The sergeant never wasted words. "Here are your orders, Jack." Normally undemonstrative, Jewell gave a wry smile and wink. Defurio didn't know what to make of it. Business went on as usual in S-1. No one mentioned or displayed any outward concern regarding his unjust penance of doing another Division patrol. This seeming lack of concern was misleading, as Defurio was soon to find out.

Sgt. Dicicco came to Defurio's office after the evening meal. "Let's have a beer, Jack."

"Sure thing, Lou."

Dicicco displayed his usual good humor. They downed swallows of beer. Dicicco turned serious and sent Symanski to buy more. He leaned close to Defurio. "Listen, we don't want you to show up at formation."

"How the fuck can I… They're mandatory."

"Don't worry about it. Jewell set something up with Fats."

"Like what?"

"Yamamoto has orders for you to do work details and guard duty until the day you leave. We're going to arrange substitutes. Fats will have Yamamoto sign the official duty roster. We'll maintain a separate roster for substitutes. Fats will assign in-transits to cover your spots."

"Shit, that sounds great."

"This is important: stay the hell away from headquarters. We don't want Yamamoto to see you and ask questions. Come back after 4:00 pm when he's gone."

"Alright, anything else I should know?"

"Let me tell you something. That motherfucker pissed us all off when he sent you to St. George, then on patrol. Total bullshit."

Unbelievable. This conspiracy to undermine Yamamoto's orders involved, in one way or another, the entire S-1 unit plus Fats. Defurio hadn't asked for any favors, hadn't solicited sympathy or support. When Dicicco left, merrily humming a tune, Sine came to have a beer. Same for Sinksen, Conrad, Lopes and others. They came individually, speaking casually. Conversation focused mostly on his plans for when he returned to the world. Yamamoto and the arrangement to trash his orders wasn't mentioned. These stalwart men weren't interested in dramatizing a circumstance for which some, if not all of them, could be court martialed.

Defurio wrote Donna about seeing Big Jim the night before. The two unlikely soul mates had gone to the beer hall. Defurio deliberately avoided exchanging addresses or phone numbers with him. He loved Jim, but he had an overwhelming desire to rid himself of Vietnam and any reminders of it.

Outside the doorway of the beer hall, he and Big Jim said a final farewell, although they didn't treat it that way. Intuitively they knew they'd always be a part of each other. Jim was leaving a month after him. "Say hello to New York for me, Jim. Don't let any of your animals or Puerto Rican women bite you in the ass." Jim did his chuckle, and they went their separate ways.

November 27, 1969

Dear Donna,

Today is Thanksgiving. It doesn't seem like it. It's just another day in an unbelievably slow progression of days. Its only significance is bringing me closer to you.

It doesn't look like I'll be coming home early. Nobody has received a drop (accelerated Deros) for November or December. Also, it won't do any good for us to meet in San Francisco. Sgt. Jewell said the Presidio and Ft. Ord are in the 6th Army and Ft. Carson is the 5th Army, whatever those designations mean. The point is that the S-1 at the Presidio won't have authorization to change my orders.

Donna, it's hard to believe I'll be home in a little over a week. Stay at my parent's house the last few days before I come. I'll fly to Fresno. I don't want to take the time to meet you in Bakersfield.

This letter should get to you a couple of days before I do. In fact, I'll address it to my parent's house. I'm continuing this in the evening. I had to help my replacement prepare a complicated court martial case. Donna, it dawned on me this will be the last letter you get from me before I get home. It's so incredible to think I'll be home soon. It's difficult for me to get my arms around the idea. I don't think I'll have trouble readjusting to civilian life. That damn six wasted months at Ft. Carson will be a pain in the neck. It's okay, though. Being with you will be like living in a dream world no matter where I am.

I think of you almost every moment. Passionately. I love you in every way. I only hope I can make you as happy as you make me.

I've been thinking about our future. The next few years, we'll be building a foundation on which to build the rest of our lives. Be patient with me. I'll be working days and studying nights. However, there should be a couple of little kids running around to keep you busy. You're going to make such a good mother. It'll be hard for me to keep from showing my pride in you. Donna, you're more than anything I'd ever dreamed of. I didn't think anyone so good and perfect as you could ever exist.

I love you,
Jack

He spent daylight hours playing hide and seek with Yamamoto. He exercised in his private gym, read Donna's letters in the barracks, bought odds and ends at the PX, drank beer at the hall, and played basketball in the afternoons.

He toyed with the idea of going to Pleiku to buy souvenirs. He decided not to, not wanting to risk a VC booby trap or ambush. He began packing. His locker overflowed with 325 letters from Donna. He wouldn't have room in his suitcase to transport correspondence. He reread every word, her letters inseparable in expression of love and sentiment. He decided to burn them, to build a funeral pyre and eliminate another reminder of lurid Vietnam history. Burn the past. He went behind the barracks to submit Donna's loving words to the fire. The cremation made sense but didn't seem right. Placing her letters in the fire hurt him. She wouldn't be hurt. The letters represented a year they both wished hadn't happened. Ashes floated skyward. He wished he could see her words again.

"Here's to you, you lucky son of a bitch." Sine clinked his beer can to Defurio's.

"Who's going to make Yamamoto jump through his ass?" asked Dicicco.

"You leaving us alone with that asshole?" said Lopes.

"What are we going to do for entertainment, Jack?" asked Sinksen, the usually quiet Iowan. Garinger, postponing his sleepover with his Pleiku whore, stumbled to congratulate him. He also had a criticism. Garinger, so bright during duty hours became a sloppy drunk at night. In garbled speech, he chastised Defurio for displaying Wood's insulting caricatures of the UCMJ represented by that Simon Legree character holding the scales of justice while revealing a hairy scrotum hanging below a black robe. These and other such drawings were packed in Defurio's Samsonite.

Drunken send-offs were an S-1 tradition. Everyone got drunk. Defurio would be leaving the next day. Midway through the evening, party goers crowded his work station as he sat soaking in the attention. Weaving drunkenly on his heels, the thin as paper Sgt. Jewell hushed the group. Displaying his usual peculiar posture, a caved in appearance, as though his lungs were missing, he made an improbable master of ceremonies. He presented Defurio with a slender square box. He hadn't seen this done before.

"Jack, on behalf of the men," he said through smoke from his cigarette. He spoke with a noticeable slur. He stopped and started again. "On behalf of the men of S-1, we would like to present this stuff." Jewell wasn't known for his eloquence. However, the simplicity of the gesture made it more meaningful.

Defurio opened it. Inscribed on its lower right hand corner was "Han Ill Enterprises Co., Ltd, Seoul, Korea." A new business had sprung up in Pleiku. Inside were three impressive mementos. A laminated plaque in the form of a shield had affixed metal insignias of the Fourth Division as well as replicas of an American flag, CIB, and two images of golden dragons. The bottom of the plaque read:

Sergeant Jack Defurio
From all the men in S-1 and the mail room.
For a job well done
and best of luck in the future.

A cigarette lighter had the inscription, "Bravo Company, 1st Battalion, 14th Infantry," and had a raised emblem of a golden dragon. Finally, a handsome eight inch chrome bayonet letter opener with a red plastic handle and the dragon logo on its blade completed the gift package.

Defurio didn't give a speech. He simply said, "Thanks, guys." There were shouts and hollers as they saluted him in a show of raised beer cans. This is as it should be, tried and tested soldiers celebrating life.

After the presentation, there was a slight lull in the partying, giving Defurio a chance to satisfy a mild curiosity. "Hey, Sarge, let me ask you something," he said, gaining Sgt. Jewell's attention. Defurio, examining his gifts, had never looked closely at the Battalion Golden Dragon insignia. The figure featured a bug-eyed Chinese day parade dragon head atop a scaly bow-legged serpent body that squatted as if defecating. "Do you know where the name 'Golden Dragon' originated?"

"Nope," replied the disinterested staff sergeant, his cigarette drooping from his lower lip. "I think it had something to do with when the battalion did some fighting in China in the early days." This was obviously a poor guess. Defurio, not really that interested himself, didn't inquire further.

"Way to go, mista legal clerk." Supply Sergeant Perkins congratulated him in his happy sing-song English. Defurio had already gone to payroll, his first stop. "Say hello to da girls for me in da U S of A."

"I will. I'll say it's coming from a black bird from an island of yellow canaries." "Heh, heh, you do dat, mista legal clerk. You do dat."

"Perkins, how long you been in Dnam?"

"Been here since '67. Goin' to stay 'til da damn war stop."

Defurio knew why. Supply sergeants controlled the black market. Career sergeants knew how to convert and smuggle cash out of the country. He let Defurio keep a pair of jungle boots, which were supposed to have been turned in.

He handed Defurio freshly pressed Class A's, the same he had on when he came to Nam. His Army issue black dress shoes were also returned nicely shined. He would change in the barracks, returning his custom tailored fatigues to supply. They wouldn't be recycled for Army use. Vietnamese males for miles around wore Army fatigues, no doubt traded in exchange for premium dope. Defurio reluctantly relinquished his trusted companion for a year, his M-16. He'd formed an attachment to it. He turned in grenades, which had given him so much reassurance; bandoliers, old boots, and web gear were also given up. He hated being reduced to the same state of helplessness as when he came to Nam—no weapon and dressed like an idiot ready to attend a military ball.

A jeep came for him at 4:00 pm. He waited outside S-1. It was a pleasant day for Vietnam. The sun was shining. There was still the same heat and humidity, but not disabling, perhaps because he wasn't carrying a heavy pack up an overgrown trail. When the jeep arrived, he stepped inside S-1 and from the doorway waved a final goodbye. The seated clerks happily acknowledged his farewell. They didn't get up. No need for an emotional display.

He poked around the terminal at Pleiku airbase. He checked in his Samsonite suitcases containing civilian clothes, mementos, and his pair of unauthorized jungle boots. He'd wear civilian clothes to Ft. Carson, where he would be issued winter wear. Not wanting to carry luggage, he arranged for it to be shipped to his parent's address. He bought a bottle of whiskey, intending to drink away Vietnam on the flight. He purchased some magazines to reacquaint himself with news of the world. His experiences in Vietnam or current news did not truly interest him. Instead, he was thinking, "Jesus, it'll be so good to be in Donna's arms to stay."

At 9:15 pm, soldiers began boarding the commercial aircraft, welcomed by the same plastic-smiled stewardesses as when he had departed for Vietnam. Same shit. Soldiers as strangers. On the way to Vietnam, he knew Fox and Walters and two or three others. Here, he didn't know anyone. Not that he cared. He wanted to be alone with his thoughts. However, he couldn't help but notice the difference from then to now. These were serious, mature men, although many retained faces of boys. This wasn't a party atmosphere. Everyone here had suffered a year of pain and loss. They also displayed an unease and uncertainty about reentering the world. These soldiers, mostly infantrymen, wanted more than anything to go home, yet they had doubts and fears about it. They weren't the same. To adjust, they would have to undo and unlearn what they'd seen and done.

Defurio had no such qualms. He had had no illusions about war, the Army, or Vietnam. He got what he expected. Shit. He would never experience guilt or shame. He hadn't given a damn about duty, honor, or propriety. He had followed his own moral code. He had the luck of avoiding his greatest fears—disfigurement and crippling injury. He would come home unhurt. There were hidden scars. So what? He had Donna, his ego, his arrogance, and his will. He would adjust, starting with a purposeful effort to forget Vietnam.

He settled in a window seat. He preferred seeing outside. Starlight found its way through a falling mist of humidity. The plane taxied to the runway. As it rolled, thoughts of Donna began crowding Vietnam from his brain. Already large chunks of Nam were falling into his self-made oblivion of memory. Names, faces, places, dates, and incidents were condensing to a formless ball kicked to the corner of his mind.

The plane stopped for an hour to refuel in Tokyo. He bought another bottle of whiskey because he'd finished the first. Less than twelve hours to go. He wanted to leave Tokyo badly. He didn't like throngs of Japanese at the terminal. They were ugly reminders of Yamamoto and besides, they looked too similar to Vietnamese. Defurio wanted to get away from the presence of swarming Orientals.

Soldiers on board had cheered when the pilot announced clearing the airspace of South Vietnam, and now they cheered deliriously when the pilot announced the aircraft was entering the airspace of the continental United States. They were preparing to land in thirty minutes. Tiny jolts of nervous energy pin balled through his body. Leaving Vietnam, Defurio had harbored a latent fear that something might happen to the plane; engine trouble, a lightning strike, something. In the past year, he'd thought himself safe so many times only to be laid bare to danger.

A nice, smooth landing. Almost midnight. In half an hour, it would be December 7. It may have been stupid or childish, but he did it anyway: When his feet touched the soil, he went a few steps and impulsively dropped to his knees and kissed the ground. He'd made it.

The Army did something for which he would be lastingly grateful. A simple thing. Non-coms directed the vets to a lighted hanger not far from where the jet landed. No loud mouthed abusive language. An open air kitchen had been set up. Short-order cooks prepared breakfasts to order. No waiting. No lines. Defurio sat at a table and hungrily downed four eggs over easy, five strips of medium crisp bacon, a large portion of hash browns, wheat toast, and fresh coffee. The coffee's colorful swirls unexpectedly brought a memory of Big Jim. A variety of condiments were on the table. He sprinkled Tabasco sauce on his eggs. Grunts in the field often dabbed Tabasco on C-rations to liven up the taste.

At a nearby table, a personnel sergeant handed him a manila folder containing verified copies of travel vouchers and his orders for Ft. Carson. He was free to go. He put his picture album in the folder. Some distance away, a waiting line of cabs coughed white puffs of smoke in the winter air. Shivering from the cold, he went in their direction. He watched condensation coming from his mouth. On a clear, icy evening, this isolated section of Ft. Lewis seemed abandoned. Passengers from the plane straggled in ones and twos, looking insignificant in the vastness of the base. Defurio walked alone. His feet were unused to the hardness of cold ground, or rather the large smooth rocks covering it, so unlike the poor quality pebbles found from Bien Hoa to Ennari. Accustomed to the soft loam of Vietnam, his thin-soled shoes crunching on the stones hurt his feet. Steel shanked jungle boots would have been helpful.

The drastic shift in one day from warm to cold, from conflict to tranquility, was disorienting. His mind clicked from one thing to another. Something disturbed him, something intangibly palpable. The stillness.

He looked at the sky. Strange not to see an orange flecked horizon of floating flares or fiery tracers falling from the heavens, or hear the braying of mini-guns, the beating of helicopter blades cutting through the air, or the booming of outgoing and sometimes incoming. He'd become unfamiliar to the appurtenances of a civilized world.

He repositioned the pint bottle jostling inside his tucked shirt. It had kept company with Donna's picture album on the flight.

He tried to think of her. The cold disrupted him. Negatives prevailed. Impatience nipped at his heels. He wished he could speed forward the movement of time. The final flight from Seattle-Tacoma airport to San Francisco, then to Fresno, was going to seem like forever. Damn cabs were a long ways off. Fucking rocks. He quickened his pace. He talked to himself as if he were settling an argument. "Okay, okay, Defurio, so you were a fucking grunt. Forget it. A jungle fighter. A low level jungle fighter. A jungle fighter nevertheless. A killer of men. I don't give a fuck. I did what I had to do. Forget it." He carried on this conversation until reaching a cab. Good. Turning the freezing handle touched off a last cold thought. He had killed. He could never again be an ordinary man. He entered the warmth of the cab. He slammed the door, shutting out the cold.

"Sea-tac," he told the driver while blowing warm breath into his cupped hands.

"Welcome home," the grey-haired cabbie said respectfully over his shoulder.

"Thanks." There hadn't been any dignitaries or bands to wish him well when he departed for Vietnam and none to welcome him home. Just as well. He wasn't interested in wasting time listening to blow hard politicians or some overstuffed general prattle on about how proud they were of these returning killers who they had so ardently recruited, indoctrinated, and trained. For what purpose, to uphold the virtues of American society?

The cab silently traversed the five or six miles to a security gate. A dribble of cabs could be seen in the distance, head lights beaming a swath through the lonely isolation, taillights disappearing behind bends in the road. Scattered street lights were insufficient to brighten the outstretched reaches of this part of Ft. Lewis. Dispelling a residual chill, Defurio drank from his bottle of whiskey. He'd splurged at the Tokyo airport, buying a bottle of Jack Daniels. The security gate loomed ahead, its booth and immediate vicinity aglow from the intensity of a high powered overhead light. Several MPs were in the booth, waiting to take their turn at the gate. Cabs flowed evenly through it. MPs knew the cabs' passengers were returning Vietnam vets. A single MP stood at attention to the side of the gate facing the vehicles. The serious faced sentry wearing a white helmet and gloves and braiding in his epaulets gave a formal signal, bringing his right elbow to his waist and raising his forearm straight up. He snapped his wrist and hand, waving the cab to go through. The cab slowed but didn't stop. The MP had an M-16 strapped to his shoulder. An M-16. Disordered recollections suddenly shot through Defurio's mind. Charmaine, Tiffany, Brillo Pad, Chu Pa, St. George. He tried to think of Donna. An M-16. Memories were disintegrating but persisted in fragments. Big Jim, Hernandez, Lt. Duke, Terrible Earl, Sinksen, Sine, Jewell, Woods, Yamamoto. Think of Donna. The damn M-16. His mind froze. "Don't mean nothin," "fire mission," "fire at will," "incoming." The cab passed the guard. Defurio relaxed. Wait a minute. After a year of confusion, frustration, and consternation, there came to him a final irony. An M-16. His. "I'll be damned." Never fired. He smiled. Funny. He'd never pulled the trigger. The cab veered toward the airport.

The End.